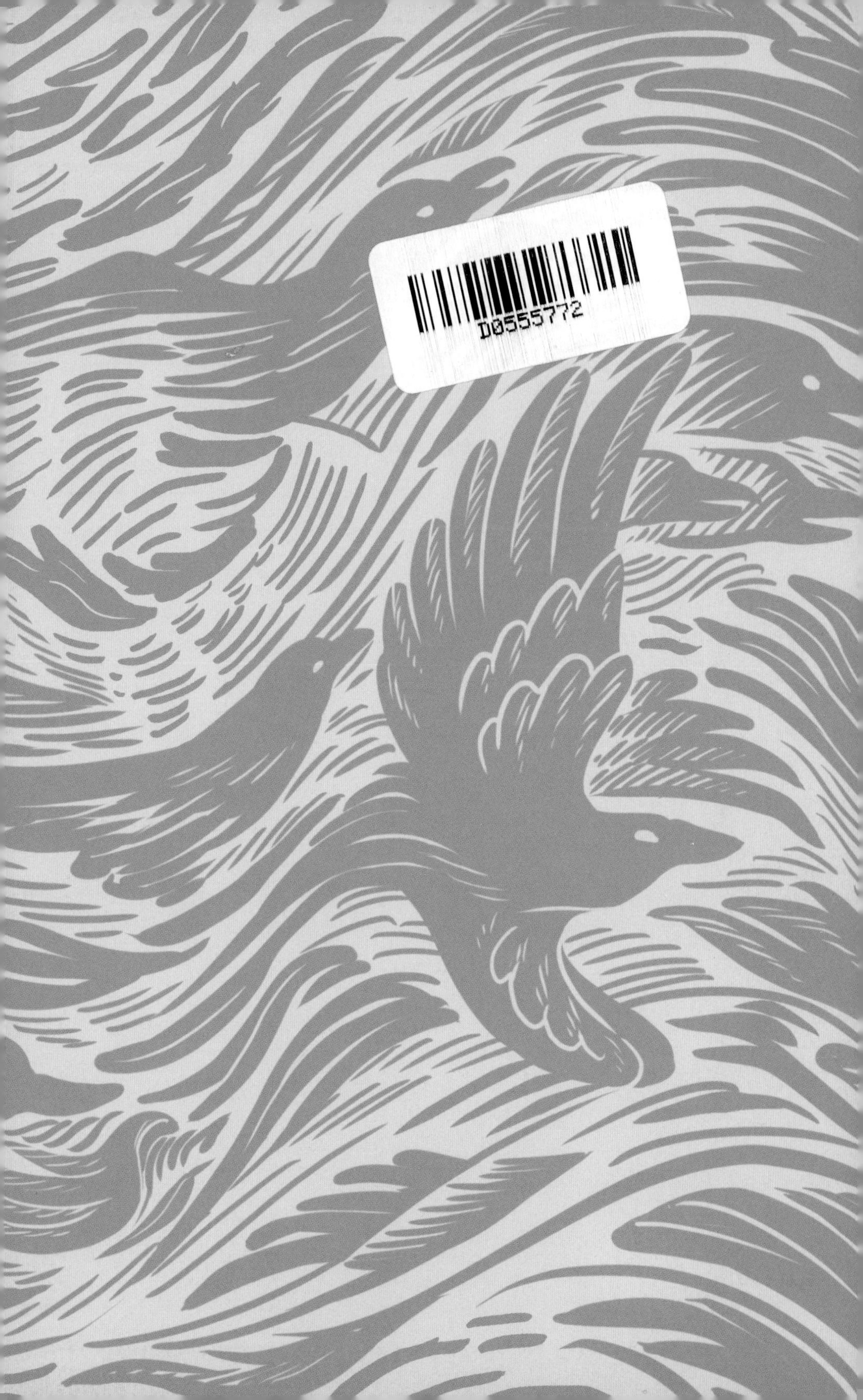

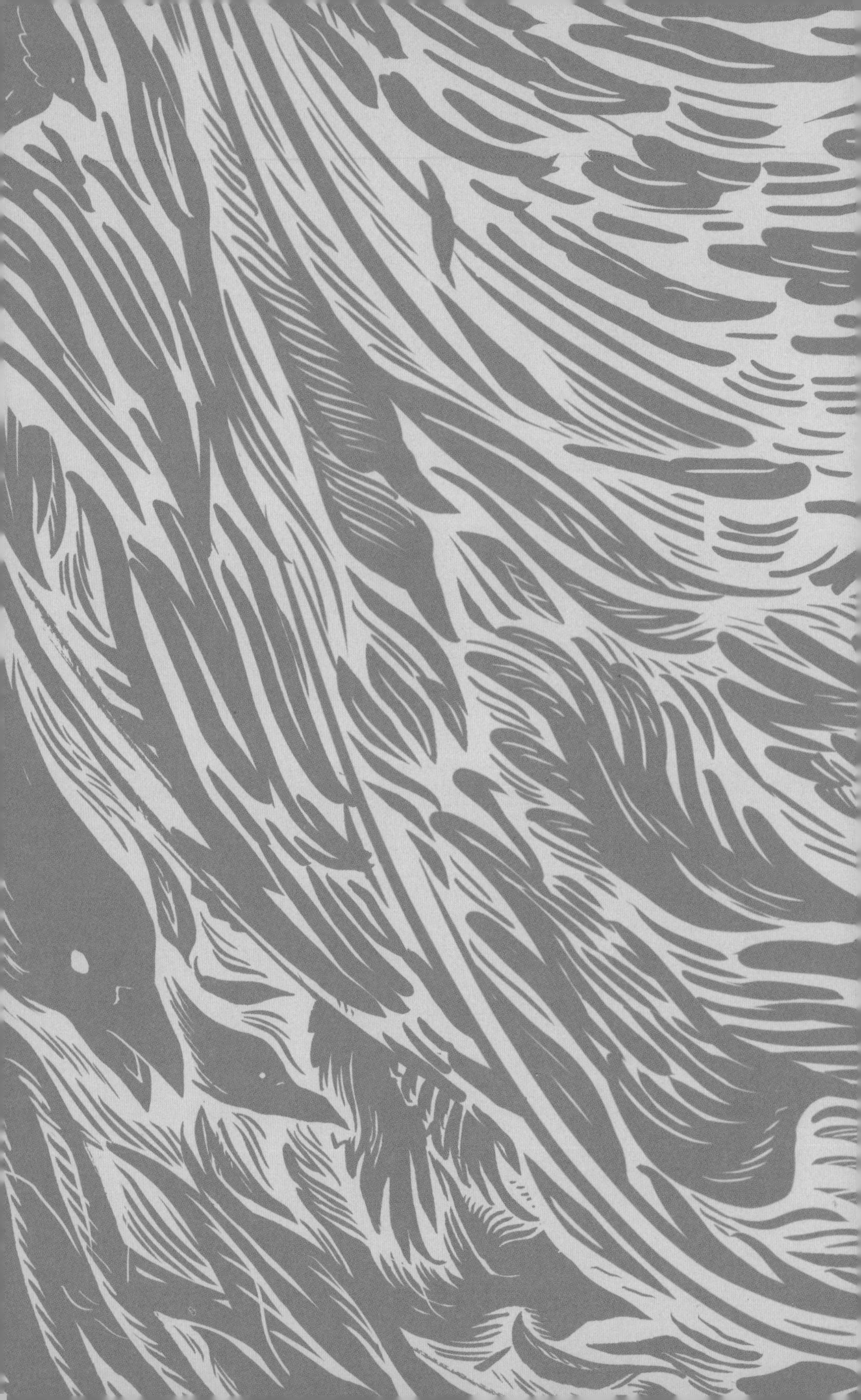

CONSPIRACY OF

Ravens™

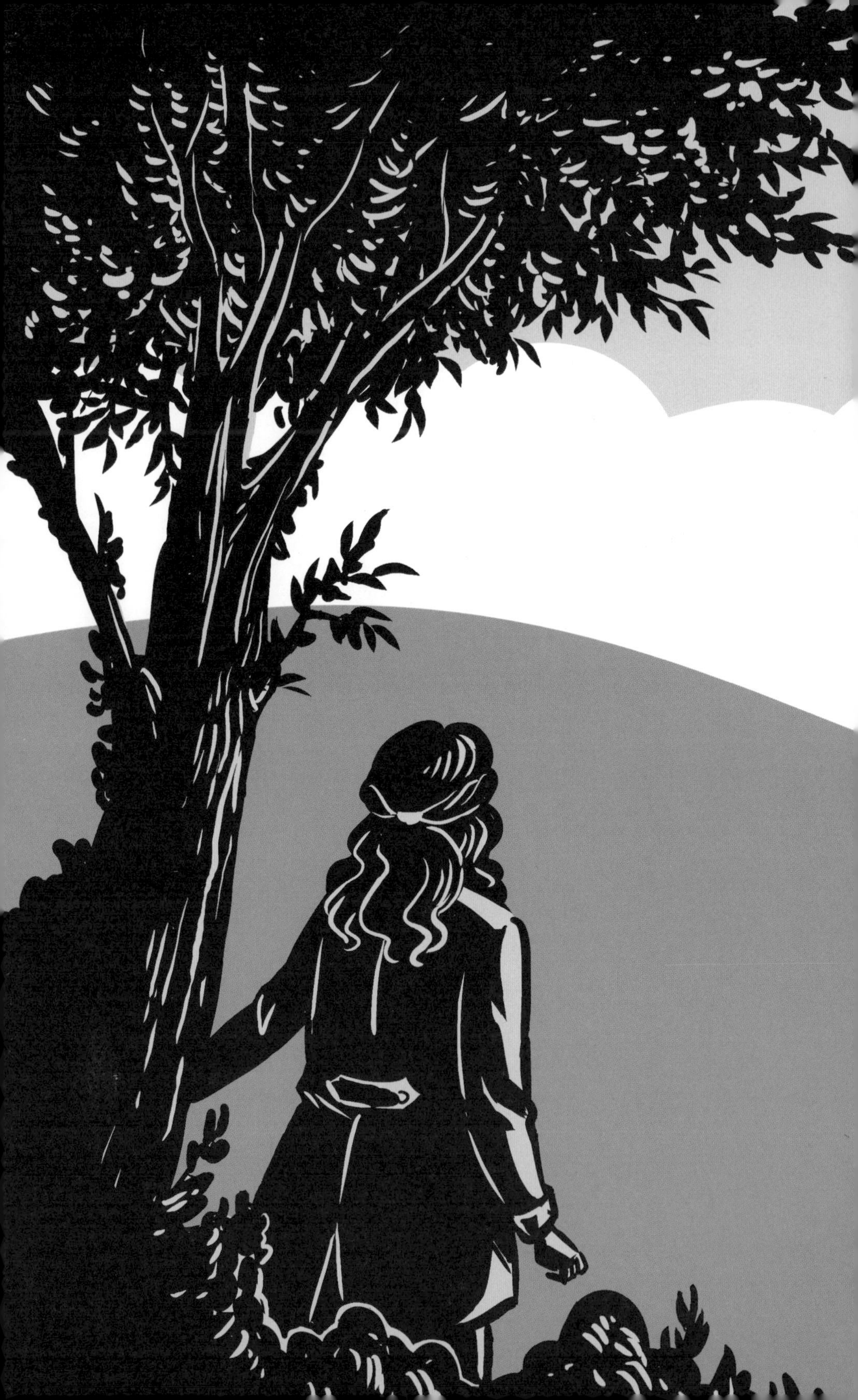

CONSPIRACY OF
Ravens™

STORY BY
LEAH MOORE & JOHN REPPION

ART AND LETTERING BY
SALLY JANE THOMPSON

TONE ASSISTANCE BY
NIKI SMITH

PUBLISHER ✦ Mike Richardson
EDITOR ✦ Katii O'Brien
ASSISTANT EDITOR ✦ Jenny Blenk
DESIGNER ✦ Anita Magaña
DIGITAL ART TECHNICIAN ✦ Allyson Haller

DARK HORSE BOOKS

Special thanks to Hannah Means-Shannon.

DarkHorse.com
Facebook.com/DarkHorseComics
Twitter.com/DarkHorseComics

Published by Dark Horse Books
A division of Dark Horse Comics, Inc.
10956 SE Main Street
Milwaukie, OR 97222

Advertising Sales (503) 905-2237
Comic Shop Locator Service:
Comicshoplocator.com

First edition: October 2018
ISBN: 978-1-50670-883-6

10 9 8 7 6 5 4 3 2 1
Printed in China

Neil Hankerson, Executive Vice President · Tom
Weddle, Chief Financial Officer · Randy Stradley,
Vice President of Publishing · Nick McWhorter,
Chief Business Development Officer · Matt
Parkinson, Vice President of Marketing · Dale
LaFountain, Vice President of Information
Technology · Cara Niece, Vice President of
Production and Scheduling · Mark Bernard , Vice
President of Book Trade and Digital Sales · Ken
Lizzi, General Counsel · Dave Marshall, Editor
in Chief · Davey Estrada, Editorial Director ·
Chris Warner, Senior Books Editor · Cary
Grazzini, Director of Specialty Projects · Lia
Ribacchi, Art Director. Vanessa Todd-Holmes,
Director of Print Purchasing · Matt Dryer,
Director of Digital Art and Prepress · Michael
Gombos, Director of International Publishing
and Licensing · Kari Yadro, Director of Custom
Programs

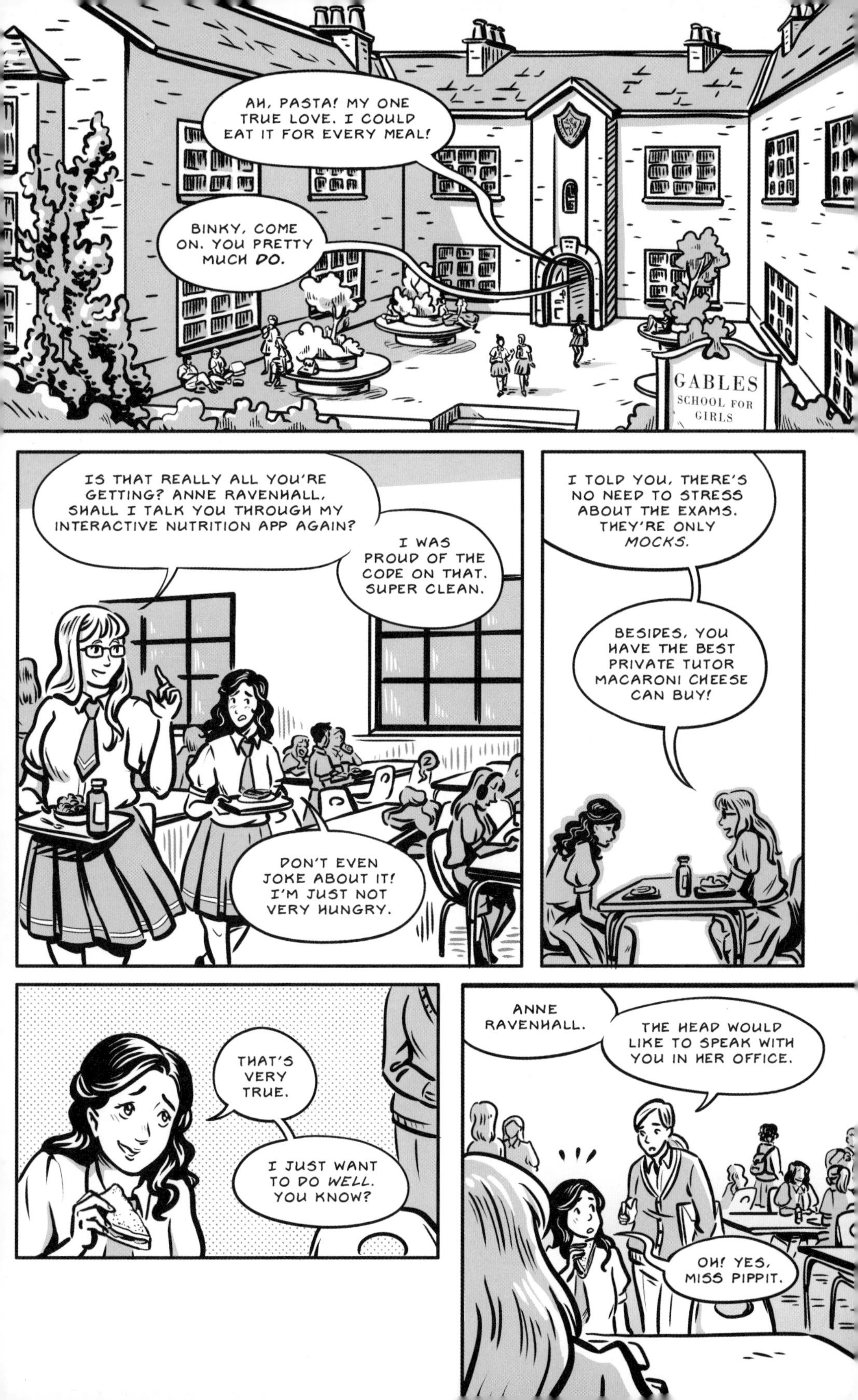
AH, PASTA! MY ONE TRUE LOVE. I COULD EAT IT FOR EVERY MEAL!
BINKY, COME ON. YOU PRETTY MUCH *DO.*
GABLES SCHOOL FOR GIRLS
IS THAT REALLY ALL YOU'RE GETTING? ANNE RAVENHALL, SHALL I TALK YOU THROUGH MY INTERACTIVE NUTRITION APP AGAIN?
I WAS PROUD OF THE CODE ON THAT. SUPER CLEAN.
DON'T EVEN JOKE ABOUT IT! I'M JUST NOT VERY HUNGRY.
I TOLD YOU, THERE'S NO NEED TO STRESS ABOUT THE EXAMS. THEY'RE ONLY *MOCKS.*
BESIDES, YOU HAVE THE BEST PRIVATE TUTOR MACARONI CHEESE CAN BUY!
THAT'S VERY TRUE.
I JUST WANT TO DO *WELL.* YOU KNOW?
ANNE RAVENHALL.
THE HEAD WOULD LIKE TO SPEAK WITH YOU IN HER OFFICE.
OH! YES, MISS PIPPIT.

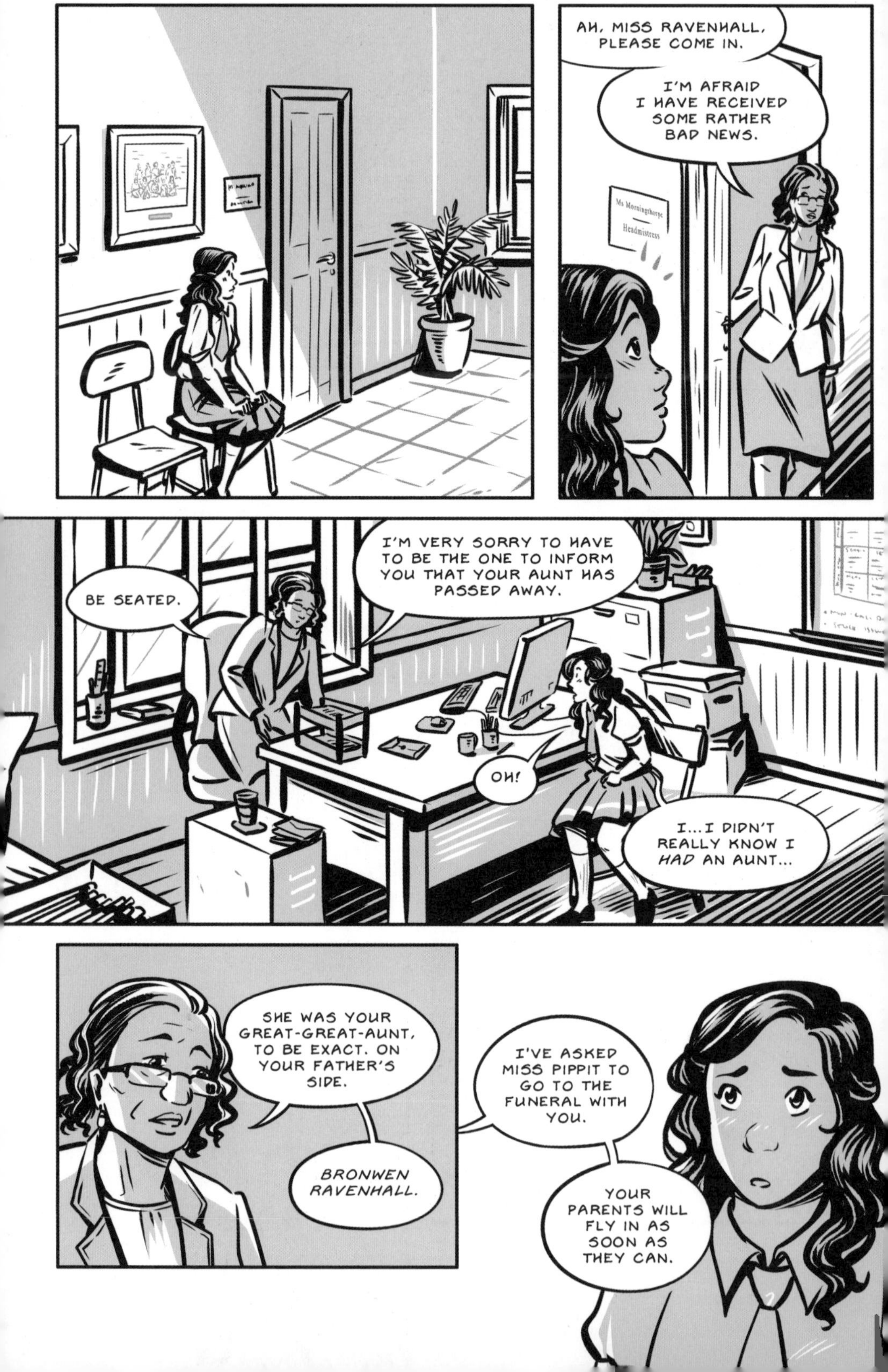

AH, MISS RAVENHALL, PLEASE COME IN.
I'M AFRAID I HAVE RECEIVED SOME RATHER BAD NEWS.
Ms Morningthorpe
Headmistress
BE SEATED.
I'M VERY SORRY TO HAVE TO BE THE ONE TO INFORM YOU THAT YOUR AUNT HAS PASSED AWAY.
OH!
I...I DIDN'T REALLY KNOW I *HAD* AN AUNT...
SHE WAS YOUR GREAT-GREAT-AUNT, TO BE EXACT. ON YOUR FATHER'S SIDE.
BRONWEN RAVENHALL.
I'VE ASKED MISS PIPPIT TO GO TO THE FUNERAL WITH YOU.
YOUR PARENTS WILL FLY IN AS SOON AS THEY CAN.

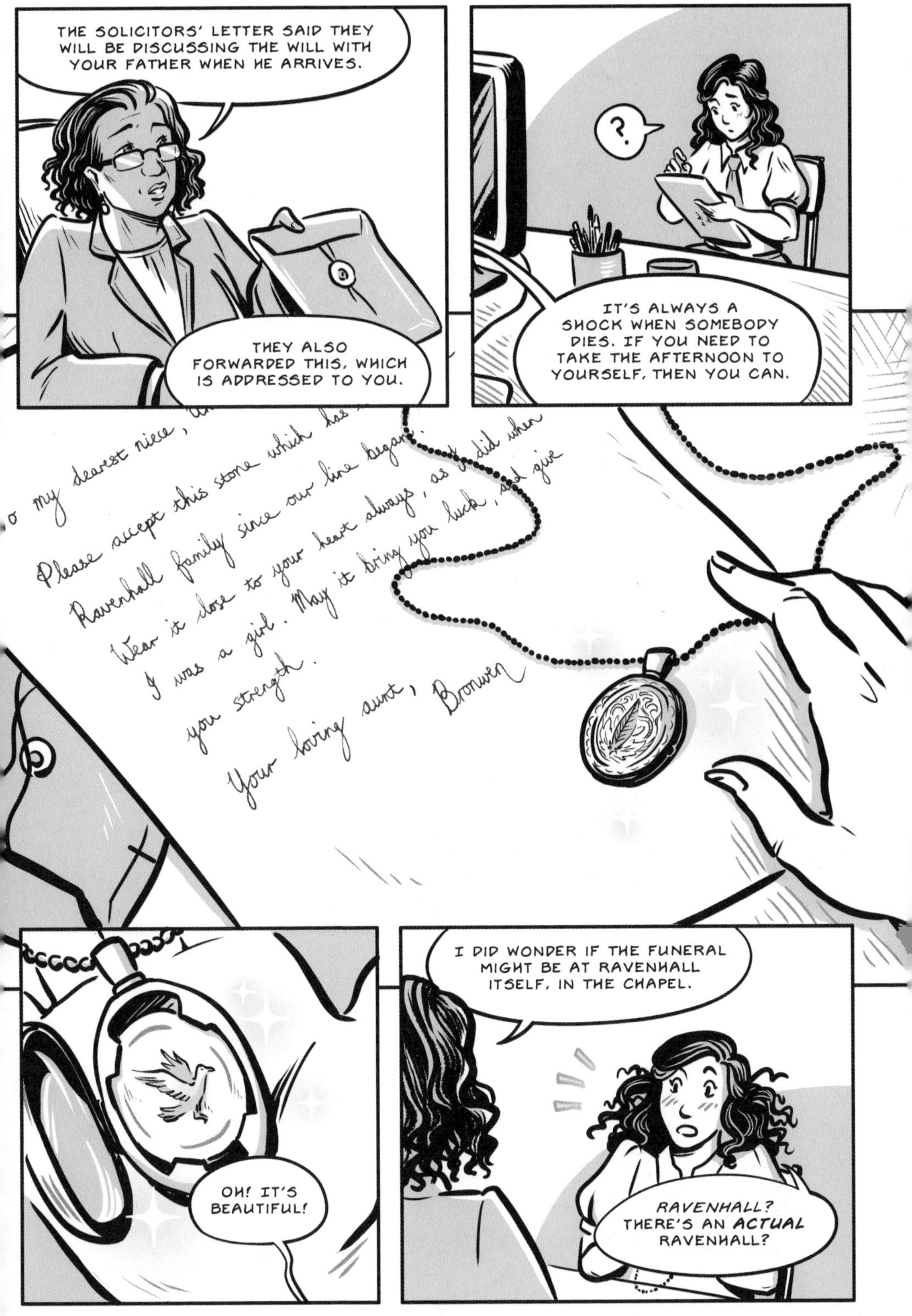
THE SOLICITORS' LETTER SAID THEY WILL BE DISCUSSING THE WILL WITH YOUR FATHER WHEN HE ARRIVES.
THEY ALSO FORWARDED THIS, WHICH IS ADDRESSED TO YOU.
?
IT'S ALWAYS A SHOCK WHEN SOMEBODY DIES. IF YOU NEED TO TAKE THE AFTERNOON TO YOURSELF, THEN YOU CAN.
o my dearest niece,
Please accept this stone which has
Ravenhall family since our line began.
Wear it close to your heart always, as I did when
I was a girl. May it bring you luck, and give
you strength.
Your loving aunt, Bronwen
OH! IT'S BEAUTIFUL!
I DID WONDER IF THE FUNERAL MIGHT BE AT RAVENHALL ITSELF, IN THE CHAPEL.
RAVENHALL? THERE'S AN ACTUAL RAVENHALL?

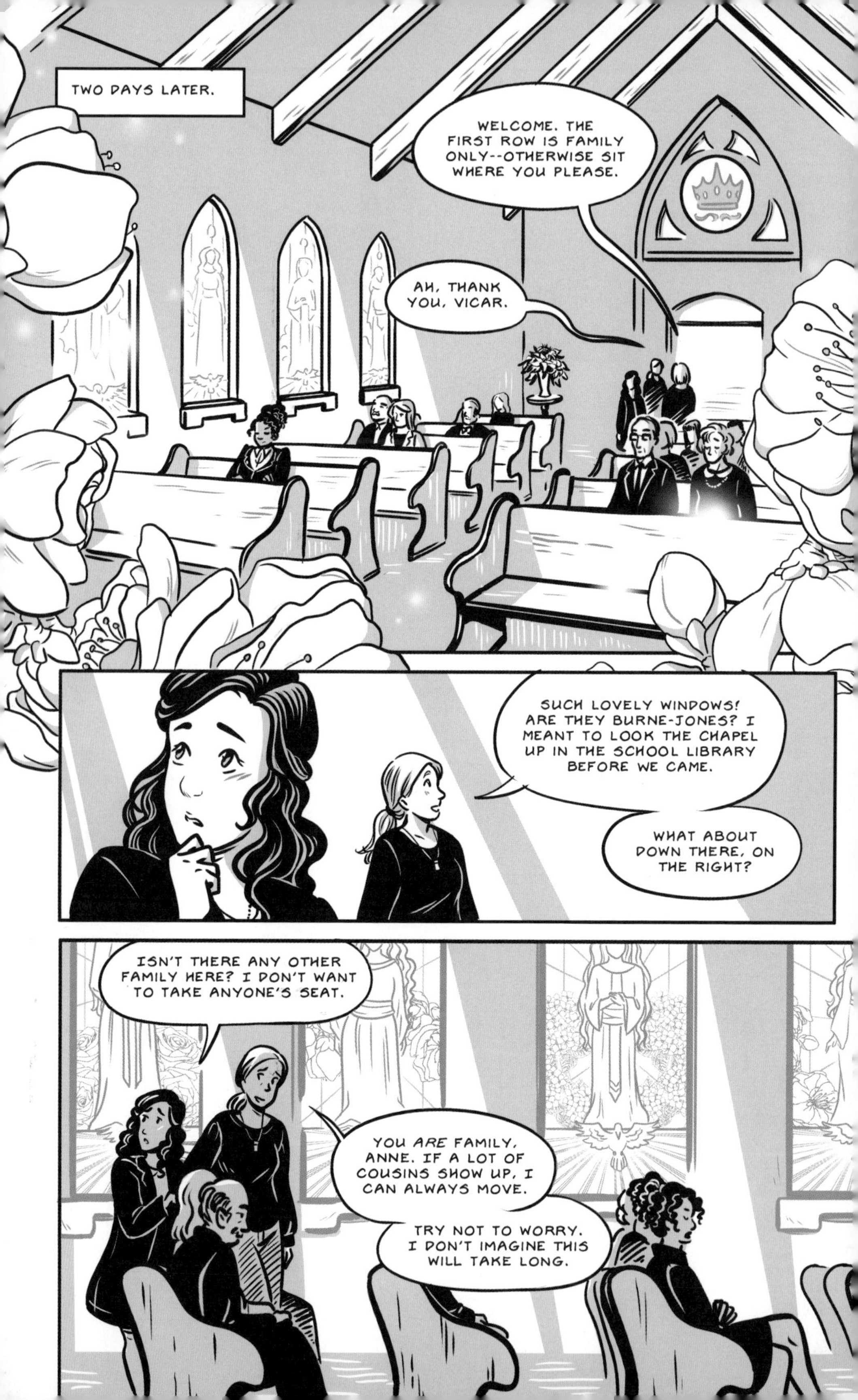
TWO DAYS LATER.
WELCOME. THE FIRST ROW IS FAMILY ONLY--OTHERWISE SIT WHERE YOU PLEASE.
AH, THANK YOU, VICAR.
SUCH LOVELY WINDOWS! ARE THEY BURNE-JONES? I MEANT TO LOOK THE CHAPEL UP IN THE SCHOOL LIBRARY BEFORE WE CAME.
WHAT ABOUT DOWN THERE, ON THE RIGHT?
ISN'T THERE ANY OTHER FAMILY HERE? I DON'T WANT TO TAKE ANYONE'S SEAT.
YOU *ARE* FAMILY, ANNE. IF A LOT OF COUSINS SHOW UP, I CAN ALWAYS MOVE.
TRY NOT TO WORRY. I DON'T IMAGINE THIS WILL TAKE LONG.

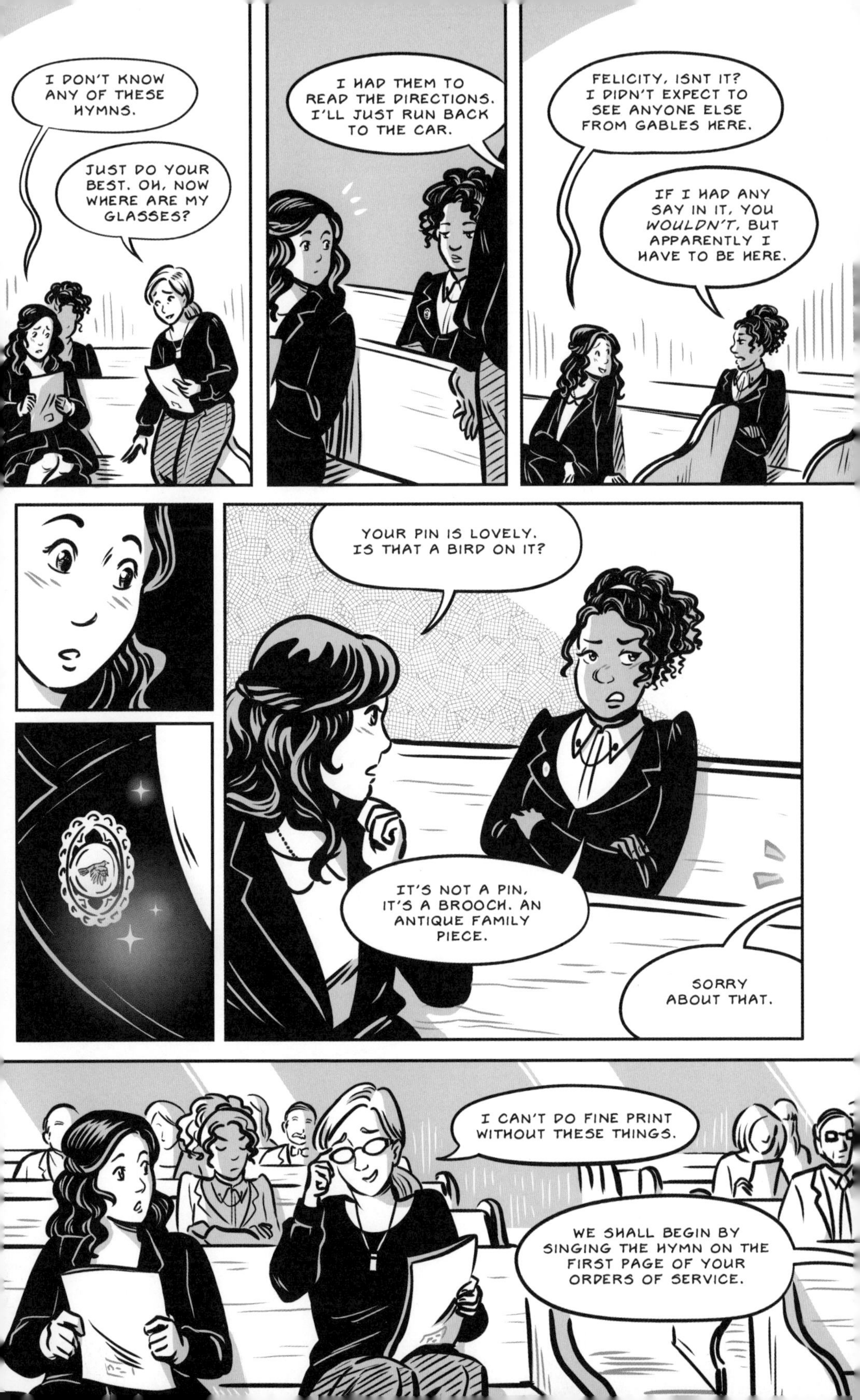
I DON'T KNOW ANY OF THESE HYMNS.
JUST DO YOUR BEST. OH, NOW WHERE ARE MY GLASSES?
I HAD THEM TO READ THE DIRECTIONS. I'LL JUST RUN BACK TO THE CAR.
FELICITY, ISNT IT? I DIDN'T EXPECT TO SEE ANYONE ELSE FROM GABLES HERE.
IF I HAD ANY SAY IN IT, YOU *WOULDN'T*, BUT APPARENTLY I HAVE TO BE HERE.
YOUR PIN IS LOVELY. IS THAT A BIRD ON IT?
IT'S NOT A PIN, IT'S A BROOCH. AN ANTIQUE FAMILY PIECE.
SORRY ABOUT THAT.
I CAN'T DO FINE PRINT WITHOUT THESE THINGS.
WE SHALL BEGIN BY SINGING THE HYMN ON THE FIRST PAGE OF YOUR ORDERS OF SERVICE.

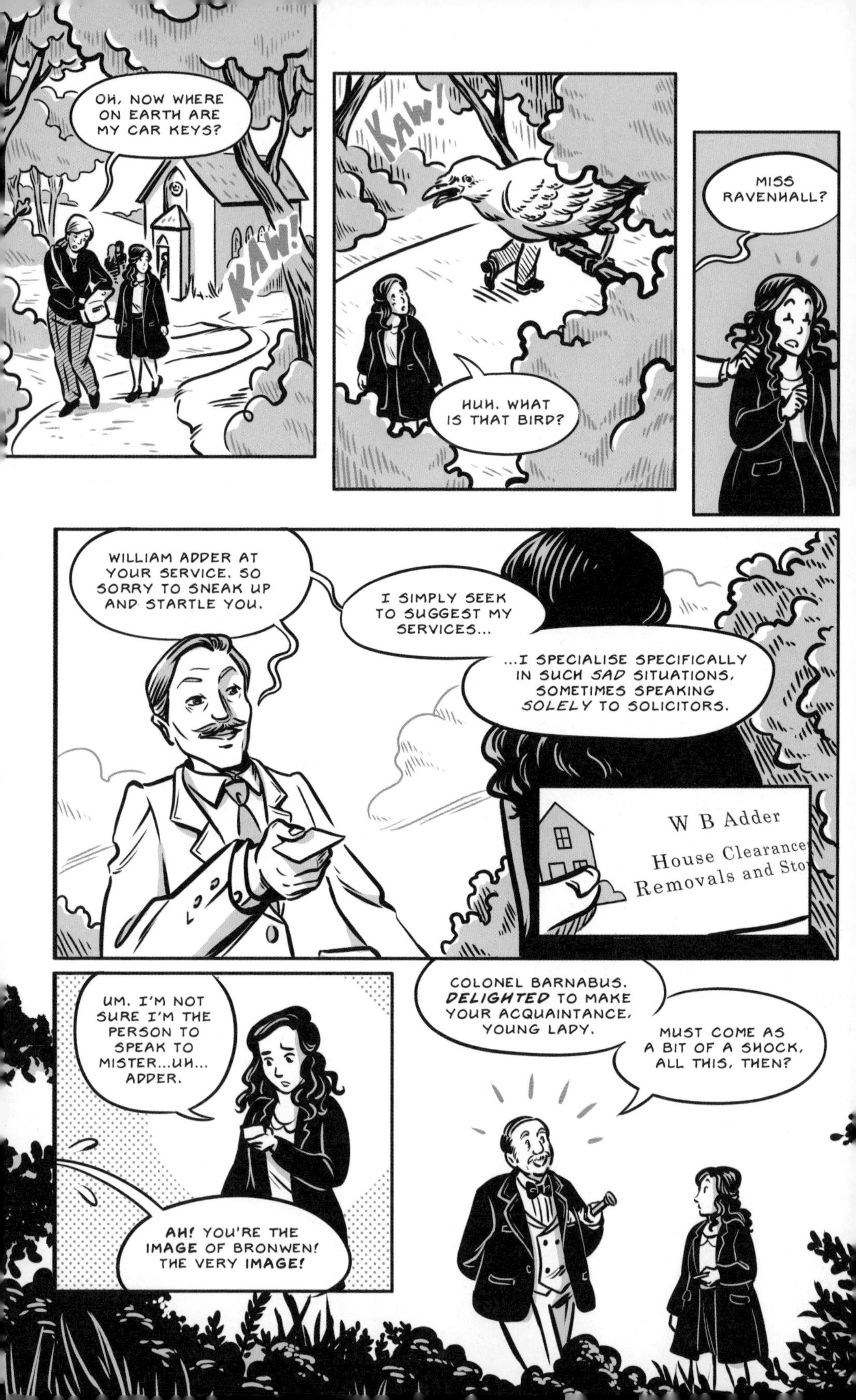

OH, NOW WHERE ON EARTH ARE MY CAR KEYS?
KAW!
KAW!
HUH. WHAT IS THAT BIRD?
MISS RAVENHALL?
WILLIAM ADDER AT YOUR SERVICE. SO SORRY TO SNEAK UP AND STARTLE YOU.
I SIMPLY SEEK TO SUGGEST MY SERVICES...
...I SPECIALISE SPECIFICALLY IN SUCH SAD SITUATIONS, SOMETIMES SPEAKING SOLELY TO SOLICITORS.
W B Adder
House Clearance
Removals and Sto
UM. I'M NOT SURE I'M THE PERSON TO SPEAK TO MISTER...UH... ADDER.
AH! YOU'RE THE IMAGE OF BRONWEN! THE VERY IMAGE!
COLONEL BARNABUS. DELIGHTED TO MAKE YOUR ACQUAINTANCE, YOUNG LADY.
MUST COME AS A BIT OF A SHOCK, ALL THIS, THEN?

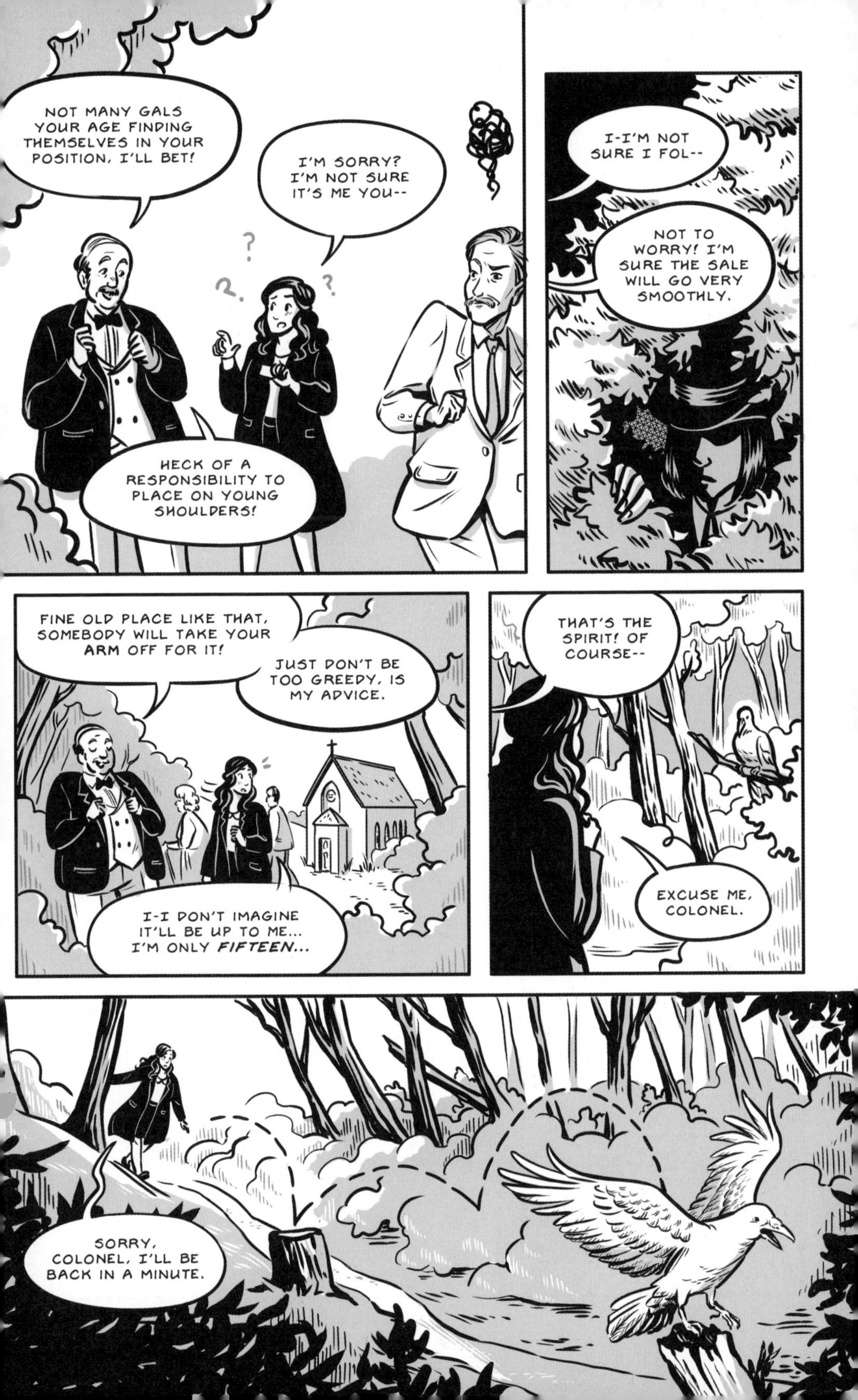
NOT MANY GALS YOUR AGE FINDING THEMSELVES IN YOUR POSITION, I'LL BET!
I'M SORRY? I'M NOT SURE IT'S ME YOU--
HECK OF A RESPONSIBILITY TO PLACE ON YOUNG SHOULDERS!
I-I'M NOT SURE I FOL--
NOT TO WORRY! I'M SURE THE SALE WILL GO VERY SMOOTHLY.
FINE OLD PLACE LIKE THAT, SOMEBODY WILL TAKE YOUR **ARM** OFF FOR IT!
JUST DON'T BE TOO GREEDY, IS MY ADVICE.
I-I DON'T IMAGINE IT'LL BE UP TO ME... I'M ONLY ***FIFTEEN...***
THAT'S THE SPIRIT! OF COURSE--
EXCUSE ME, COLONEL.
SORRY, COLONEL, I'LL BE BACK IN A MINUTE.

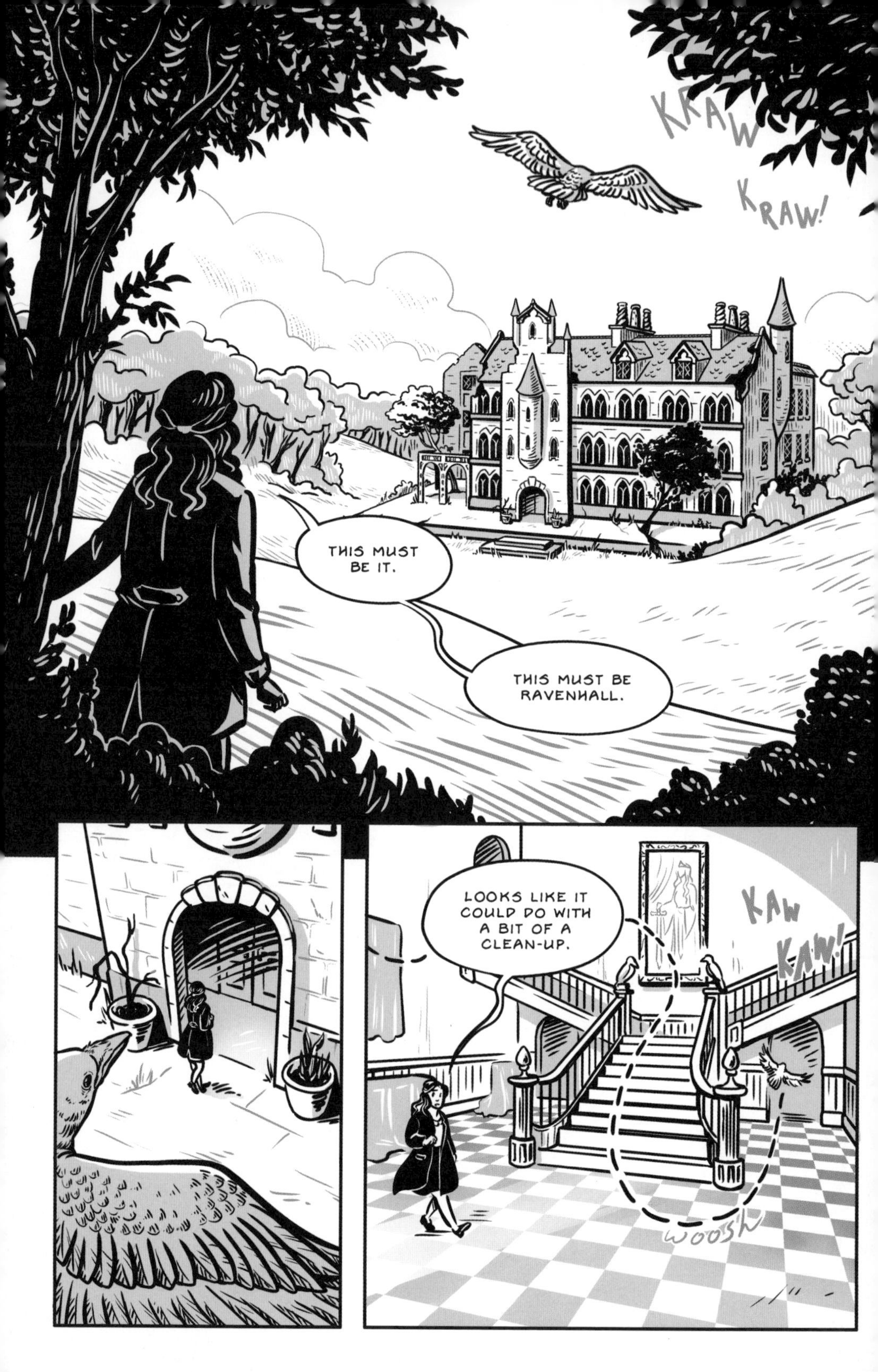
KRAW
KRAW!
THIS MUST BE IT.
THIS MUST BE RAVENHALL.
LOOKS LIKE IT COULD DO WITH A BIT OF A CLEAN-UP.
KAW
KAW!
WOOSH

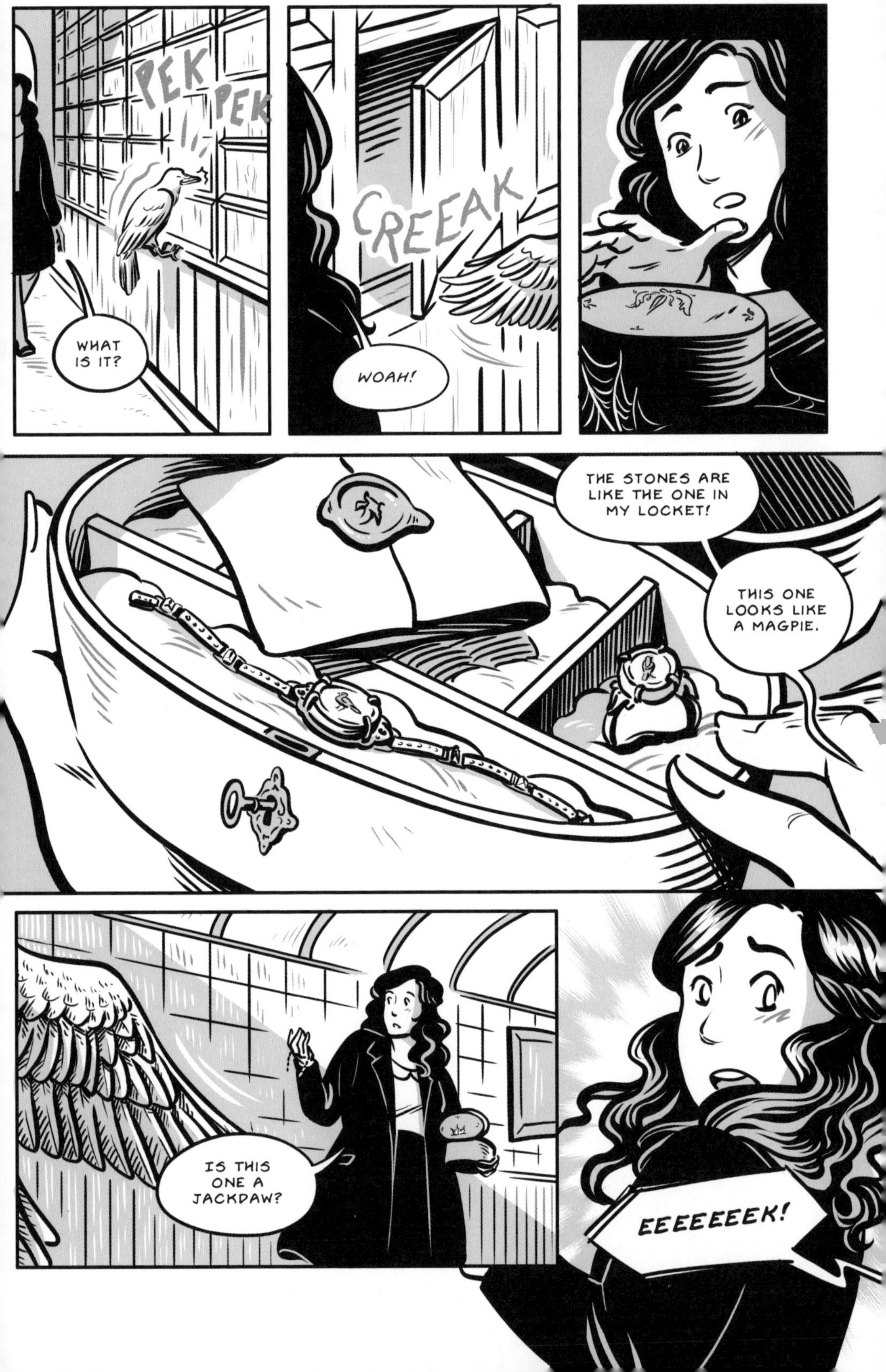
PEK PEK
WHAT IS IT?
CREEAK
WOAH!
THE STONES ARE LIKE THE ONE IN MY LOCKET!
THIS ONE LOOKS LIKE A MAGPIE.
IS THIS ONE A JACKDAW?
EEEEEEEK!

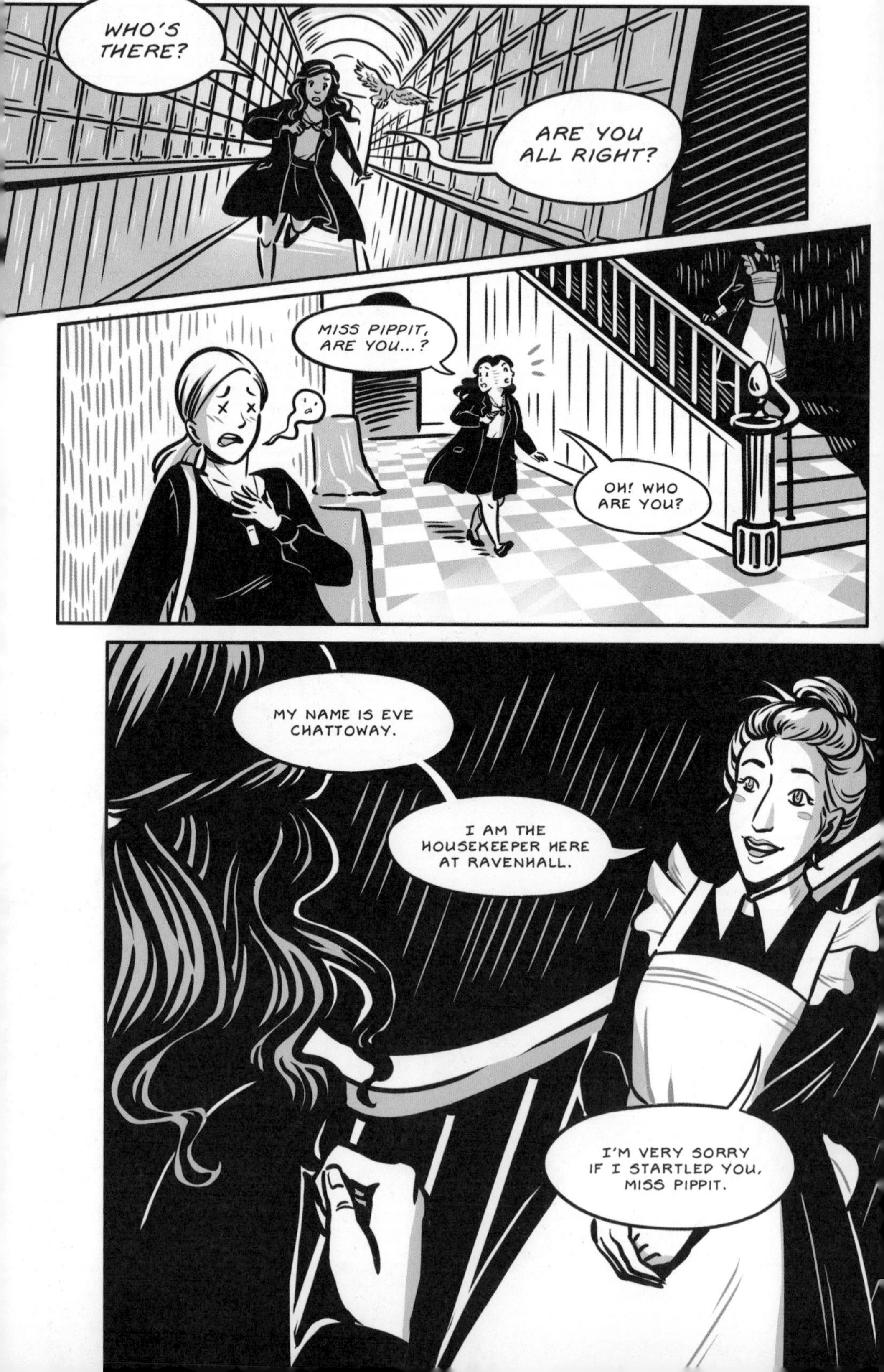
WHO'S THERE?
ARE YOU ALL RIGHT?
MISS PIPPIT, ARE YOU...?
OH! WHO ARE YOU?
MY NAME IS EVE CHATTOWAY.
I AM THE HOUSEKEEPER HERE AT RAVENHALL.
I'M VERY SORRY IF I STARTLED YOU, MISS PIPPIT.

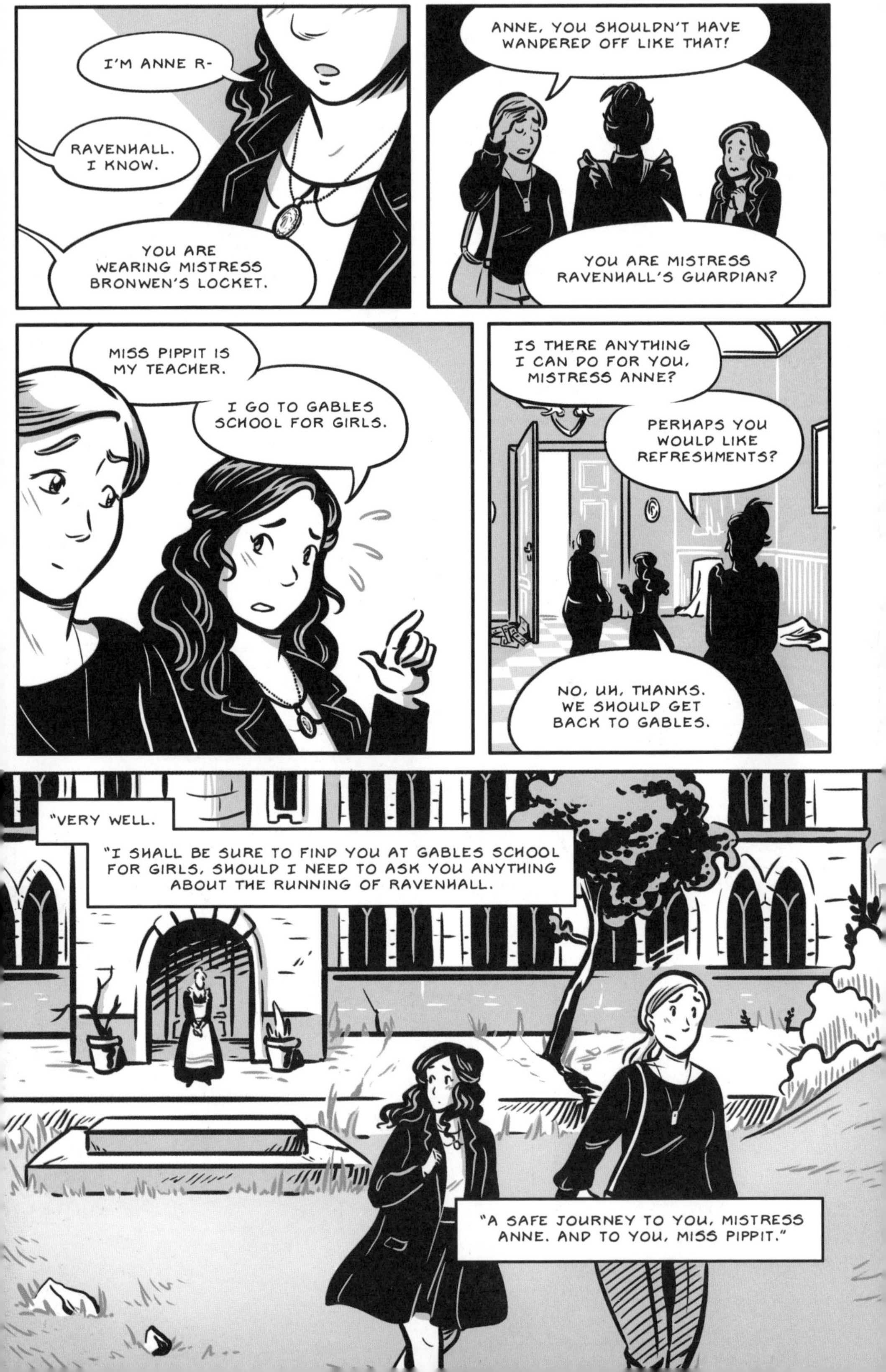
I'M ANNE R-
RAVENHALL. I KNOW.
YOU ARE WEARING MISTRESS BRONWEN'S LOCKET.
ANNE, YOU SHOULDN'T HAVE WANDERED OFF LIKE THAT!
YOU ARE MISTRESS RAVENHALL'S GUARDIAN?
MISS PIPPIT IS MY TEACHER.
I GO TO GABLES SCHOOL FOR GIRLS.
IS THERE ANYTHING I CAN DO FOR YOU, MISTRESS ANNE?
PERHAPS YOU WOULD LIKE REFRESHMENTS?
NO, UH, THANKS. WE SHOULD GET BACK TO GABLES.
"VERY WELL.
"I SHALL BE SURE TO FIND YOU AT GABLES SCHOOL FOR GIRLS, SHOULD I NEED TO ASK YOU ANYTHING ABOUT THE RUNNING OF RAVENHALL.
"A SAFE JOURNEY TO YOU, MISTRESS ANNE. AND TO YOU, MISS PIPPIT."

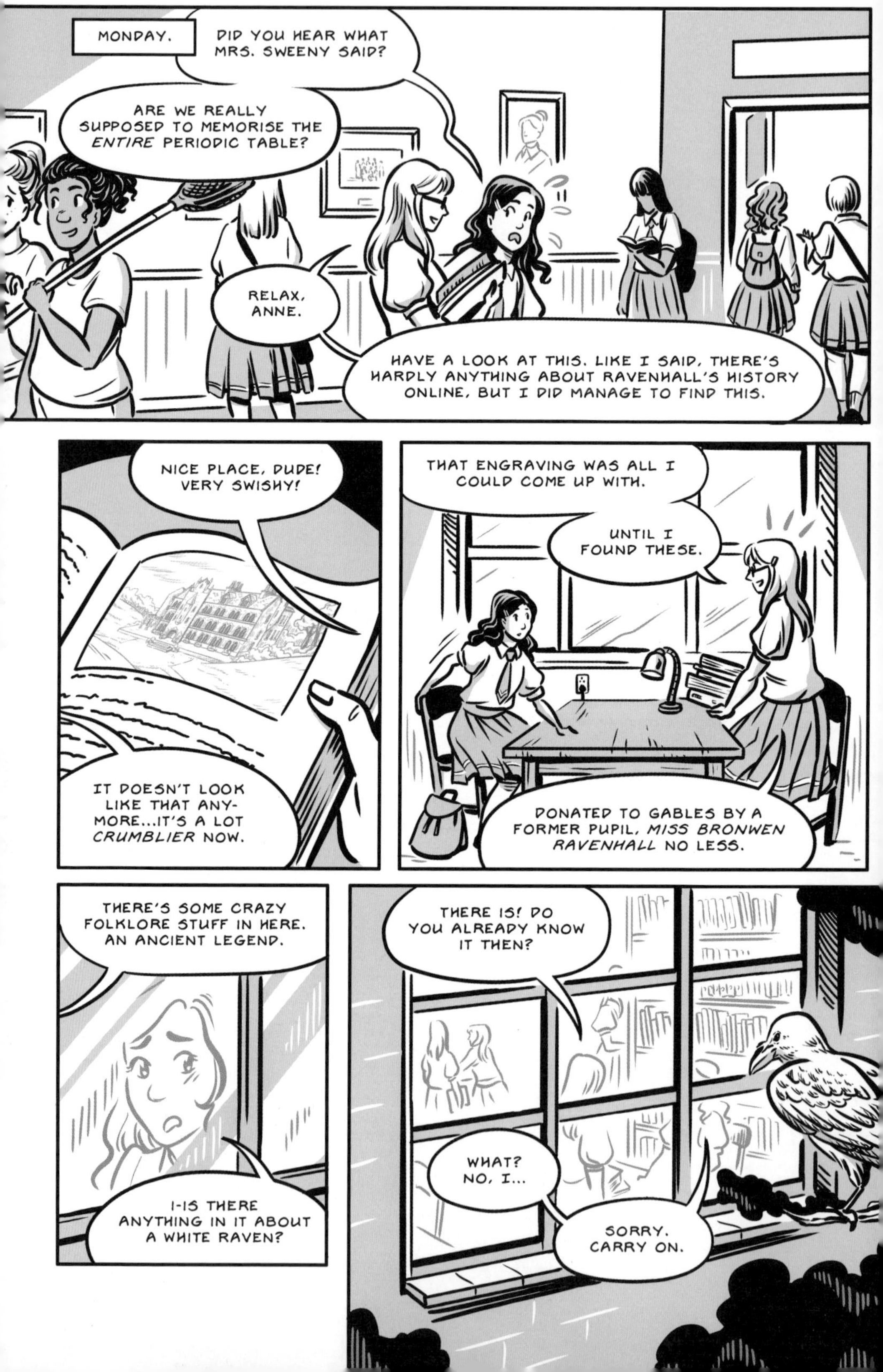

MONDAY.
DID YOU HEAR WHAT MRS. SWEENY SAID?
ARE WE REALLY SUPPOSED TO MEMORISE THE *ENTIRE* PERIODIC TABLE?
RELAX, ANNE.
HAVE A LOOK AT THIS. LIKE I SAID, THERE'S HARDLY ANYTHING ABOUT RAVENHALL'S HISTORY ONLINE, BUT I DID MANAGE TO FIND THIS.
NICE PLACE, DUDE! VERY SWISHY!
IT DOESN'T LOOK LIKE THAT ANY-MORE...IT'S A LOT *CRUMBLIER* NOW.
THAT ENGRAVING WAS ALL I COULD COME UP WITH.
UNTIL I FOUND THESE.
DONATED TO GABLES BY A FORMER PUPIL, *MISS BRONWEN RAVENHALL* NO LESS.
THERE'S SOME CRAZY FOLKLORE STUFF IN HERE. AN ANCIENT LEGEND.
I-IS THERE ANYTHING IN IT ABOUT A WHITE RAVEN?
THERE IS! DO YOU ALREADY KNOW IT THEN?
WHAT? NO, I...
SORRY. CARRY ON.

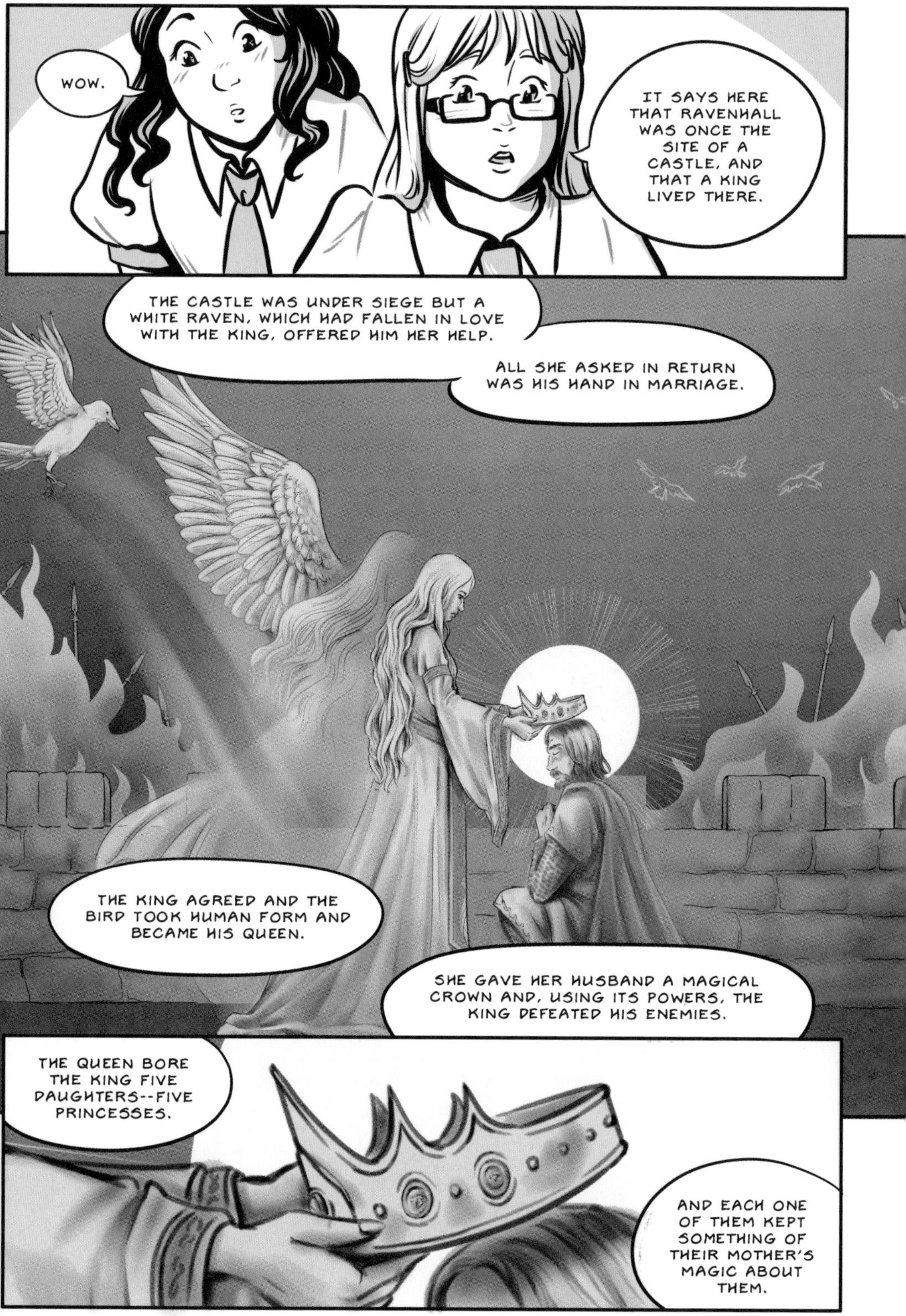
WOW.
IT SAYS HERE THAT RAVENHALL WAS ONCE THE SITE OF A CASTLE, AND THAT A KING LIVED THERE.
THE CASTLE WAS UNDER SIEGE BUT A WHITE RAVEN, WHICH HAD FALLEN IN LOVE WITH THE KING, OFFERED HIM HER HELP.
ALL SHE ASKED IN RETURN WAS HIS HAND IN MARRIAGE.
THE KING AGREED AND THE BIRD TOOK HUMAN FORM AND BECAME HIS QUEEN.
SHE GAVE HER HUSBAND A MAGICAL CROWN AND, USING ITS POWERS, THE KING DEFEATED HIS ENEMIES.
THE QUEEN BORE THE KING FIVE DAUGHTERS--FIVE PRINCESSES.
AND EACH ONE OF THEM KEPT SOMETHING OF THEIR MOTHER'S MAGIC ABOUT THEM.

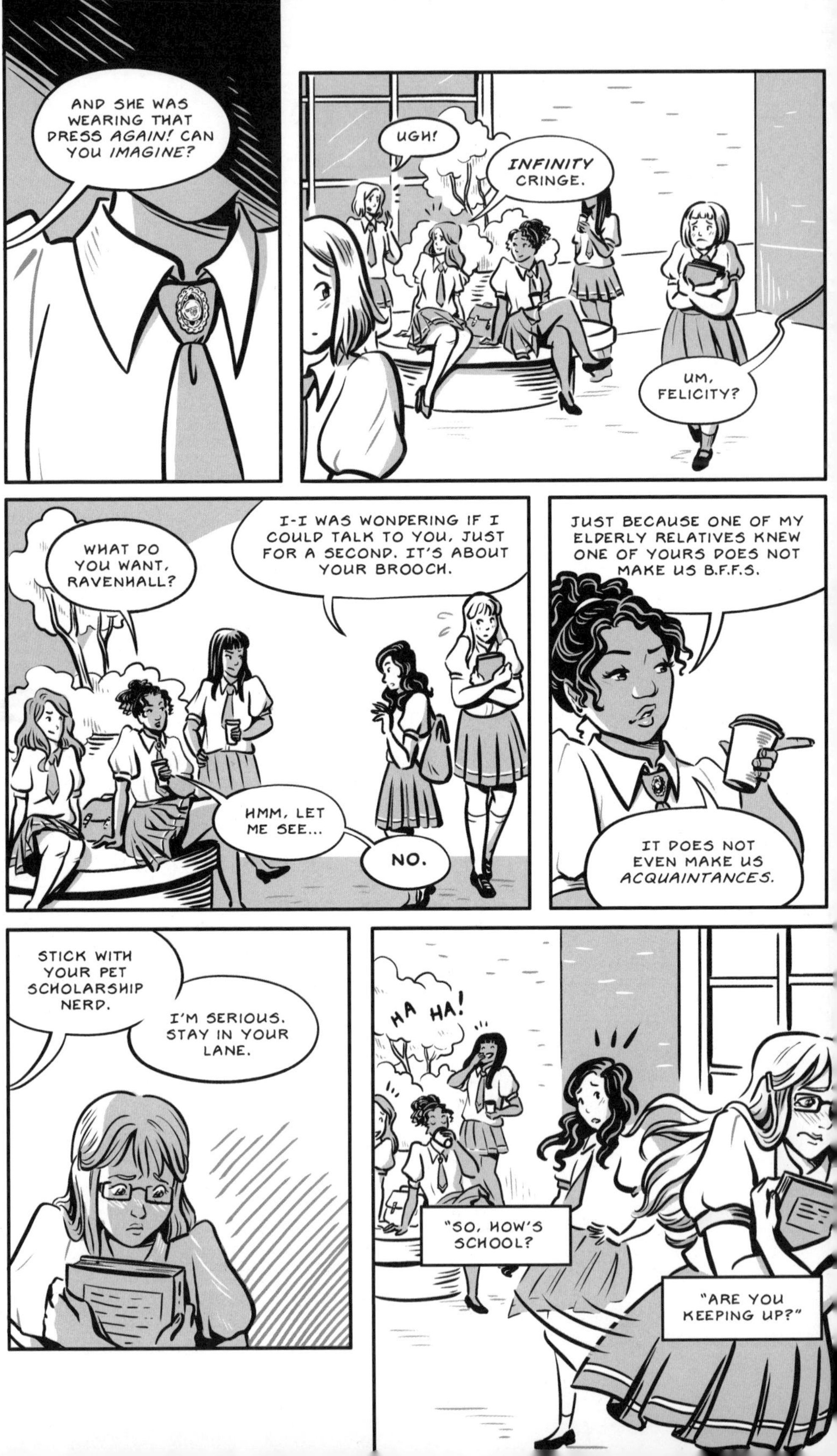
AND SHE WAS WEARING THAT DRESS *AGAIN!* CAN YOU *IMAGINE?*
UGH!
INFINITY CRINGE.
UM, FELICITY?
WHAT DO YOU WANT, RAVENHALL?
I-I WAS WONDERING IF I COULD TALK TO YOU, JUST FOR A SECOND. IT'S ABOUT YOUR BROOCH.
HMM, LET ME SEE...
NO.
JUST BECAUSE ONE OF MY ELDERLY RELATIVES KNEW ONE OF YOURS DOES NOT MAKE US B.F.F.S.
IT DOES NOT EVEN MAKE US *ACQUAINTANCES.*
STICK WITH YOUR PET SCHOLARSHIP NERD.
I'M SERIOUS. STAY IN YOUR LANE.
HA HA!
"SO, HOW'S SCHOOL?
"ARE YOU KEEPING UP?"

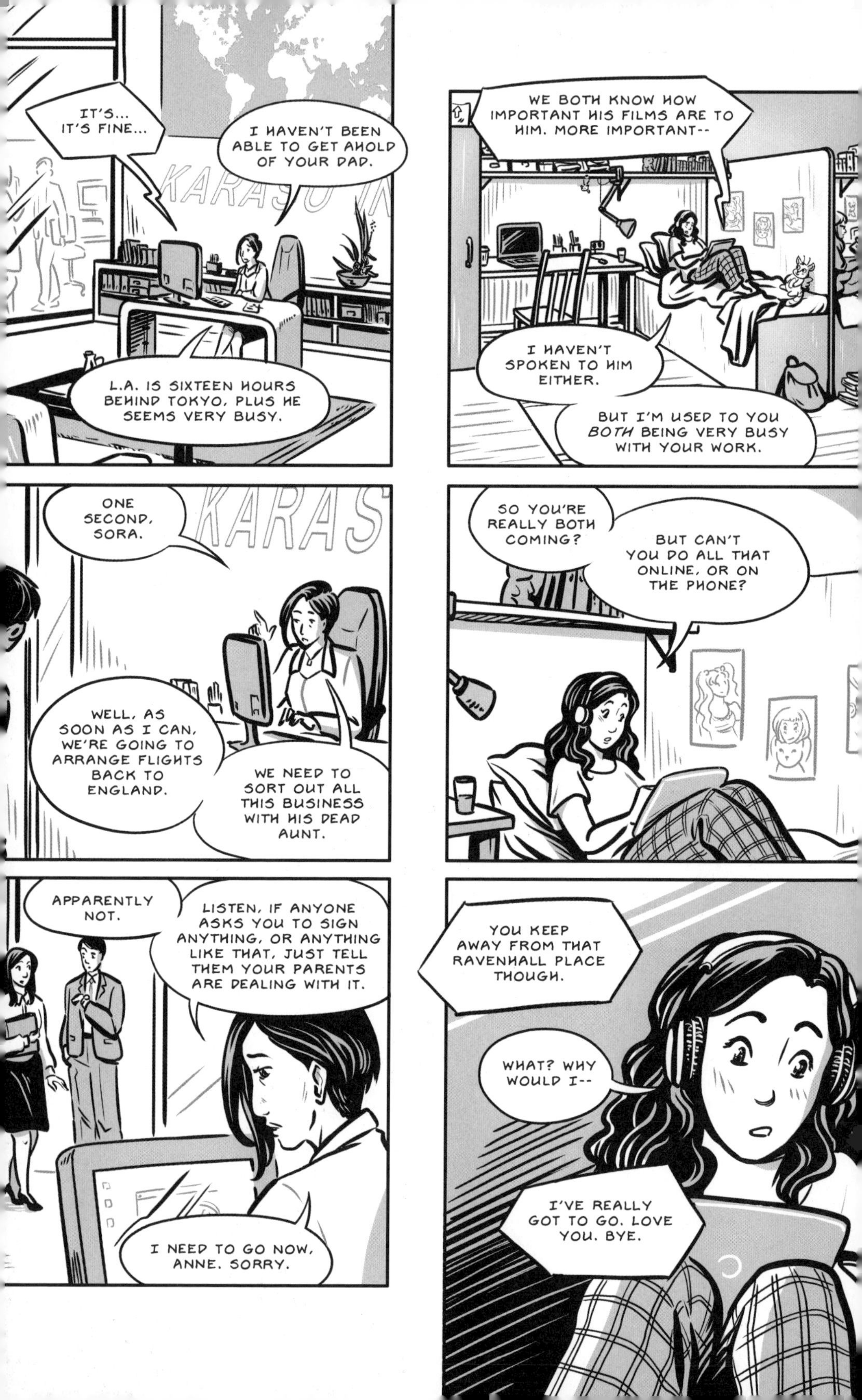

IT'S... IT'S FINE...
I HAVEN'T BEEN ABLE TO GET AHOLD OF YOUR DAD.
KARASU IN
L.A. IS SIXTEEN HOURS BEHIND TOKYO, PLUS HE SEEMS VERY BUSY.
WE BOTH KNOW HOW IMPORTANT HIS FILMS ARE TO HIM. MORE IMPORTANT--
I HAVEN'T SPOKEN TO HIM EITHER.
BUT I'M USED TO YOU *BOTH* BEING VERY BUSY WITH YOUR WORK.
ONE SECOND, SORA.
KARAS
WELL, AS SOON AS I CAN, WE'RE GOING TO ARRANGE FLIGHTS BACK TO ENGLAND.
WE NEED TO SORT OUT ALL THIS BUSINESS WITH HIS DEAD AUNT.
SO YOU'RE REALLY BOTH COMING?
BUT CAN'T YOU DO ALL THAT ONLINE, OR ON THE PHONE?
APPARENTLY NOT.
LISTEN, IF ANYONE ASKS YOU TO SIGN ANYTHING, OR ANYTHING LIKE THAT, JUST TELL THEM YOUR PARENTS ARE DEALING WITH IT.
I NEED TO GO NOW, ANNE. SORRY.
YOU KEEP AWAY FROM THAT RAVENHALL PLACE THOUGH.
WHAT? WHY WOULD I--
I'VE REALLY GOT TO GO. LOVE YOU. BYE.

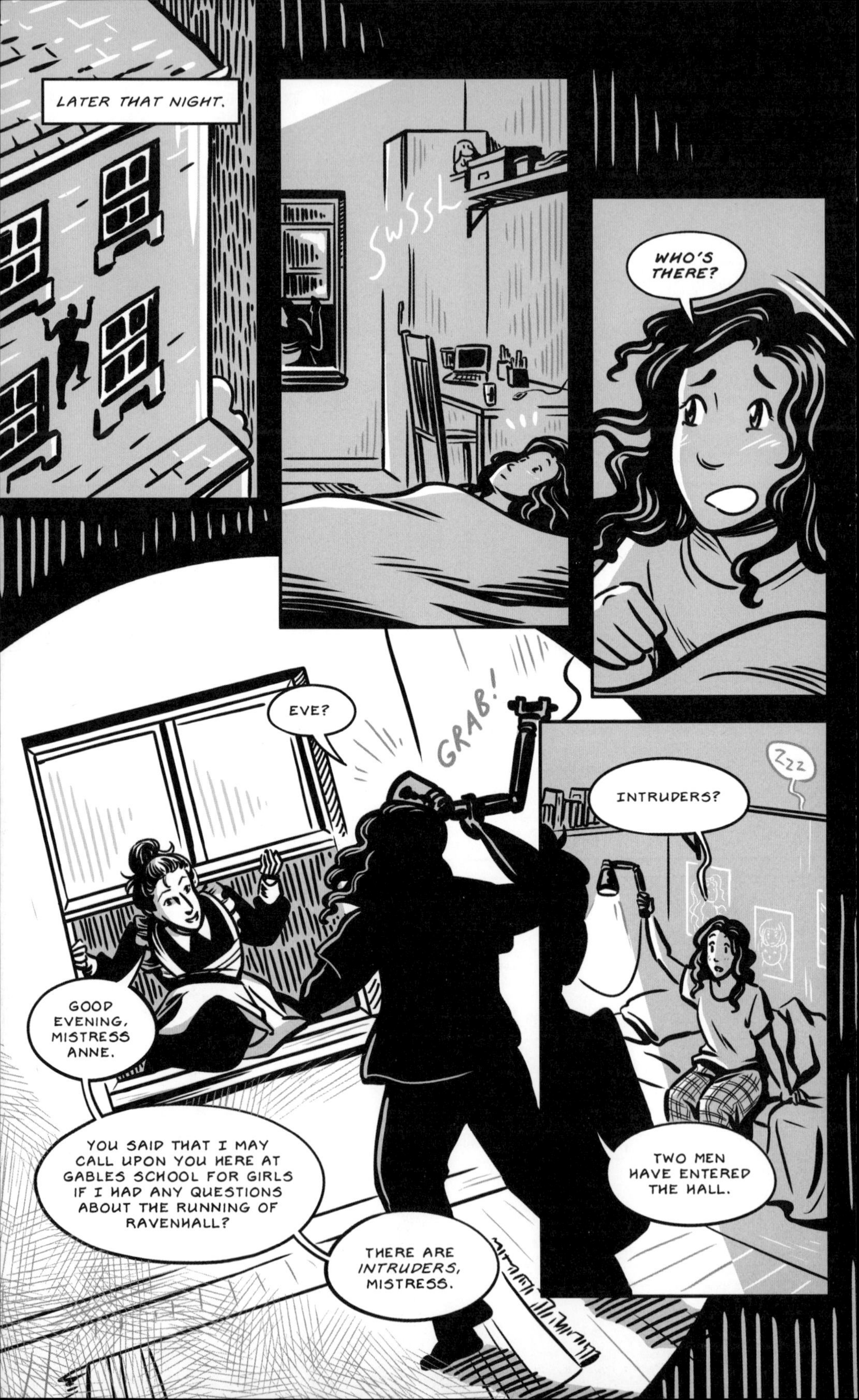
LATER THAT NIGHT.
SWSSH
WHO'S THERE?
EVE?
GRAB!
ZZZ
INTRUDERS?
GOOD EVENING, MISTRESS ANNE.
YOU SAID THAT I MAY CALL UPON YOU HERE AT GABLES SCHOOL FOR GIRLS IF I HAD ANY QUESTIONS ABOUT THE RUNNING OF RAVENHALL?
THERE ARE *INTRUDERS*, MISTRESS.
TWO MEN HAVE ENTERED THE HALL.

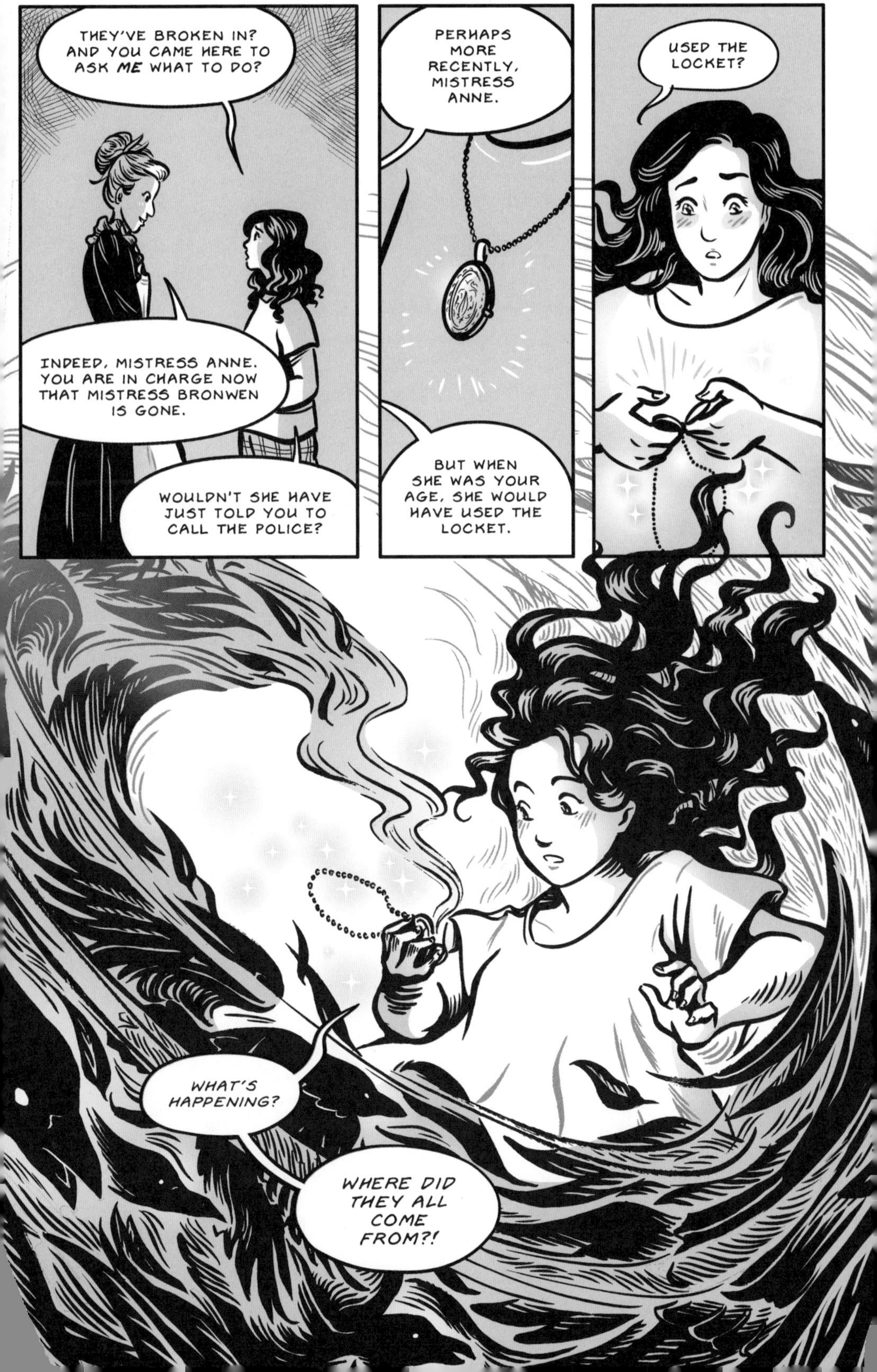
THEY'VE BROKEN IN? AND YOU CAME HERE TO ASK *ME* WHAT TO DO?
INDEED, MISTRESS ANNE. YOU ARE IN CHARGE NOW THAT MISTRESS BRONWEN IS GONE.
WOULDN'T SHE HAVE JUST TOLD YOU TO CALL THE POLICE?
PERHAPS MORE RECENTLY, MISTRESS ANNE.
BUT WHEN SHE WAS YOUR AGE, SHE WOULD HAVE USED THE LOCKET.
USED THE LOCKET?
WHAT'S HAPPENING?
WHERE DID THEY ALL COME FROM?!

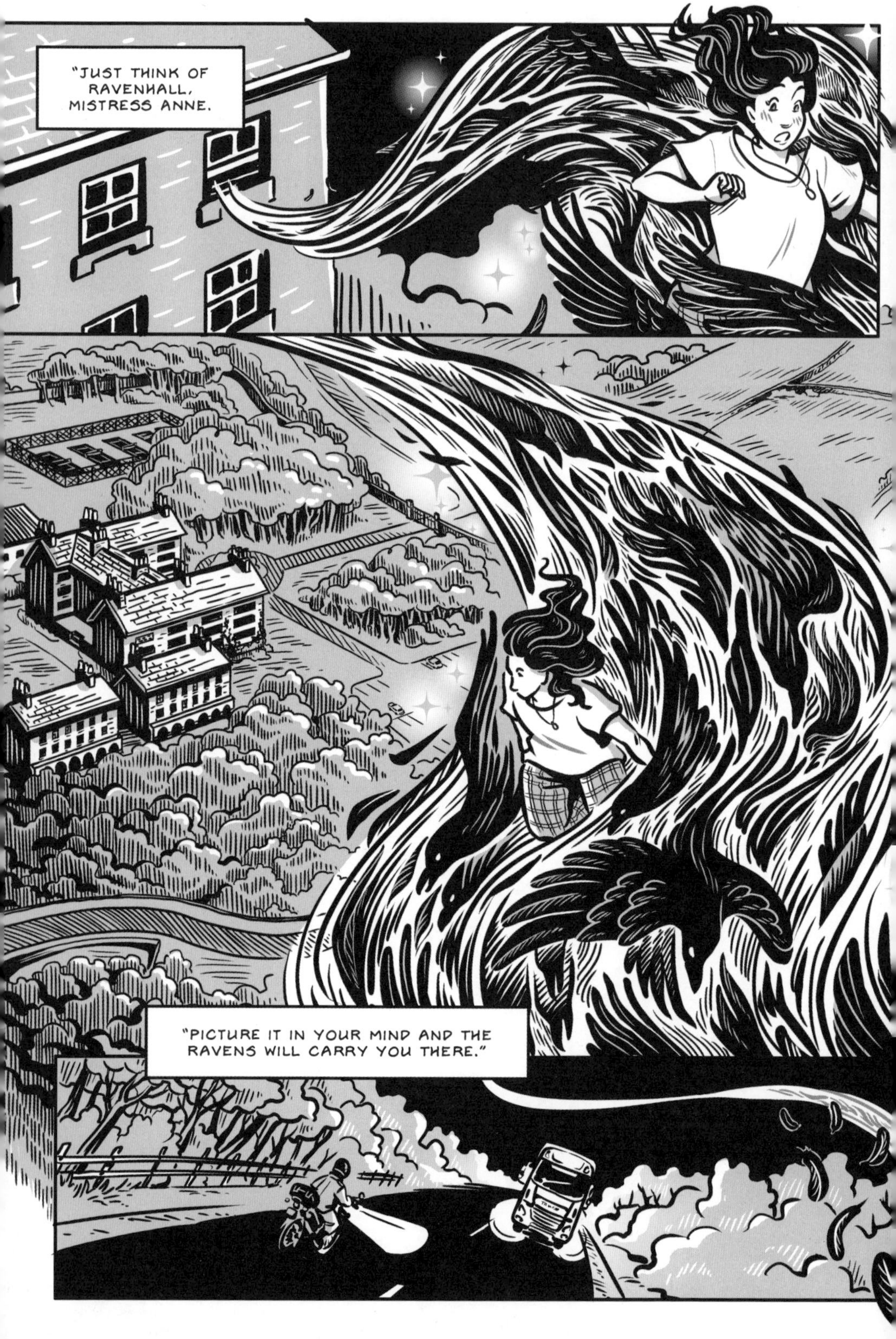
"JUST THINK OF RAVENHALL, MISTRESS ANNE.
"PICTURE IT IN YOUR MIND AND THE RAVENS WILL CARRY YOU THERE."

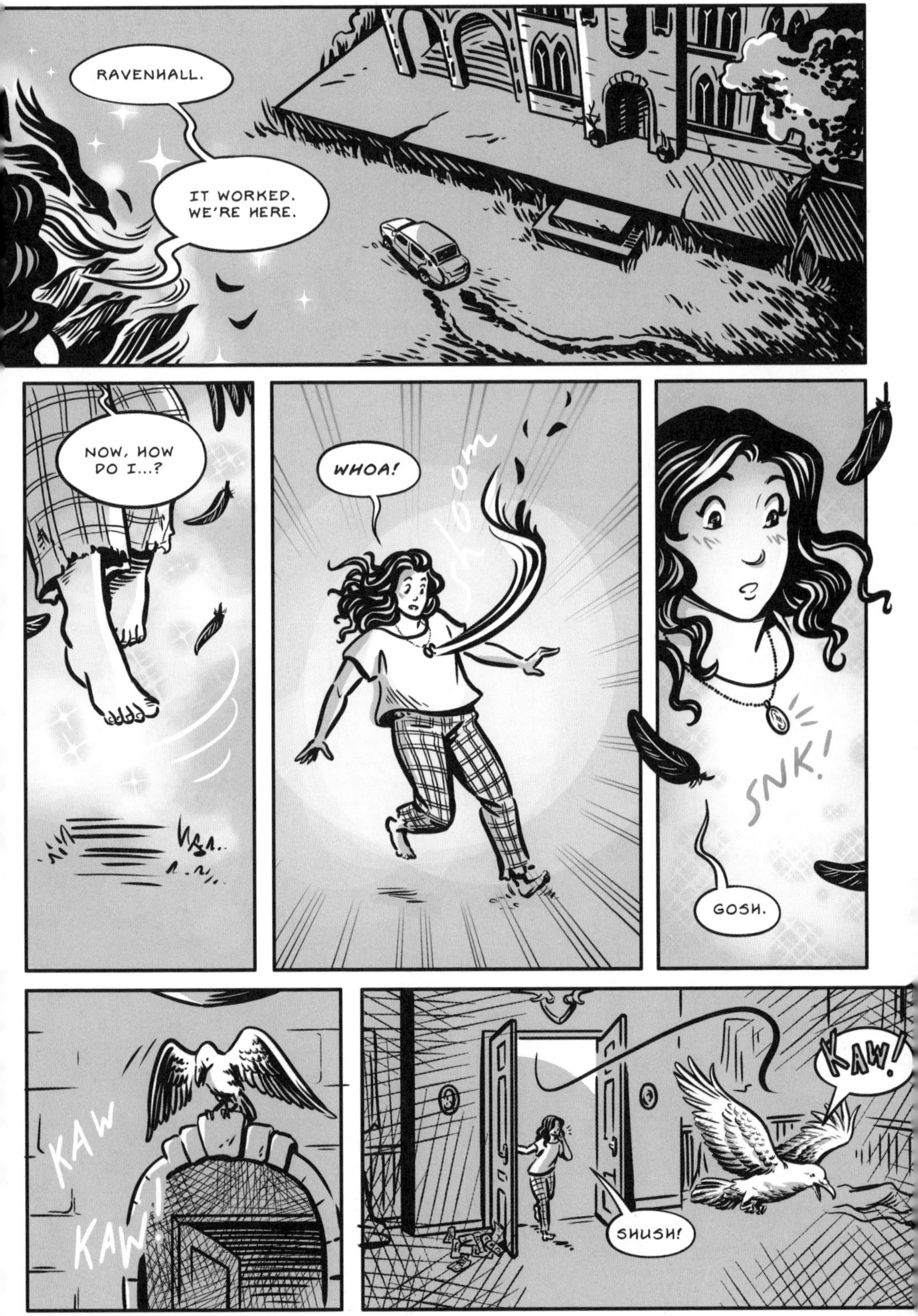
RAVENHALL.
IT WORKED. WE'RE HERE.
NOW, HOW DO I...?
WHOA!
shoom
SNK!
GOSH.
KAW KAW!
KAW!
SHUSH!

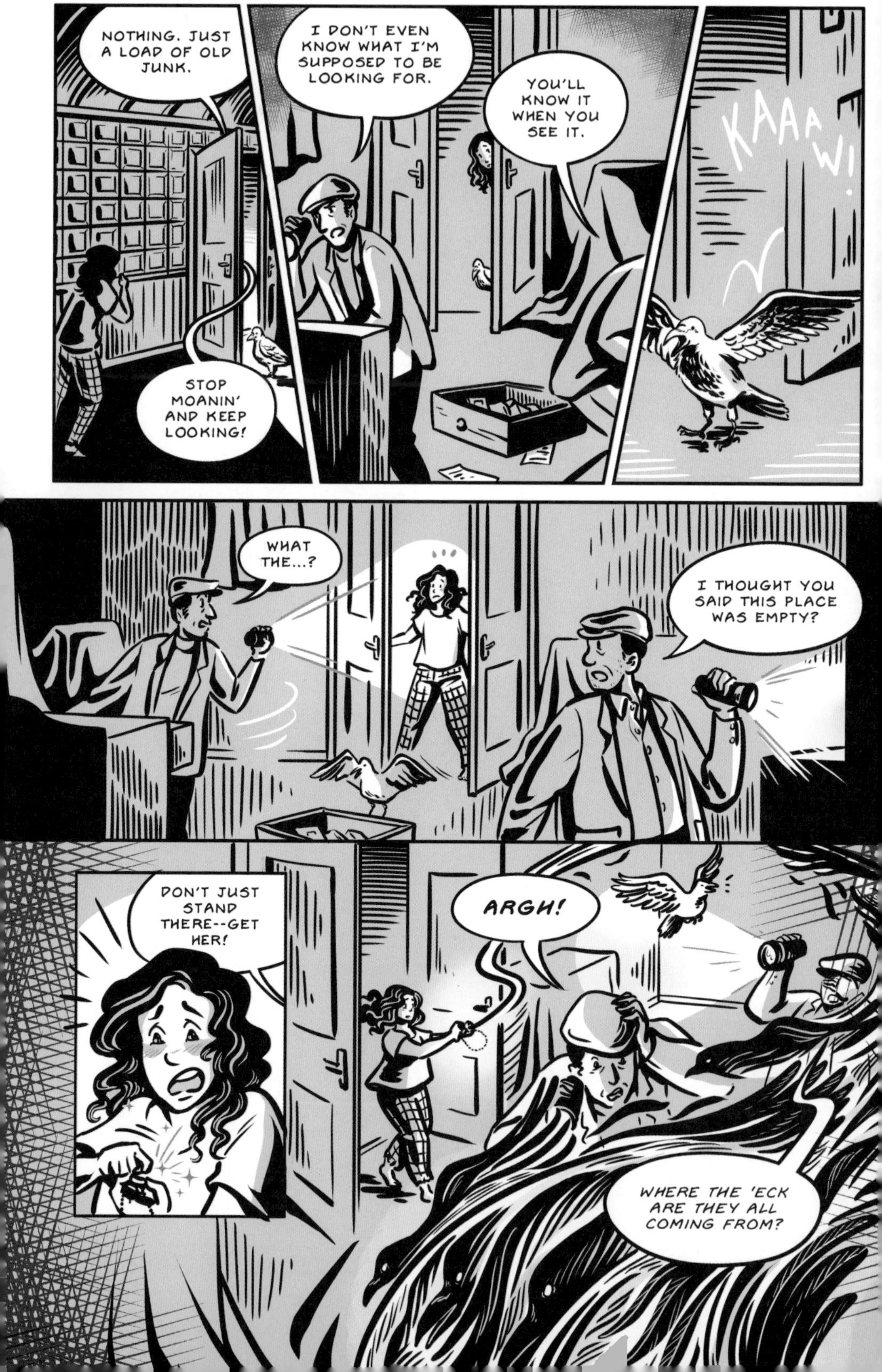
NOTHING. JUST A LOAD OF OLD JUNK.
STOP MOANIN' AND KEEP LOOKING!
I DON'T EVEN KNOW WHAT I'M SUPPOSED TO BE LOOKING FOR.
YOU'LL KNOW IT WHEN YOU SEE IT.
KAAAW!
WHAT THE...?
I THOUGHT YOU SAID THIS PLACE WAS EMPTY?
DON'T JUST STAND THERE--GET HER!
ARGH!
WHERE THE 'ECK ARE THEY ALL COMING FROM?

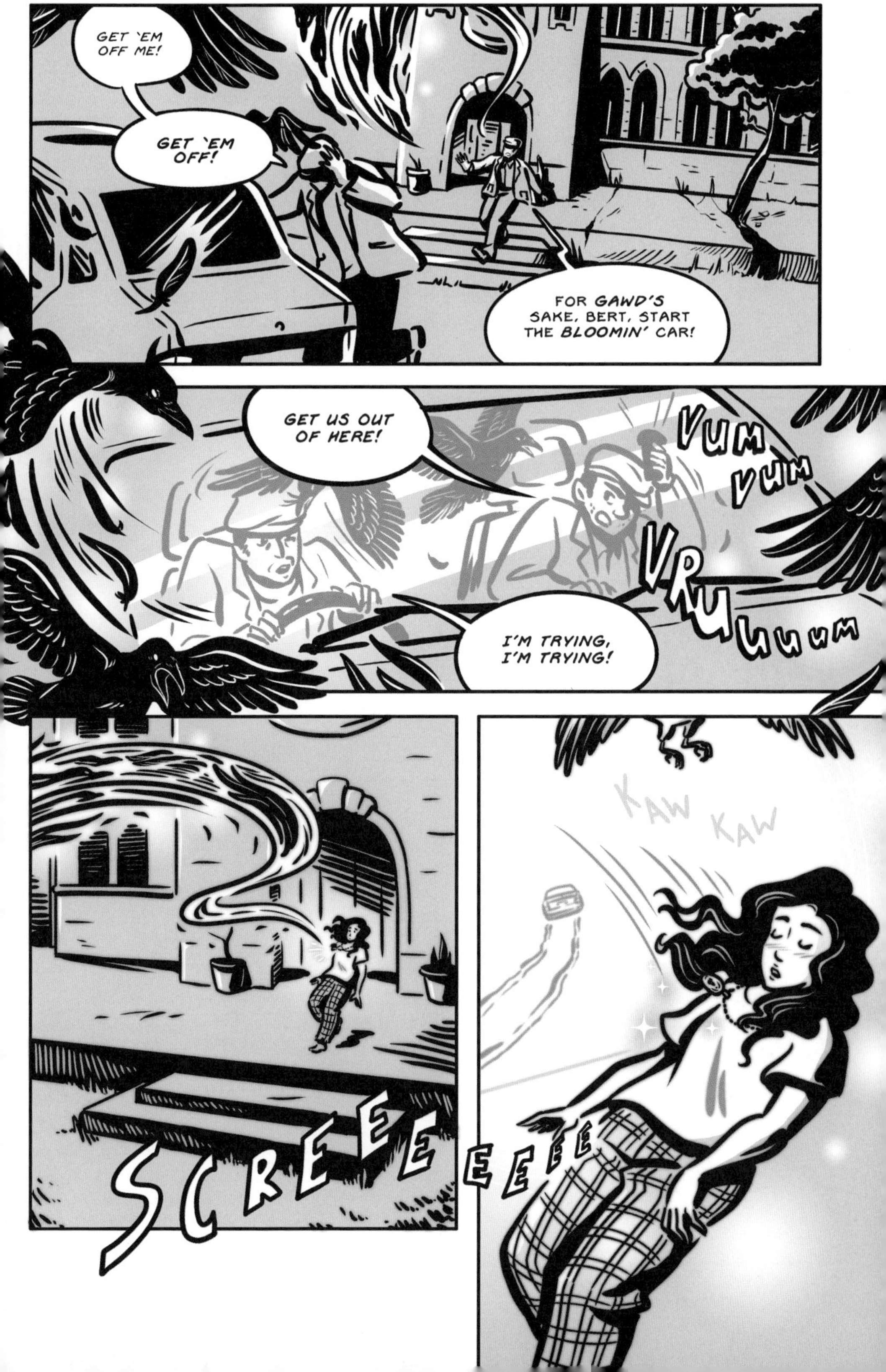
GET `EM OFF ME!
GET `EM OFF!
FOR GAWD'S SAKE, BERT, START THE BLOOMIN' CAR!
GET US OUT OF HERE!
VUM VUM
VRUUUUUM
I'M TRYING, I'M TRYING!
SCREEEEEEEE
KAW KAW

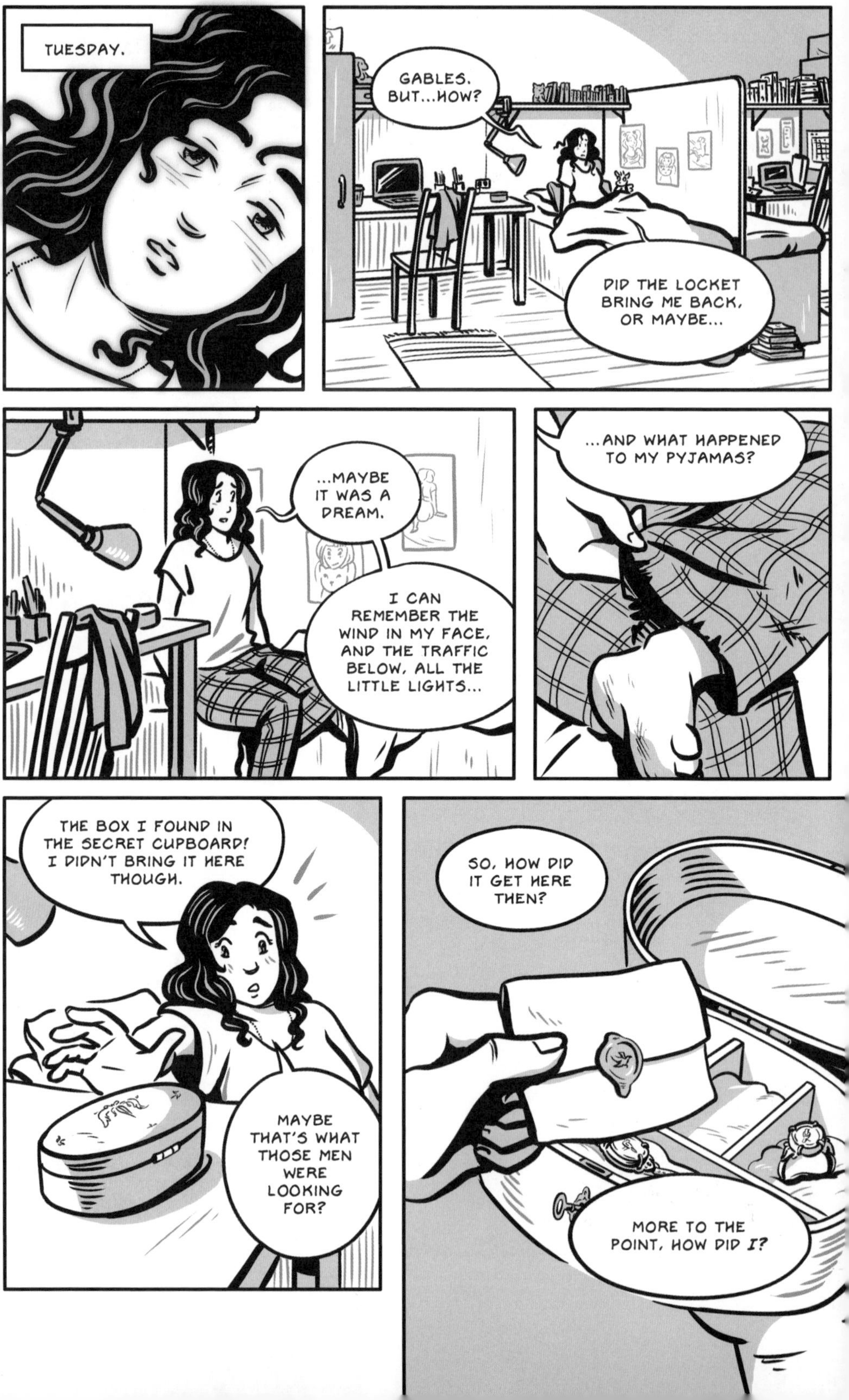
TUESDAY.
GABLES. BUT...HOW?
DID THE LOCKET BRING ME BACK, OR MAYBE...
...MAYBE IT WAS A DREAM.
I CAN REMEMBER THE WIND IN MY FACE, AND THE TRAFFIC BELOW, ALL THE LITTLE LIGHTS...
...AND WHAT HAPPENED TO MY PYJAMAS?
THE BOX I FOUND IN THE SECRET CUPBOARD! I DIDN'T BRING IT HERE THOUGH.
MAYBE THAT'S WHAT THOSE MEN WERE LOOKING FOR?
SO, HOW DID IT GET HERE THEN?
MORE TO THE POINT, HOW DID *I*?

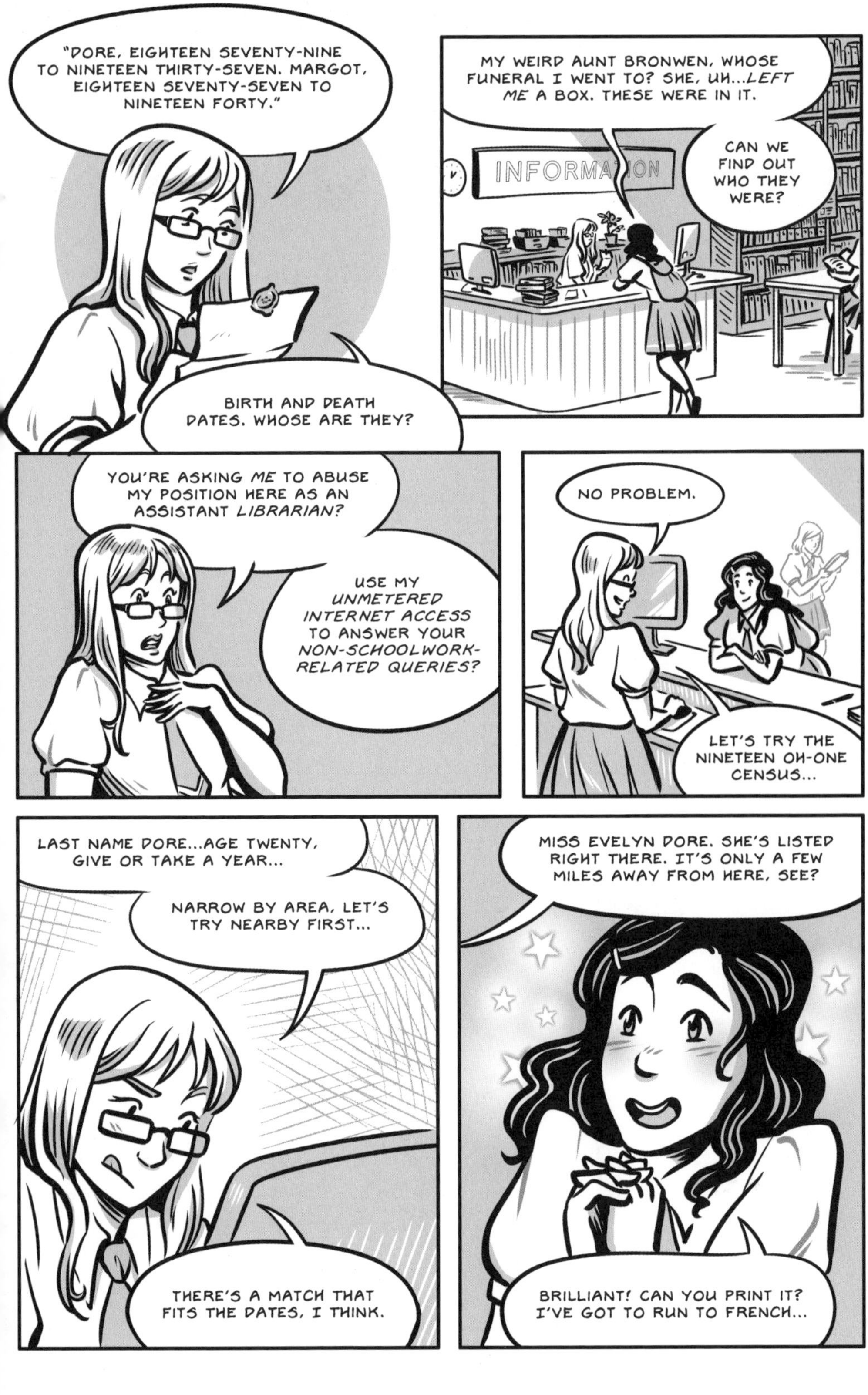
"DORE, EIGHTEEN SEVENTY-NINE TO NINETEEN THIRTY-SEVEN. MARGOT, EIGHTEEN SEVENTY-SEVEN TO NINETEEN FORTY."
BIRTH AND DEATH DATES. WHOSE ARE THEY?
MY WEIRD AUNT BRONWEN, WHOSE FUNERAL I WENT TO? SHE, UH...*LEFT ME* A BOX. THESE WERE IN IT.
INFORMATION
CAN WE FIND OUT WHO THEY WERE?
YOU'RE ASKING *ME* TO ABUSE MY POSITION HERE AS AN ASSISTANT *LIBRARIAN?*
USE MY *UNMETERED INTERNET ACCESS* TO ANSWER YOUR *NON-SCHOOLWORK-RELATED QUERIES?*
NO PROBLEM.
LET'S TRY THE NINETEEN OH-ONE CENSUS...
LAST NAME DORE...AGE TWENTY, GIVE OR TAKE A YEAR...
NARROW BY AREA, LET'S TRY NEARBY FIRST...
THERE'S A MATCH THAT FITS THE DATES, I THINK.
MISS EVELYN DORE. SHE'S LISTED RIGHT THERE. IT'S ONLY A FEW MILES AWAY FROM HERE, SEE?
BRILLIANT! CAN YOU PRINT IT? I'VE GOT TO RUN TO FRENCH...

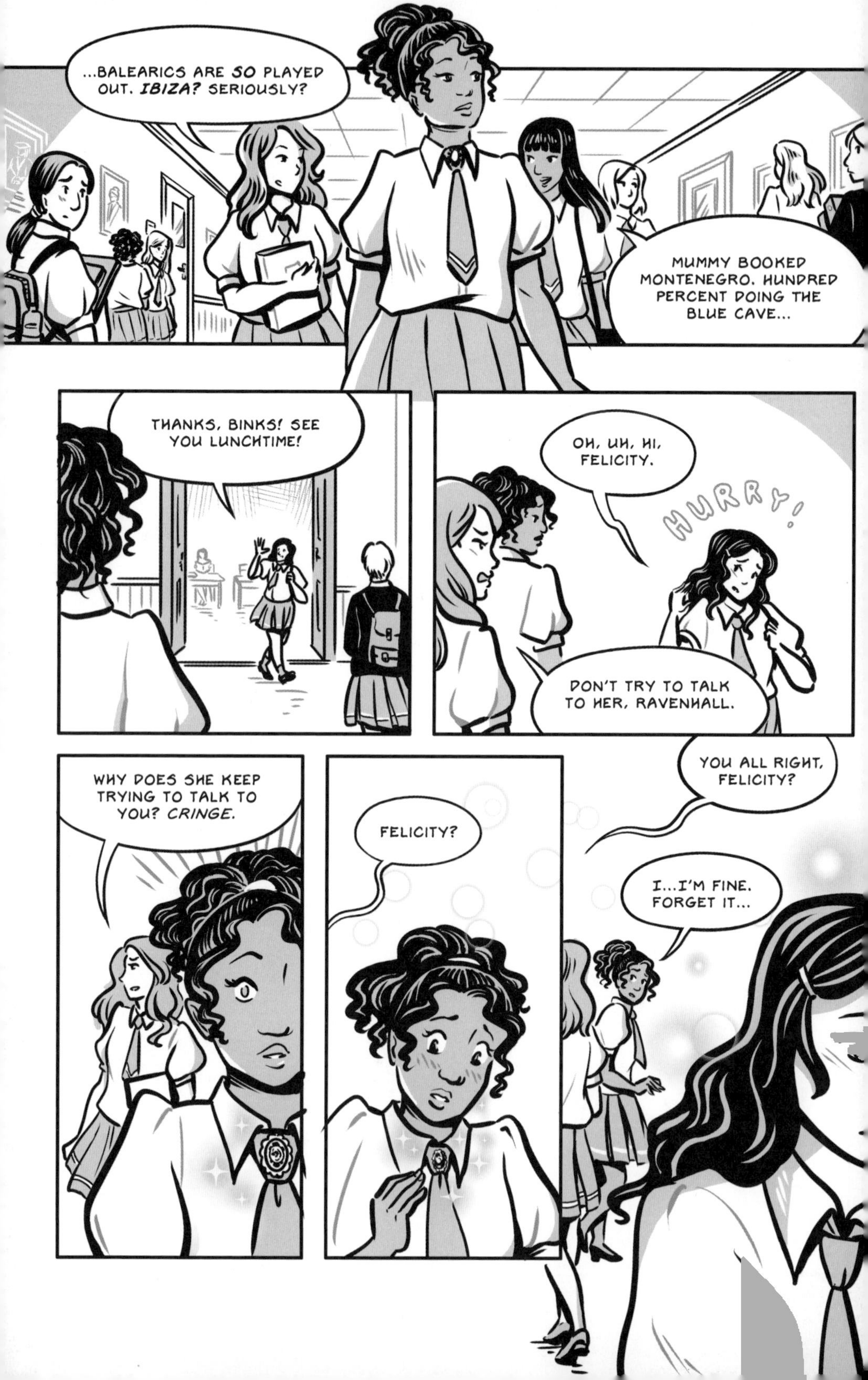
...BALEARICS ARE SO PLAYED OUT. IBIZA? SERIOUSLY?
MUMMY BOOKED MONTENEGRO. HUNDRED PERCENT DOING THE BLUE CAVE...
THANKS, BINKS! SEE YOU LUNCHTIME!
OH, UH, HI, FELICITY.
HURRY!
DON'T TRY TO TALK TO HER, RAVENHALL.
WHY DOES SHE KEEP TRYING TO TALK TO YOU? CRINGE.
FELICITY?
YOU ALL RIGHT, FELICITY?
I...I'M FINE. FORGET IT...

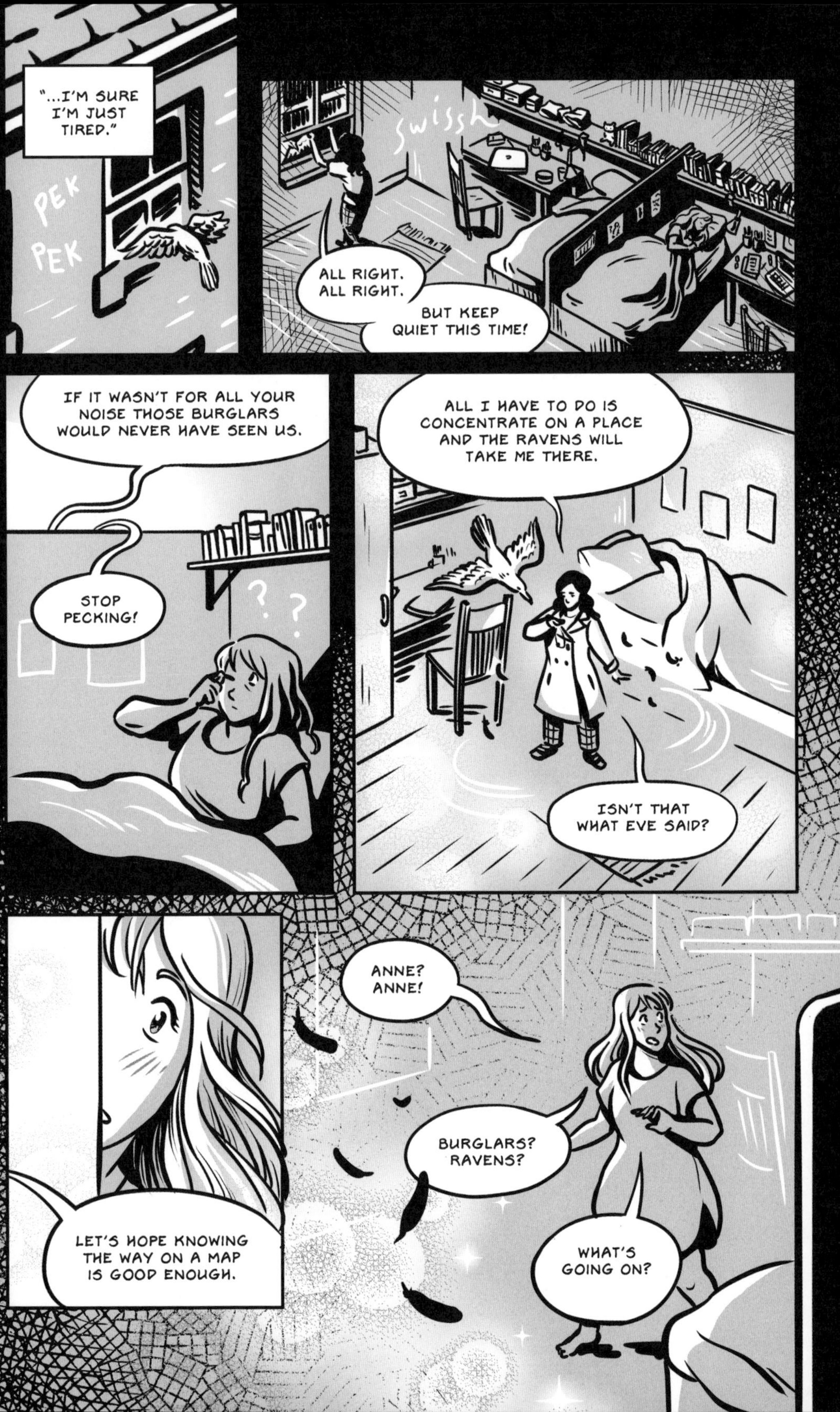
"...I'M SURE I'M JUST TIRED."
PEK PEK
swissh
ALL RIGHT. ALL RIGHT.
BUT KEEP QUIET THIS TIME!
IF IT WASN'T FOR ALL YOUR NOISE THOSE BURGLARS WOULD NEVER HAVE SEEN US.
STOP PECKING!
? ?
ALL I HAVE TO DO IS CONCENTRATE ON A PLACE AND THE RAVENS WILL TAKE ME THERE.
ISN'T THAT WHAT EVE SAID?
LET'S HOPE KNOWING THE WAY ON A MAP IS GOOD ENOUGH.
ANNE? ANNE!
BURGLARS? RAVENS?
WHAT'S GOING ON?

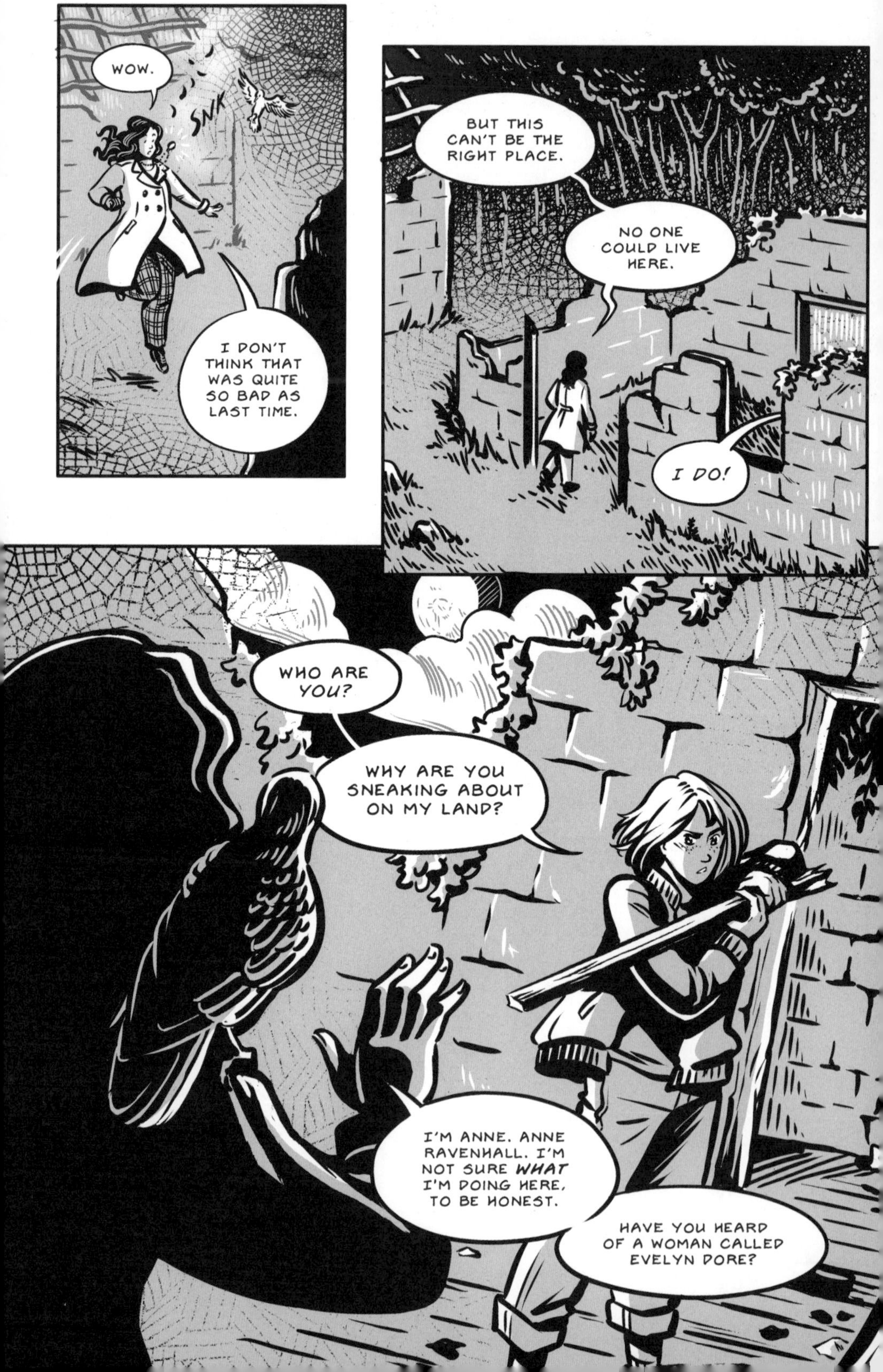
WOW.
SNK
I DON'T THINK THAT WAS QUITE SO BAD AS LAST TIME.
BUT THIS CAN'T BE THE RIGHT PLACE.
NO ONE COULD LIVE HERE.
I DO!
WHO ARE YOU?
WHY ARE YOU SNEAKING ABOUT ON MY LAND?
I'M ANNE. ANNE RAVENHALL. I'M NOT SURE WHAT I'M DOING HERE, TO BE HONEST.
HAVE YOU HEARD OF A WOMAN CALLED EVELYN DORE?

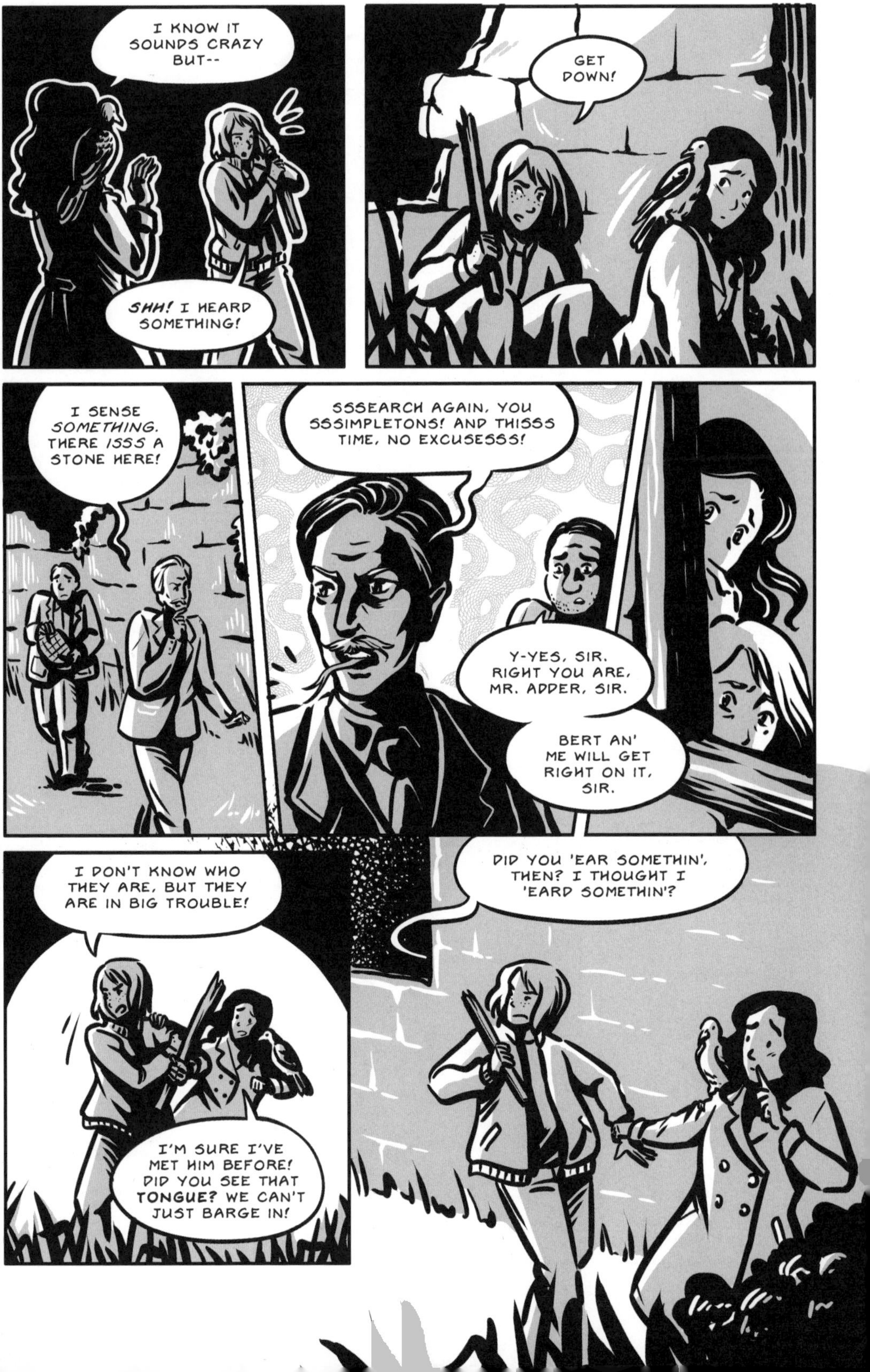
I KNOW IT SOUNDS CRAZY BUT--
SHH! I HEARD SOMETHING!
GET DOWN!
I SENSE SOMETHING. THERE ISSS A STONE HERE!
SSSEARCH AGAIN, YOU SSSIMPLETONS! AND THISSS TIME, NO EXCUSESSS!
Y-YES, SIR. RIGHT YOU ARE, MR. ADDER, SIR.
BERT AN' ME WILL GET RIGHT ON IT, SIR.
I DON'T KNOW WHO THEY ARE, BUT THEY ARE IN BIG TROUBLE!
I'M SURE I'VE MET HIM BEFORE! DID YOU SEE THAT TONGUE? WE CAN'T JUST BARGE IN!
DID YOU 'EAR SOMETHIN', THEN? I THOUGHT I 'EARD SOMETHIN'?

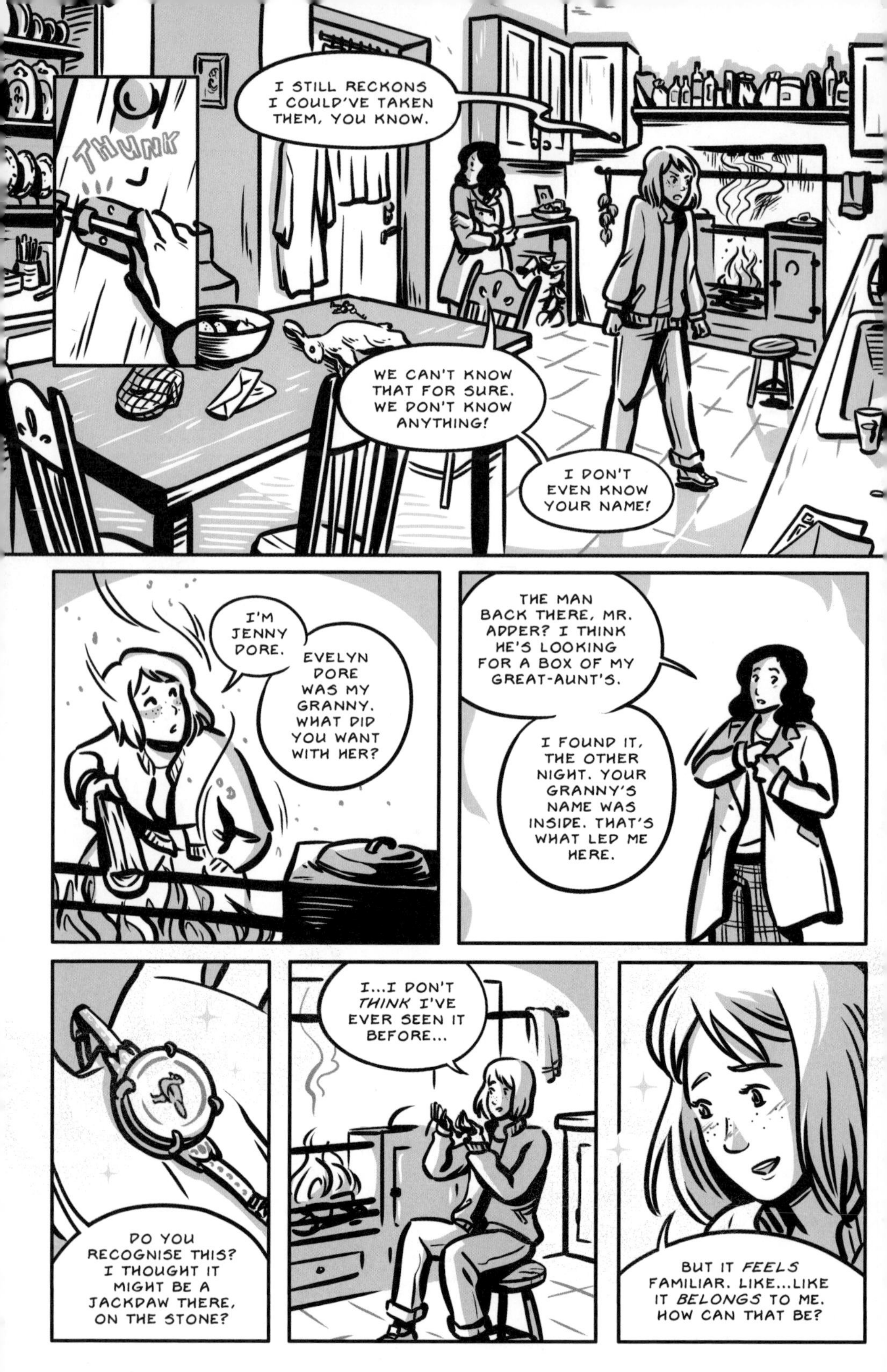
THUNK
I STILL RECKONS I COULD'VE TAKEN THEM, YOU KNOW.
WE CAN'T KNOW THAT FOR SURE. WE DON'T KNOW ANYTHING!
I DON'T EVEN KNOW YOUR NAME!
I'M JENNY DORE.
EVELYN DORE WAS MY GRANNY. WHAT DID YOU WANT WITH HER?
THE MAN BACK THERE, MR. ADDER? I THINK HE'S LOOKING FOR A BOX OF MY GREAT-AUNT'S.
I FOUND IT, THE OTHER NIGHT. YOUR GRANNY'S NAME WAS INSIDE. THAT'S WHAT LED ME HERE.
DO YOU RECOGNISE THIS? I THOUGHT IT MIGHT BE A JACKDAW THERE, ON THE STONE?
I...I DON'T *THINK* I'VE EVER SEEN IT BEFORE...
BUT IT *FEELS* FAMILIAR. LIKE...LIKE IT *BELONGS* TO ME. HOW CAN THAT BE?

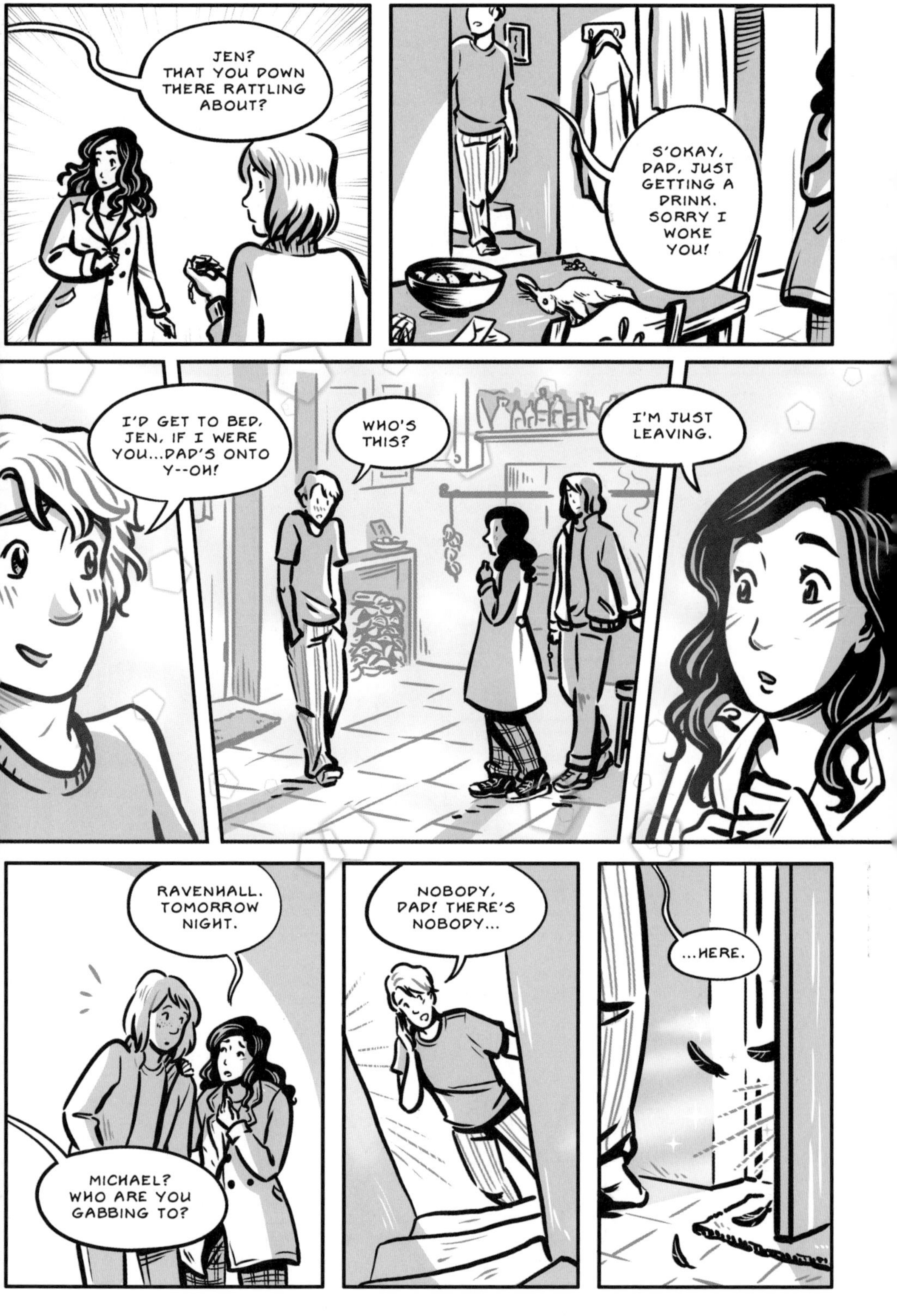
JEN? THAT YOU DOWN THERE RATTLING ABOUT?
S'OKAY, DAD, JUST GETTING A DRINK. SORRY I WOKE YOU!
I'D GET TO BED, JEN, IF I WERE YOU...DAD'S ONTO Y--OH!
WHO'S THIS?
I'M JUST LEAVING.
RAVENHALL. TOMORROW NIGHT.
MICHAEL? WHO ARE YOU GABBING TO?
NOBODY, DAD! THERE'S NOBODY...
...HERE.

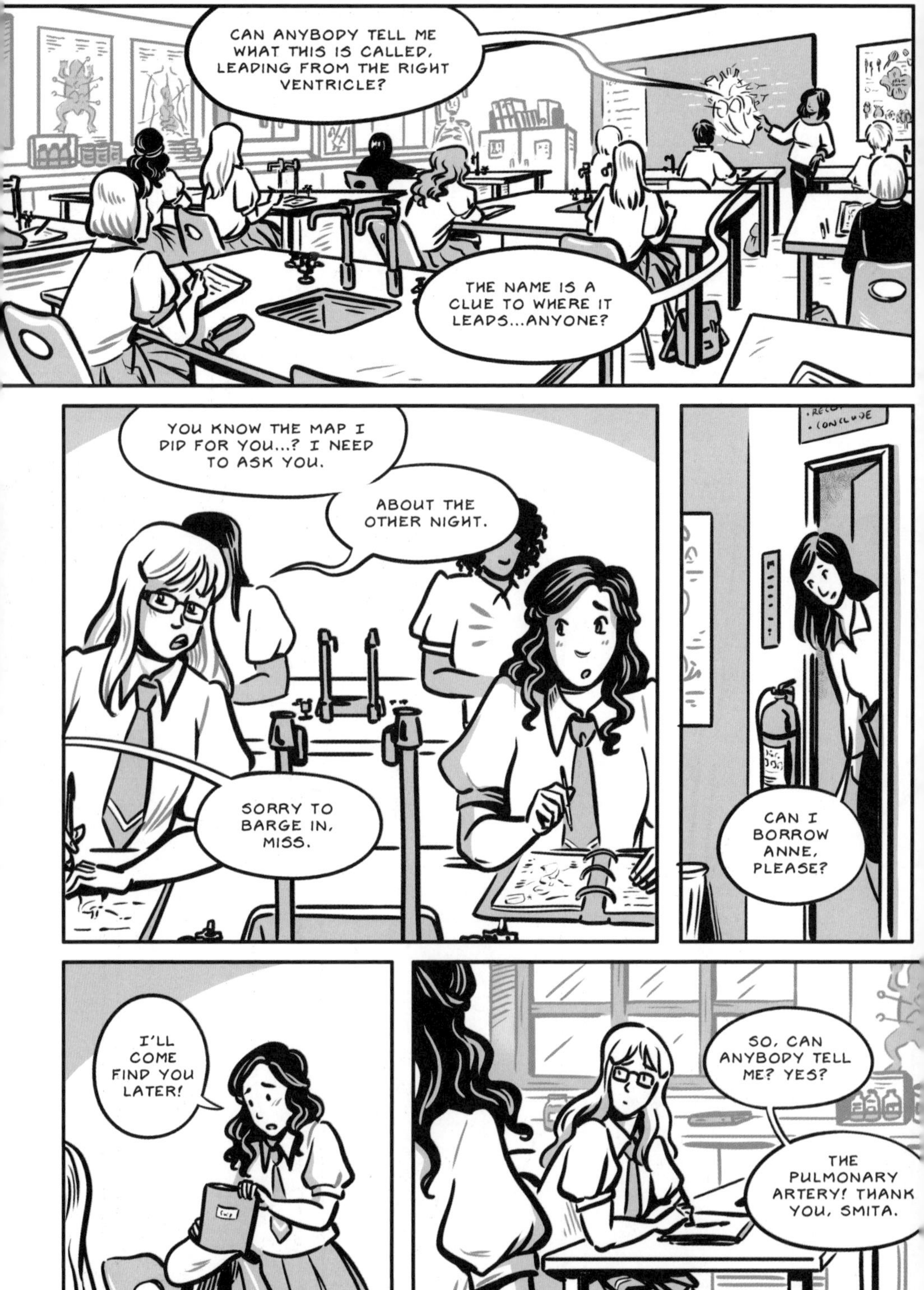
CAN ANYBODY TELL ME WHAT THIS IS CALLED, LEADING FROM THE RIGHT VENTRICLE?
THE NAME IS A CLUE TO WHERE IT LEADS...ANYONE?
YOU KNOW THE MAP I DID FOR YOU...? I NEED TO ASK YOU.
ABOUT THE OTHER NIGHT.
SORRY TO BARGE IN, MISS.
CAN I BORROW ANNE, PLEASE?
I'LL COME FIND YOU LATER!
SO, CAN ANYBODY TELL ME? YES?
THE PULMONARY ARTERY! THANK YOU, SMITA.

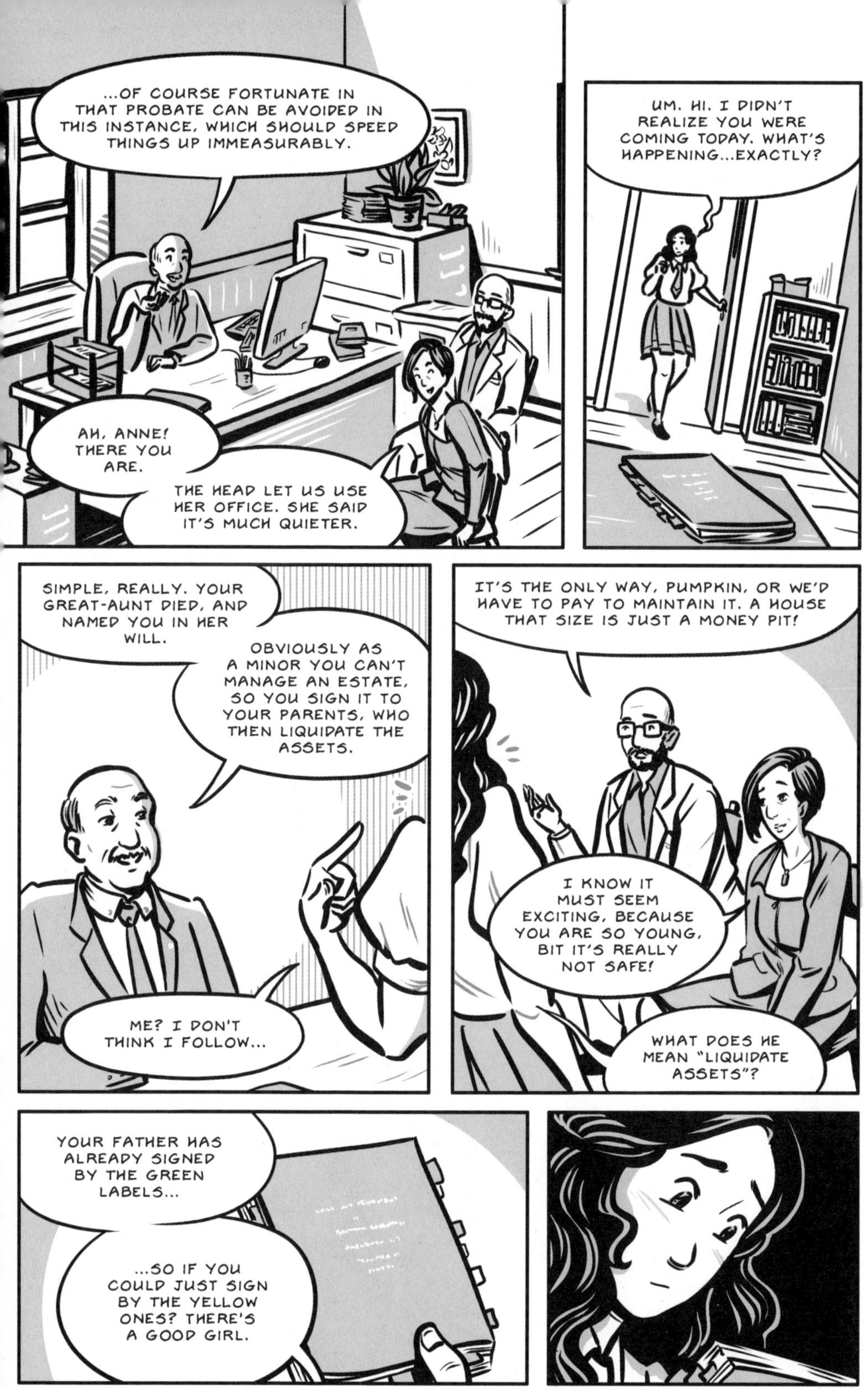
...OF COURSE FORTUNATE IN THAT PROBATE CAN BE AVOIDED IN THIS INSTANCE, WHICH SHOULD SPEED THINGS UP IMMEASURABLY.
AH, ANNE! THERE YOU ARE.
THE HEAD LET US USE HER OFFICE. SHE SAID IT'S MUCH QUIETER.
UM. HI. I DIDN'T REALIZE YOU WERE COMING TODAY. WHAT'S HAPPENING...EXACTLY?
SIMPLE, REALLY. YOUR GREAT-AUNT DIED, AND NAMED YOU IN HER WILL.
OBVIOUSLY AS A MINOR YOU CAN'T MANAGE AN ESTATE, SO YOU SIGN IT TO YOUR PARENTS, WHO THEN LIQUIDATE THE ASSETS.
ME? I DON'T THINK I FOLLOW...
IT'S THE ONLY WAY, PUMPKIN, OR WE'D HAVE TO PAY TO MAINTAIN IT. A HOUSE THAT SIZE IS JUST A MONEY PIT!
I KNOW IT MUST SEEM EXCITING, BECAUSE YOU ARE SO YOUNG, BIT IT'S REALLY NOT SAFE!
WHAT DOES HE MEAN "LIQUIDATE ASSETS"?
YOUR FATHER HAS ALREADY SIGNED BY THE GREEN LABELS...
...SO IF YOU COULD JUST SIGN BY THE YELLOW ONES? THERE'S A GOOD GIRL.

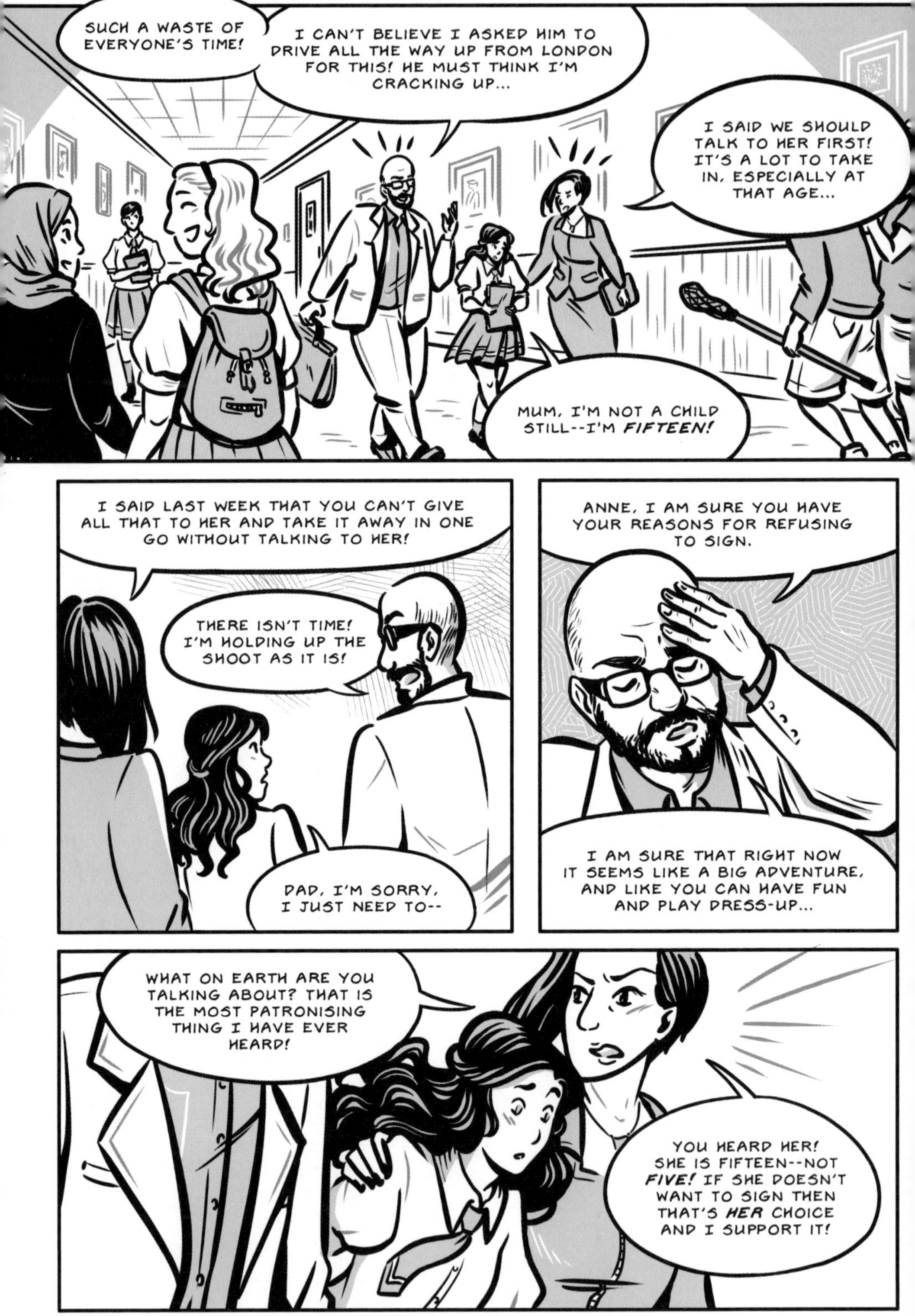
SUCH A WASTE OF EVERYONE'S TIME!
I CAN'T BELIEVE I ASKED HIM TO DRIVE ALL THE WAY UP FROM LONDON FOR THIS! HE MUST THINK I'M CRACKING UP...
I SAID WE SHOULD TALK TO HER FIRST! IT'S A LOT TO TAKE IN, ESPECIALLY AT THAT AGE...
MUM, I'M NOT A CHILD STILL--I'M *FIFTEEN!*
I SAID LAST WEEK THAT YOU CAN'T GIVE ALL THAT TO HER AND TAKE IT AWAY IN ONE GO WITHOUT TALKING TO HER!
THERE ISN'T TIME! I'M HOLDING UP THE SHOOT AS IT IS!
DAD, I'M SORRY, I JUST NEED TO--
ANNE, I AM SURE YOU HAVE YOUR REASONS FOR REFUSING TO SIGN.
I AM SURE THAT RIGHT NOW IT SEEMS LIKE A BIG ADVENTURE, AND LIKE YOU CAN HAVE FUN AND PLAY DRESS-UP...
WHAT ON EARTH ARE YOU TALKING ABOUT? THAT IS THE MOST PATRONISING THING I HAVE EVER HEARD!
YOU HEARD HER! SHE IS FIFTEEN--NOT *FIVE!* IF SHE DOESN'T WANT TO SIGN THEN THAT'S *HER* CHOICE AND I SUPPORT IT!

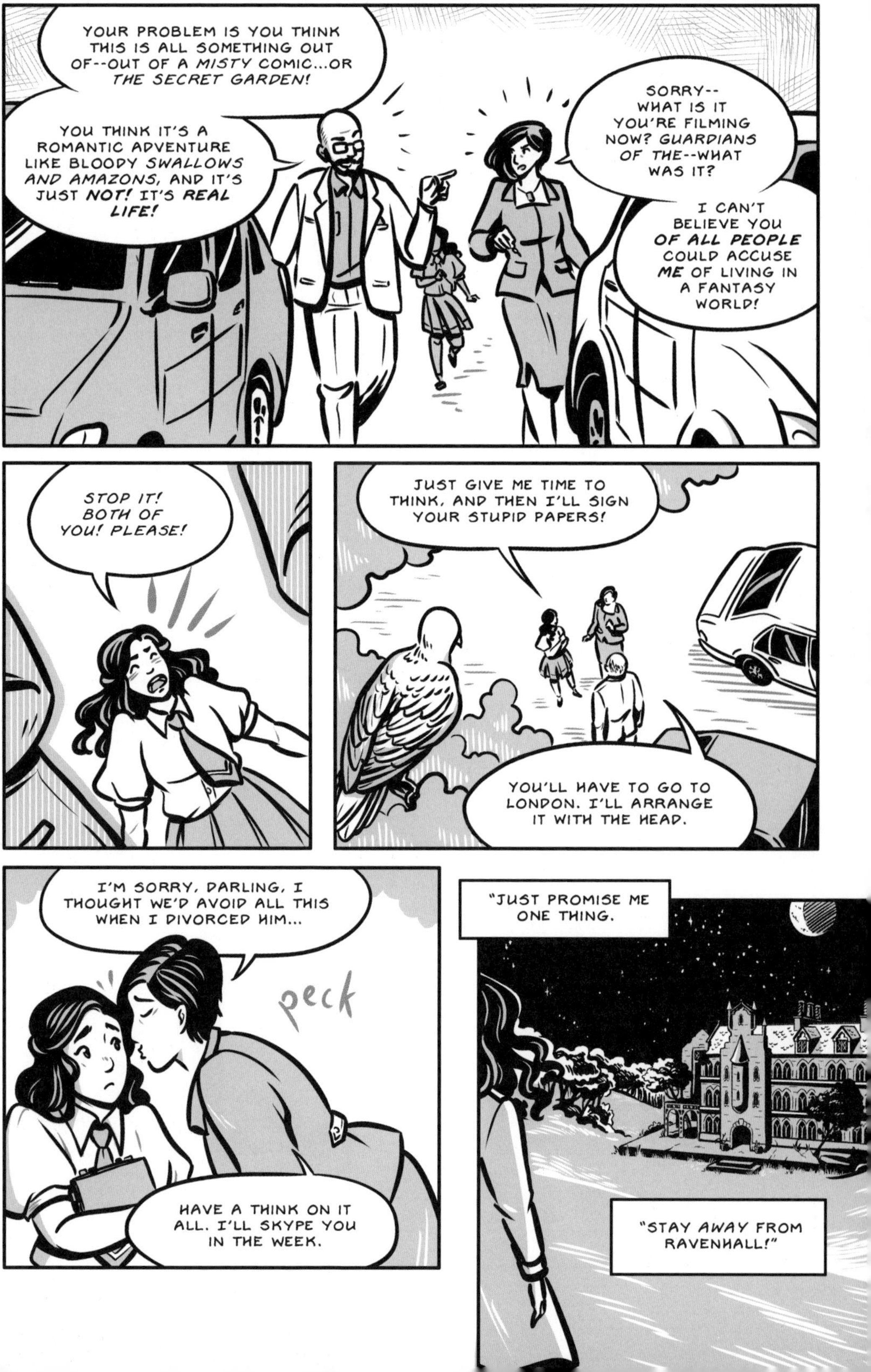

YOUR PROBLEM IS YOU THINK THIS IS ALL SOMETHING OUT OF--OUT OF A *MISTY* COMIC...OR *THE SECRET GARDEN!*
YOU THINK IT'S A ROMANTIC ADVENTURE LIKE BLOODY *SWALLOWS AND AMAZONS*, AND IT'S JUST ***NOT!*** IT'S ***REAL LIFE!***
SORRY-- WHAT IS IT YOU'RE FILMING NOW? *GUARDIANS OF THE*--WHAT WAS IT?
I CAN'T BELIEVE YOU ***OF ALL PEOPLE*** COULD ACCUSE ***ME*** OF LIVING IN A FANTASY WORLD!
STOP IT! BOTH OF YOU! PLEASE!
JUST GIVE ME TIME TO THINK, AND THEN I'LL SIGN YOUR STUPID PAPERS!
YOU'LL HAVE TO GO TO LONDON. I'LL ARRANGE IT WITH THE HEAD.
I'M SORRY, DARLING, I THOUGHT WE'D AVOID ALL THIS WHEN I DIVORCED HIM...
peck
HAVE A THINK ON IT ALL. I'LL SKYPE YOU IN THE WEEK.
"JUST PROMISE ME ONE THING.
"STAY AWAY FROM RAVENHALL!"

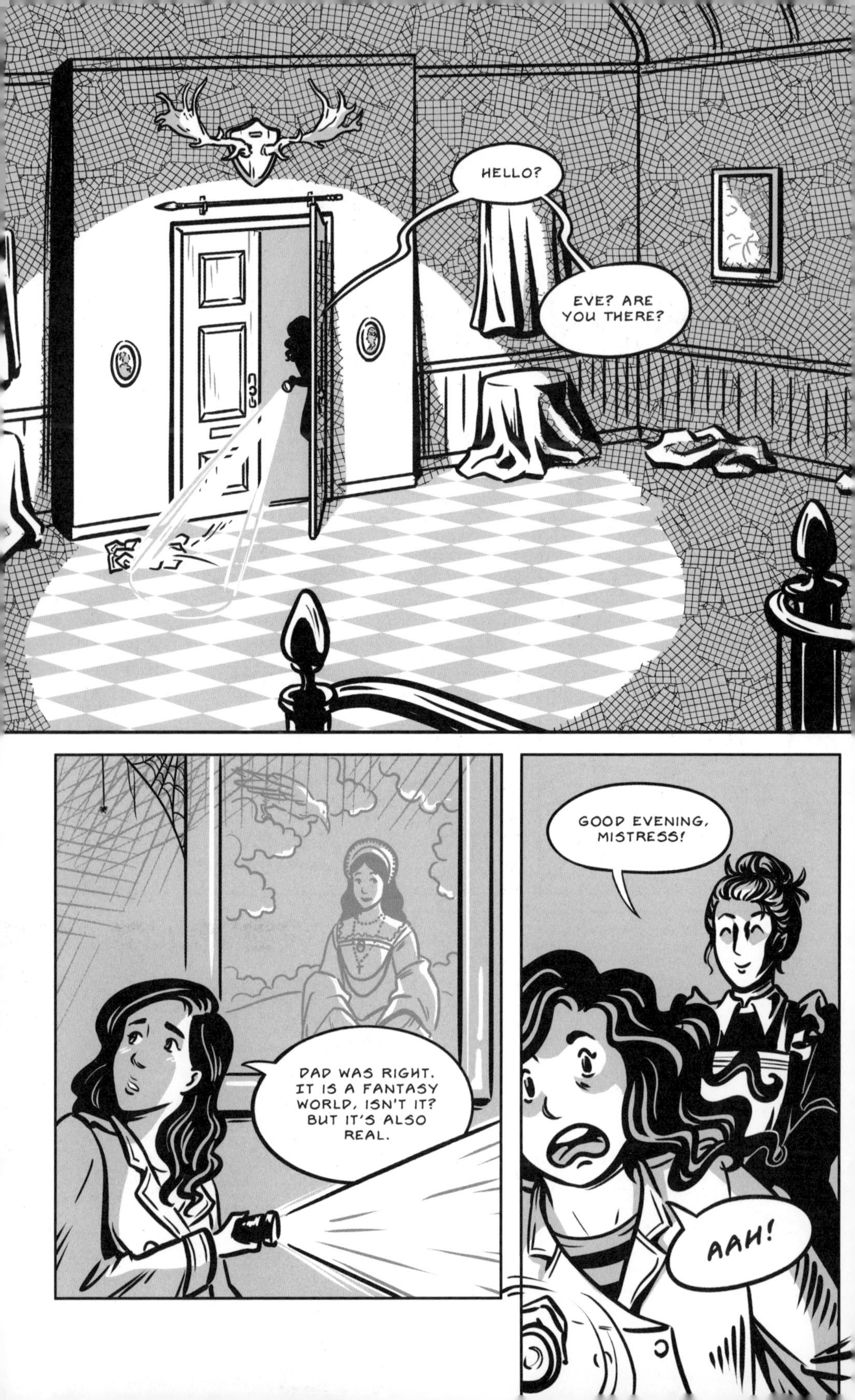
HELLO?
EVE? ARE YOU THERE?
DAD WAS RIGHT. IT IS A FANTASY WORLD, ISN'T IT? BUT IT'S ALSO REAL.
GOOD EVENING, MISTRESS!
AAH!

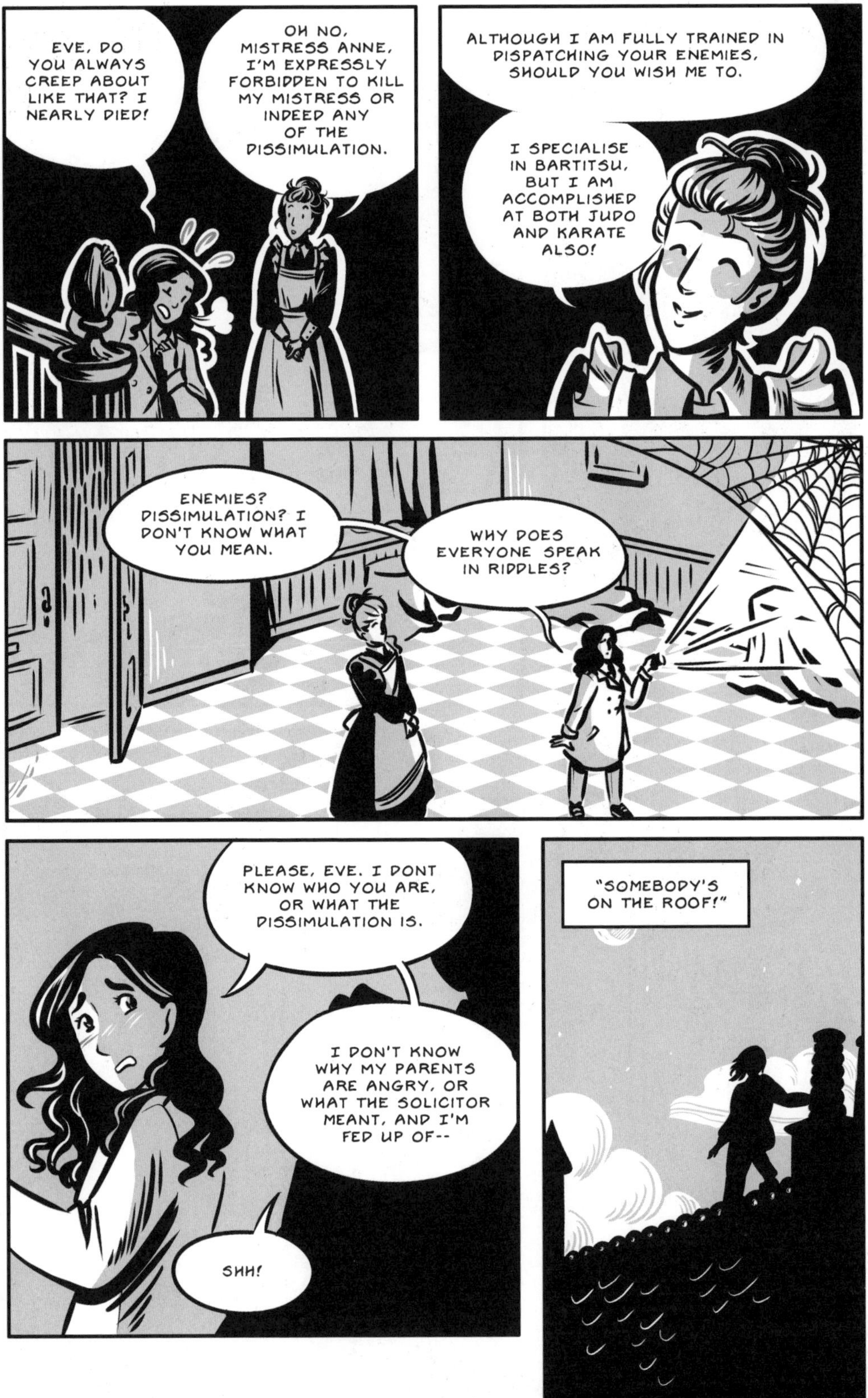
EVE, DO YOU ALWAYS CREEP ABOUT LIKE THAT? I NEARLY DIED!
OH NO, MISTRESS ANNE, I'M EXPRESSLY FORBIDDEN TO KILL MY MISTRESS OR INDEED ANY OF THE DISSIMULATION.
ALTHOUGH I AM FULLY TRAINED IN DISPATCHING YOUR ENEMIES, SHOULD YOU WISH ME TO.
I SPECIALISE IN BARTITSU, BUT I AM ACCOMPLISHED AT BOTH JUDO AND KARATE ALSO!
ENEMIES? DISSIMULATION? I DON'T KNOW WHAT YOU MEAN.
WHY DOES EVERYONE SPEAK IN RIDDLES?
PLEASE, EVE. I DONT KNOW WHO YOU ARE, OR WHAT THE DISSIMULATION IS.
I DON'T KNOW WHY MY PARENTS ARE ANGRY, OR WHAT THE SOLICITOR MEANT, AND I'M FED UP OF--
SHH!
"SOMEBODY'S ON THE ROOF!"

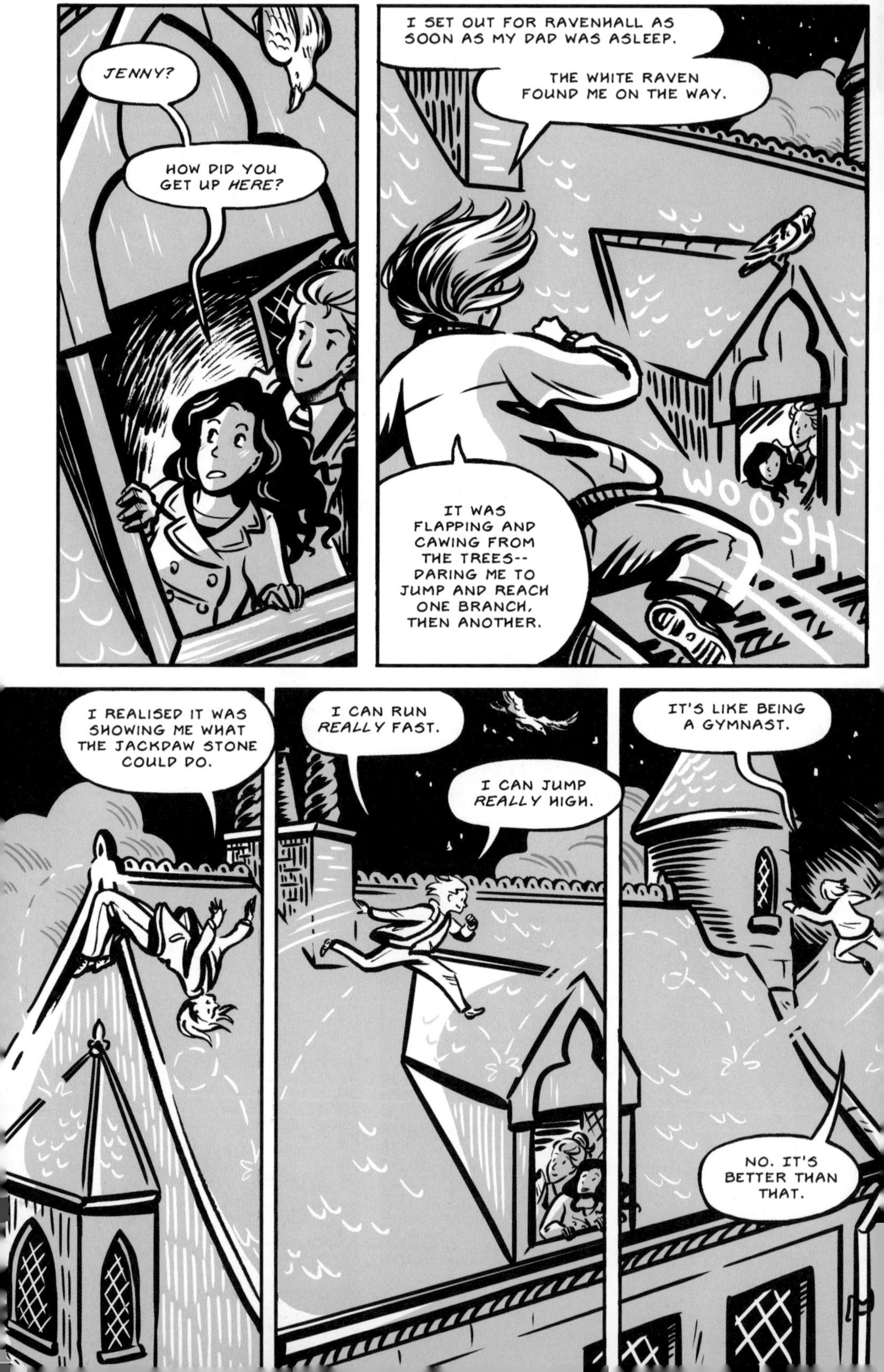

JENNY?
HOW DID YOU GET UP HERE?
I SET OUT FOR RAVENHALL AS SOON AS MY DAD WAS ASLEEP.
THE WHITE RAVEN FOUND ME ON THE WAY.
IT WAS FLAPPING AND CAWING FROM THE TREES-- DARING ME TO JUMP AND REACH ONE BRANCH, THEN ANOTHER.
WOOSH
I REALISED IT WAS SHOWING ME WHAT THE JACKDAW STONE COULD DO.
I CAN RUN REALLY FAST.
I CAN JUMP REALLY HIGH.
IT'S LIKE BEING A GYMNAST.
NO. IT'S BETTER THAN THAT.

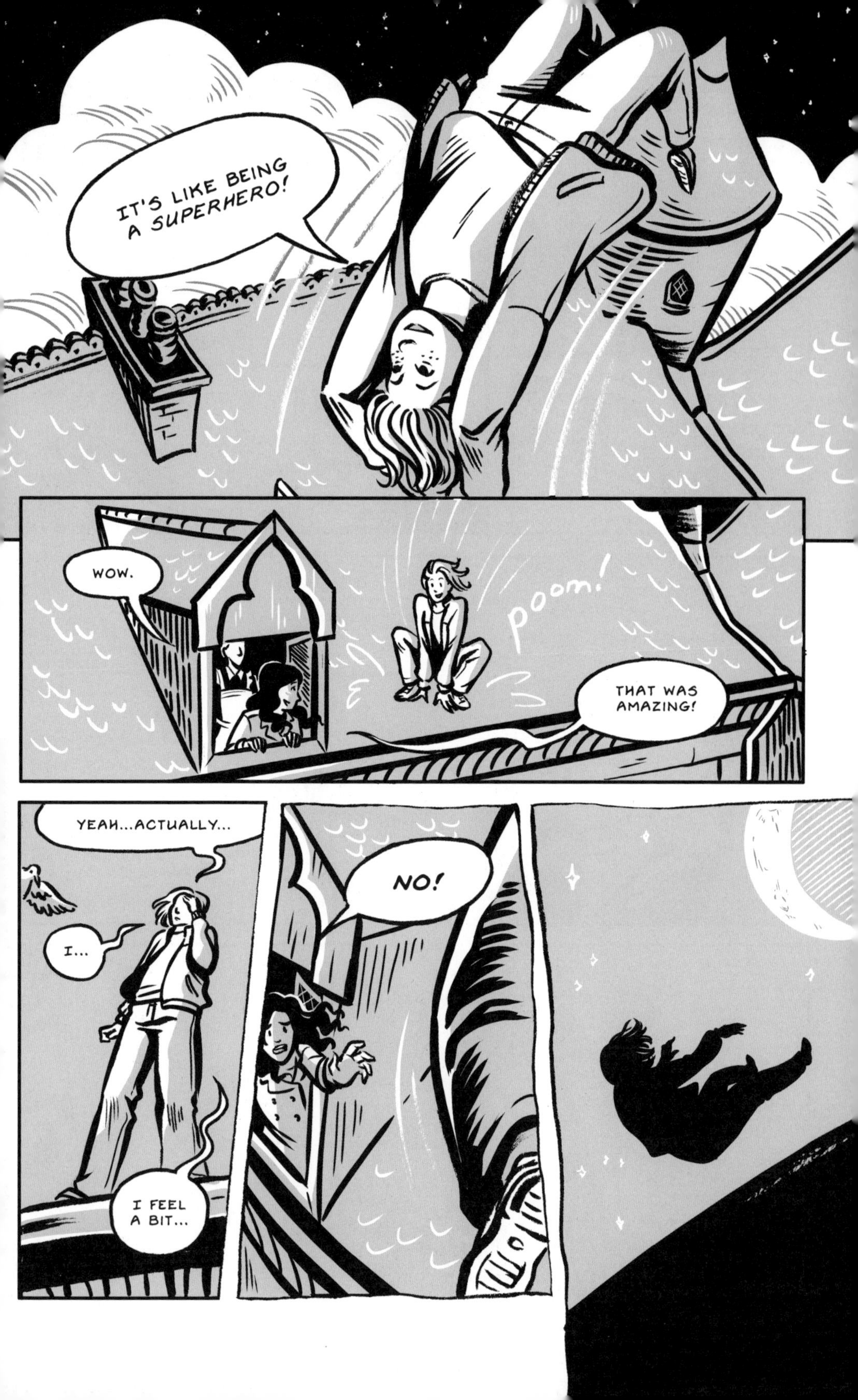
IT'S LIKE BEING A SUPERHERO!
WOW.
poom!
THAT WAS AMAZING!
YEAH...ACTUALLY...
I...
I FEEL A BIT...
NO!

JENNY?

JENNY!

EVE? B-BUT HOW?

WHAT ARE YOU, A MAGICIAN?

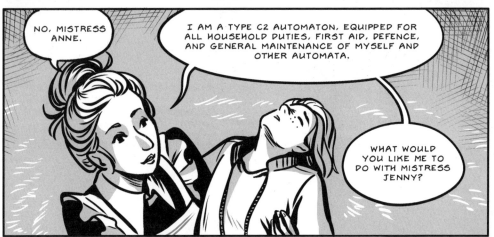

NO, MISTRESS ANNE.

I AM A TYPE C2 AUTOMATON, EQUIPPED FOR ALL HOUSEHOLD DUTIES, FIRST AID, DEFENCE, AND GENERAL MAINTENANCE OF MYSELF AND OTHER AUTOMATA.

WHAT WOULD YOU LIKE ME TO DO WITH MISTRESS JENNY?

...

WELL...TAKE HER SOMEWHERE, I SUPPOSE. SOMEWHERE WARM AND SAFE, TO RECOVER?

CERTAINLY, MISTRESS ANNE.

WOULD YOU LIKE ME TO TAKE HER TO YOUR AUNT'S ROOM, OR DOWN TO THE SECRET HEADQUARTERS?

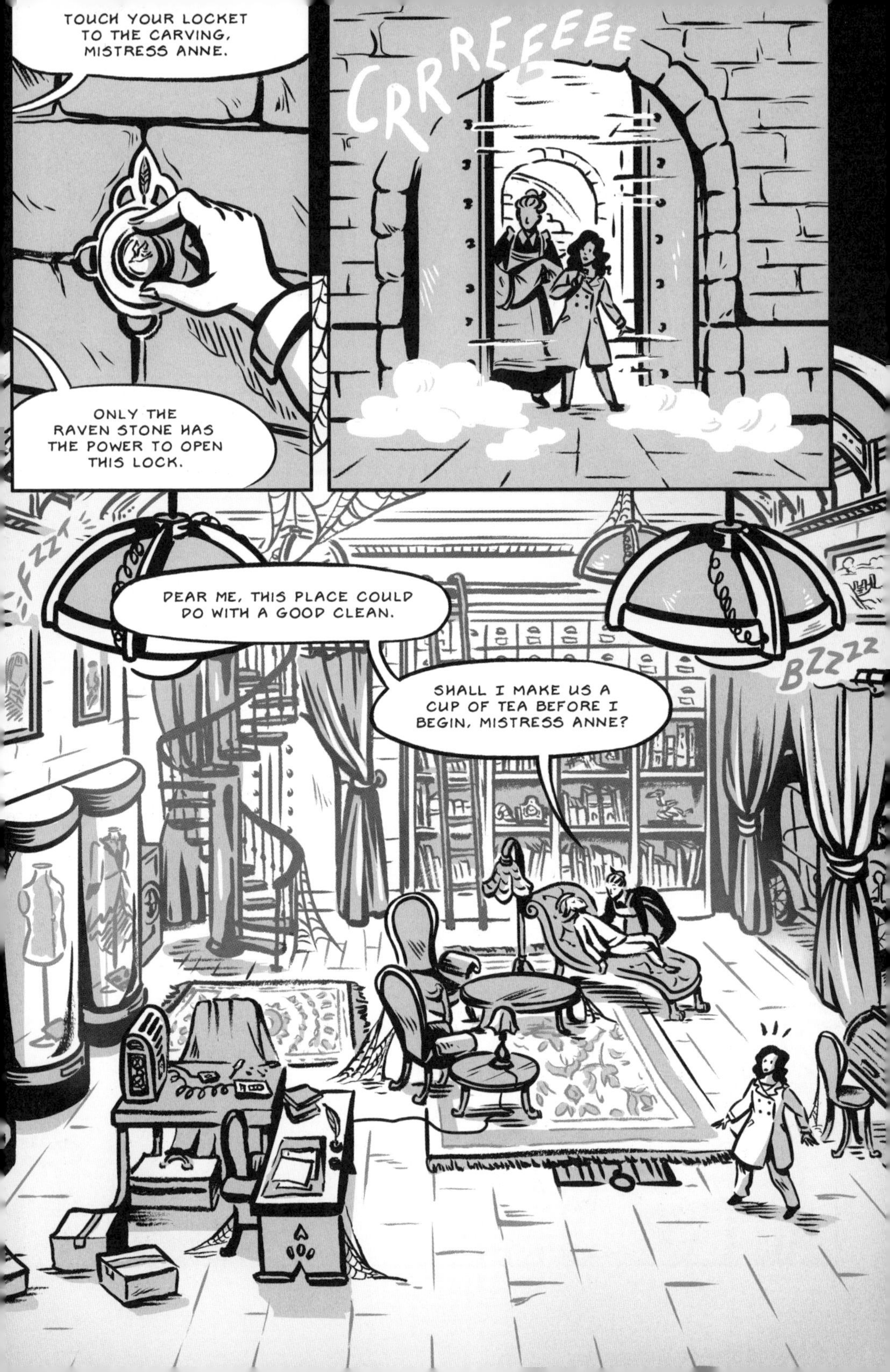
TOUCH YOUR LOCKET TO THE CARVING, MISTRESS ANNE.
ONLY THE RAVEN STONE HAS THE POWER TO OPEN THIS LOCK.
CRRREEEEEE
FZZZT
DEAR ME, THIS PLACE COULD DO WITH A GOOD CLEAN.
BZZZZ
SHALL I MAKE US A CUP OF TEA BEFORE I BEGIN, MISTRESS ANNE?

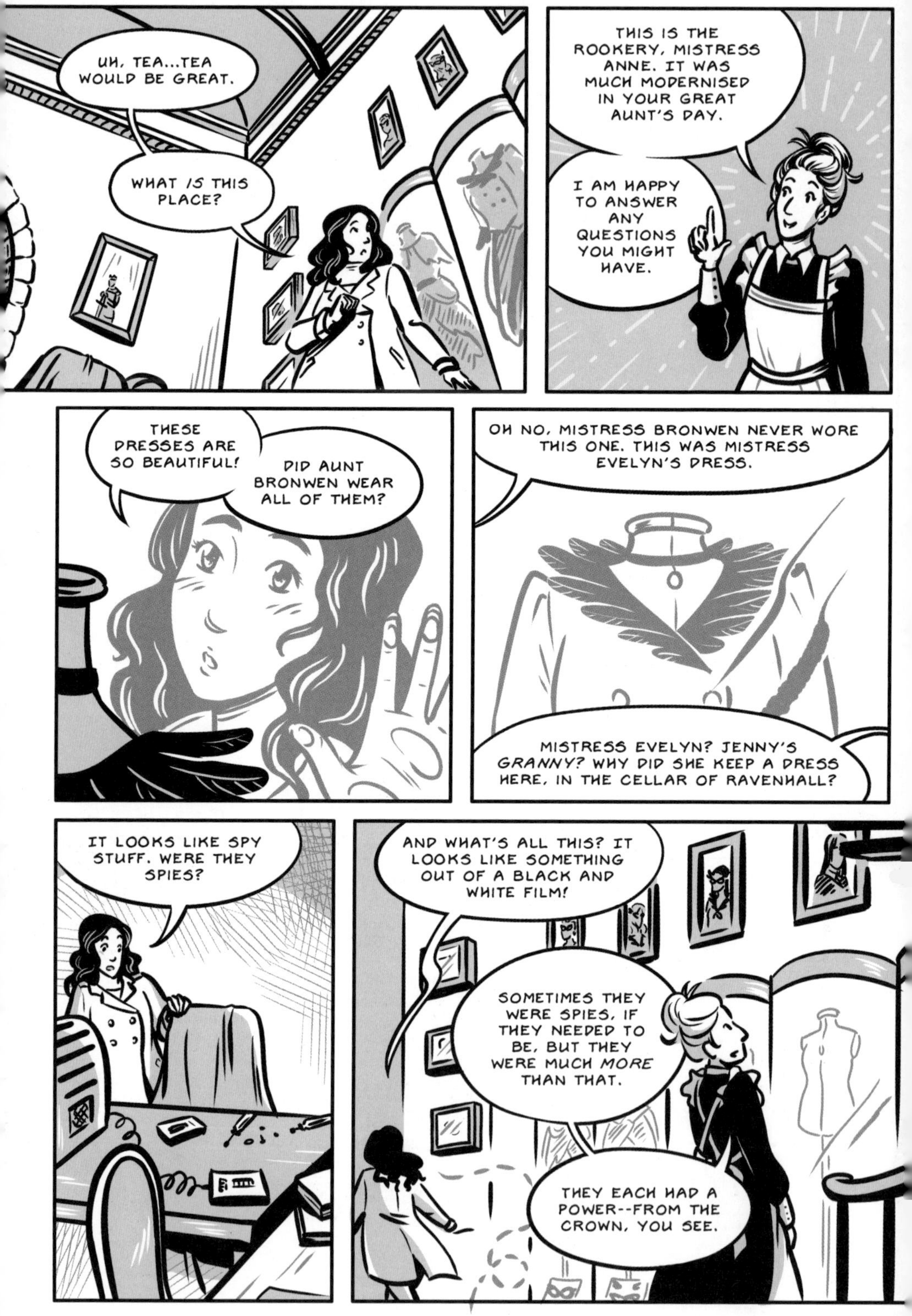
UH, TEA...TEA WOULD BE GREAT.
WHAT *IS* THIS PLACE?
THIS IS THE ROOKERY, MISTRESS ANNE. IT WAS MUCH MODERNISED IN YOUR GREAT AUNT'S DAY.
I AM HAPPY TO ANSWER ANY QUESTIONS YOU MIGHT HAVE.
THESE DRESSES ARE SO BEAUTIFUL!
DID AUNT BRONWEN WEAR ALL OF THEM?
OH NO, MISTRESS BRONWEN NEVER WORE THIS ONE. THIS WAS MISTRESS EVELYN'S DRESS.
MISTRESS EVELYN? JENNY'S *GRANNY*? WHY DID SHE KEEP A DRESS HERE, IN THE CELLAR OF RAVENHALL?
IT LOOKS LIKE SPY STUFF. WERE THEY SPIES?
AND WHAT'S ALL THIS? IT LOOKS LIKE SOMETHING OUT OF A BLACK AND WHITE FILM!
SOMETIMES THEY WERE SPIES, IF THEY NEEDED TO BE, BUT THEY WERE MUCH *MORE* THAN THAT.
THEY EACH HAD A POWER--FROM THE CROWN, YOU SEE.

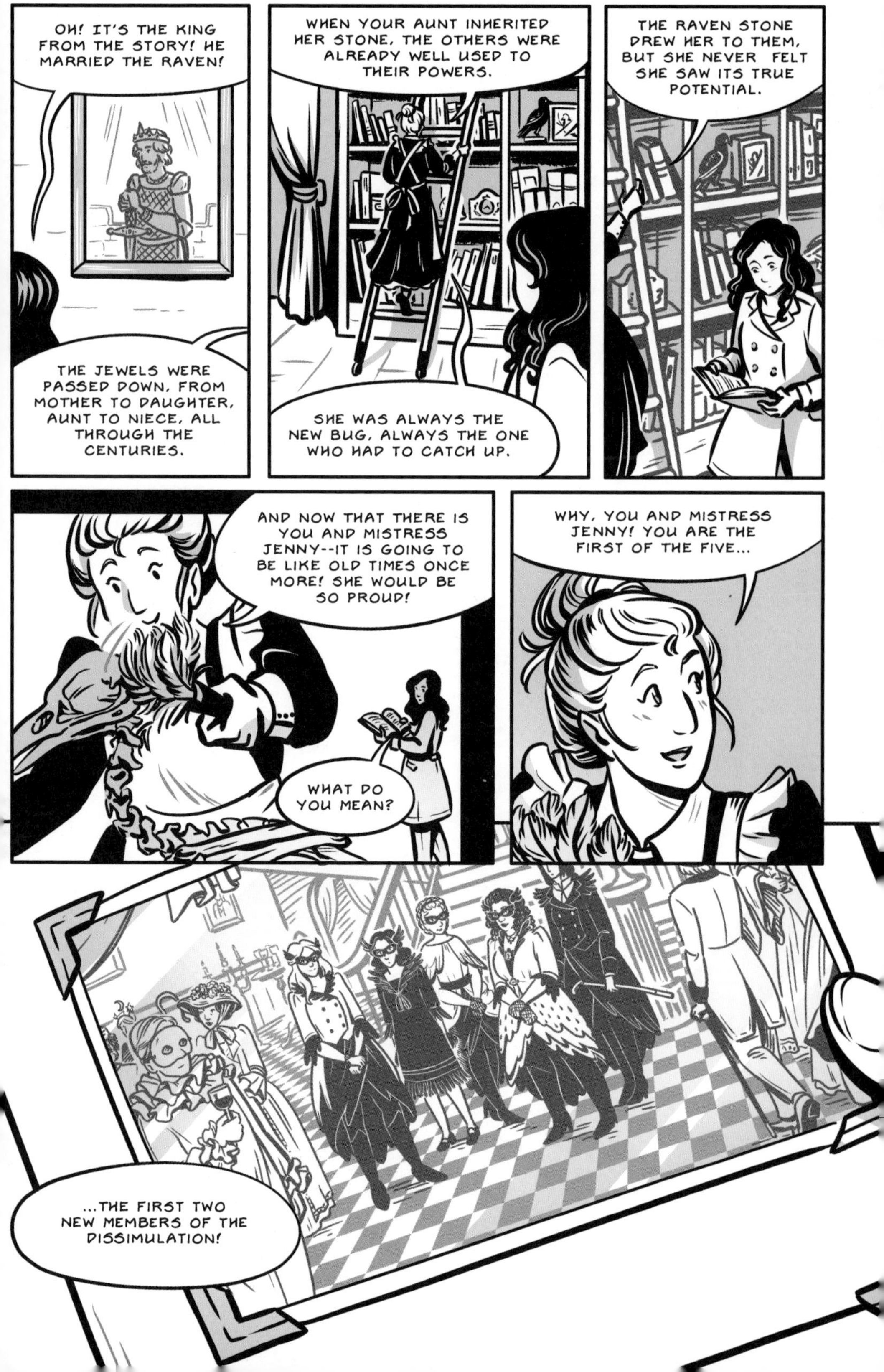
OH! IT'S THE KING FROM THE STORY! HE MARRIED THE RAVEN!
THE JEWELS WERE PASSED DOWN, FROM MOTHER TO DAUGHTER, AUNT TO NIECE, ALL THROUGH THE CENTURIES.
WHEN YOUR AUNT INHERITED HER STONE, THE OTHERS WERE ALREADY WELL USED TO THEIR POWERS.
SHE WAS ALWAYS THE NEW BUG, ALWAYS THE ONE WHO HAD TO CATCH UP.
THE RAVEN STONE DREW HER TO THEM, BUT SHE NEVER FELT SHE SAW ITS TRUE POTENTIAL.
AND NOW THAT THERE IS YOU AND MISTRESS JENNY--IT IS GOING TO BE LIKE OLD TIMES ONCE MORE! SHE WOULD BE SO PROUD!
WHAT DO YOU MEAN?
WHY, YOU AND MISTRESS JENNY! YOU ARE THE FIRST OF THE FIVE...
...THE FIRST TWO NEW MEMBERS OF THE DISSIMULATION!

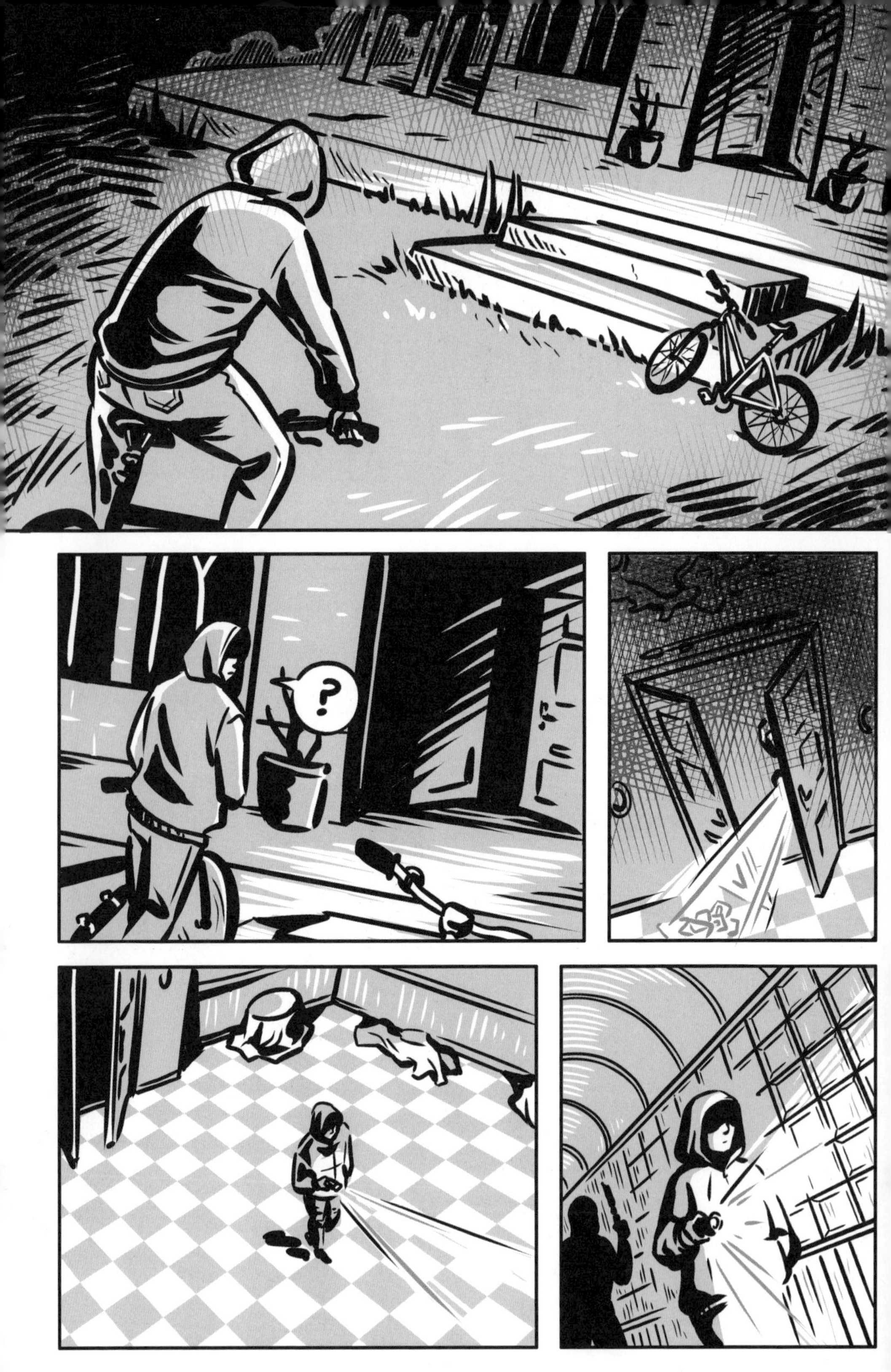
?

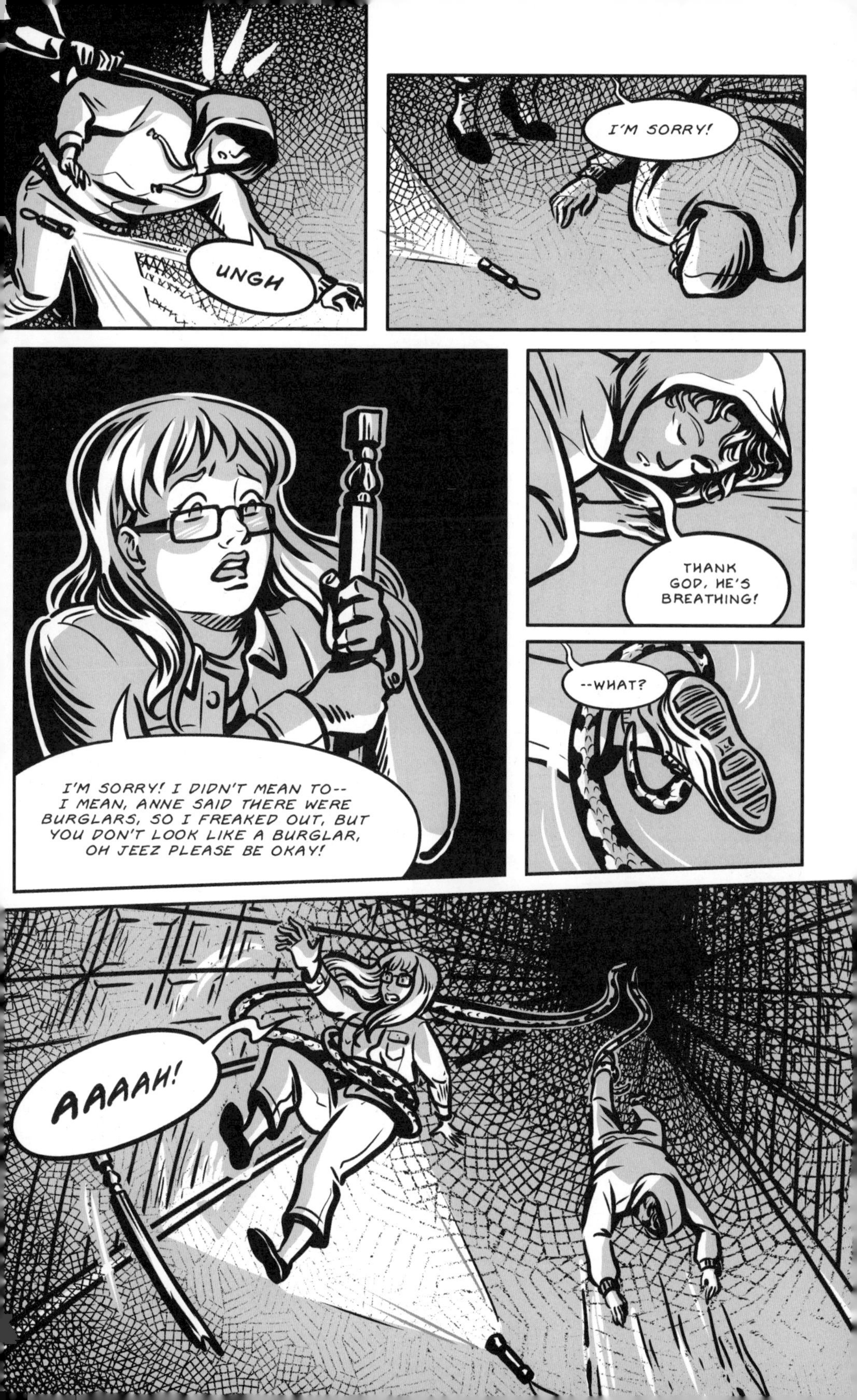
UNGH
I'M SORRY!
I'M SORRY! I DIDN'T MEAN TO-- I MEAN, ANNE SAID THERE WERE BURGLARS, SO I FREAKED OUT, BUT YOU DON'T LOOK LIKE A BURGLAR, OH JEEZ PLEASE BE OKAY!
THANK GOD, HE'S BREATHING!
--WHAT?
AAAAH!

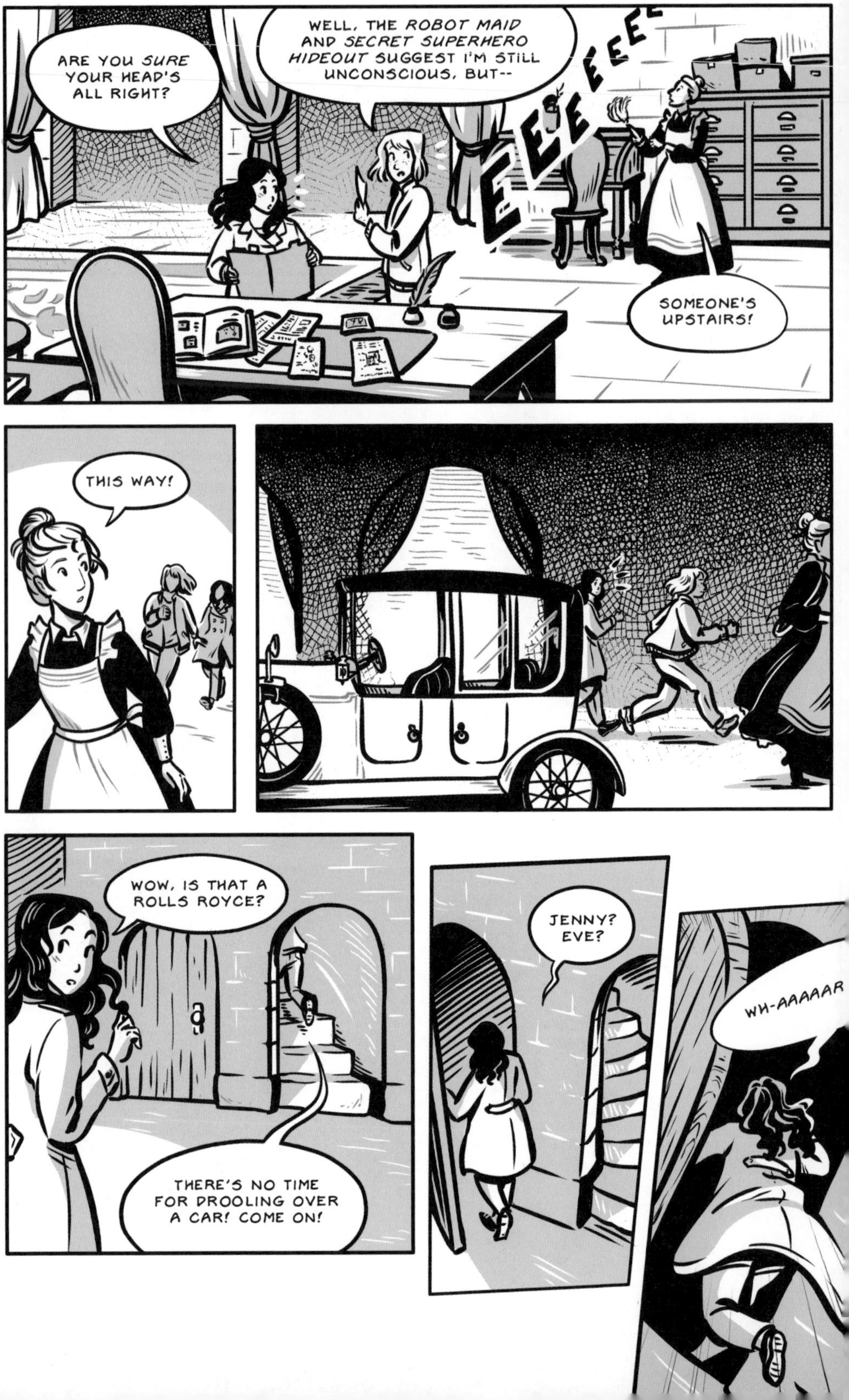
ARE YOU SURE YOUR HEAD'S ALL RIGHT?
WELL, THE ROBOT MAID AND SECRET SUPERHERO HIDEOUT SUGGEST I'M STILL UNCONSCIOUS, BUT--
EEEEEEEE
SOMEONE'S UPSTAIRS!
THIS WAY!
WOW, IS THAT A ROLLS ROYCE?
THERE'S NO TIME FOR DROOLING OVER A CAR! COME ON!
JENNY? EVE?
WH-AAAAAR

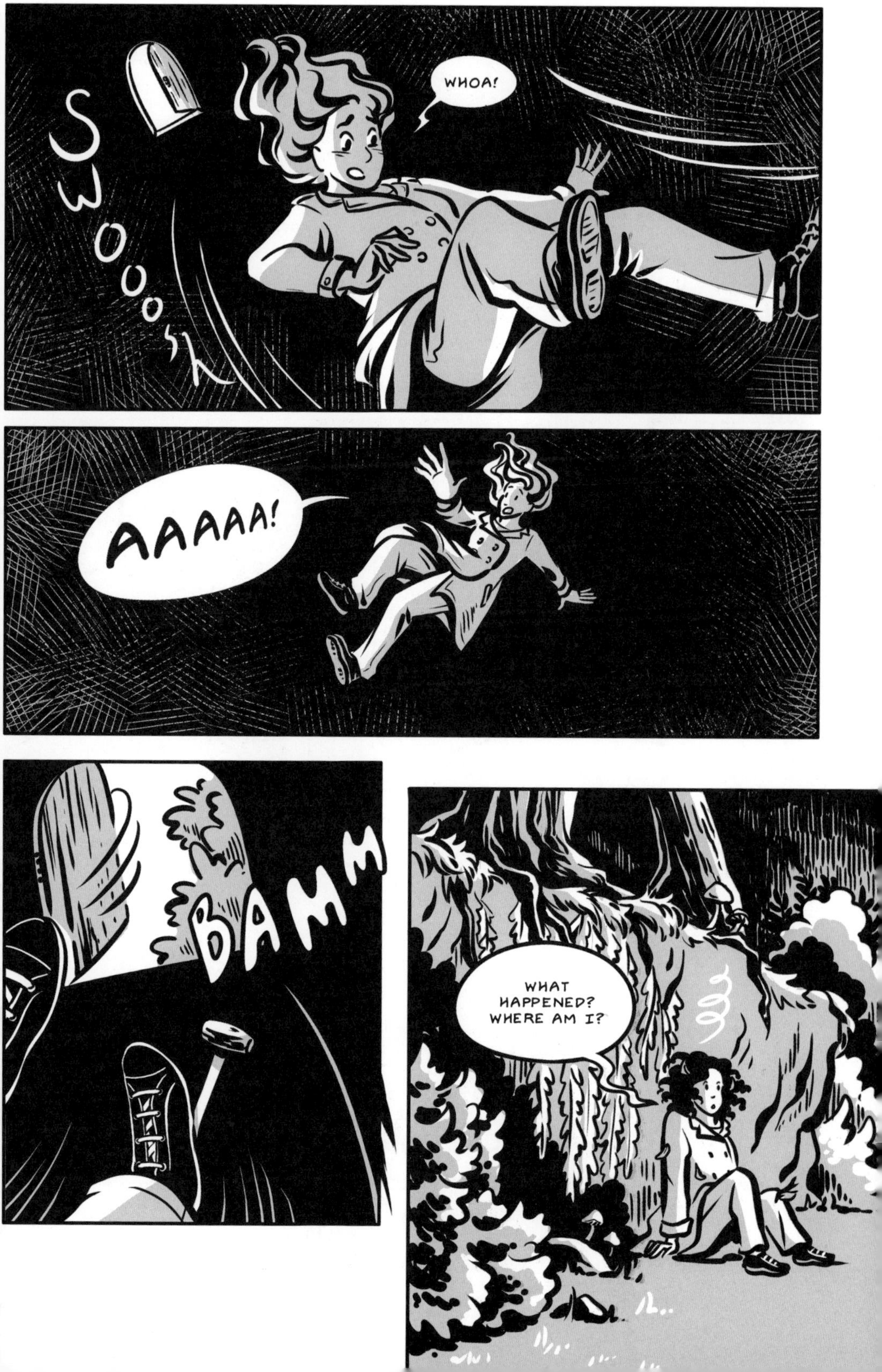
SWOOOOSH
WHOA!
AAAAA!
BAMM
WHAT HAPPENED? WHERE AM I?

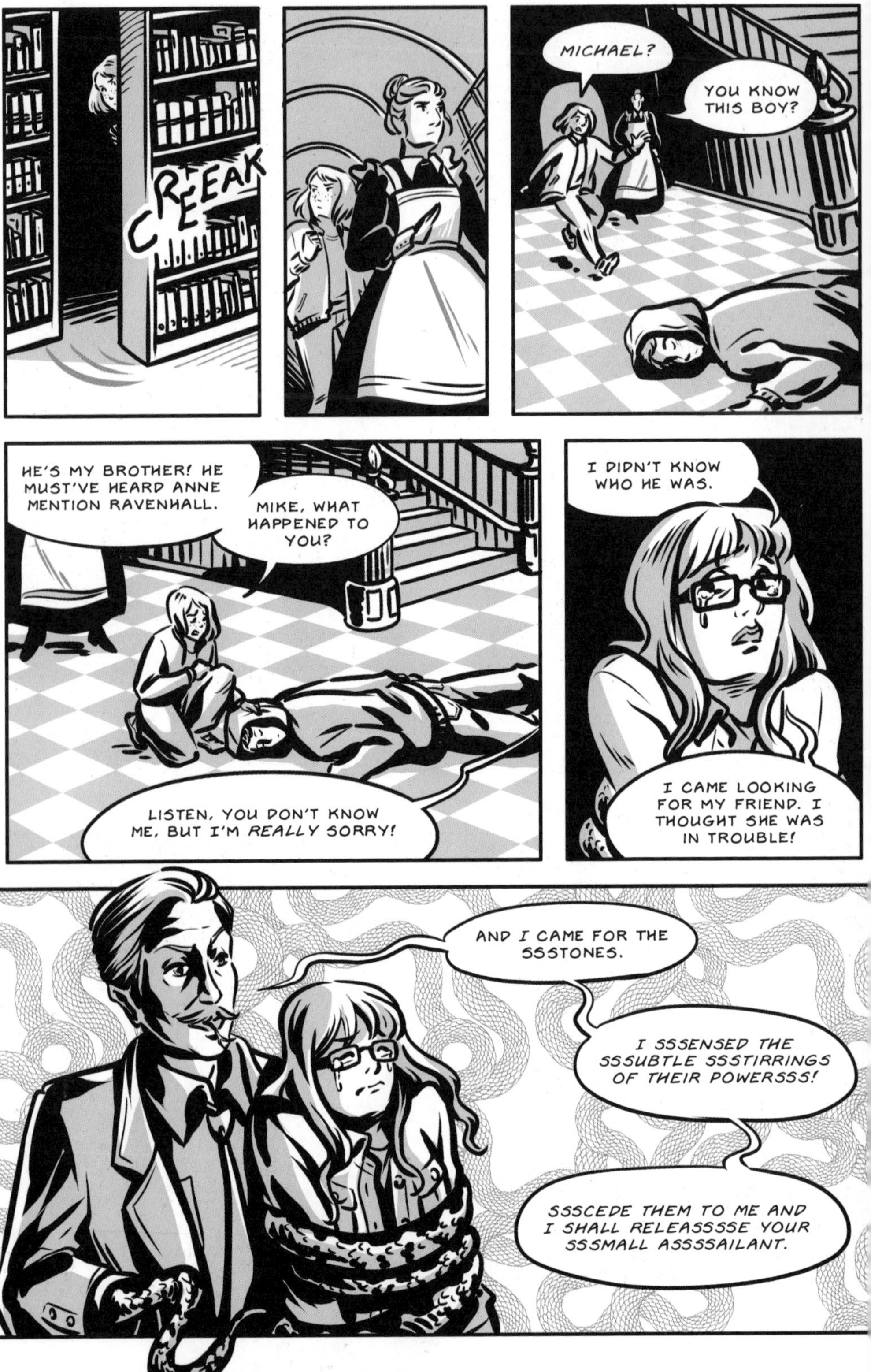
CREEAK
MICHAEL?
YOU KNOW THIS BOY?
HE'S MY BROTHER! HE MUST'VE HEARD ANNE MENTION RAVENHALL.
MIKE, WHAT HAPPENED TO YOU?
LISTEN, YOU DON'T KNOW ME, BUT I'M *REALLY* SORRY!
I DIDN'T KNOW WHO HE WAS.
I CAME LOOKING FOR MY FRIEND. I THOUGHT SHE WAS IN TROUBLE!
AND *I* CAME FOR THE SSSTONES.
I SSSENSED THE SSSUBTLE SSSTIRRINGS OF THEIR POWERSSS!
SSSCEDE THEM TO ME AND I SHALL RELEASSSSE YOUR SSSMALL ASSSSAILANT.

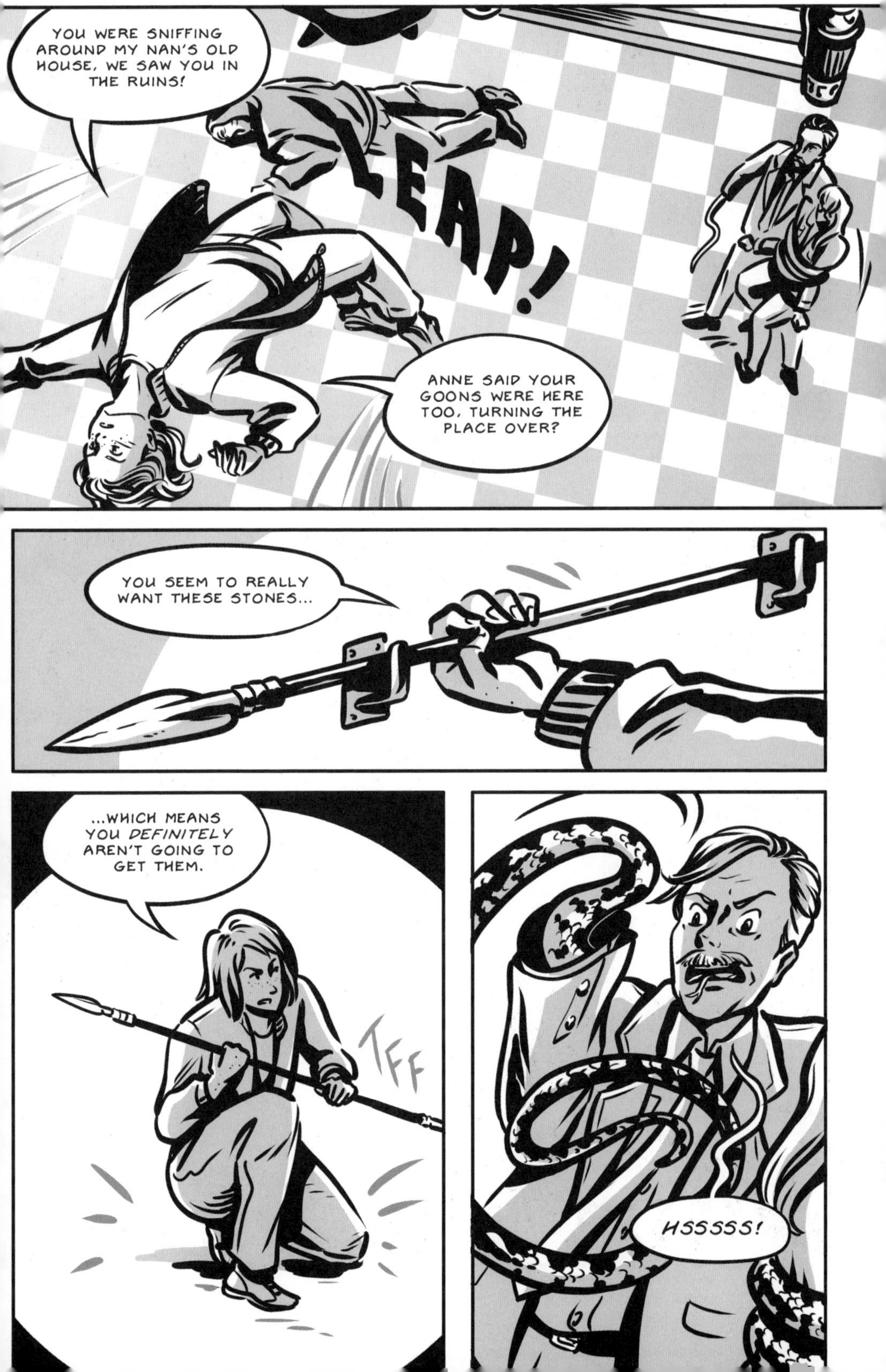
YOU WERE SNIFFING AROUND MY NAN'S OLD HOUSE, WE SAW YOU IN THE RUINS!
LEAP!
ANNE SAID YOUR GOONS WERE HERE TOO, TURNING THE PLACE OVER?
YOU SEEM TO REALLY WANT THESE STONES...
...WHICH MEANS YOU *DEFINITELY* AREN'T GOING TO GET THEM.
TFF
HSSSSS!

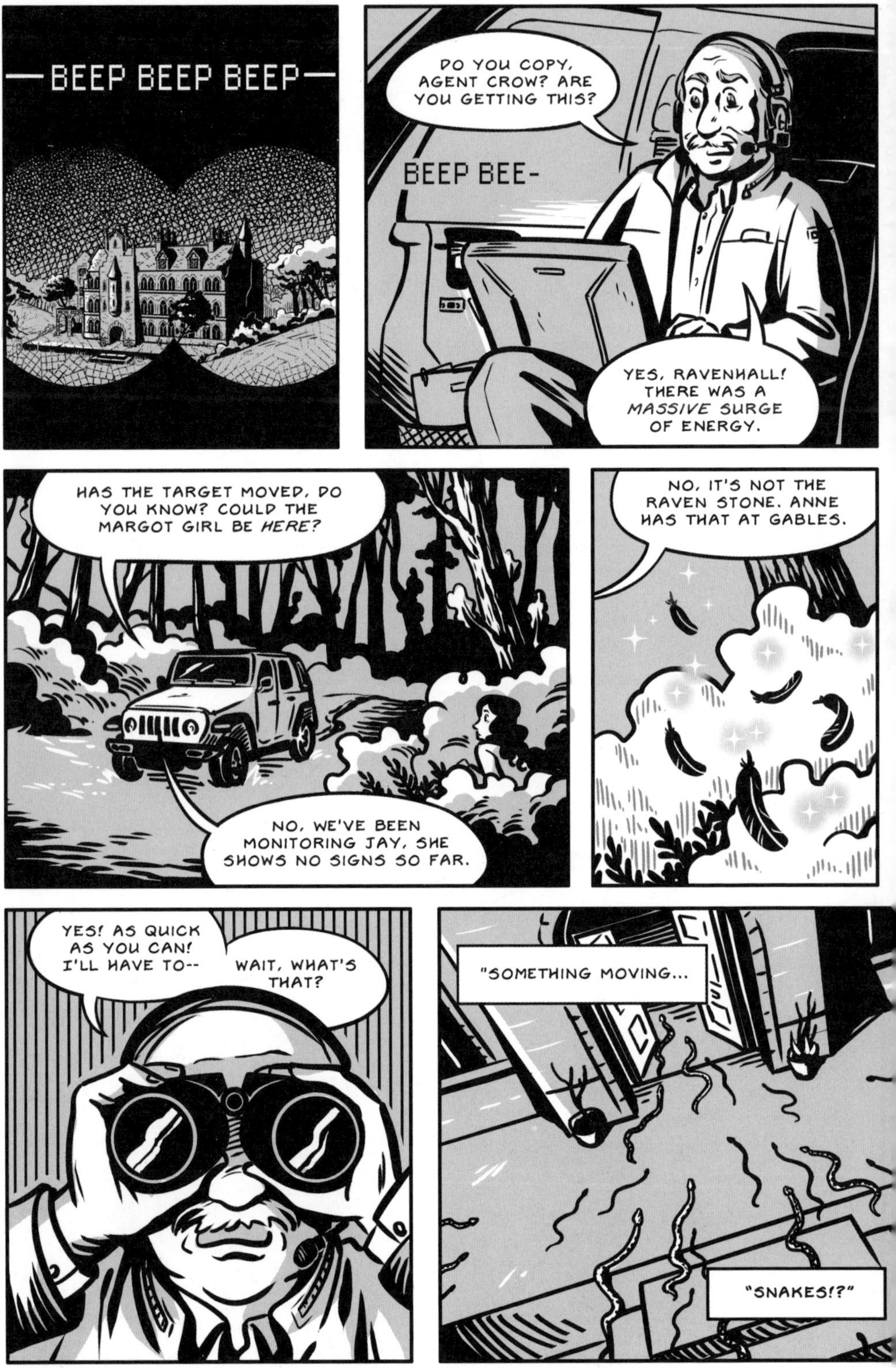
BEEP BEEP BEEP
DO YOU COPY, AGENT CROW? ARE YOU GETTING THIS?
BEEP BEE-
YES, RAVENHALL! THERE WAS A *MASSIVE* SURGE OF ENERGY.
HAS THE TARGET MOVED, DO YOU KNOW? COULD THE MARGOT GIRL BE *HERE?*
NO, WE'VE BEEN MONITORING JAY, SHE SHOWS NO SIGNS SO FAR.
NO, IT'S NOT THE RAVEN STONE. ANNE HAS THAT AT GABLES.
YES! AS QUICK AS YOU CAN! I'LL HAVE TO--
WAIT, WHAT'S THAT?
"SOMETHING MOVING...
"SNAKES!?"

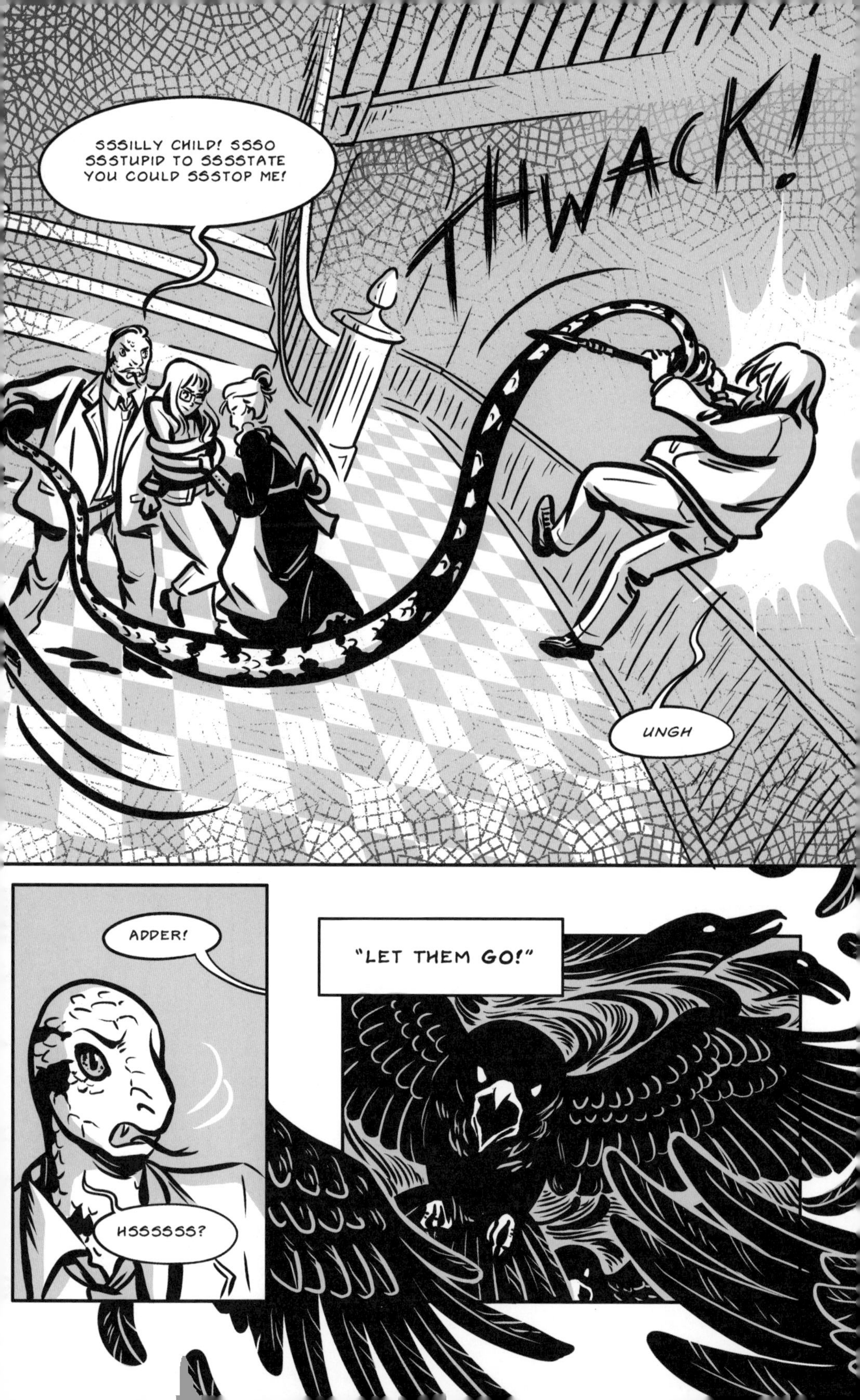
SSSILLY CHILD! SSSO SSSTUPID TO SSSSTATE YOU COULD SSSTOP ME!
THWACK!
UNGH
ADDER!
HSSSSSS?
"LET THEM GO!"

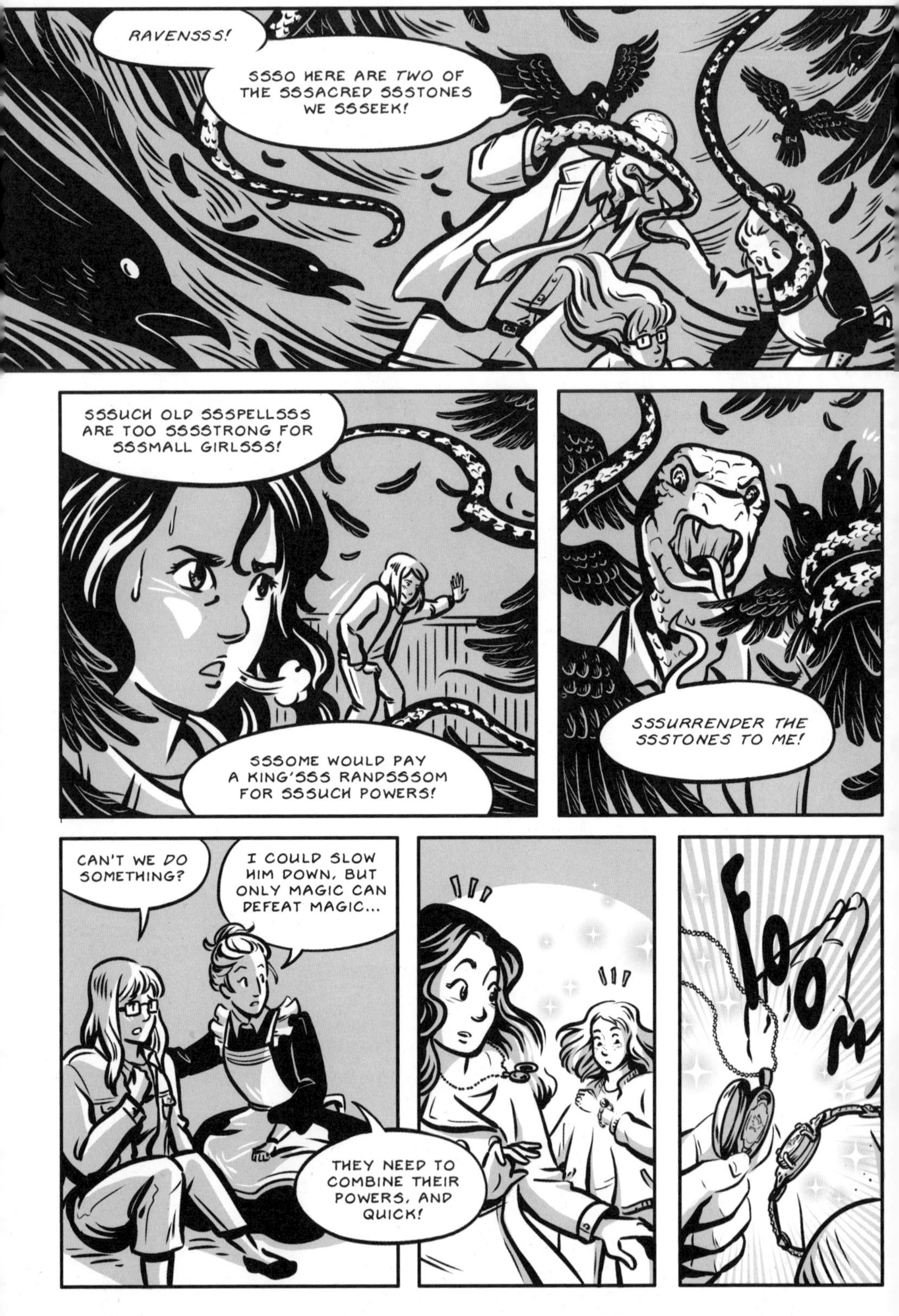
RAVENSSS!
SSSO HERE ARE TWO OF THE SSSACRED SSSTONES WE SSSEEK!
SSSUCH OLD SSSPELLSSS ARE TOO SSSSTRONG FOR SSSMALL GIRLSSS!
SSSOME WOULD PAY A KING'SSS RANDSSSOM FOR SSSUCH POWERS!
SSSURRENDER THE SSSTONES TO ME!
CAN'T WE DO SOMETHING?
I COULD SLOW HIM DOWN, BUT ONLY MAGIC CAN DEFEAT MAGIC...
THEY NEED TO COMBINE THEIR POWERS, AND QUICK!
FOOOM

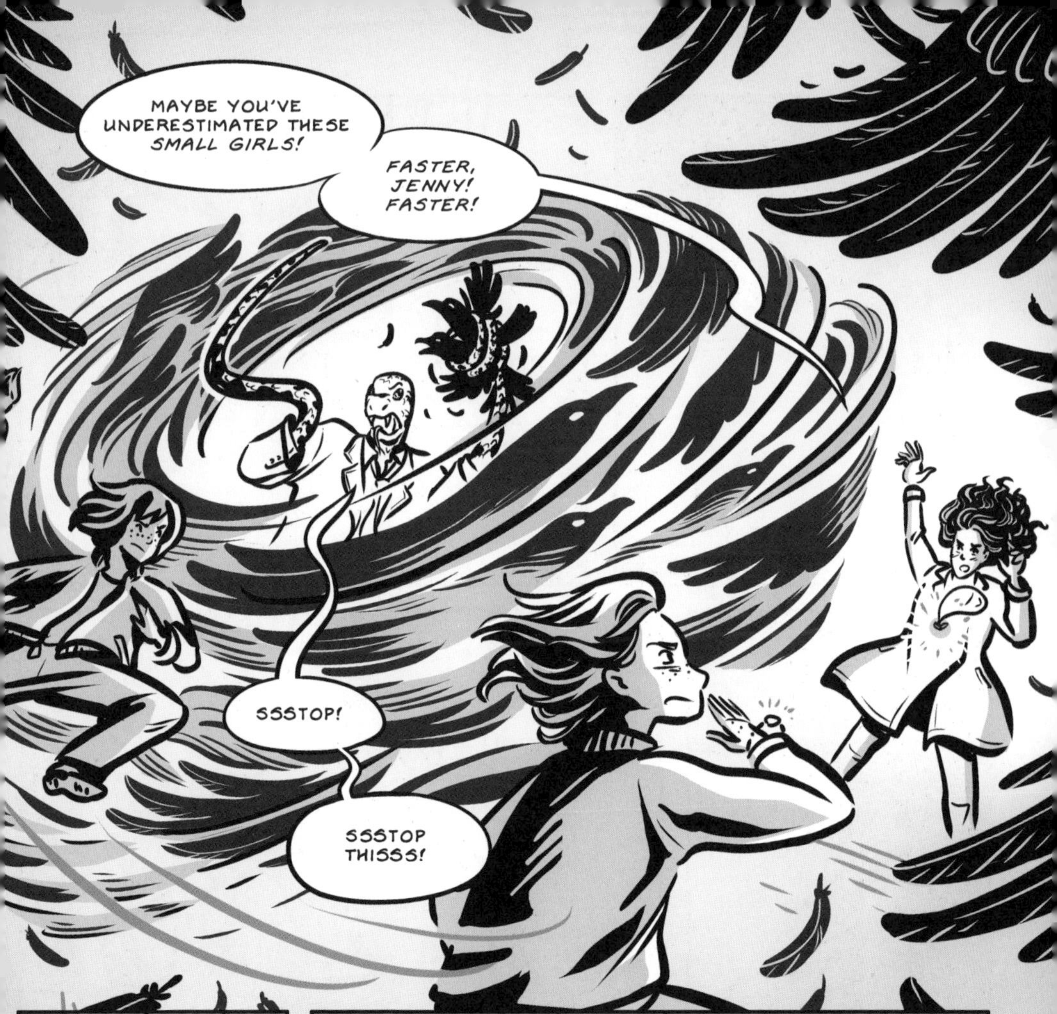
MAYBE YOU'VE UNDERESTIMATED THESE *SMALL GIRLS!*
FASTER, JENNY! FASTER!
SSSTOP!
SSSTOP THISSS!

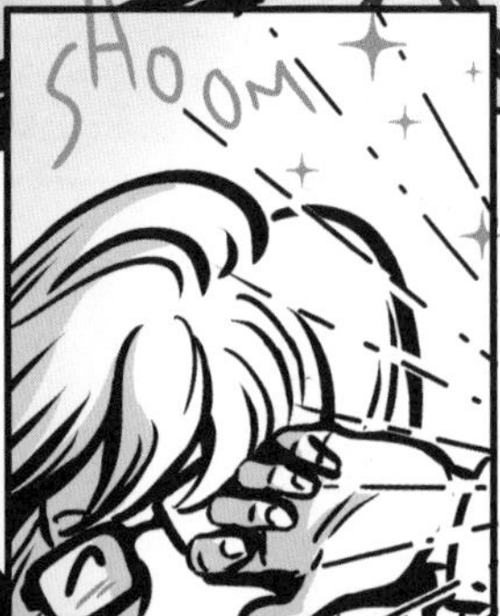
SHOOM

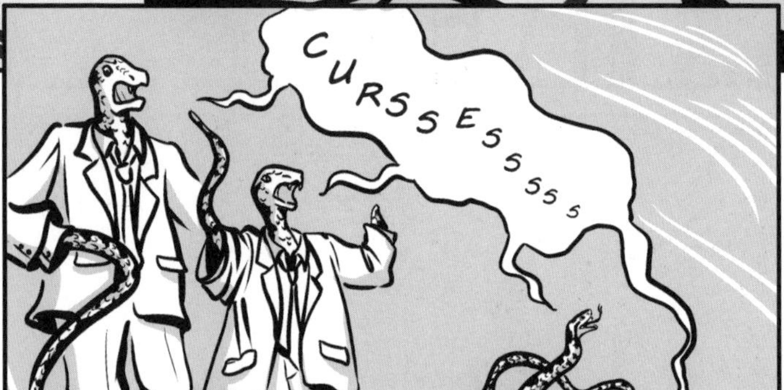
CURSSESSSSSS

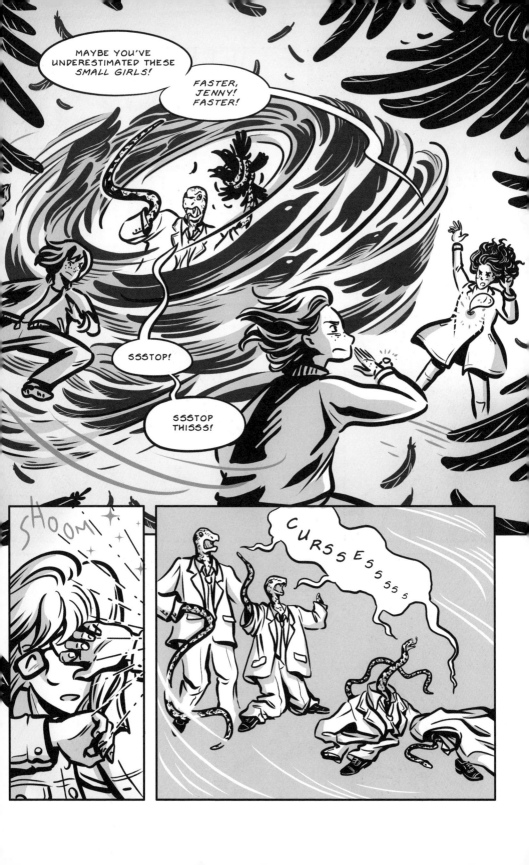

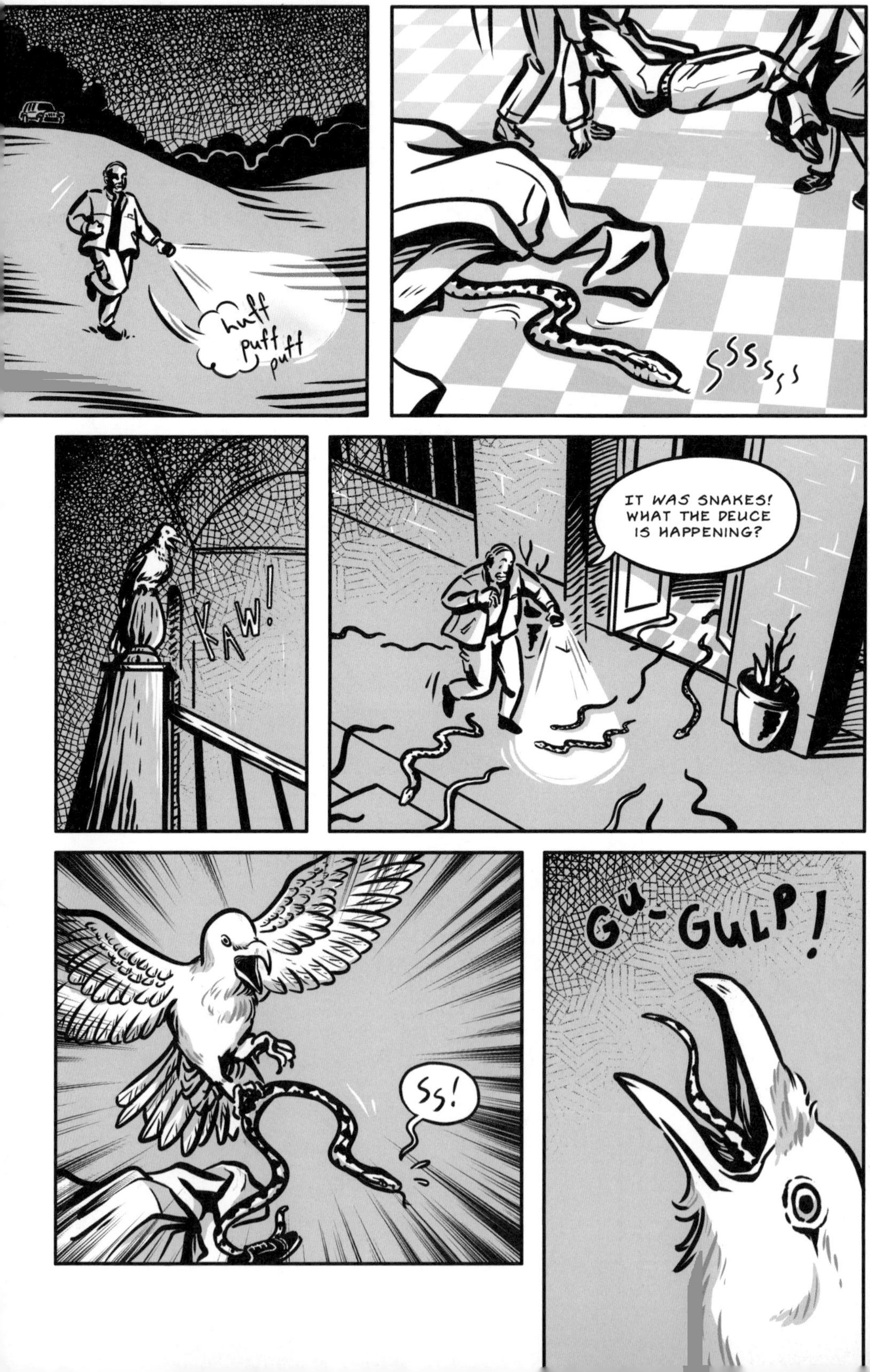
huff puff puff
SSSSSS
KAW!
IT WAS SNAKES! WHAT THE DEUCE IS HAPPENING?
Ss!
GU-GULP!

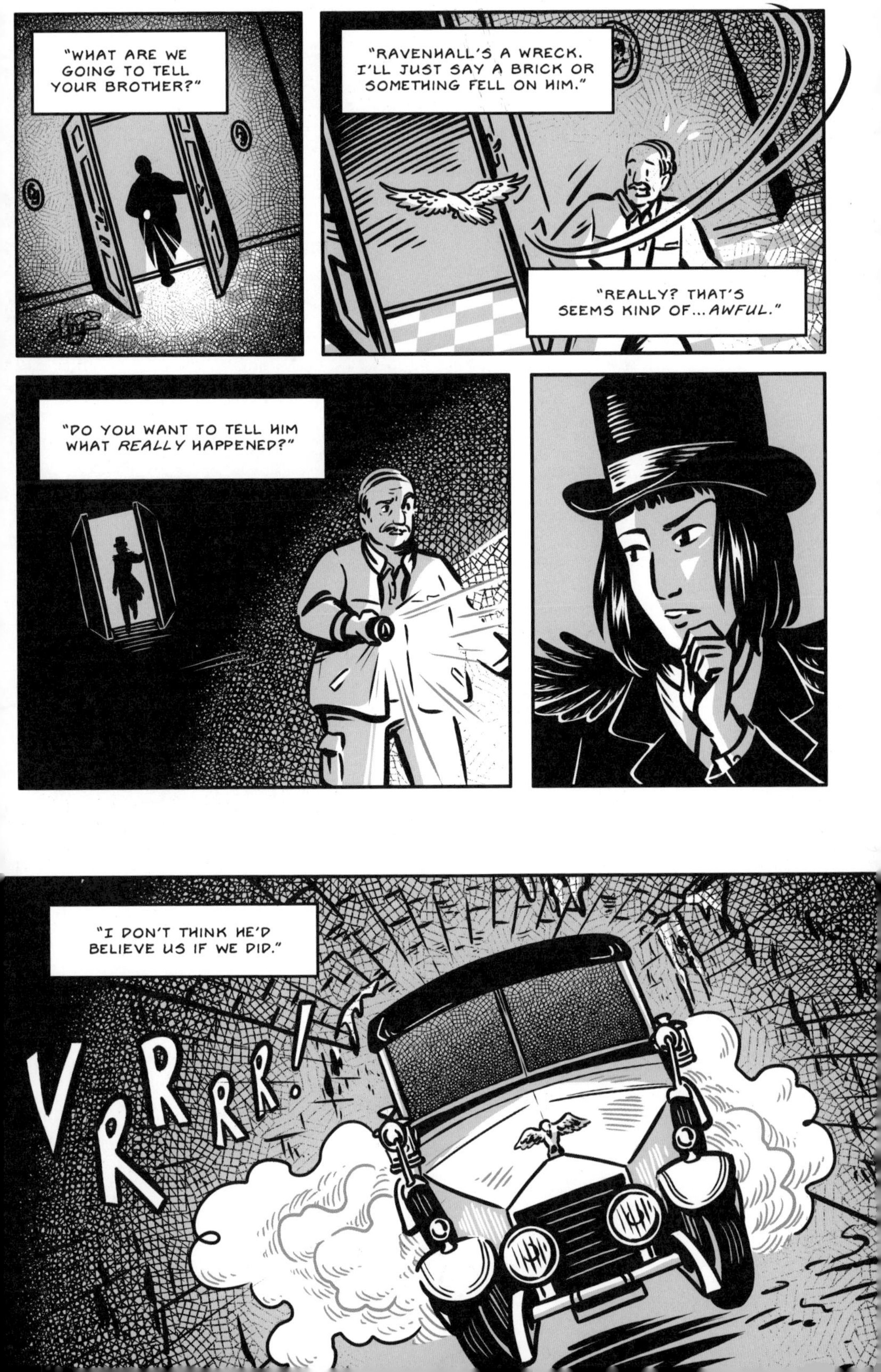
"WHAT ARE WE GOING TO TELL YOUR BROTHER?"
"RAVENHALL'S A WRECK. I'LL JUST SAY A BRICK OR SOMETHING FELL ON HIM."
"REALLY? THAT'S SEEMS KIND OF... *AWFUL.*"
"DO YOU WANT TO TELL HIM WHAT *REALLY* HAPPENED?"
"I DON'T THINK HE'D BELIEVE US IF WE DID."
VRRRR!

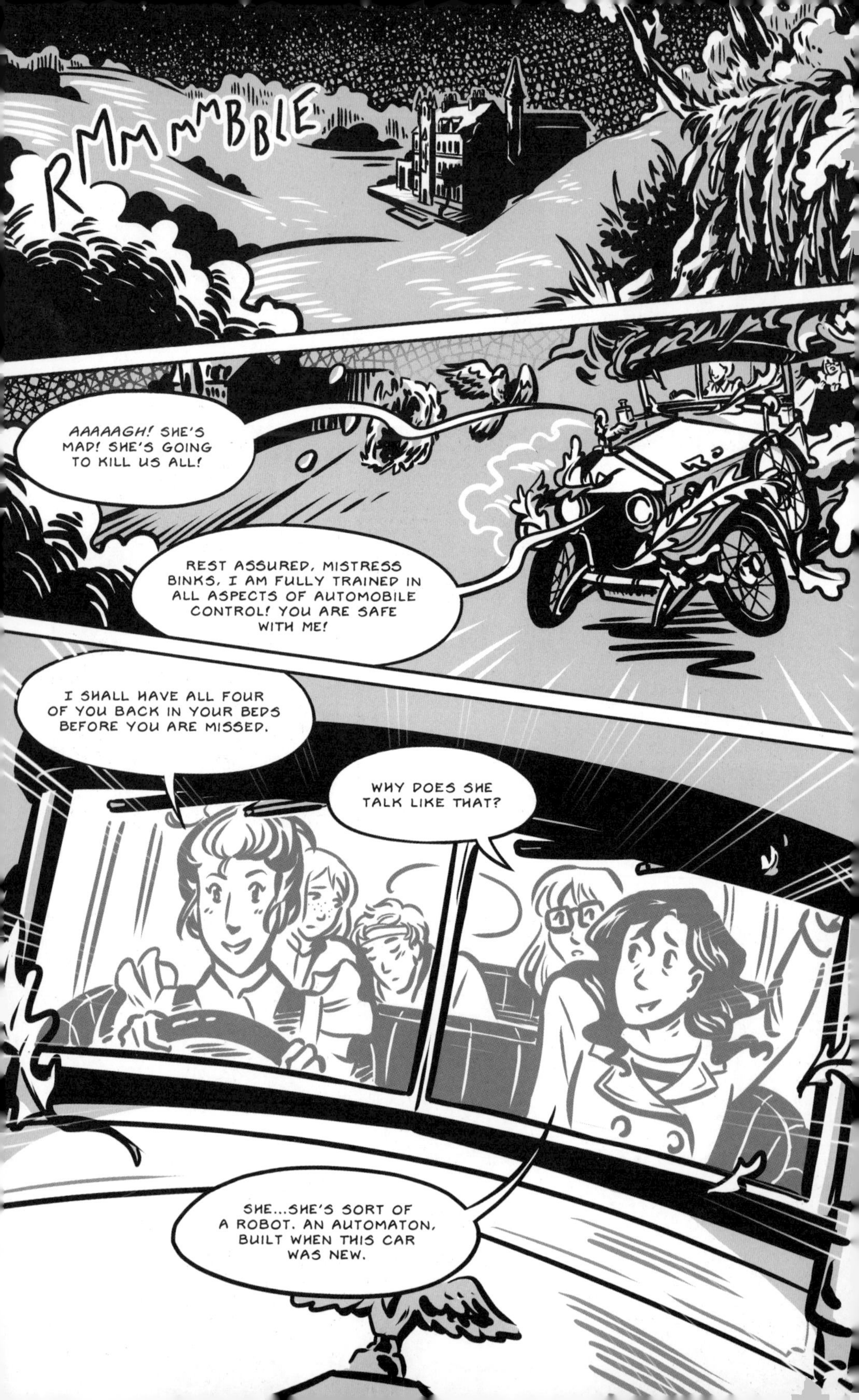
RMMMMBBLE
AAAAAGH! SHE'S MAD! SHE'S GOING TO KILL US ALL!
REST ASSURED, MISTRESS BINKS, I AM FULLY TRAINED IN ALL ASPECTS OF AUTOMOBILE CONTROL! YOU ARE SAFE WITH ME!
I SHALL HAVE ALL FOUR OF YOU BACK IN YOUR BEDS BEFORE YOU ARE MISSED.
WHY DOES SHE TALK LIKE THAT?
SHE...SHE'S SORT OF A ROBOT. AN AUTOMATON, BUILT WHEN THIS CAR WAS NEW.

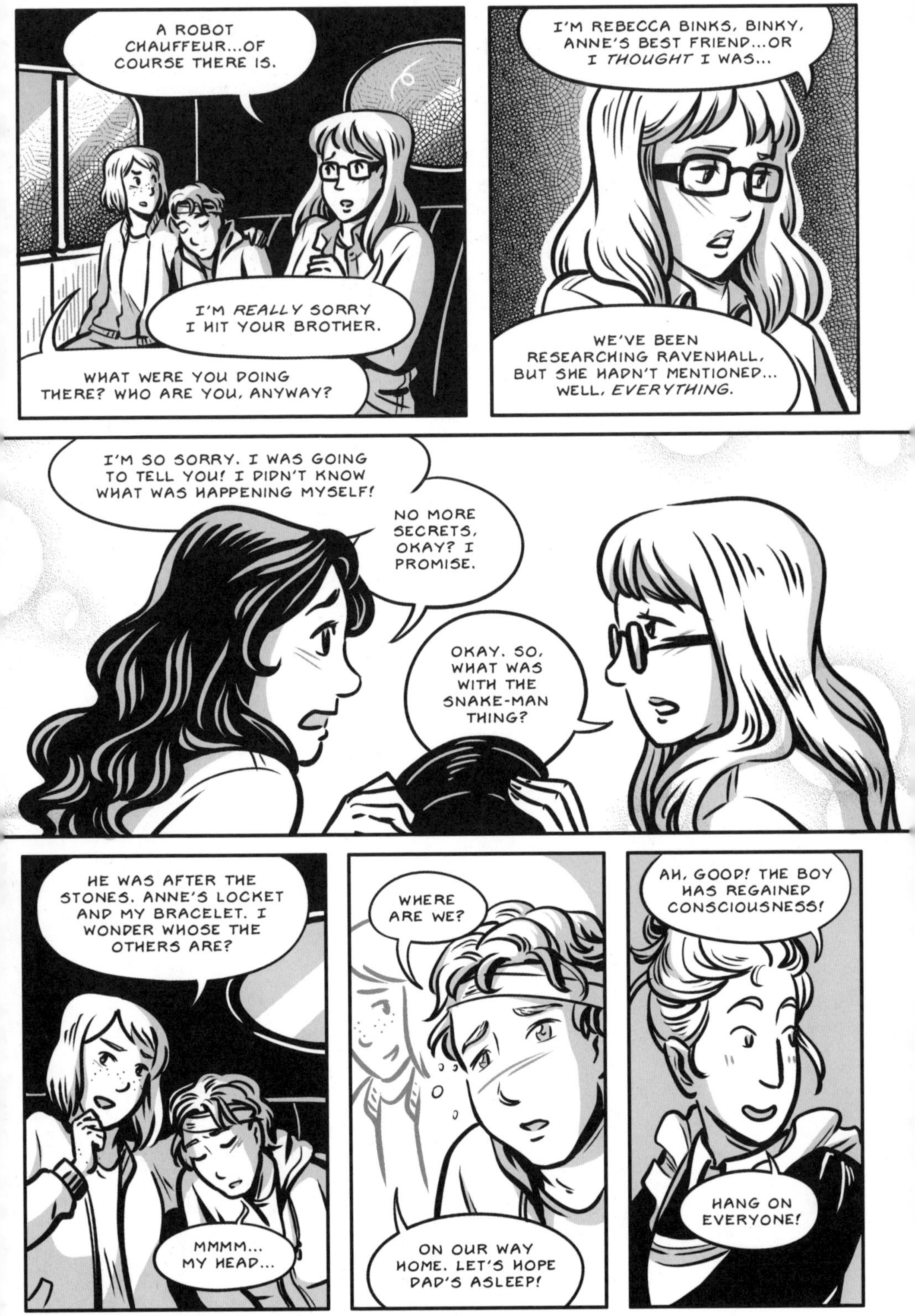
A ROBOT CHAUFFEUR...OF COURSE THERE IS.
I'M *REALLY* SORRY I HIT YOUR BROTHER.
WHAT WERE YOU DOING THERE? WHO ARE YOU, ANYWAY?
I'M REBECCA BINKS, BINKY, ANNE'S BEST FRIEND...OR I *THOUGHT* I WAS...
WE'VE BEEN RESEARCHING RAVENHALL, BUT SHE HADN'T MENTIONED... WELL, *EVERYTHING.*
I'M SO SORRY. I WAS GOING TO TELL YOU! I DIDN'T KNOW WHAT WAS HAPPENING MYSELF!
NO MORE SECRETS, OKAY? I PROMISE.
OKAY. SO, WHAT WAS WITH THE SNAKE-MAN THING?
HE WAS AFTER THE STONES. ANNE'S LOCKET AND MY BRACELET. I WONDER WHOSE THE OTHERS ARE?
MMMM... MY HEAD...
WHERE ARE WE?
ON OUR WAY HOME. LET'S HOPE DAD'S ASLEEP!
AH, GOOD! THE BOY HAS REGAINED CONSCIOUSNESS!
HANG ON EVERYONE!

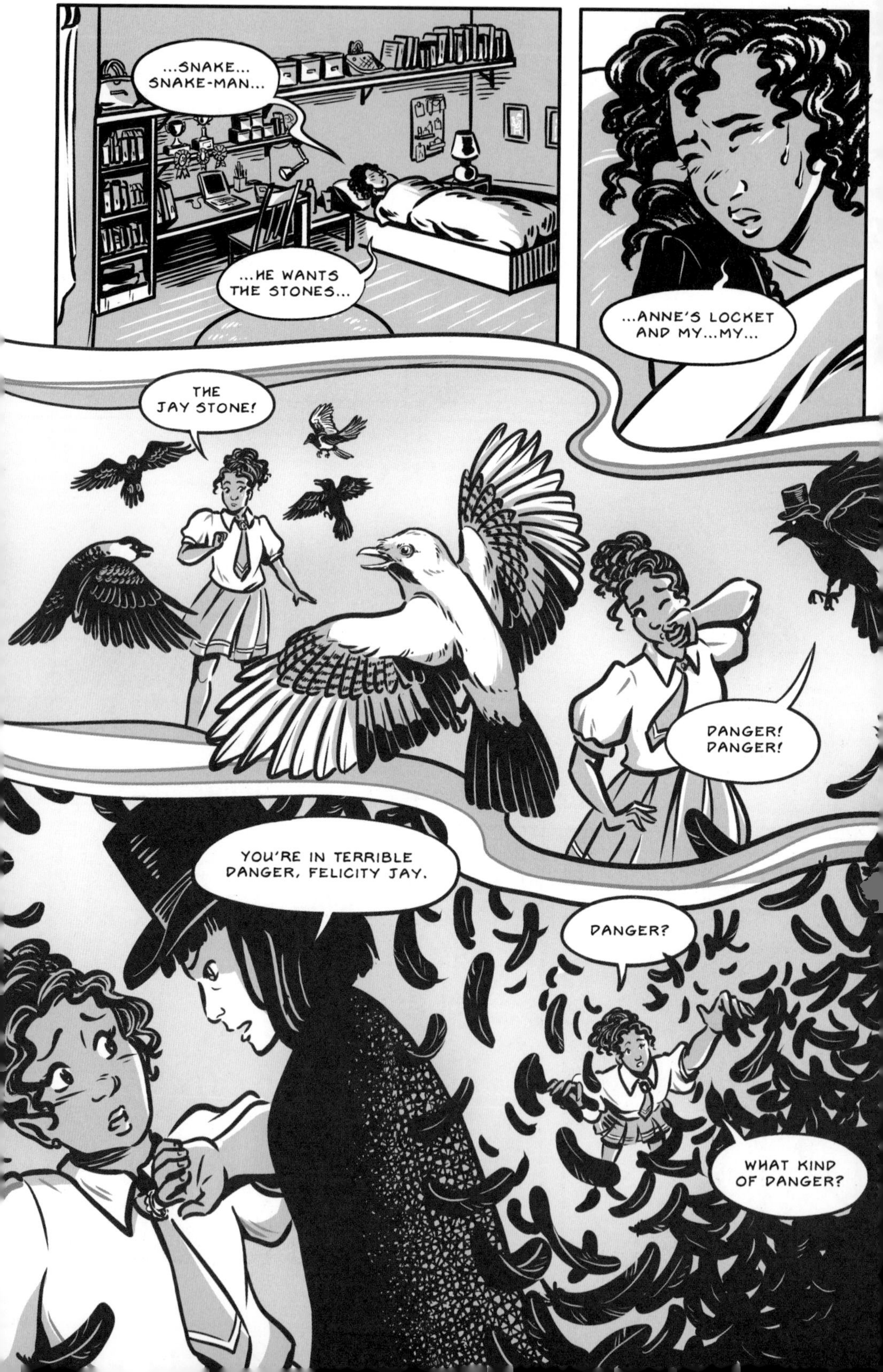
...SNAKE...
SNAKE-MAN...
...HE WANTS
THE STONES...
...ANNE'S LOCKET
AND MY...MY...
THE
JAY STONE!
DANGER!
DANGER!
YOU'RE IN TERRIBLE
DANGER, FELICITY JAY.
DANGER?
WHAT KIND
OF DANGER?

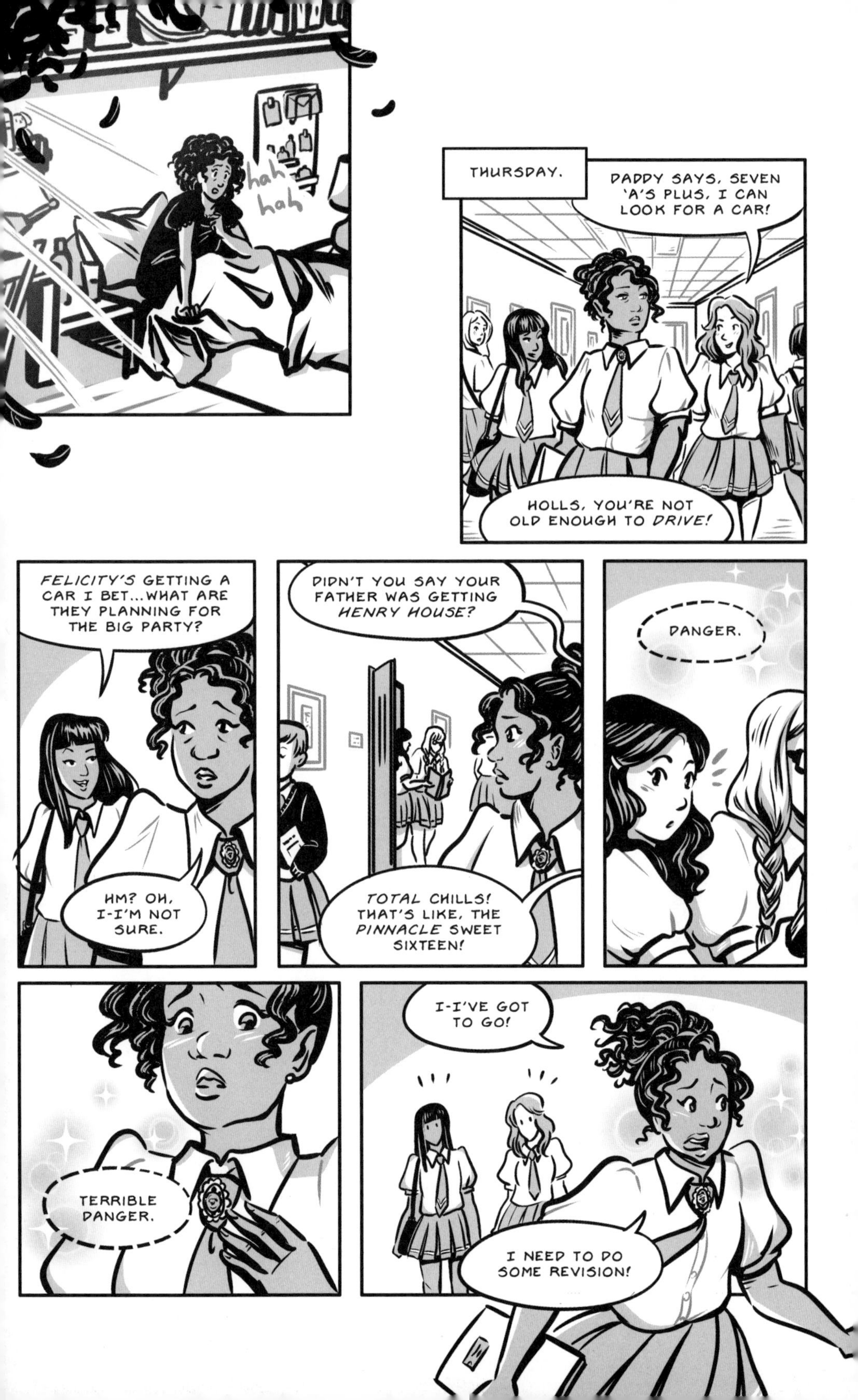
hah
hah
THURSDAY.
DADDY SAYS, SEVEN 'A'S PLUS, I CAN LOOK FOR A CAR!
HOLLS, YOU'RE NOT OLD ENOUGH TO *DRIVE!*
FELICITY'S GETTING A CAR I BET...WHAT ARE THEY PLANNING FOR THE BIG PARTY?
HM? OH, I-I'M NOT SURE.
DIDN'T YOU SAY YOUR FATHER WAS GETTING *HENRY HOUSE?*
TOTAL CHILLS! THAT'S LIKE, THE *PINNACLE* SWEET SIXTEEN!
DANGER.
TERRIBLE DANGER.
I-I'VE GOT TO GO!
I NEED TO DO SOME REVISION!

HAVE A LOOK AT THIS...

THIS *REALLY* DOESN'T LOOK LIKE REVISION, BINKY.

Treatise concerning the Language of Birds

Thomas Lanchester

OH, BUT IT IS!

THIS IS IMPORTANT DISSIMULATION BUSINESS.

LISTEN...

"THERE IS NO OLDER NOR PURER FORM OF MAGIC THAN THAT OF THE BIRDS.

"NO TALES MORE ANCIENT NOR PROPHETIC THAN THOSE TOLD OF THE FEATHERED KINGS AND QUEENS OF THE AIR."

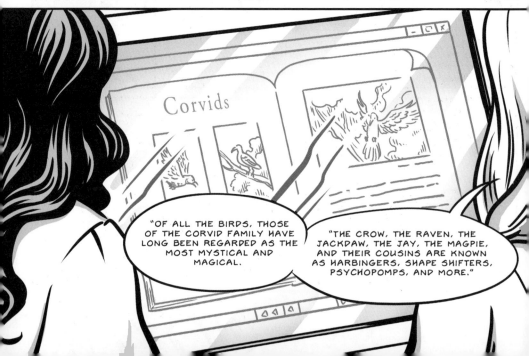

Corvids

"OF ALL THE BIRDS, THOSE OF THE CORVID FAMILY HAVE LONG BEEN REGARDED AS THE MOST MYSTICAL AND MAGICAL.

"THE CROW, THE RAVEN, THE JACKDAW, THE JAY, THE MAGPIE, AND THEIR COUSINS ARE KNOWN AS HARBINGERS, SHAPE SHIFTERS, PSYCHOPOMPS, AND MORE."

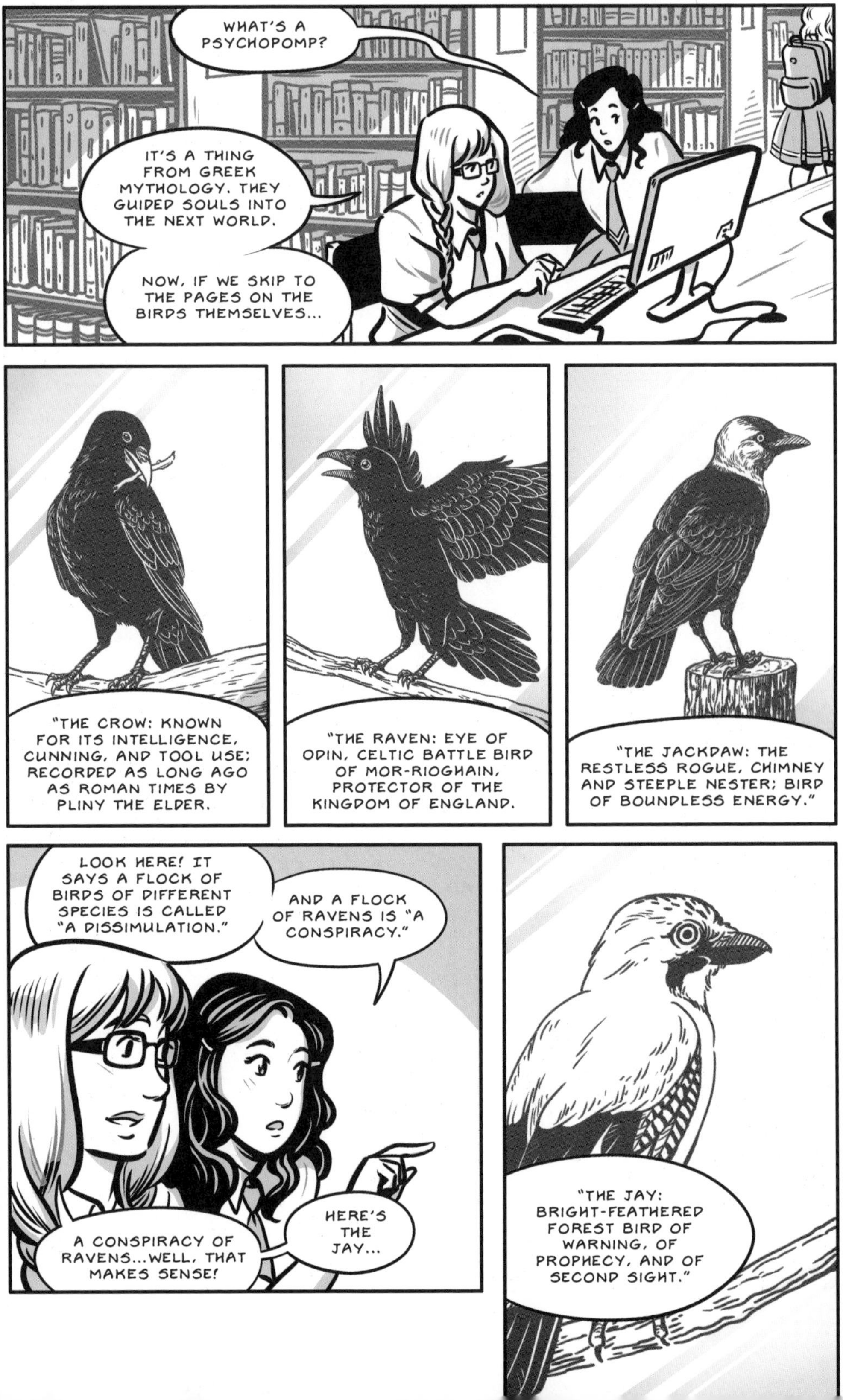
WHAT'S A PSYCHOPOMP?
IT'S A THING FROM GREEK MYTHOLOGY. THEY GUIDED SOULS INTO THE NEXT WORLD.
NOW, IF WE SKIP TO THE PAGES ON THE BIRDS THEMSELVES...
"THE CROW: KNOWN FOR ITS INTELLIGENCE, CUNNING, AND TOOL USE; RECORDED AS LONG AGO AS ROMAN TIMES BY PLINY THE ELDER.
"THE RAVEN: EYE OF ODIN, CELTIC BATTLE BIRD OF MOR-RIOGHAIN, PROTECTOR OF THE KINGDOM OF ENGLAND.
"THE JACKDAW: THE RESTLESS ROGUE, CHIMNEY AND STEEPLE NESTER; BIRD OF BOUNDLESS ENERGY."
LOOK HERE! IT SAYS A FLOCK OF BIRDS OF DIFFERENT SPECIES IS CALLED "A DISSIMULATION."
AND A FLOCK OF RAVENS IS "A CONSPIRACY."
A CONSPIRACY OF RAVENS...WELL, THAT MAKES SENSE!
HERE'S THE JAY...
"THE JAY: BRIGHT-FEATHERED FOREST BIRD OF WARNING, OF PROPHECY, AND OF SECOND SIGHT."

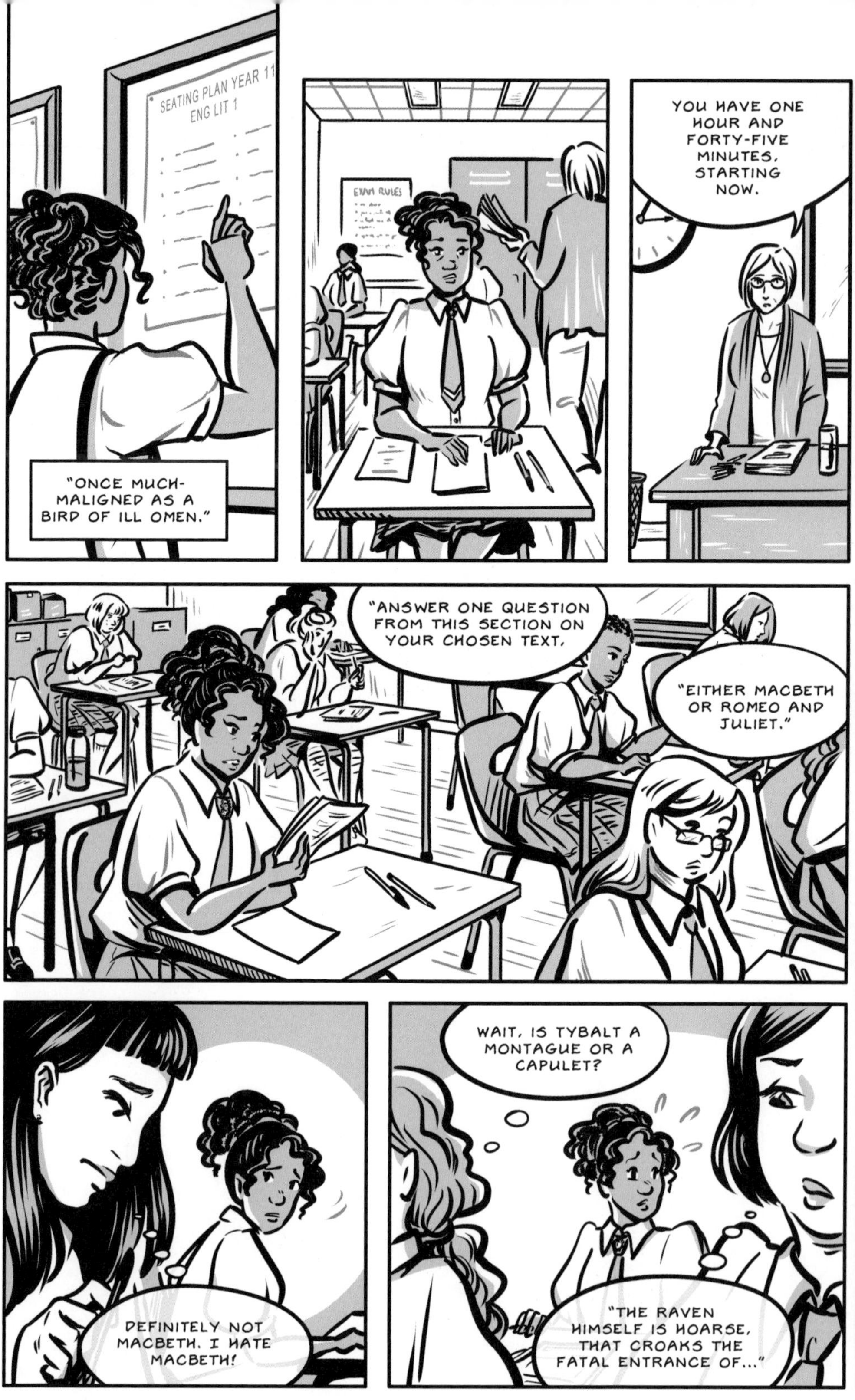
SEATING PLAN YEAR 11
ENG LIT 1
"ONCE MUCH-MALIGNED AS A BIRD OF ILL OMEN."
EXAM RULES
YOU HAVE ONE HOUR AND FORTY-FIVE MINUTES, STARTING NOW.
"ANSWER ONE QUESTION FROM THIS SECTION ON YOUR CHOSEN TEXT,
"EITHER MACBETH OR ROMEO AND JULIET."
DEFINITELY NOT MACBETH. I HATE MACBETH!
WAIT, IS TYBALT A MONTAGUE OR A CAPULET?
"THE RAVEN HIMSELF IS HOARSE, THAT CROAKS THE FATAL ENTRANCE OF..."

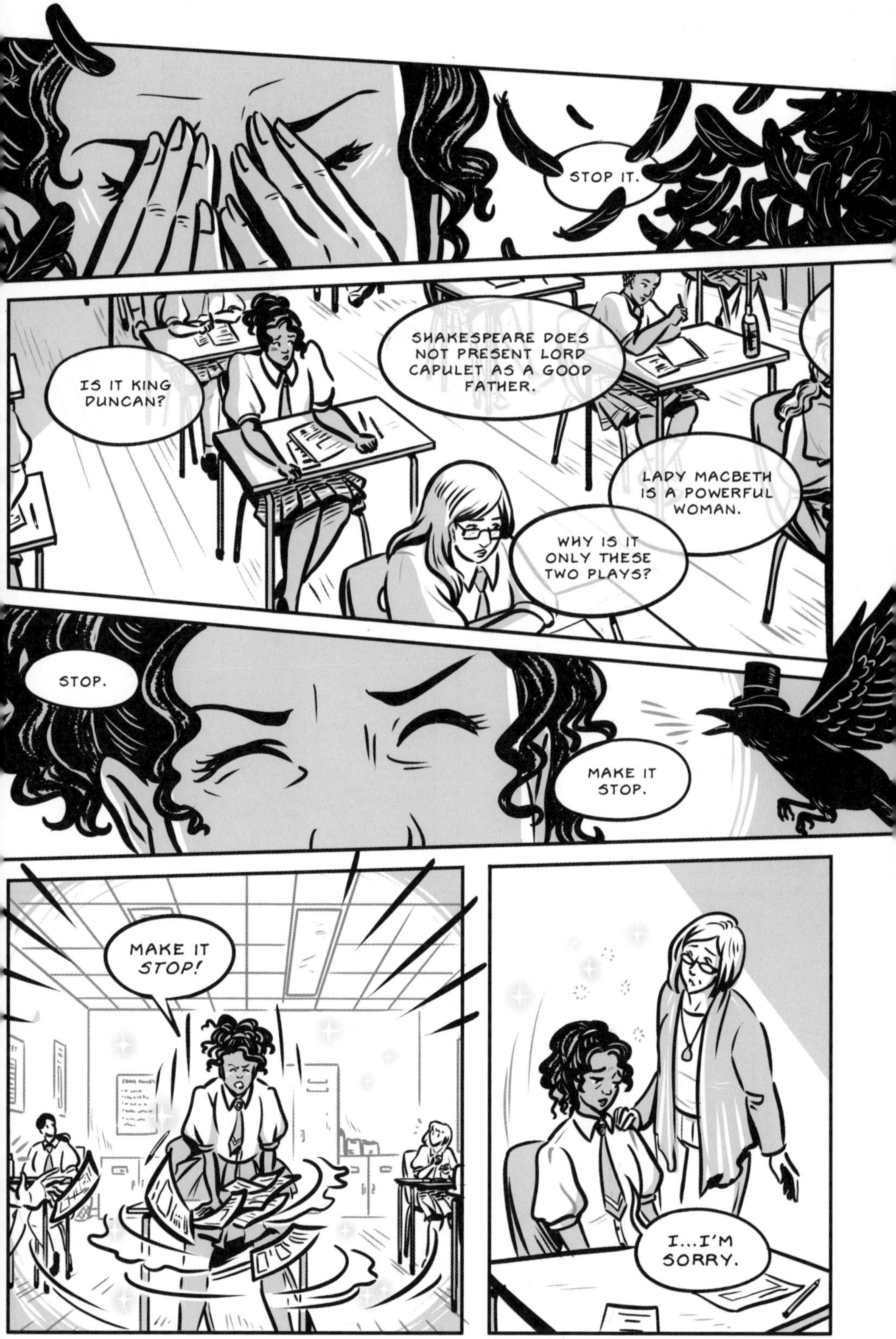
STOP IT.
IS IT KING DUNCAN?
SHAKESPEARE DOES NOT PRESENT LORD CAPULET AS A GOOD FATHER.
LADY MACBETH IS A POWERFUL WOMAN.
WHY IS IT ONLY THESE TWO PLAYS?
STOP.
MAKE IT STOP.
MAKE IT *STOP!*
I...I'M SORRY.

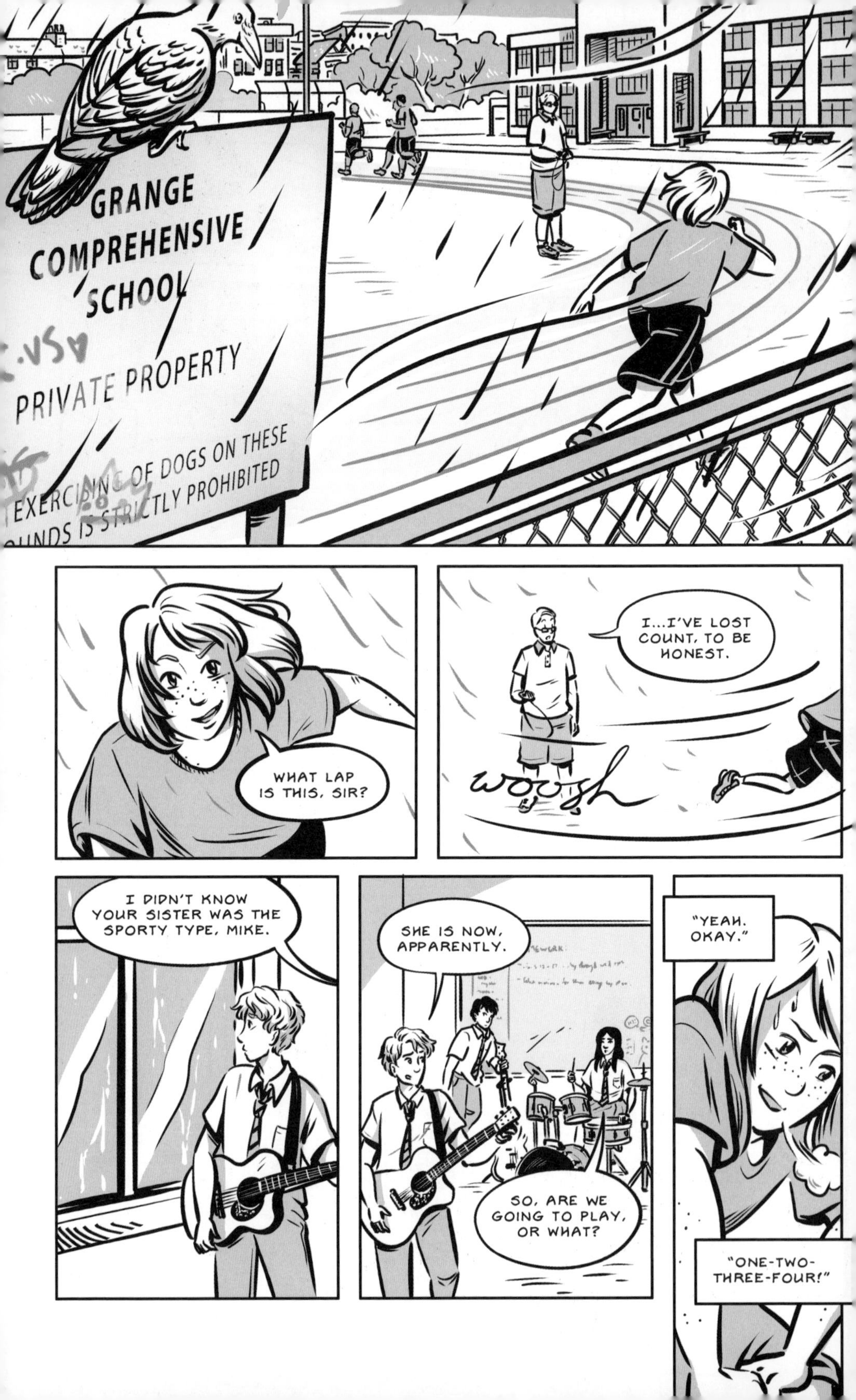
GRANGE
COMPREHENSIVE
SCHOOL
PRIVATE PROPERTY
EXERCISING OF DOGS ON THESE
GROUNDS IS STRICTLY PROHIBITED
WHAT LAP IS THIS, SIR?
I...I'VE LOST COUNT, TO BE HONEST.
WOOSH
I DIDN'T KNOW YOUR SISTER WAS THE SPORTY TYPE, MIKE.
SHE IS NOW, APPARENTLY.
SO, ARE WE GOING TO PLAY, OR WHAT?
"YEAH. OKAY."
"ONE-TWO-THREE-FOUR!"

SLOW DOWN, YOU KIDS! ONE AT A TIME!

beep!

GETTING THE BUS?

YEAH, WHY?

AFTER TODAY, I THOUGHT YOU MIGHT HAVE RUN INSTEAD...

FUNNY.

WHAT'S GOING ON, JEN?

NOTHING! WHY?

ALL THE SNEAKING ABOUT? THAT WRECK OF A HOUSE? HOW I GOT THIS LUMP?

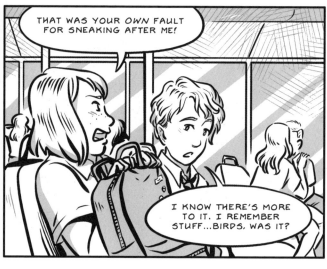

THAT WAS YOUR OWN FAULT FOR SNEAKING AFTER ME!

I KNOW THERE'S MORE TO IT. I REMEMBER STUFF...BIRDS, WAS IT?

JUST LEAVE IT, MIKE. SERIOUSLY.

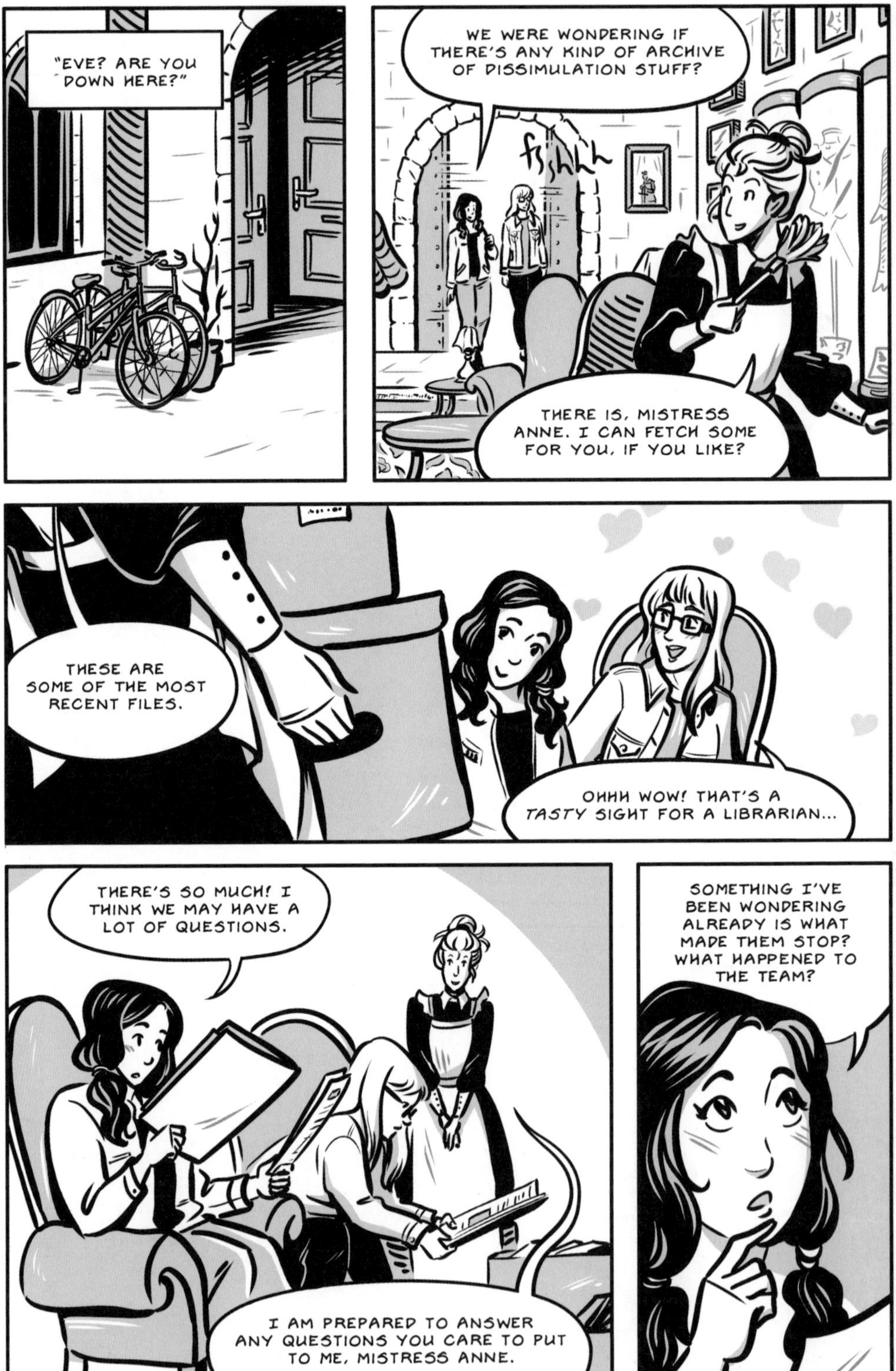
"EVE? ARE YOU DOWN HERE?"
WE WERE WONDERING IF THERE'S ANY KIND OF ARCHIVE OF DISSIMULATION STUFF?
fshhh
THERE IS, MISTRESS ANNE. I CAN FETCH SOME FOR YOU, IF YOU LIKE?
THESE ARE SOME OF THE MOST RECENT FILES.
OHHH WOW! THAT'S A *TASTY* SIGHT FOR A LIBRARIAN...
THERE'S SO MUCH! I THINK WE MAY HAVE A LOT OF QUESTIONS.
I AM PREPARED TO ANSWER ANY QUESTIONS YOU CARE TO PUT TO ME, MISTRESS ANNE.
SOMETHING I'VE BEEN WONDERING ALREADY IS WHAT MADE THEM STOP? WHAT HAPPENED TO THE TEAM?

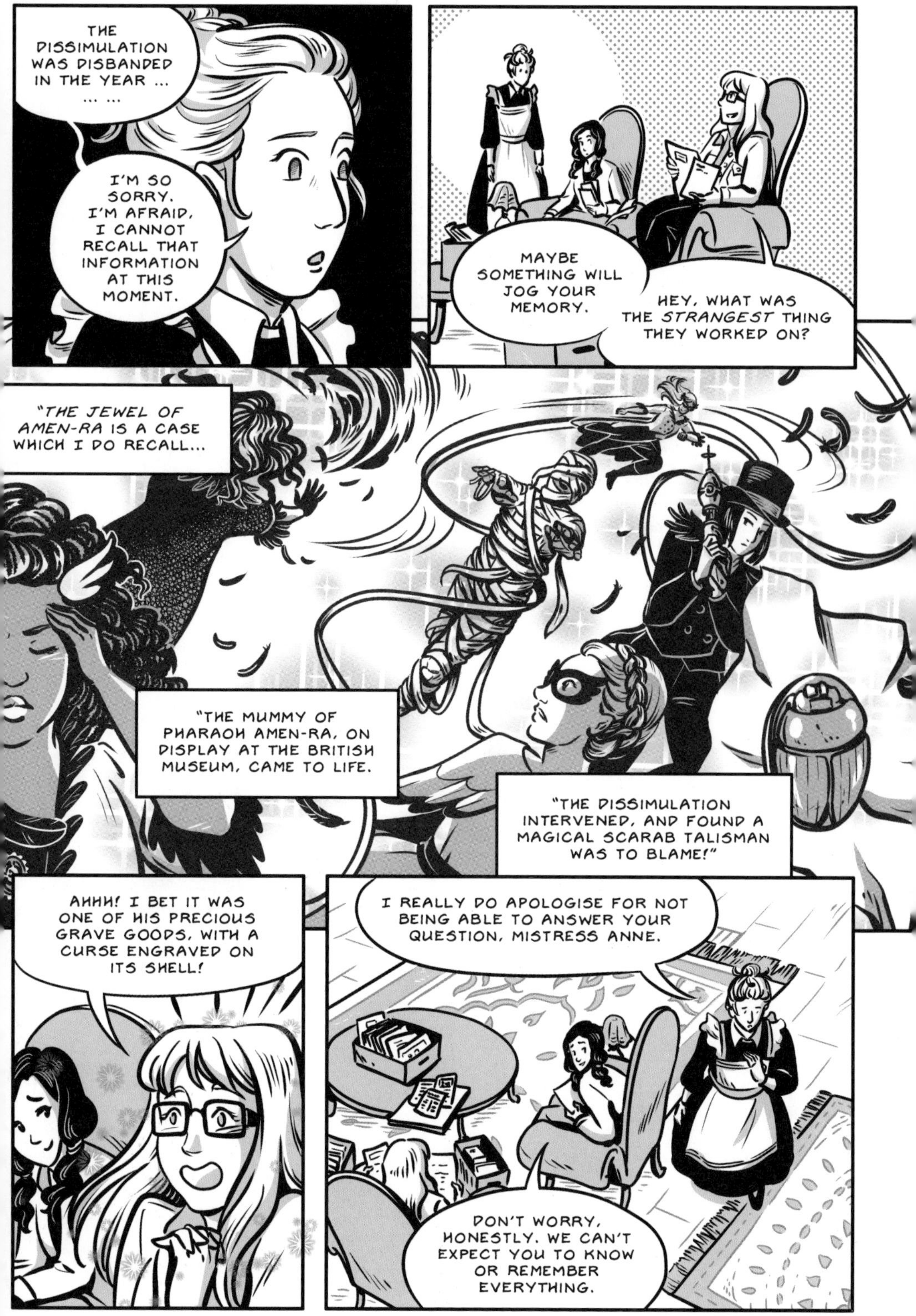
THE DISSIMULATION WAS DISBANDED IN THE YEAR ... ...
I'M SO SORRY. I'M AFRAID, I CANNOT RECALL THAT INFORMATION AT THIS MOMENT.
MAYBE SOMETHING WILL JOG YOUR MEMORY.
HEY, WHAT WAS THE STRANGEST THING THEY WORKED ON?
"THE JEWEL OF AMEN-RA IS A CASE WHICH I DO RECALL...
"THE MUMMY OF PHARAOH AMEN-RA, ON DISPLAY AT THE BRITISH MUSEUM, CAME TO LIFE.
"THE DISSIMULATION INTERVENED, AND FOUND A MAGICAL SCARAB TALISMAN WAS TO BLAME!"
AHHH! I BET IT WAS ONE OF HIS PRECIOUS GRAVE GOODS, WITH A CURSE ENGRAVED ON ITS SHELL!
I REALLY DO APOLOGISE FOR NOT BEING ABLE TO ANSWER YOUR QUESTION, MISTRESS ANNE.
DON'T WORRY, HONESTLY. WE CAN'T EXPECT YOU TO KNOW OR REMEMBER EVERYTHING.

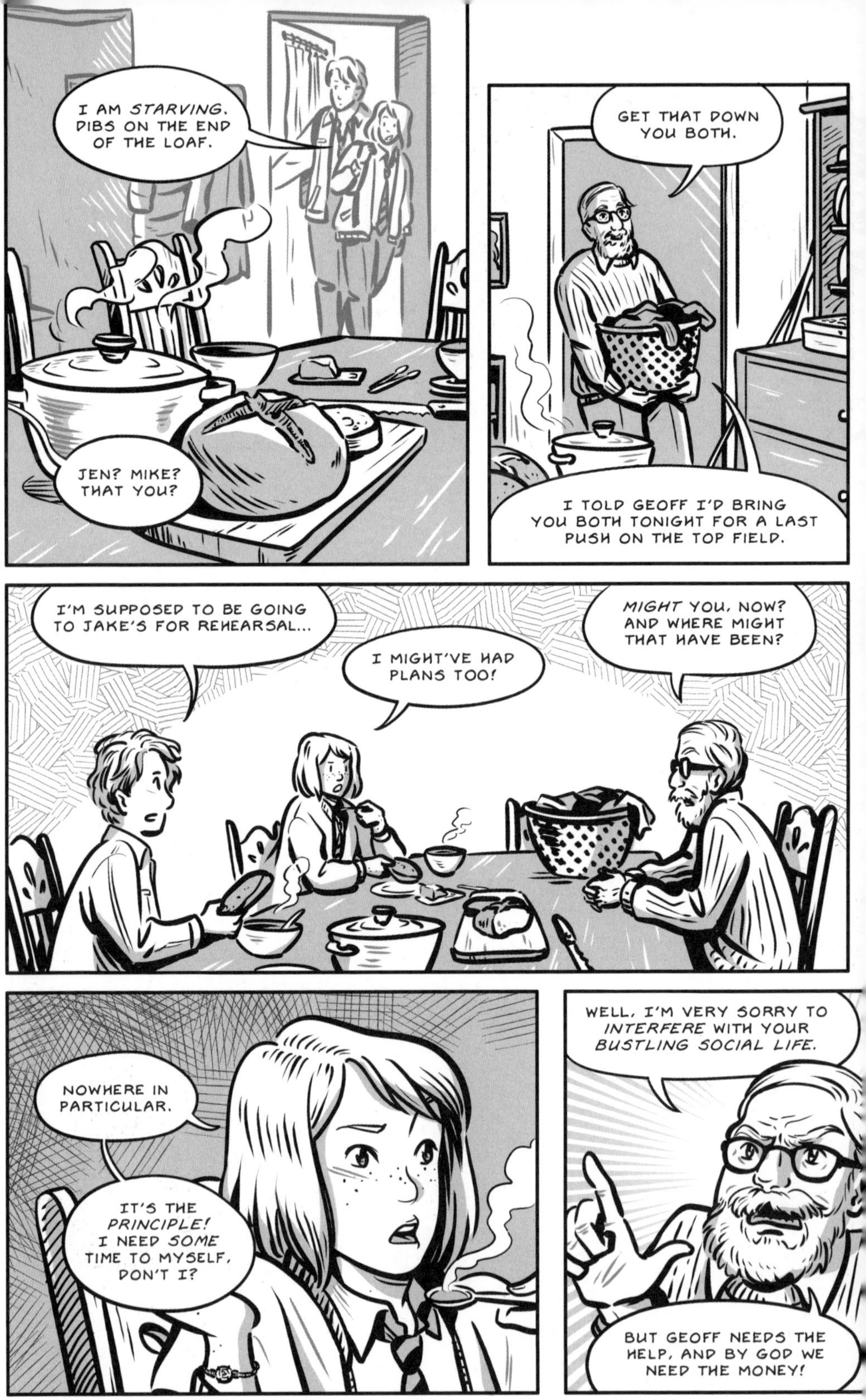
I AM *STARVING*. DIBS ON THE END OF THE LOAF.
JEN? MIKE? THAT YOU?
GET THAT DOWN YOU BOTH.
I TOLD GEOFF I'D BRING YOU BOTH TONIGHT FOR A LAST PUSH ON THE TOP FIELD.
I'M SUPPOSED TO BE GOING TO JAKE'S FOR REHEARSAL...
I MIGHT'VE HAD PLANS TOO!
MIGHT YOU, NOW? AND WHERE MIGHT THAT HAVE BEEN?
NOWHERE IN PARTICULAR.
IT'S THE *PRINCIPLE!* I NEED *SOME* TIME TO MYSELF, DON'T I?
WELL, I'M VERY SORRY TO *INTERFERE* WITH YOUR *BUSTLING SOCIAL LIFE.*
BUT GEOFF NEEDS THE HELP, AND BY GOD WE NEED THE MONEY!

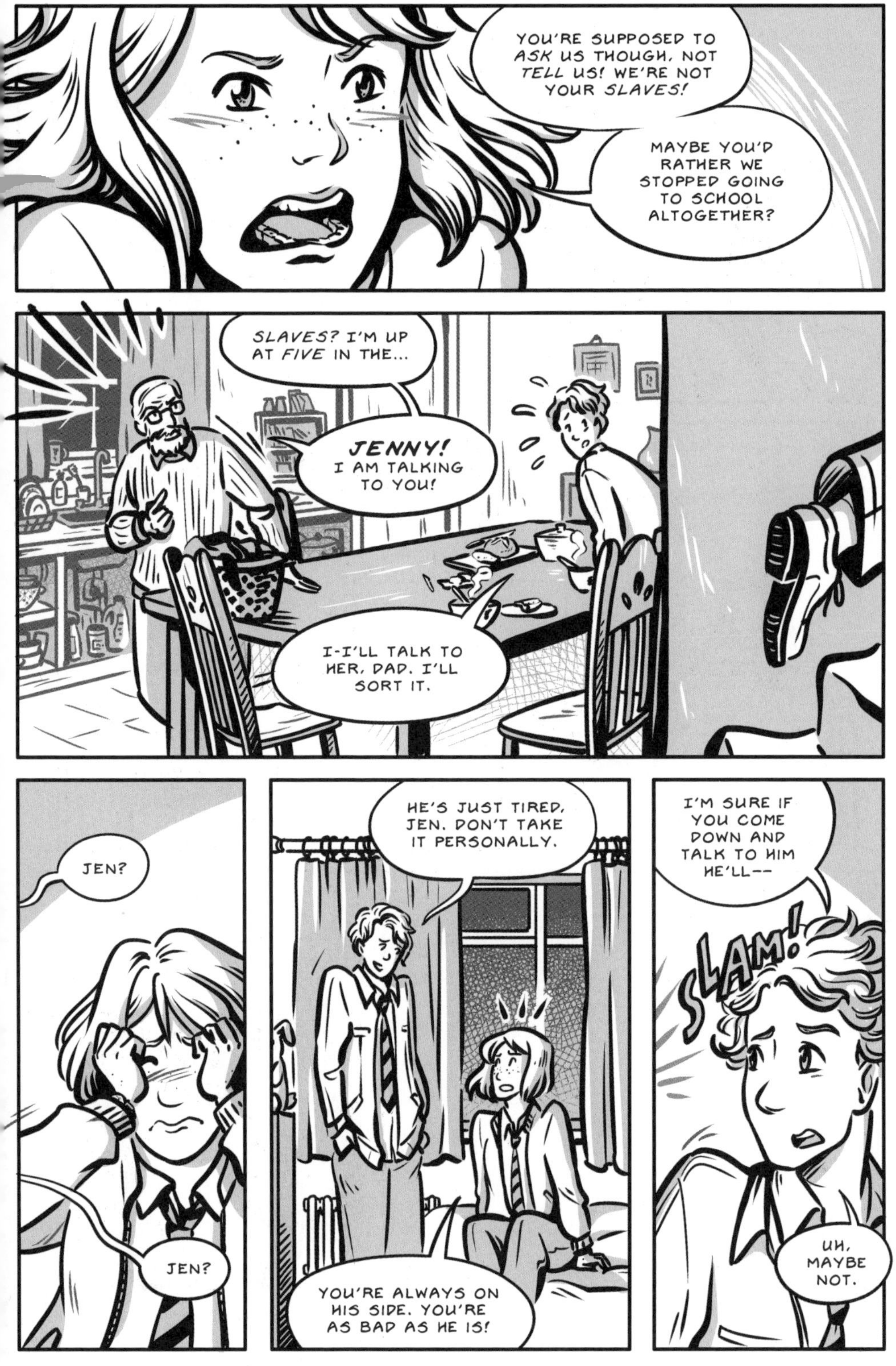
YOU'RE SUPPOSED TO ASK US THOUGH, NOT TELL US! WE'RE NOT YOUR SLAVES!
MAYBE YOU'D RATHER WE STOPPED GOING TO SCHOOL ALTOGETHER?
SLAVES? I'M UP AT FIVE IN THE...
JENNY! I AM TALKING TO YOU!
I-I'LL TALK TO HER, DAD. I'LL SORT IT.
JEN?
JEN?
HE'S JUST TIRED, JEN. DON'T TAKE IT PERSONALLY.
YOU'RE ALWAYS ON HIS SIDE. YOU'RE AS BAD AS HE IS!
I'M SURE IF YOU COME DOWN AND TALK TO HIM HE'LL--
SLAM!
UH, MAYBE NOT.

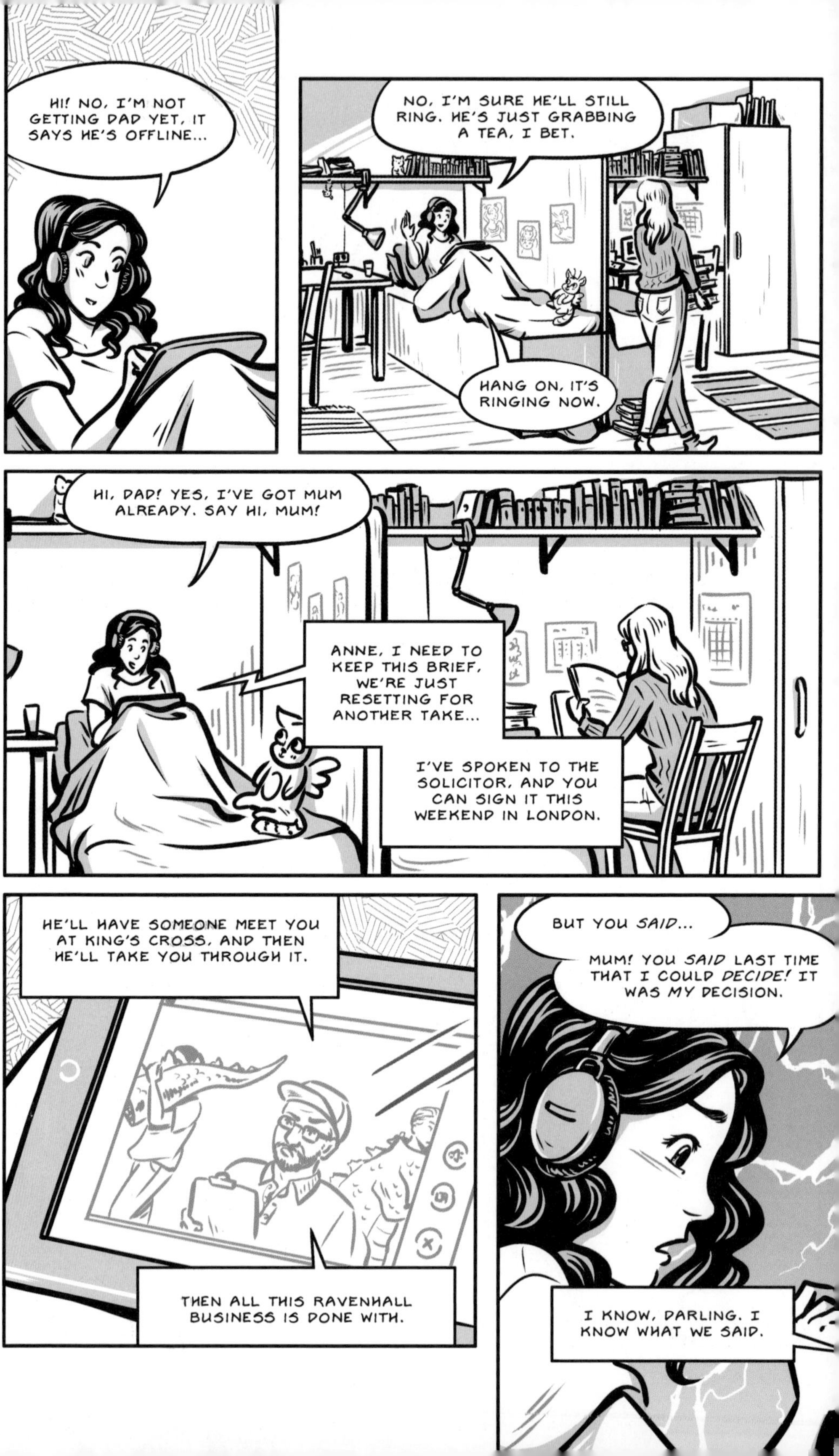
HI! NO, I'M NOT GETTING DAD YET, IT SAYS HE'S OFFLINE...
NO, I'M SURE HE'LL STILL RING. HE'S JUST GRABBING A TEA, I BET.
HANG ON, IT'S RINGING NOW.
HI, DAD! YES, I'VE GOT MUM ALREADY. SAY HI, MUM!
ANNE, I NEED TO KEEP THIS BRIEF, WE'RE JUST RESETTING FOR ANOTHER TAKE...
I'VE SPOKEN TO THE SOLICITOR, AND YOU CAN SIGN IT THIS WEEKEND IN LONDON.
HE'LL HAVE SOMEONE MEET YOU AT KING'S CROSS, AND THEN HE'LL TAKE YOU THROUGH IT.
THEN ALL THIS RAVENHALL BUSINESS IS DONE WITH.
BUT YOU *SAID*...
MUM! YOU *SAID* LAST TIME THAT I COULD *DECIDE!* IT WAS MY DECISION.
I KNOW, DARLING. I KNOW WHAT WE SAID.

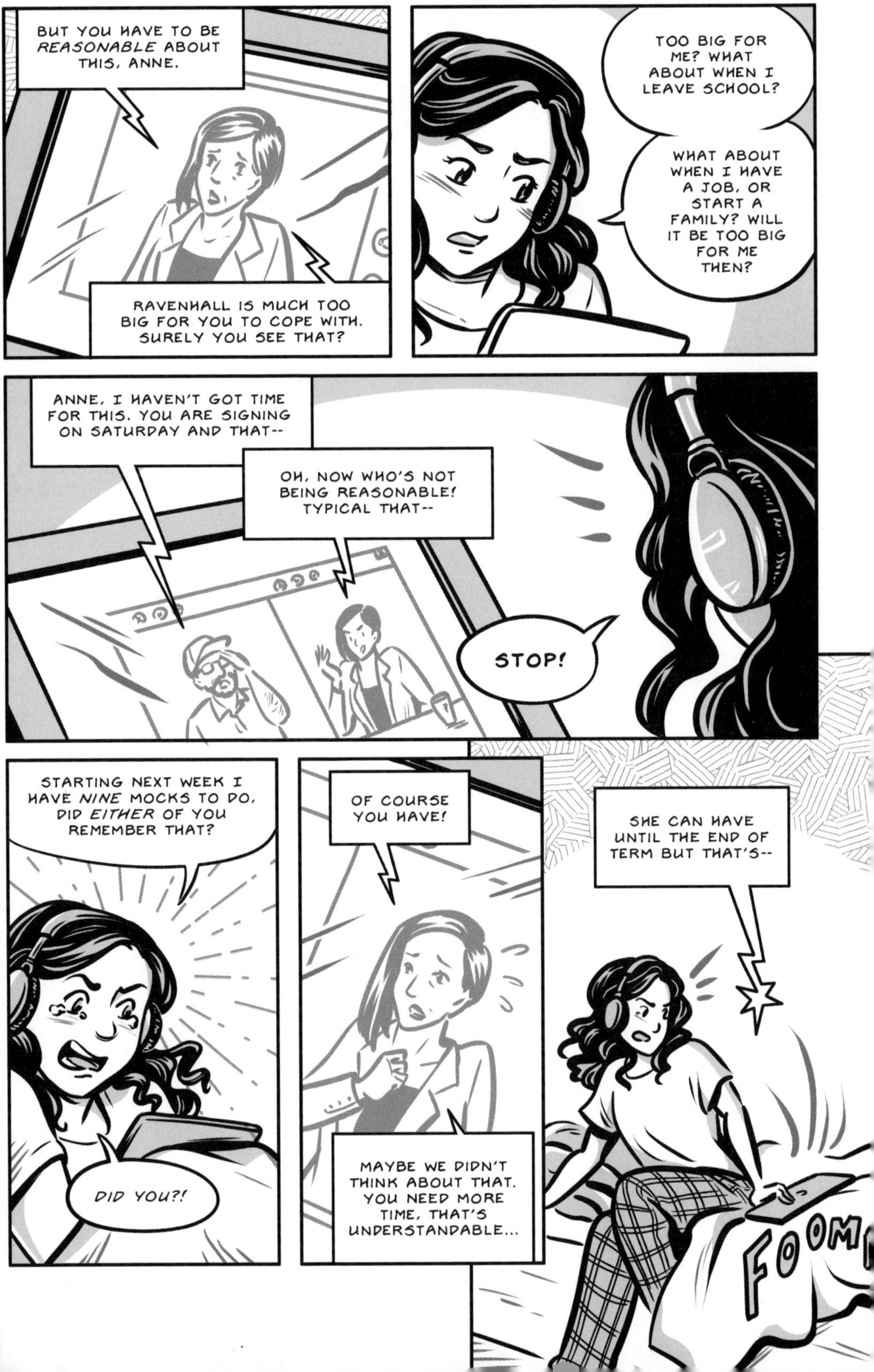
BUT YOU HAVE TO BE *REASONABLE* ABOUT THIS, ANNE.
RAVENHALL IS MUCH TOO BIG FOR YOU TO COPE WITH. SURELY YOU SEE THAT?
TOO BIG FOR ME? WHAT ABOUT WHEN I LEAVE SCHOOL?
WHAT ABOUT WHEN I HAVE A JOB, OR START A FAMILY? WILL IT BE TOO BIG FOR ME THEN?
ANNE, I HAVEN'T GOT TIME FOR THIS. YOU ARE SIGNING ON SATURDAY AND THAT--
OH, NOW WHO'S NOT BEING REASONABLE! TYPICAL THAT--
STOP!
STARTING NEXT WEEK I HAVE *NINE* MOCKS TO DO. DID *EITHER* OF YOU REMEMBER THAT?
DID YOU?!
OF COURSE YOU HAVE!
MAYBE WE DIDN'T THINK ABOUT THAT. YOU NEED MORE TIME, THAT'S UNDERSTANDABLE...
SHE CAN HAVE UNTIL THE END OF TERM BUT THAT'S--
FOOM

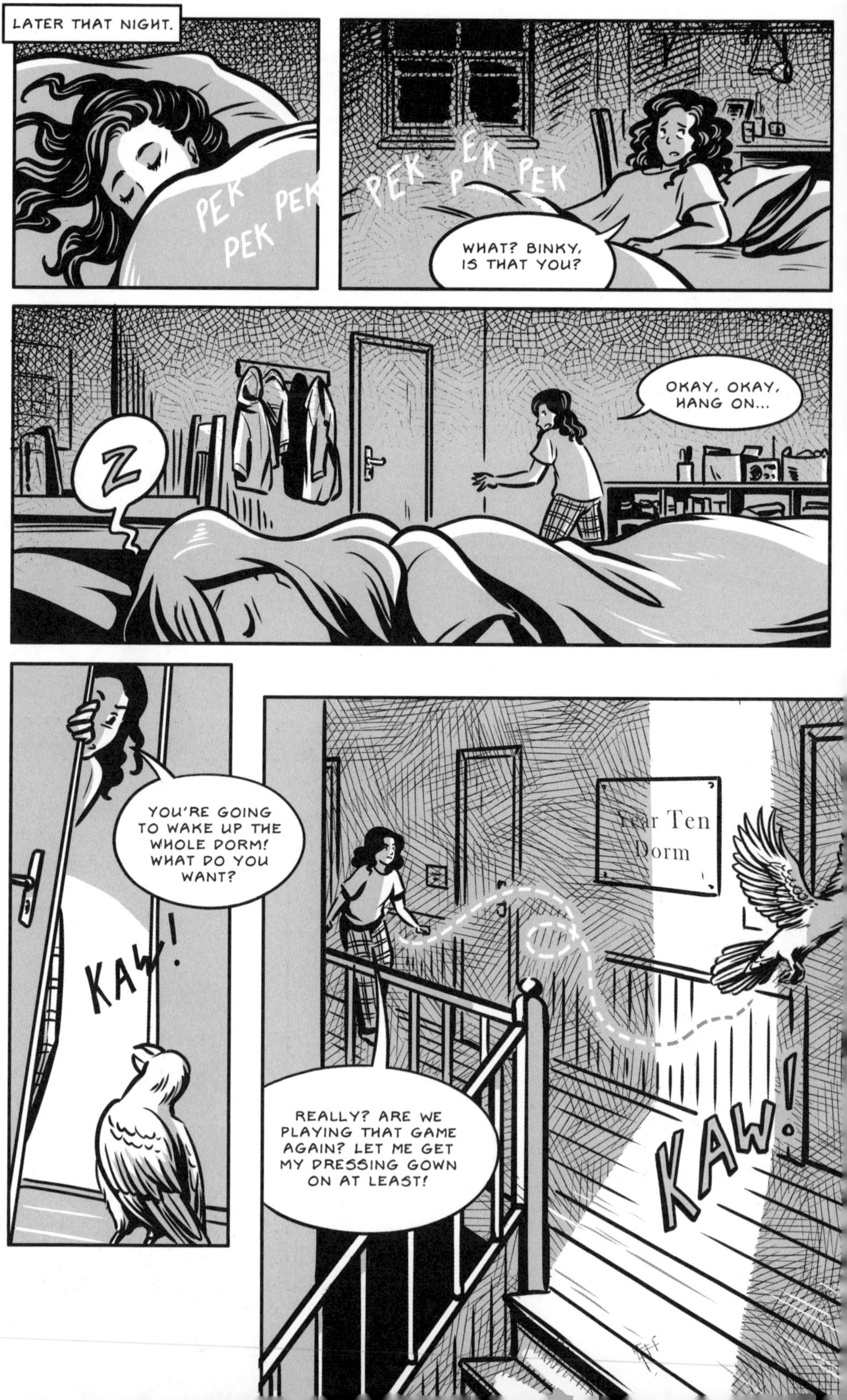
LATER THAT NIGHT.
PEK
PEK PEK
PEK PEK
PEK P EK PEK
WHAT? BINKY, IS THAT YOU?
Z
OKAY, OKAY, HANG ON...
YOU'RE GOING TO WAKE UP THE WHOLE DORM! WHAT DO YOU WANT?
KAW!
Year Ten Dorm
REALLY? ARE WE PLAYING THAT GAME AGAIN? LET ME GET MY DRESSING GOWN ON AT LEAST!
KAW!

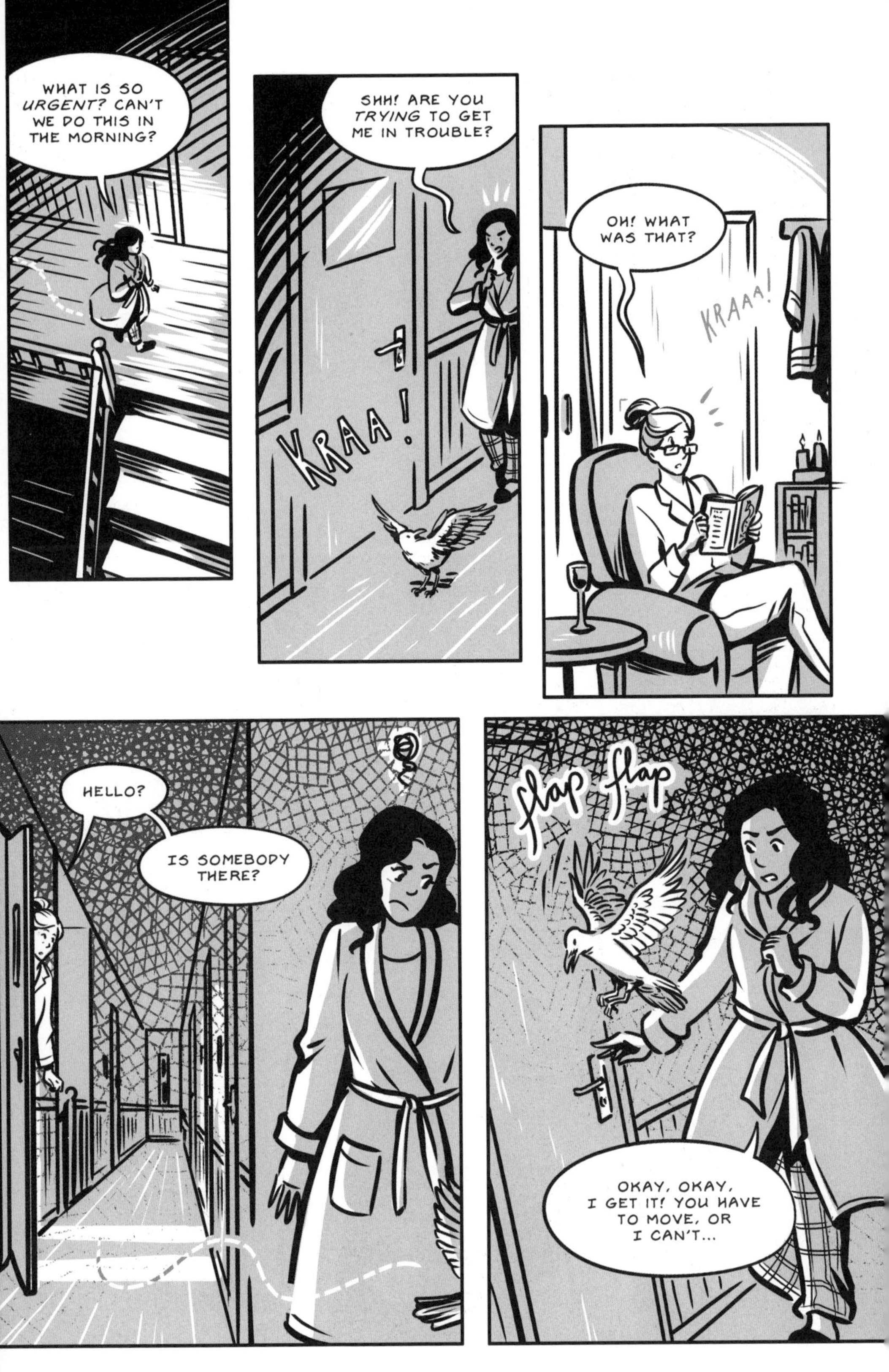
WHAT IS SO URGENT? CAN'T WE DO THIS IN THE MORNING?
SHH! ARE YOU TRYING TO GET ME IN TROUBLE?
KRAA!
OH! WHAT WAS THAT?
KRAAA!
HELLO?
IS SOMEBODY THERE?
flap flap
OKAY, OKAY, I GET IT! YOU HAVE TO MOVE, OR I CAN'T...

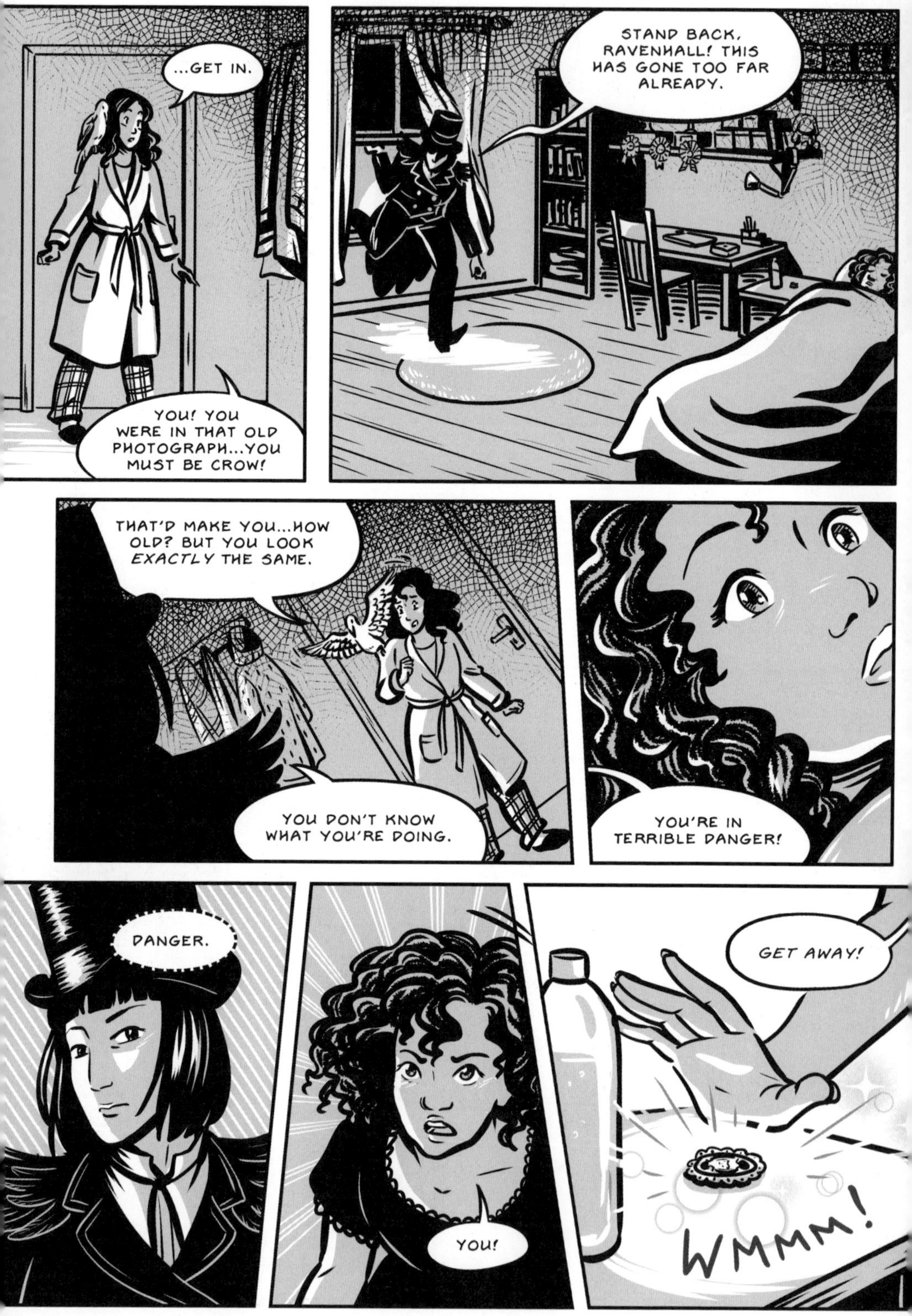
...GET IN.
YOU! YOU WERE IN THAT OLD PHOTOGRAPH...YOU MUST BE CROW!
STAND BACK, RAVENHALL! THIS HAS GONE TOO FAR ALREADY.
THAT'D MAKE YOU...HOW OLD? BUT YOU LOOK *EXACTLY* THE SAME.
YOU DON'T KNOW WHAT YOU'RE DOING.
YOU'RE IN TERRIBLE DANGER!
DANGER.
YOU!
GET AWAY!
WMMM!

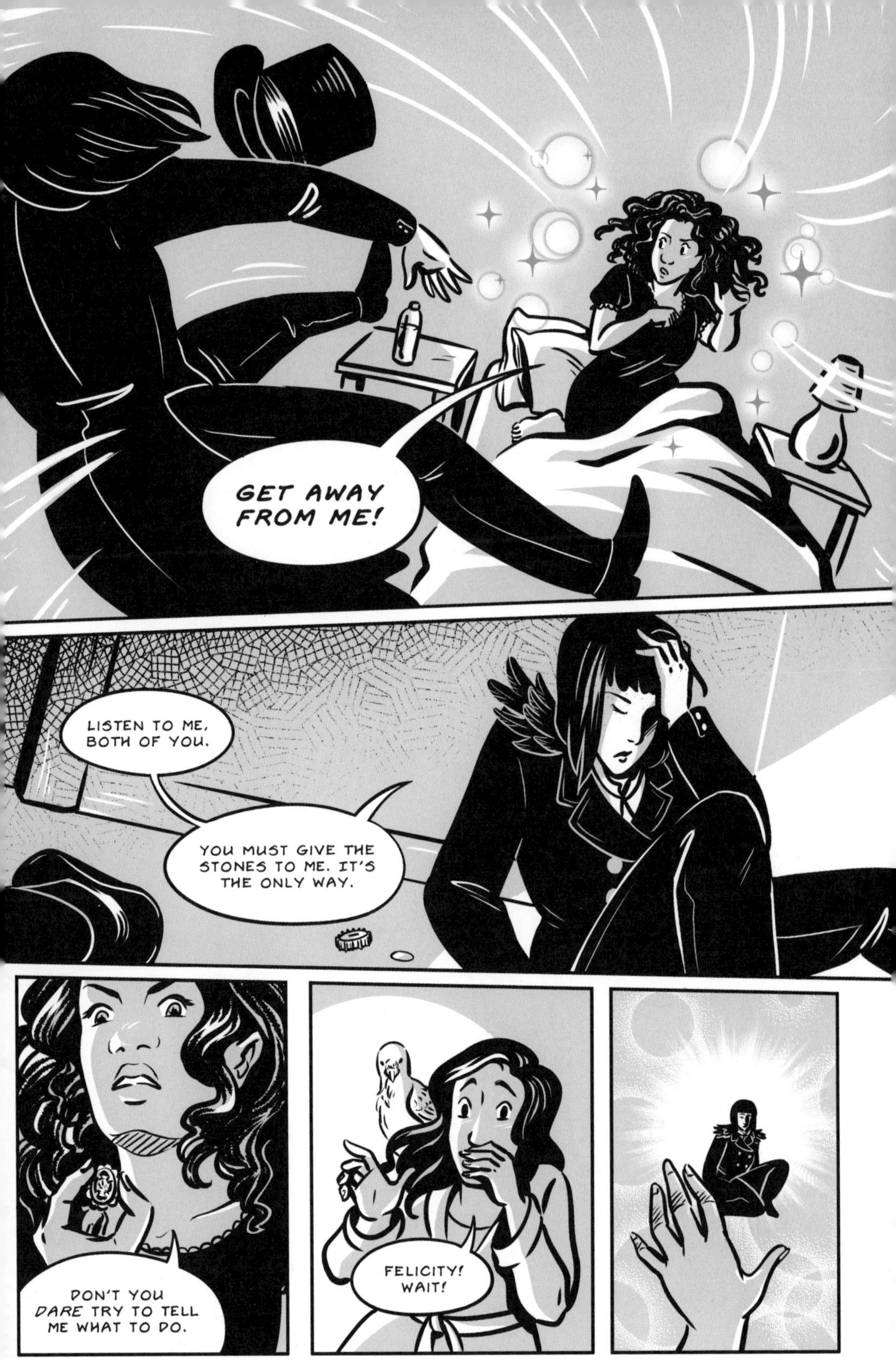
GET AWAY FROM ME!
LISTEN TO ME, BOTH OF YOU.
YOU MUST GIVE THE STONES TO ME. IT'S THE ONLY WAY.
DON'T YOU *DARE* TRY TO TELL ME WHAT TO DO.
FELICITY! WAIT!

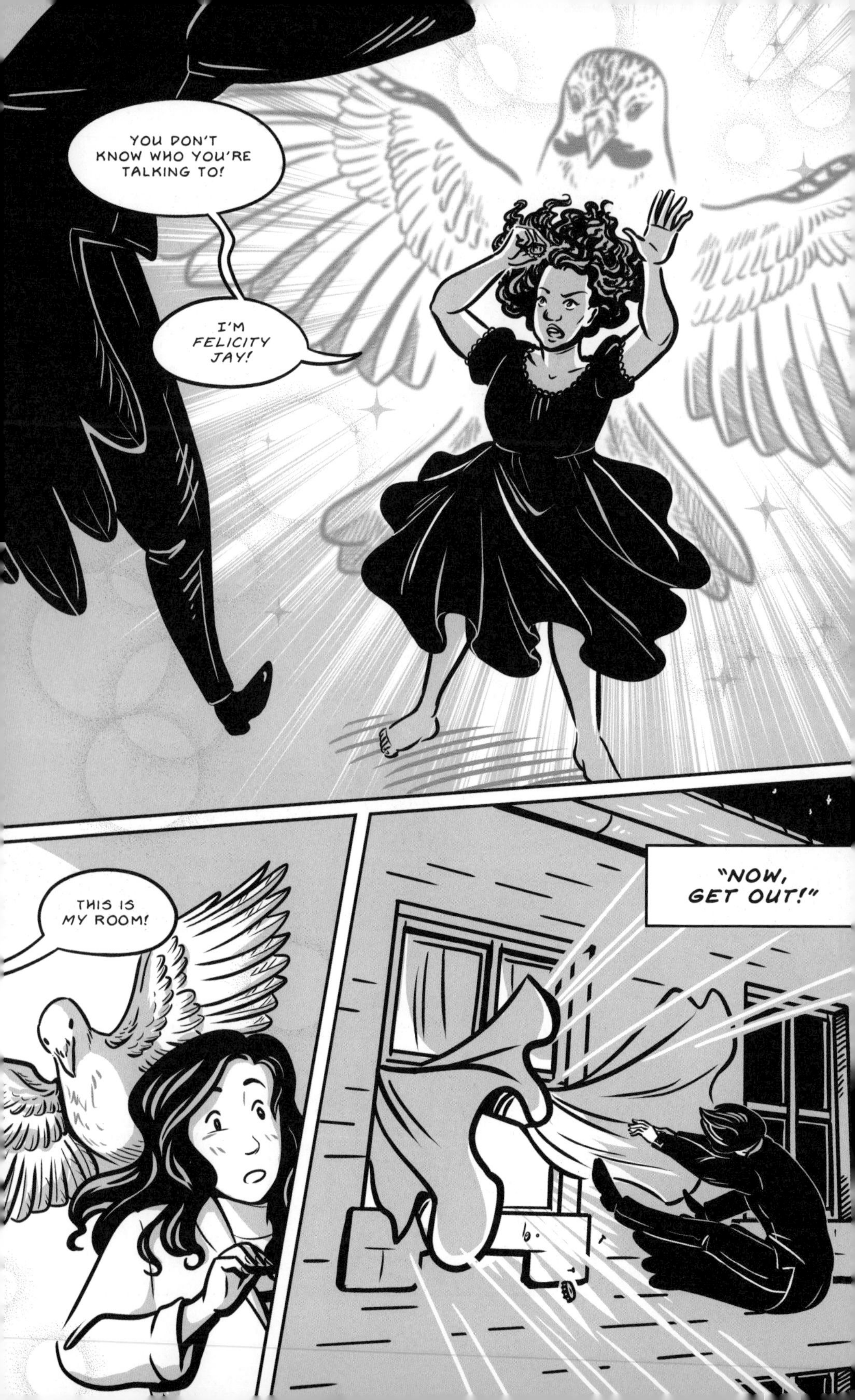
YOU DON'T KNOW WHO YOU'RE TALKING TO!
I'M FELICITY JAY!
THIS IS MY ROOM!
"NOW, GET OUT!"

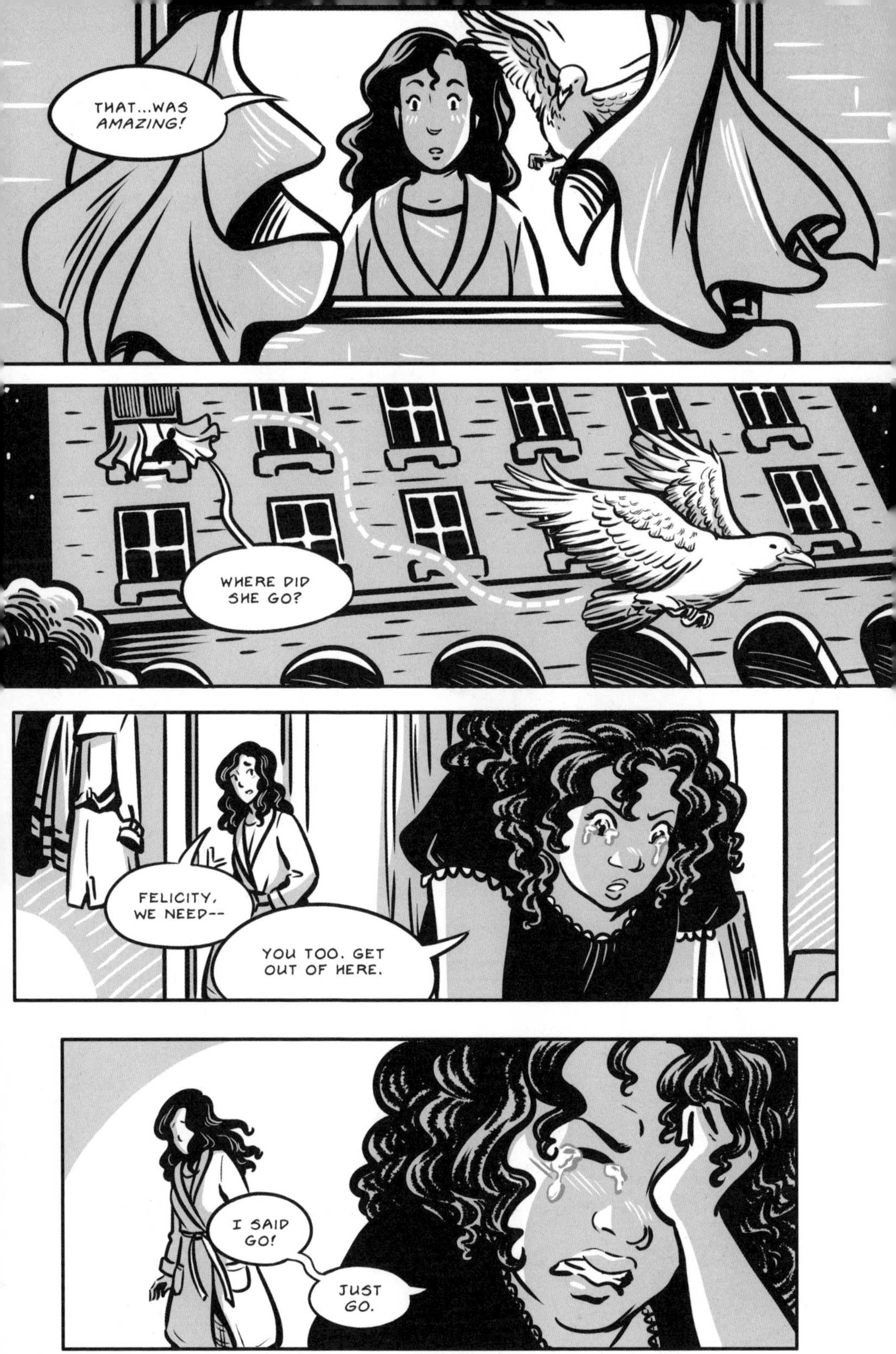
THAT...WAS AMAZING!
WHERE DID SHE GO?
FELICITY, WE NEED--
YOU TOO. GET OUT OF HERE.
I SAID GO!
JUST GO.

ONE WEEK LATER.

Full name:
FELICITY JA[...]

Class: [...]

GCSE
History B-1: Early Modern

Time: 1 hour 30 minutes
Materials: This paper, excerpt, 3 sheets foolsc[...]

Instructions:

"I DON'T KNOW WHAT TO DO.

Only black ink or ballpoint pens to be used

"SHE WAS SO UPSET, I DON'T WANT TO FREAK HER OUT.

"ESPECIALLY NOW I KNOW WHAT CAN HAPPEN IF SHE LOSES IT!

"YOU SAW WHAT IT WAS LIKE WHEN I TRIED TO SPEAK TO HER ON WEDNESDAY BEFORE THE CHEMISTRY MOCK.

"SHE COMPLETELY *BLANKED* ME."

"WELL, BEING BLANKED IS STILL BETTER THAN WHAT SHE USUALLY DISHES OUT.

"OR, YOU KNOW, BEING *BLASTED OUT OF A WINDOW.*"

SHHH. KEEP IT DOWN!

INFORMATION

BUT, YOU KNOW, SHE *CAN'T* JUST EXPECT US TO ACT LIKE NOTHING HAPPENED!

Early Medieva[l] Britain

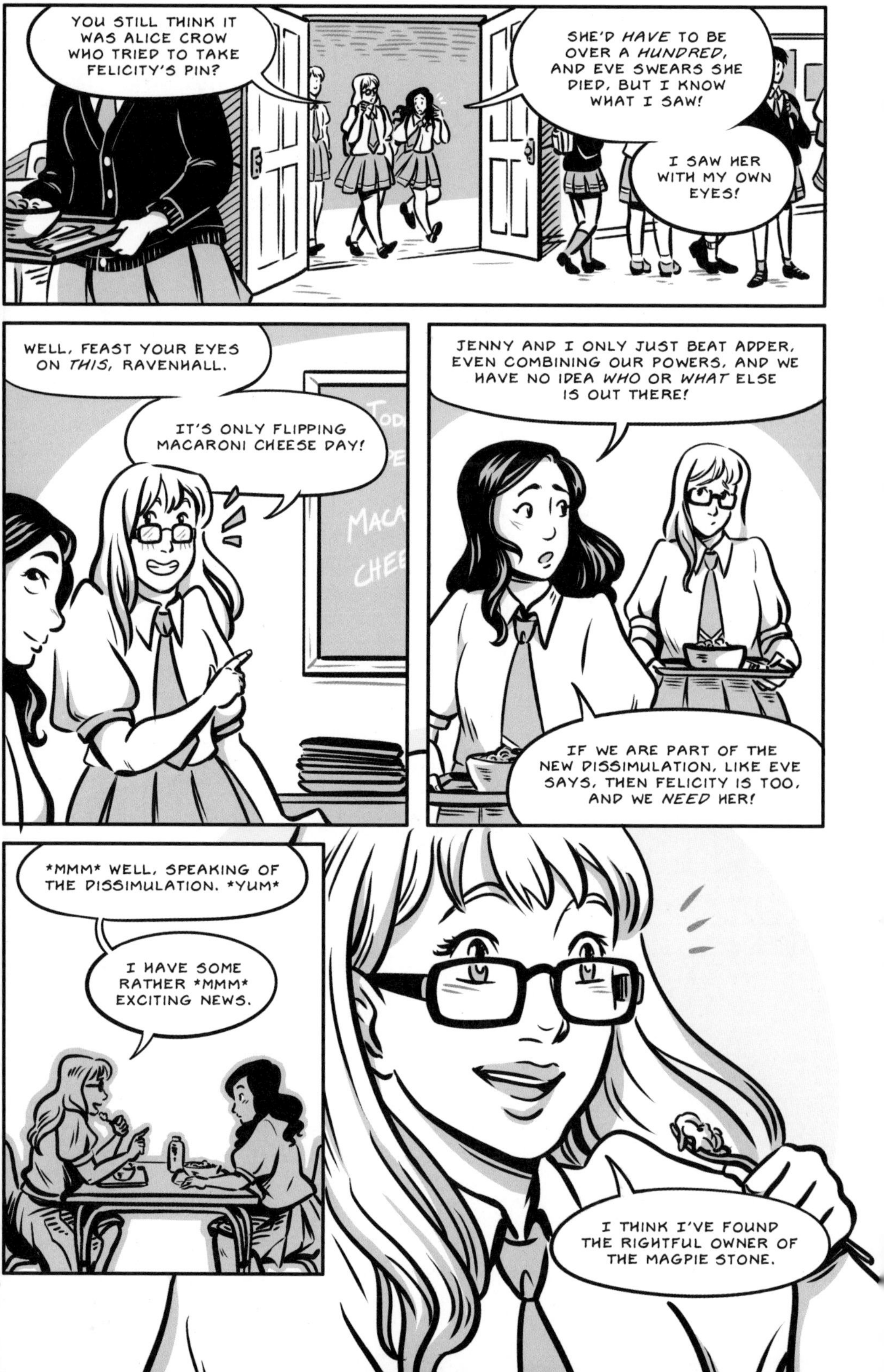
YOU STILL THINK IT WAS ALICE CROW WHO TRIED TO TAKE FELICITY'S PIN?
SHE'D HAVE TO BE OVER A HUNDRED, AND EVE SWEARS SHE DIED, BUT I KNOW WHAT I SAW!
I SAW HER WITH MY OWN EYES!
WELL, FEAST YOUR EYES ON THIS, RAVENHALL.
IT'S ONLY FLIPPING MACARONI CHEESE DAY!
JENNY AND I ONLY JUST BEAT ADDER, EVEN COMBINING OUR POWERS, AND WE HAVE NO IDEA WHO OR WHAT ELSE IS OUT THERE!
IF WE ARE PART OF THE NEW DISSIMULATION, LIKE EVE SAYS, THEN FELICITY IS TOO, AND WE NEED HER!
MMM WELL, SPEAKING OF THE DISSIMULATION. *YUM*
I HAVE SOME RATHER *MMM* EXCITING NEWS.
I THINK I'VE FOUND THE RIGHTFUL OWNER OF THE MAGPIE STONE.

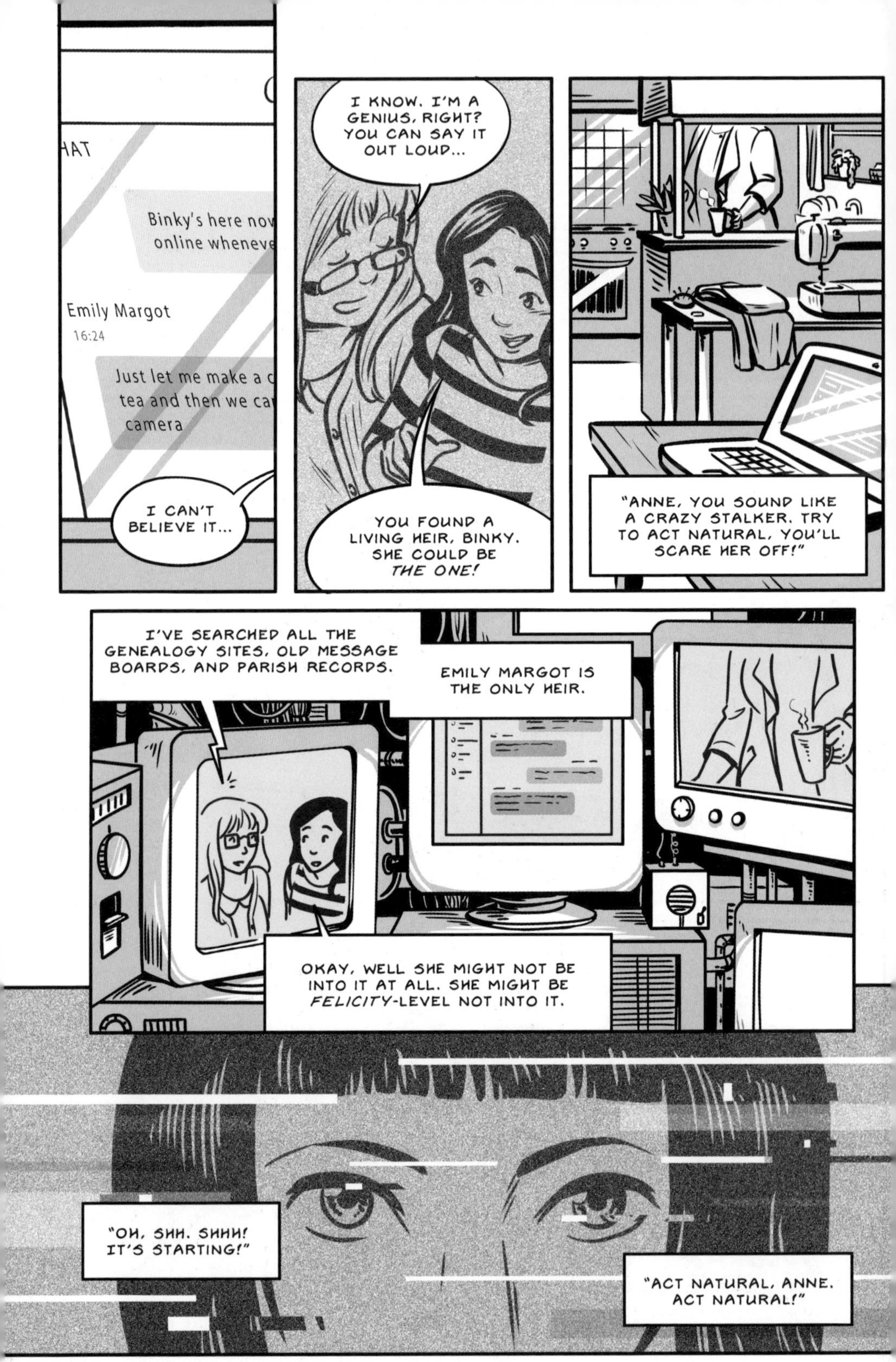
HAT
Binky's here now
online wheneve
Emily Margot
16:24
Just let me make a c
tea and then we ca
camera
I CAN'T BELIEVE IT...
I KNOW. I'M A GENIUS, RIGHT? YOU CAN SAY IT OUT LOUD...
YOU FOUND A LIVING HEIR, BINKY. SHE COULD BE *THE ONE!*
"ANNE, YOU SOUND LIKE A CRAZY STALKER. TRY TO ACT NATURAL, YOU'LL SCARE HER OFF!"
I'VE SEARCHED ALL THE GENEALOGY SITES, OLD MESSAGE BOARDS, AND PARISH RECORDS.
EMILY MARGOT IS THE ONLY HEIR.
OKAY, WELL SHE MIGHT NOT BE INTO IT AT ALL. SHE MIGHT BE *FELICITY*-LEVEL NOT INTO IT.
"OH, SHH. SHHH! IT'S STARTING!"
"ACT NATURAL, ANNE. ACT NATURAL!"

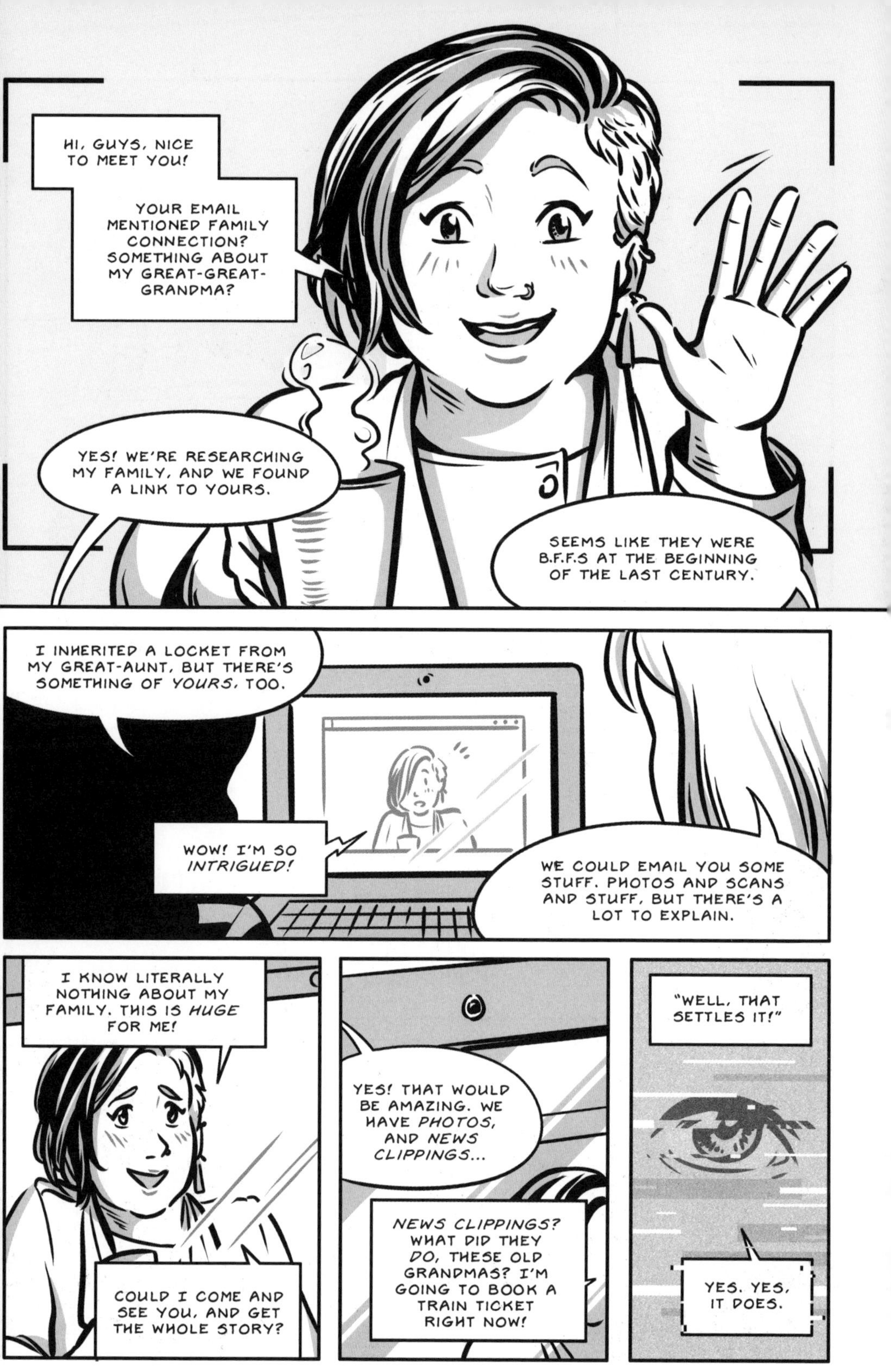

HI, GUYS, NICE TO MEET YOU!
YOUR EMAIL MENTIONED FAMILY CONNECTION? SOMETHING ABOUT MY GREAT-GREAT-GRANDMA?
YES! WE'RE RESEARCHING MY FAMILY, AND WE FOUND A LINK TO YOURS.
SEEMS LIKE THEY WERE B.F.F.S AT THE BEGINNING OF THE LAST CENTURY.
I INHERITED A LOCKET FROM MY GREAT-AUNT, BUT THERE'S SOMETHING OF *YOURS*, TOO.
WOW! I'M SO *INTRIGUED!*
WE COULD EMAIL YOU SOME STUFF. PHOTOS AND SCANS AND STUFF, BUT THERE'S A LOT TO EXPLAIN.
I KNOW LITERALLY NOTHING ABOUT MY FAMILY. THIS IS *HUGE* FOR ME!
COULD I COME AND SEE YOU, AND GET THE WHOLE STORY?
YES! THAT WOULD BE AMAZING. WE HAVE *PHOTOS*, AND *NEWS CLIPPINGS*...
NEWS CLIPPINGS? WHAT DID THEY *DO*, THESE OLD GRANDMAS? I'M GOING TO BOOK A TRAIN TICKET RIGHT NOW!
"WELL, THAT SETTLES IT!"
YES. YES, IT DOES.

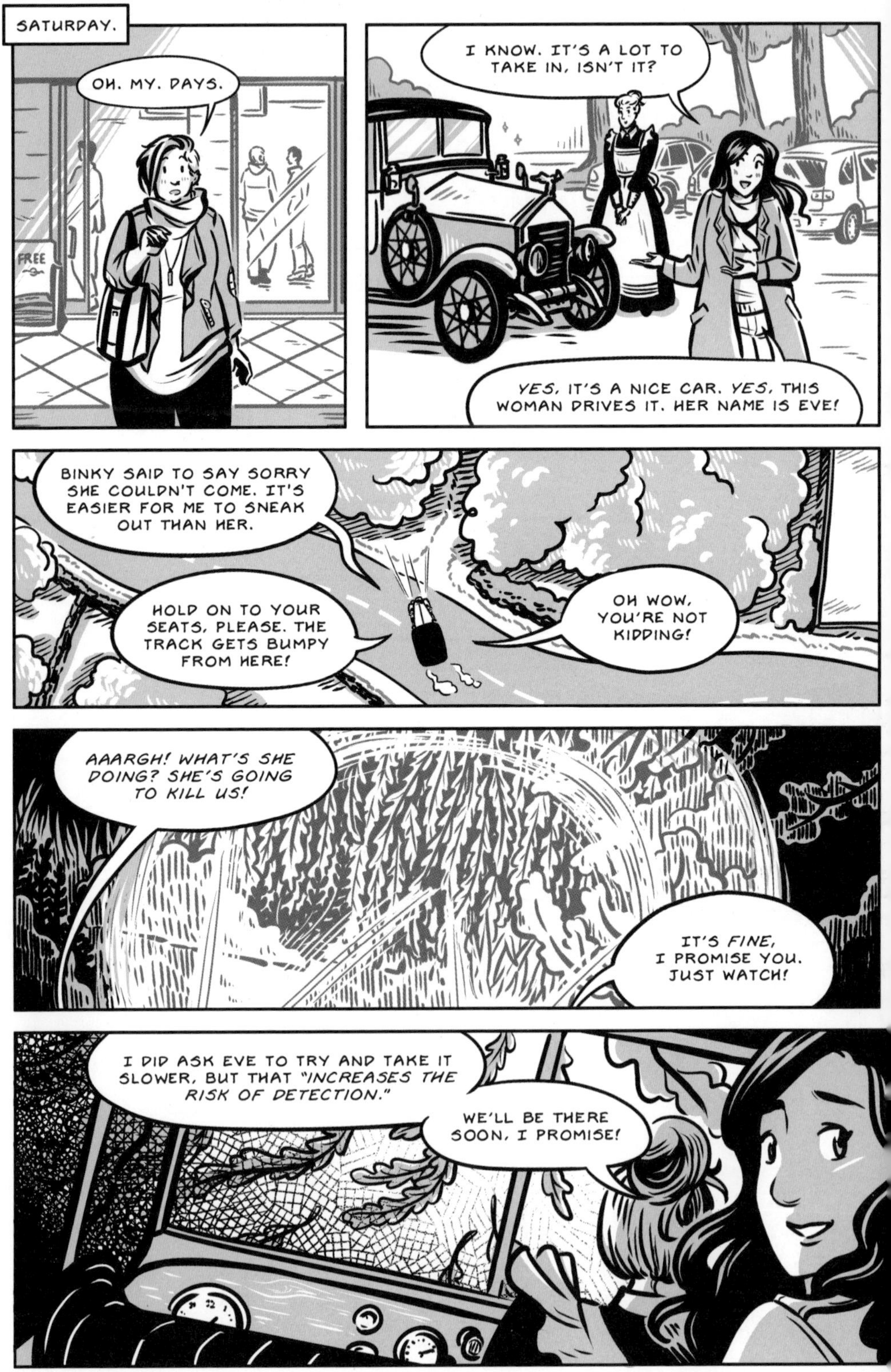
SATURDAY.
OH. MY. DAYS.
I KNOW. IT'S A LOT TO TAKE IN, ISN'T IT?
FREE
YES, IT'S A NICE CAR. *YES,* THIS WOMAN DRIVES IT. HER NAME IS EVE!
BINKY SAID TO SAY SORRY SHE COULDN'T COME. IT'S EASIER FOR ME TO SNEAK OUT THAN HER.
HOLD ON TO YOUR SEATS, PLEASE. THE TRACK GETS BUMPY FROM HERE!
OH WOW, YOU'RE NOT KIDDING!
AAARGH! WHAT'S SHE DOING? SHE'S GOING TO KILL US!
IT'S *FINE,* I PROMISE YOU. JUST WATCH!
I DID ASK EVE TO TRY AND TAKE IT SLOWER, BUT THAT *"INCREASES THE RISK OF DETECTION."*
WE'LL BE THERE SOON, I PROMISE!

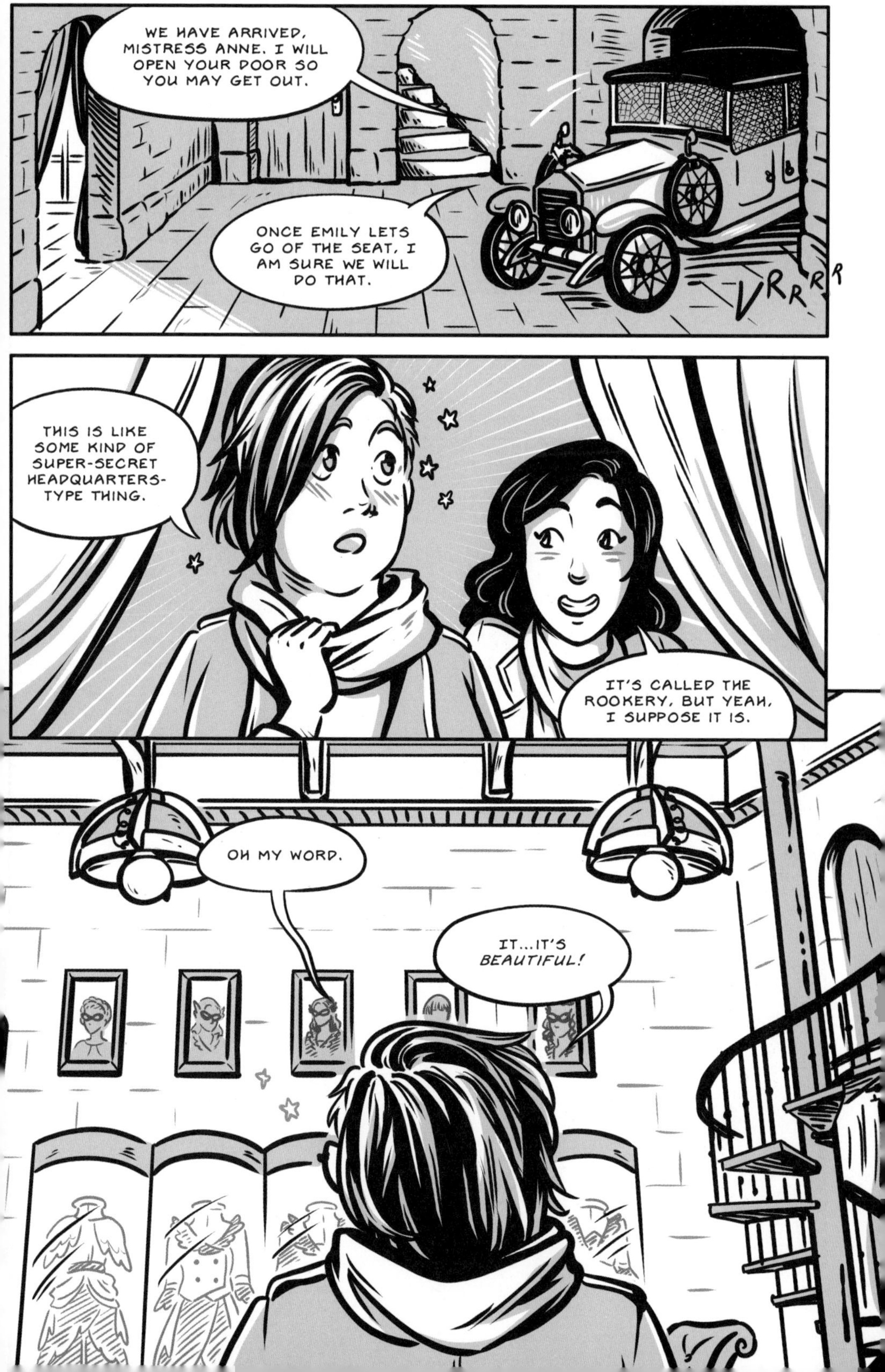
WE HAVE ARRIVED, MISTRESS ANNE. I WILL OPEN YOUR DOOR SO YOU MAY GET OUT.
ONCE EMILY LETS GO OF THE SEAT, I AM SURE WE WILL DO THAT.
VRRRRR
THIS IS LIKE SOME KIND OF SUPER-SECRET HEADQUARTERS-TYPE THING.
IT'S CALLED THE ROOKERY, BUT YEAH, I SUPPOSE IT IS.
OH MY WORD.
IT...IT'S *BEAUTIFUL!*

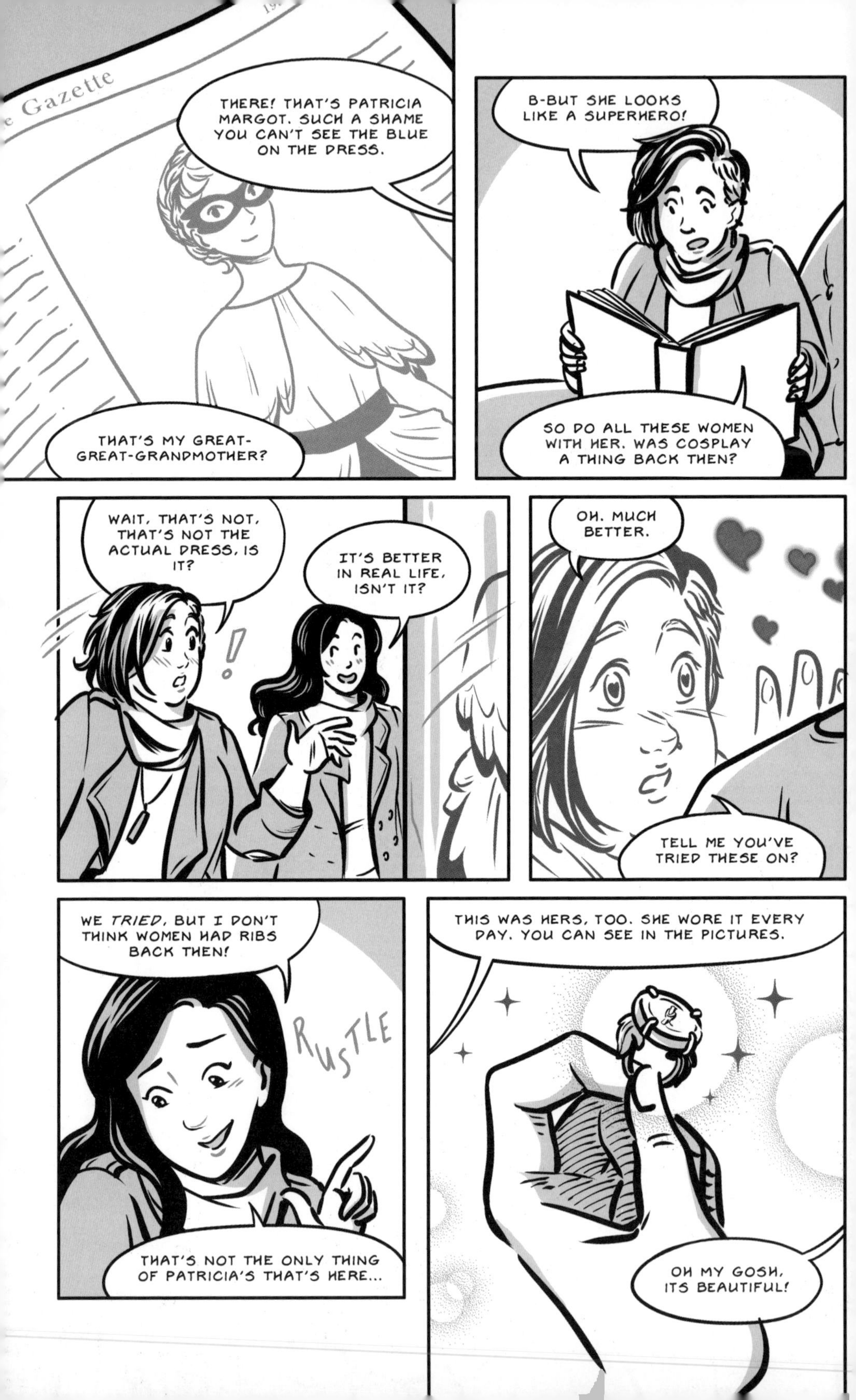
Gazette
THERE! THAT'S PATRICIA MARGOT. SUCH A SHAME YOU CAN'T SEE THE BLUE ON THE DRESS.
THAT'S MY GREAT-GREAT-GRANDMOTHER?
B-BUT SHE LOOKS LIKE A SUPERHERO!
SO DO ALL THESE WOMEN WITH HER. WAS COSPLAY A THING BACK THEN?
WAIT, THAT'S NOT, THAT'S NOT THE ACTUAL DRESS, IS IT?
!
IT'S BETTER IN REAL LIFE, ISN'T IT?
OH. MUCH BETTER.
TELL ME YOU'VE TRIED THESE ON?
WE *TRIED*, BUT I DON'T THINK WOMEN HAD RIBS BACK THEN!
RUSTLE
THAT'S NOT THE ONLY THING OF PATRICIA'S THAT'S HERE...
THIS WAS HERS, TOO. SHE WORE IT EVERY DAY. YOU CAN SEE IN THE PICTURES.
OH MY GOSH, ITS BEAUTIFUL!

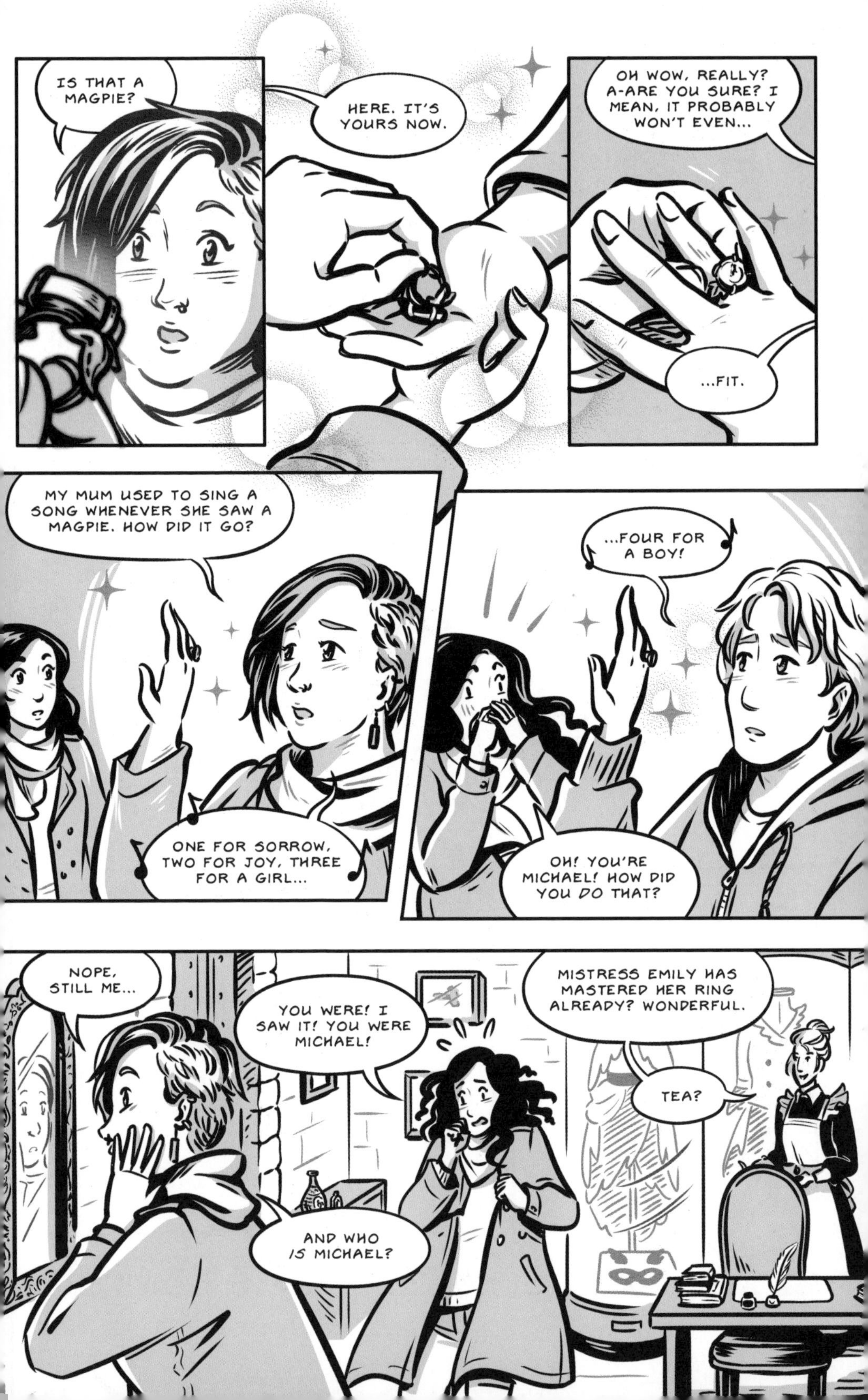
IS THAT A MAGPIE?
HERE. IT'S YOURS NOW.
OH WOW, REALLY? A-ARE YOU SURE? I MEAN, IT PROBABLY WON'T EVEN...
...FIT.
MY MUM USED TO SING A SONG WHENEVER SHE SAW A MAGPIE. HOW DID IT GO?
ONE FOR SORROW, TWO FOR JOY, THREE FOR A GIRL...
...FOUR FOR A BOY!
OH! YOU'RE MICHAEL! HOW DID YOU DO THAT?
NOPE, STILL ME...
YOU WERE! I SAW IT! YOU WERE MICHAEL!
MISTRESS EMILY HAS MASTERED HER RING ALREADY? WONDERFUL.
TEA?
AND WHO IS MICHAEL?

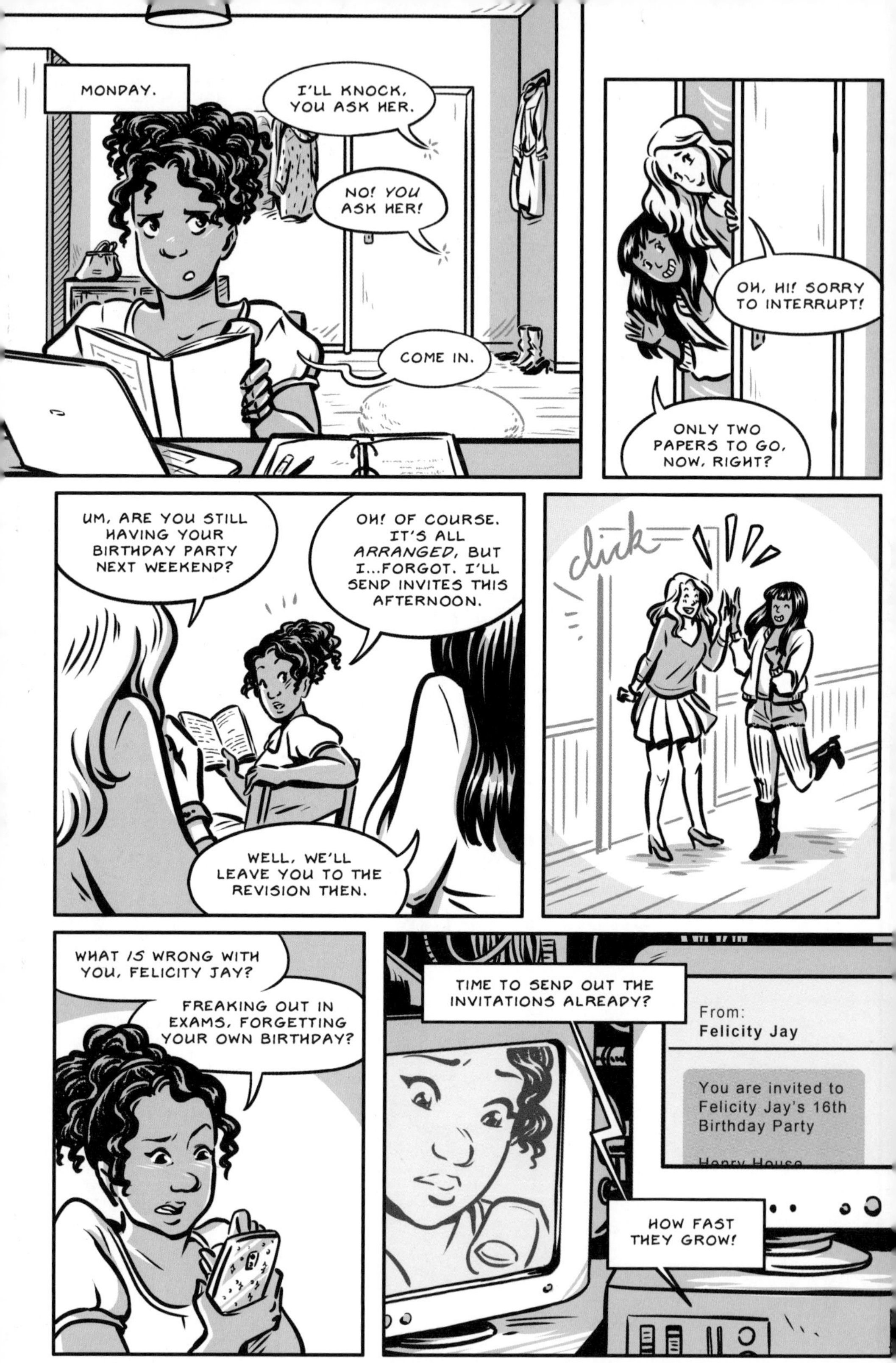
MONDAY.
I'LL KNOCK, YOU ASK HER.
NO! YOU ASK HER!
COME IN.
OH, HI! SORRY TO INTERRUPT!
ONLY TWO PAPERS TO GO, NOW, RIGHT?
UM, ARE YOU STILL HAVING YOUR BIRTHDAY PARTY NEXT WEEKEND?
OH! OF COURSE. IT'S ALL ARRANGED, BUT I...FORGOT. I'LL SEND INVITES THIS AFTERNOON.
WELL, WE'LL LEAVE YOU TO THE REVISION THEN.
click
WHAT IS WRONG WITH YOU, FELICITY JAY?
FREAKING OUT IN EXAMS, FORGETTING YOUR OWN BIRTHDAY?
TIME TO SEND OUT THE INVITATIONS ALREADY?
From:
Felicity Jay
You are invited to Felicity Jay's 16th Birthday Party
HOW FAST THEY GROW!

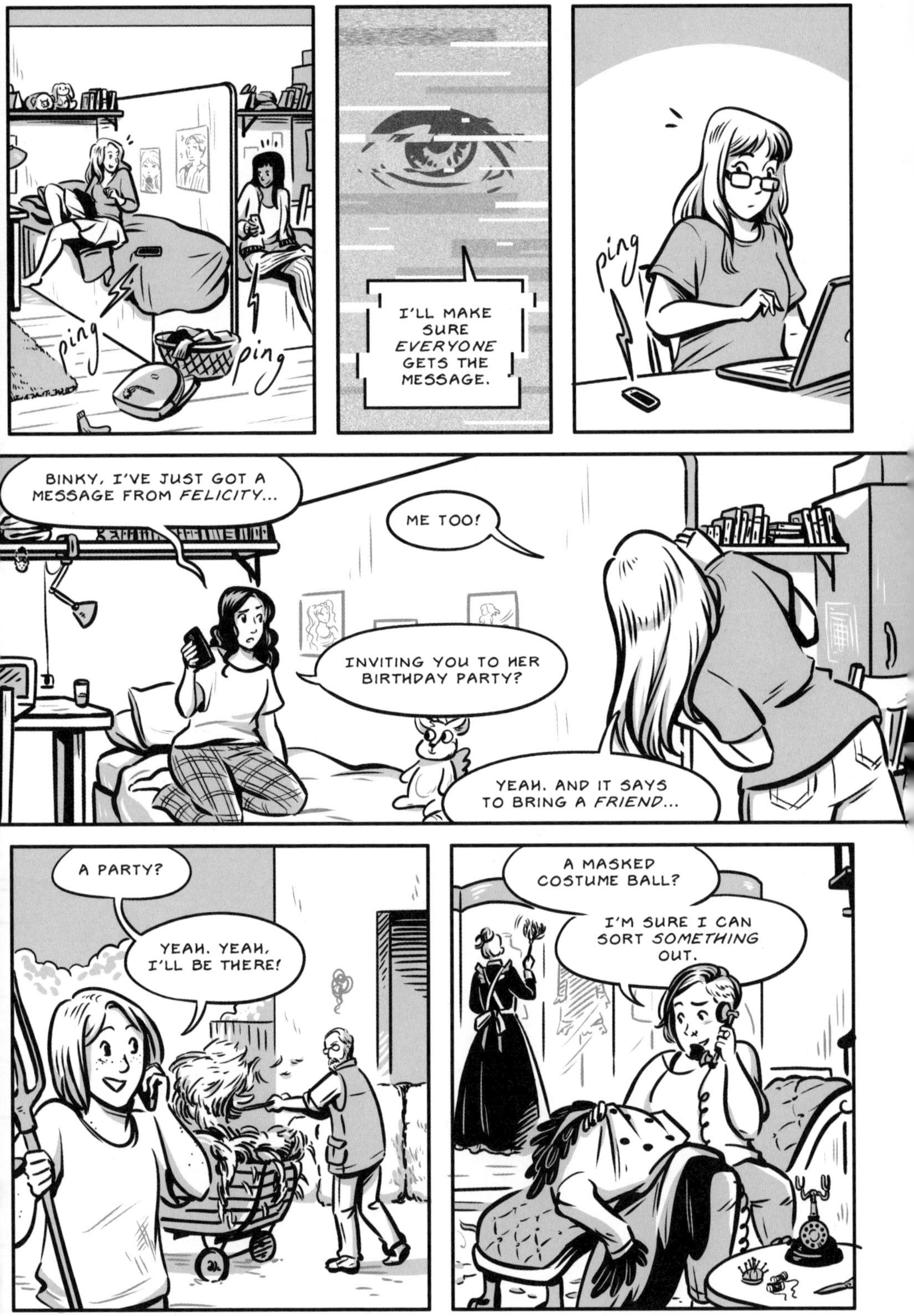
ping
ping
I'LL MAKE SURE *EVERYONE* GETS THE MESSAGE.
ping
BINKY, I'VE JUST GOT A MESSAGE FROM *FELICITY*...
ME TOO!
INVITING YOU TO HER BIRTHDAY PARTY?
YEAH. AND IT SAYS TO BRING A *FRIEND*...
A PARTY?
YEAH. YEAH, I'LL BE THERE!
A MASKED COSTUME BALL?
I'M SURE I CAN SORT *SOMETHING* OUT.

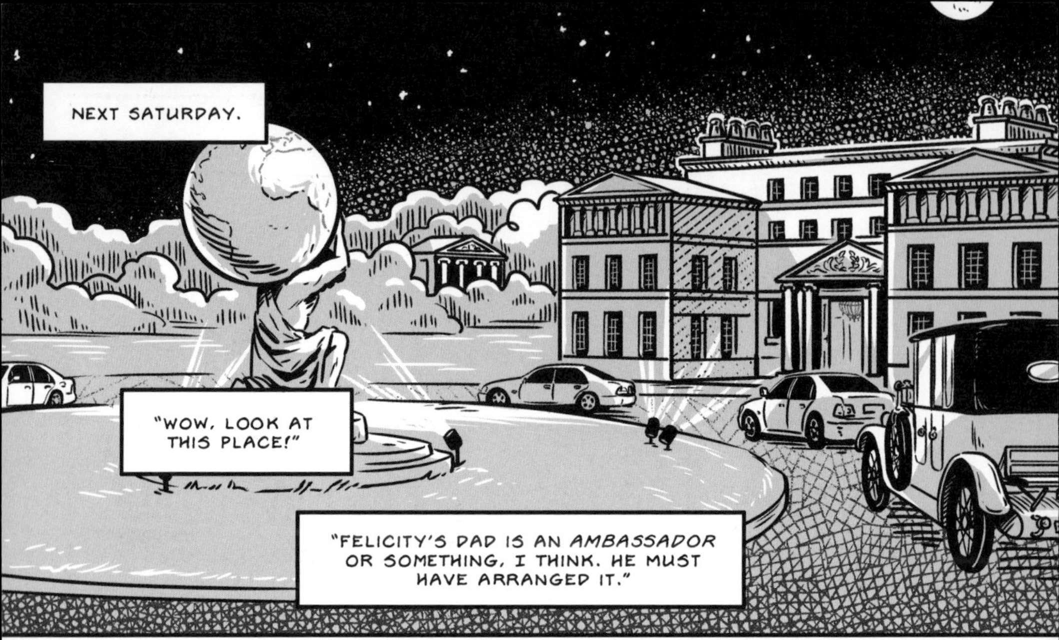
NEXT SATURDAY.
"WOW, LOOK AT THIS PLACE!"
"FELICITY'S DAD IS AN *AMBASSADOR* OR SOMETHING, I THINK. HE MUST HAVE ARRANGED IT."

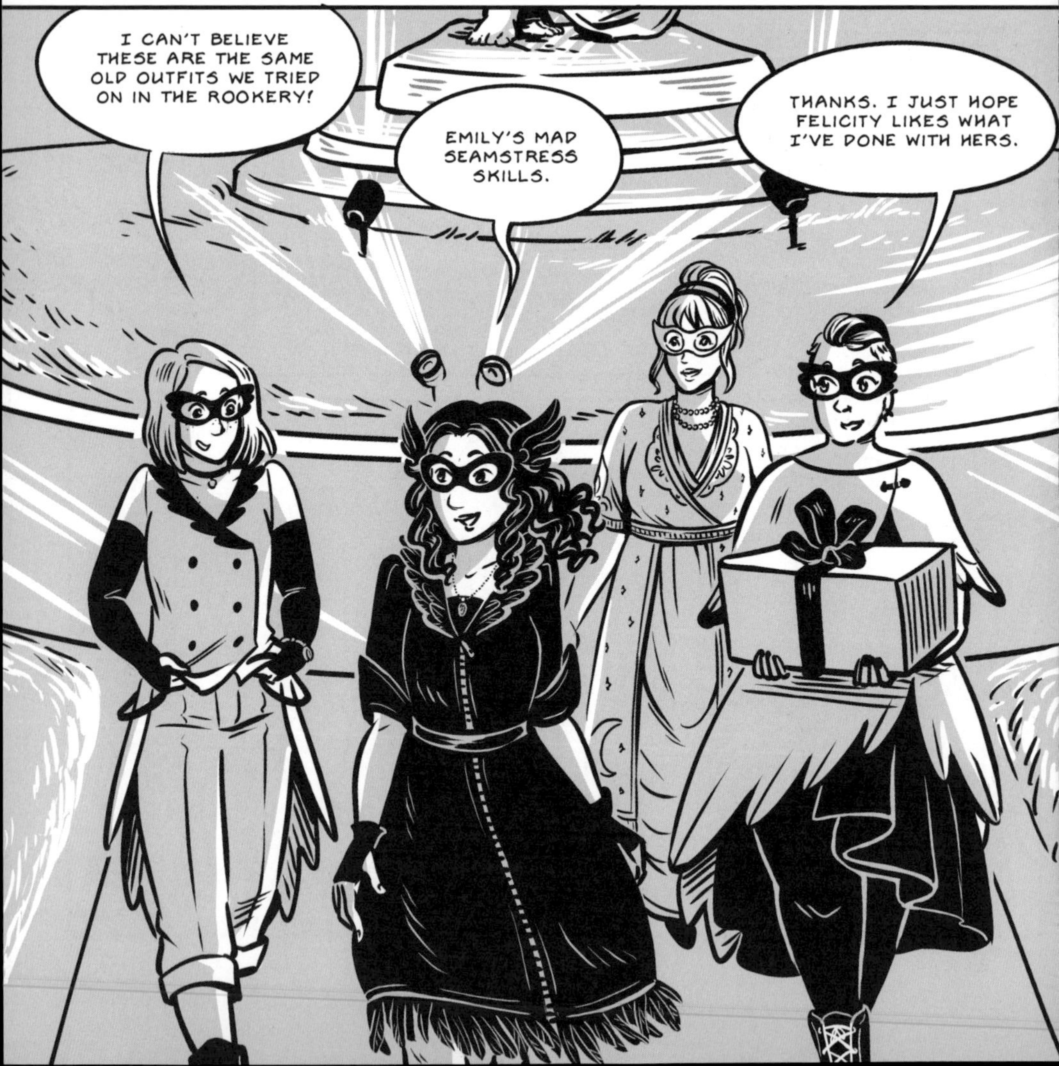
I CAN'T BELIEVE THESE ARE THE SAME OLD OUTFITS WE TRIED ON IN THE ROOKERY!
EMILY'S MAD SEAMSTRESS SKILLS.
THANKS. I JUST HOPE FELICITY LIKES WHAT I'VE DONE WITH HERS.

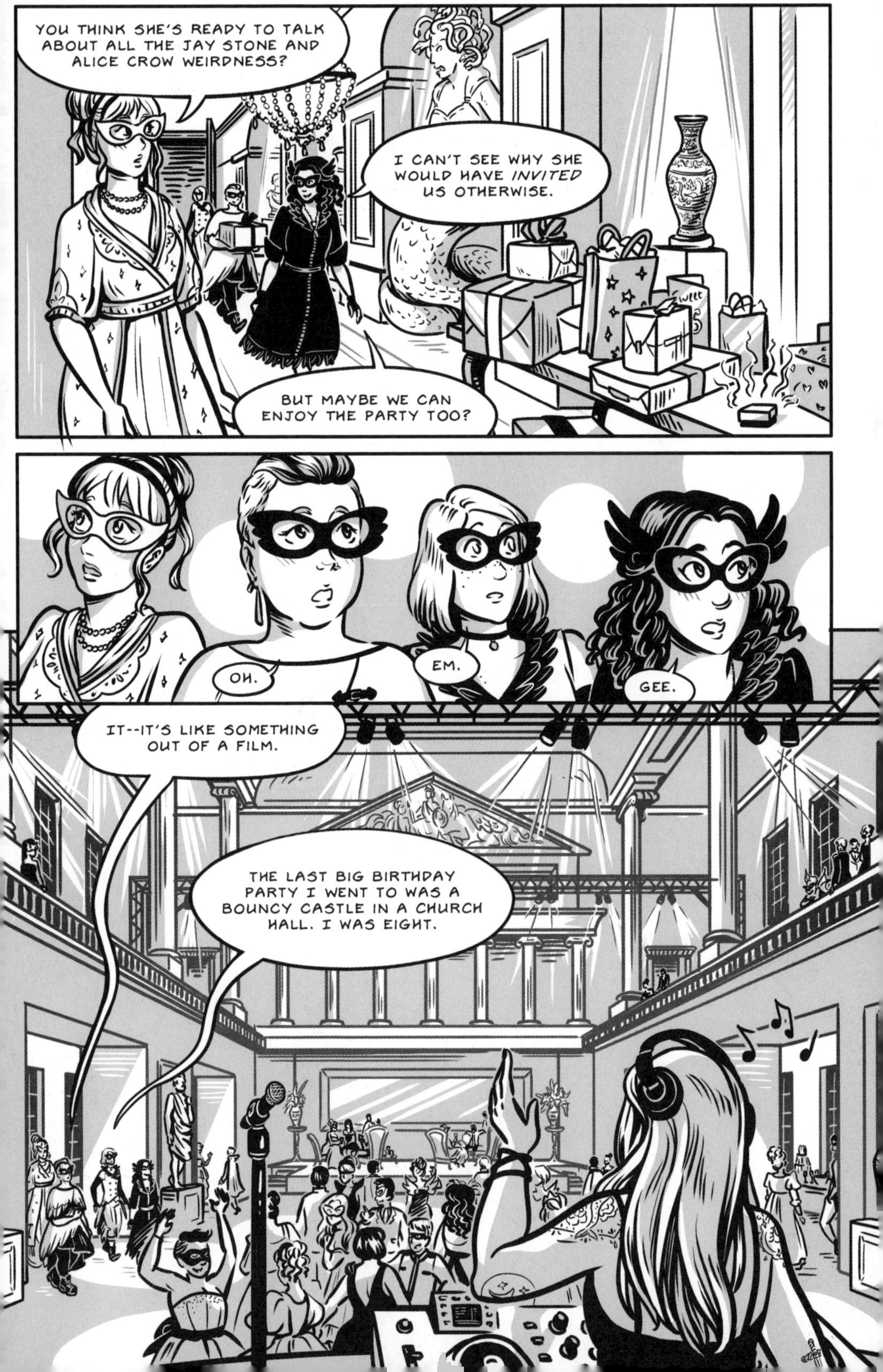
YOU THINK SHE'S READY TO TALK ABOUT ALL THE JAY STONE AND ALICE CROW WEIRDNESS?
I CAN'T SEE WHY SHE WOULD HAVE *INVITED* US OTHERWISE.
BUT MAYBE WE CAN ENJOY THE PARTY TOO?
OH.
EM.
GEE.
IT--IT'S LIKE SOMETHING OUT OF A FILM.
THE LAST BIG BIRTHDAY PARTY I WENT TO WAS A BOUNCY CASTLE IN A CHURCH HALL. I WAS EIGHT.

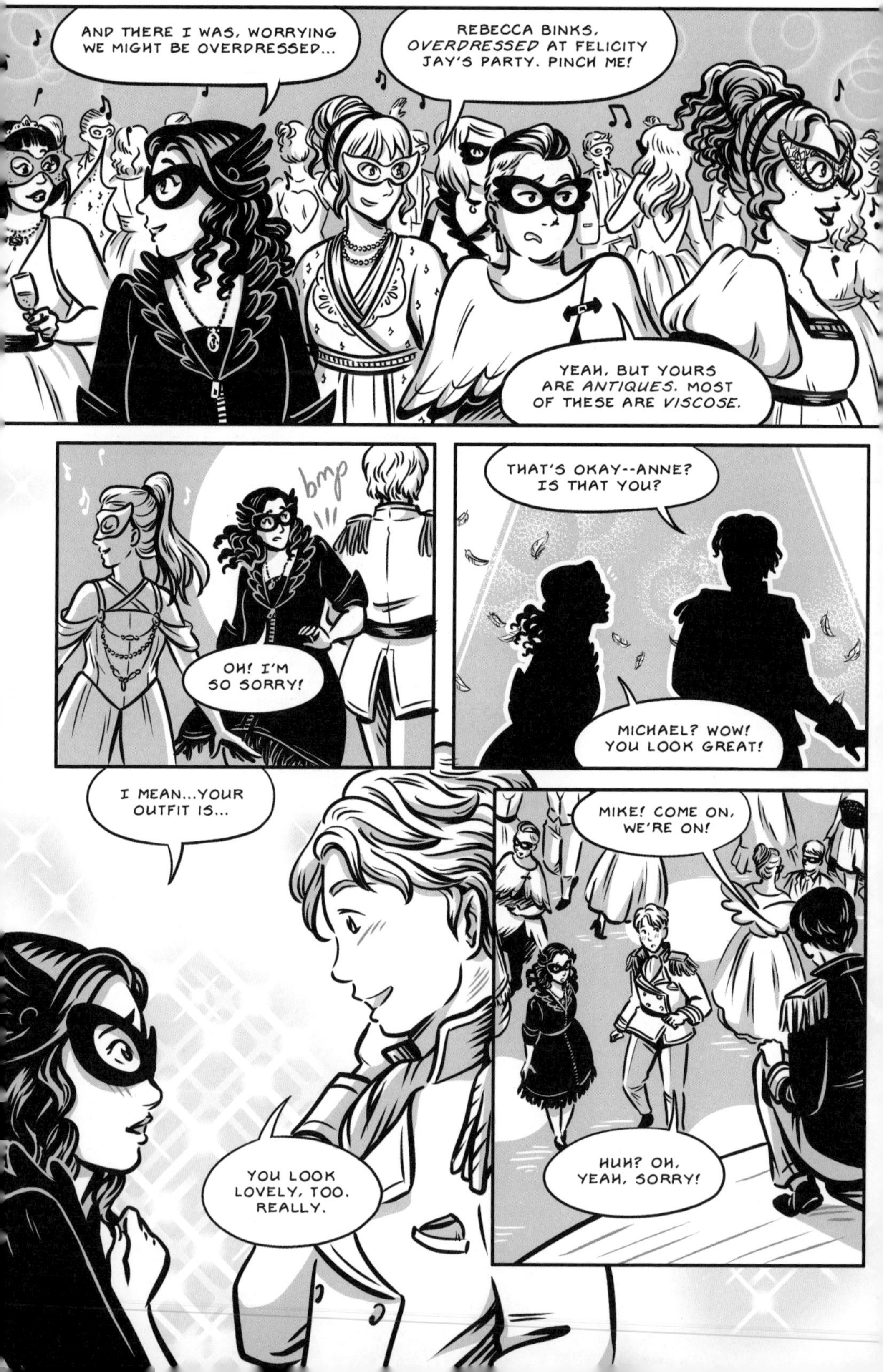
AND THERE I WAS, WORRYING WE MIGHT BE OVERDRESSED...
REBECCA BINKS, *OVERDRESSED* AT FELICITY JAY'S PARTY. PINCH ME!
YEAH, BUT YOURS ARE *ANTIQUES*. MOST OF THESE ARE *VISCOSE*.
bmp
OH! I'M SO SORRY!
THAT'S OKAY--ANNE? IS THAT YOU?
MICHAEL? WOW! YOU LOOK GREAT!
I MEAN...YOUR OUTFIT IS...
YOU LOOK LOVELY, TOO. REALLY.
MIKE! COME ON, WE'RE ON!
HUH? OH, YEAH, SORRY!

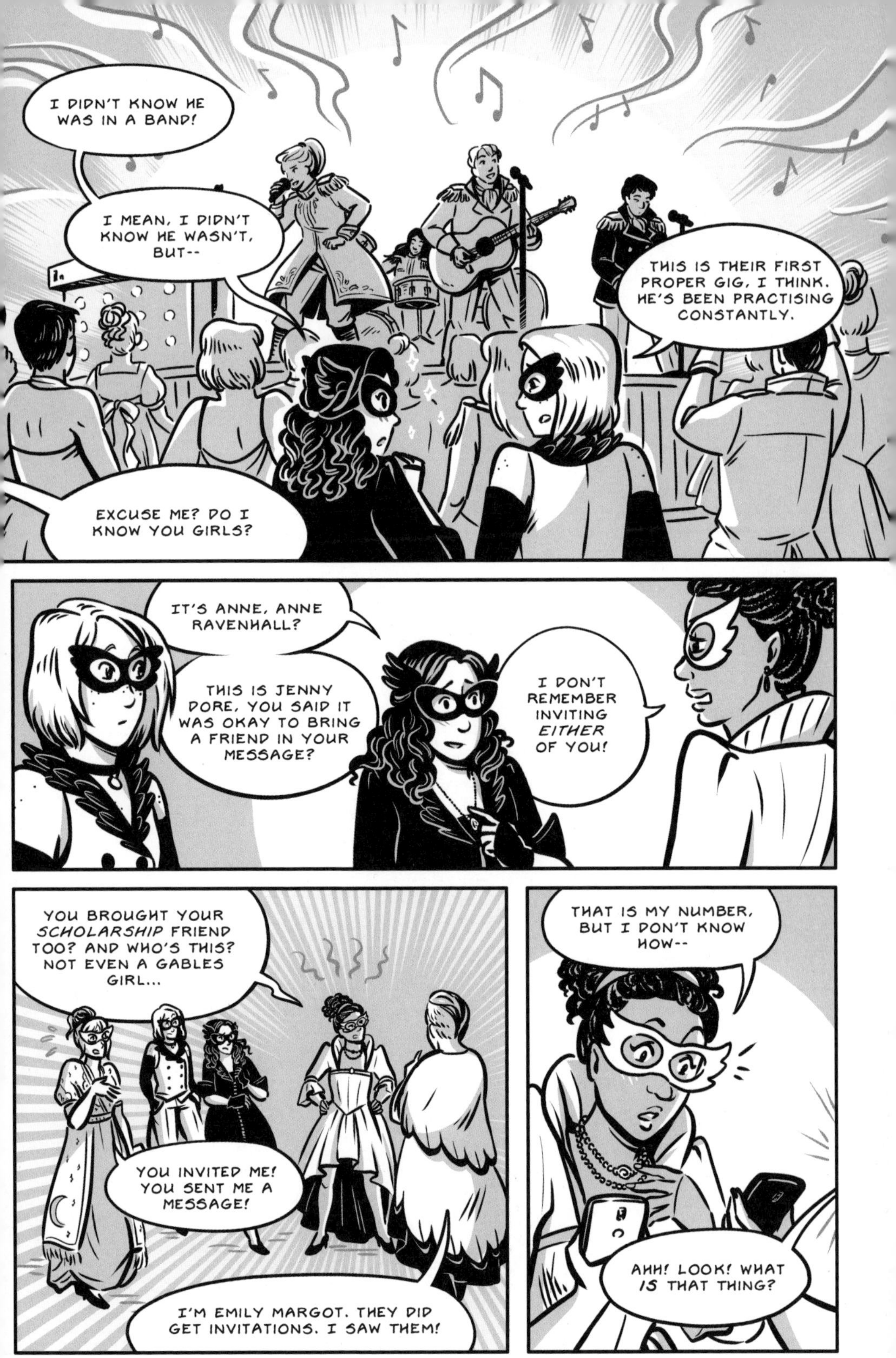
I DIDN'T KNOW HE WAS IN A BAND!
I MEAN, I DIDN'T KNOW HE WASN'T, BUT--
THIS IS THEIR FIRST PROPER GIG, I THINK. HE'S BEEN PRACTISING CONSTANTLY.
EXCUSE ME? DO I KNOW YOU GIRLS?
IT'S ANNE, ANNE RAVENHALL?
THIS IS JENNY DORE. YOU SAID IT WAS OKAY TO BRING A FRIEND IN YOUR MESSAGE?
I DON'T REMEMBER INVITING *EITHER* OF YOU!
YOU BROUGHT YOUR *SCHOLARSHIP* FRIEND TOO? AND WHO'S THIS? NOT EVEN A GABLES GIRL...
YOU INVITED ME! YOU SENT ME A MESSAGE!
I'M EMILY MARGOT. THEY DID GET INVITATIONS. I SAW THEM!
THAT IS MY NUMBER, BUT I DON'T KNOW HOW--
AHH! LOOK! WHAT *IS* THAT THING?

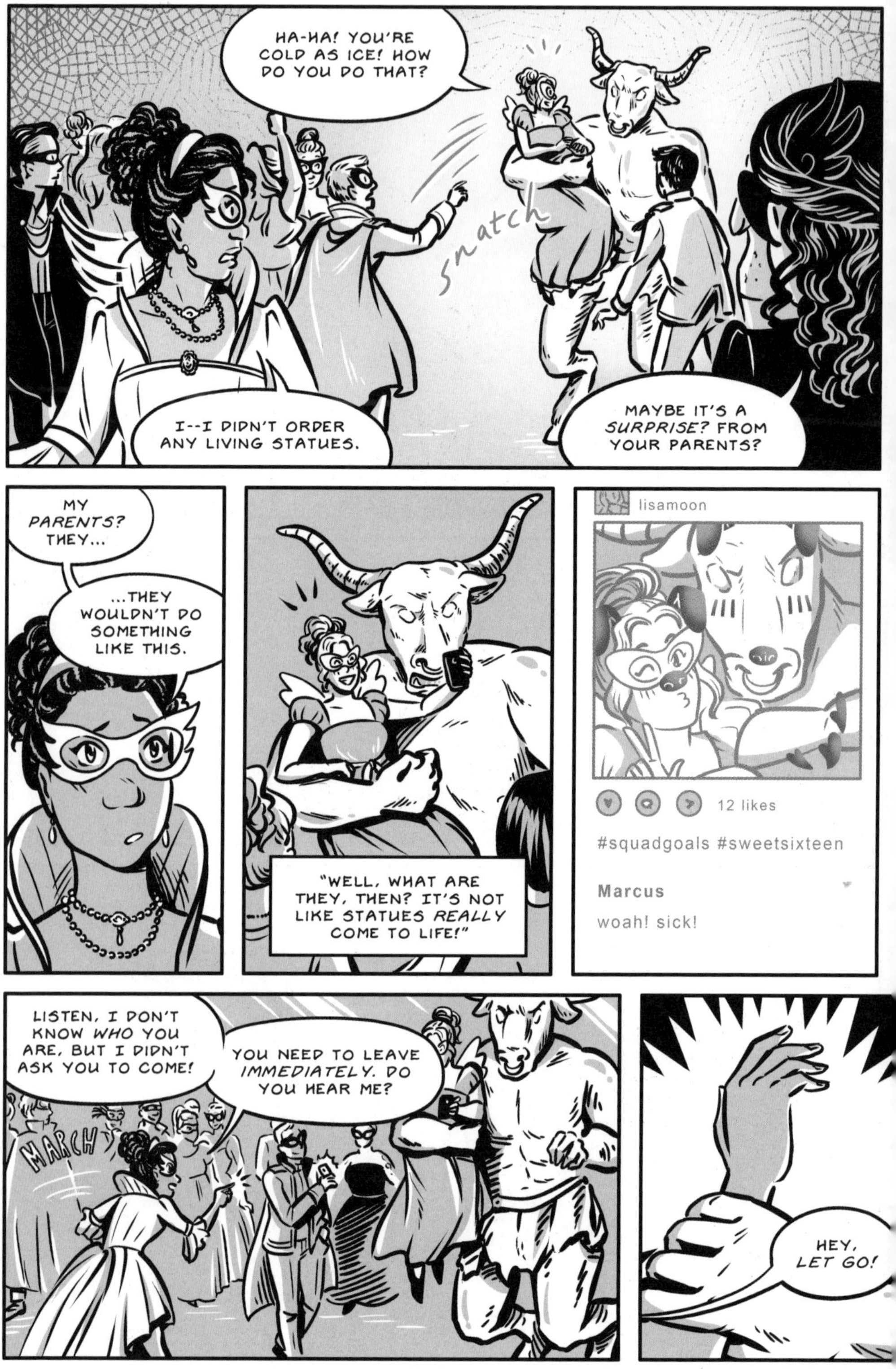
HA-HA! YOU'RE COLD AS ICE! HOW DO YOU DO THAT?
snatch
I--I DIDN'T ORDER ANY LIVING STATUES.
MAYBE IT'S A *SURPRISE?* FROM YOUR PARENTS?
MY *PARENTS?* THEY...
...THEY WOULDN'T DO SOMETHING LIKE THIS.
"WELL, WHAT ARE THEY, THEN? IT'S NOT LIKE STATUES *REALLY* COME TO LIFE!"
lisamoon
12 likes
#squadgoals #sweetsixteen
Marcus
woah! sick!
LISTEN, I DON'T KNOW *WHO* YOU ARE, BUT I DIDN'T ASK YOU TO COME!
YOU NEED TO LEAVE *IMMEDIATELY*. DO YOU HEAR ME?
MARCH
HEY, *LET GO!*

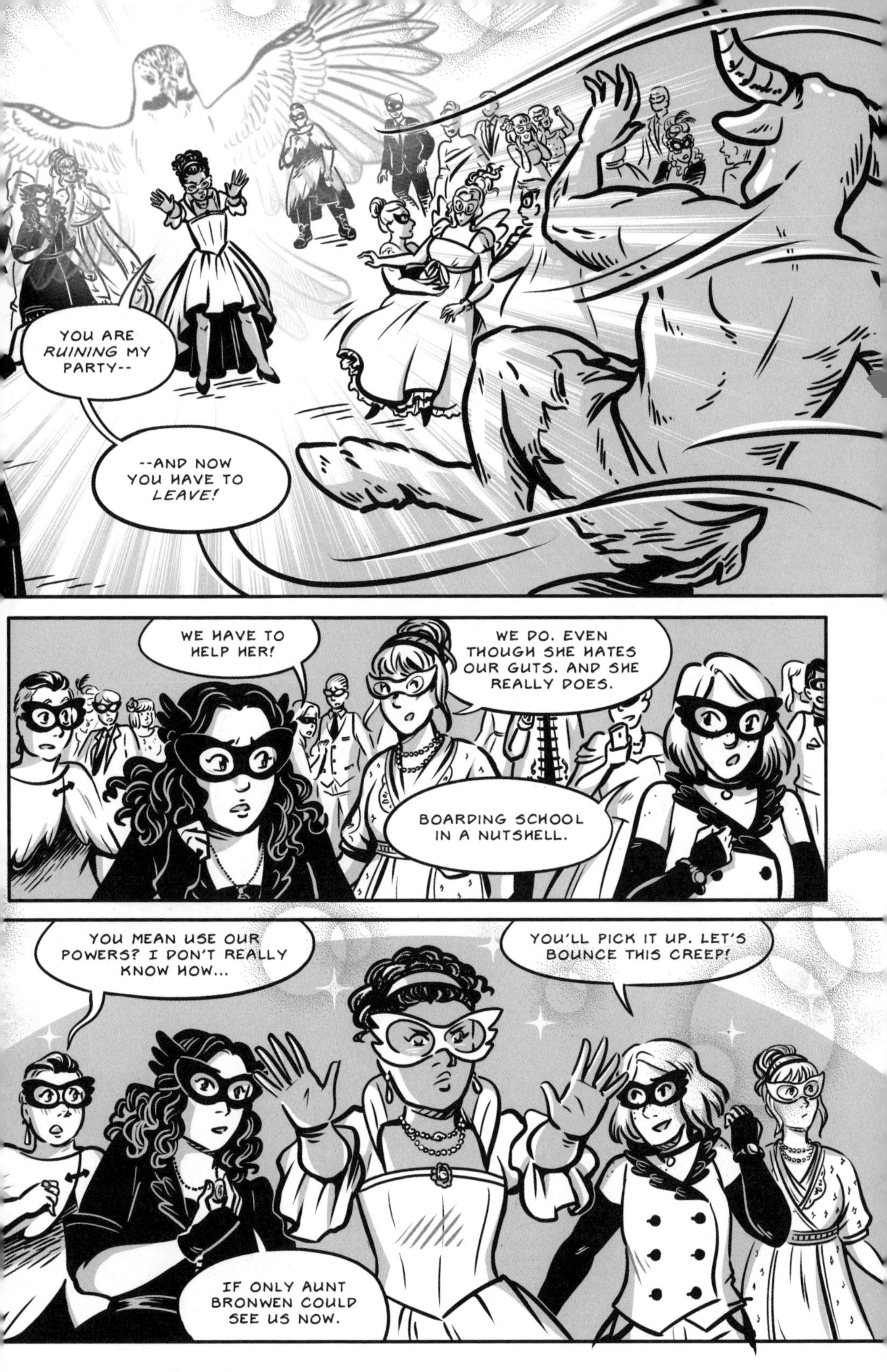
YOU ARE *RUINING* MY PARTY--
--AND NOW YOU HAVE TO *LEAVE!*
WE HAVE TO HELP HER!
WE DO. EVEN THOUGH SHE HATES OUR GUTS. AND SHE REALLY DOES.
BOARDING SCHOOL IN A NUTSHELL.
YOU MEAN USE OUR POWERS? I DON'T REALLY KNOW HOW...
YOU'LL PICK IT UP. LET'S BOUNCE THIS CREEP!
IF ONLY AUNT BRONWEN COULD SEE US NOW.

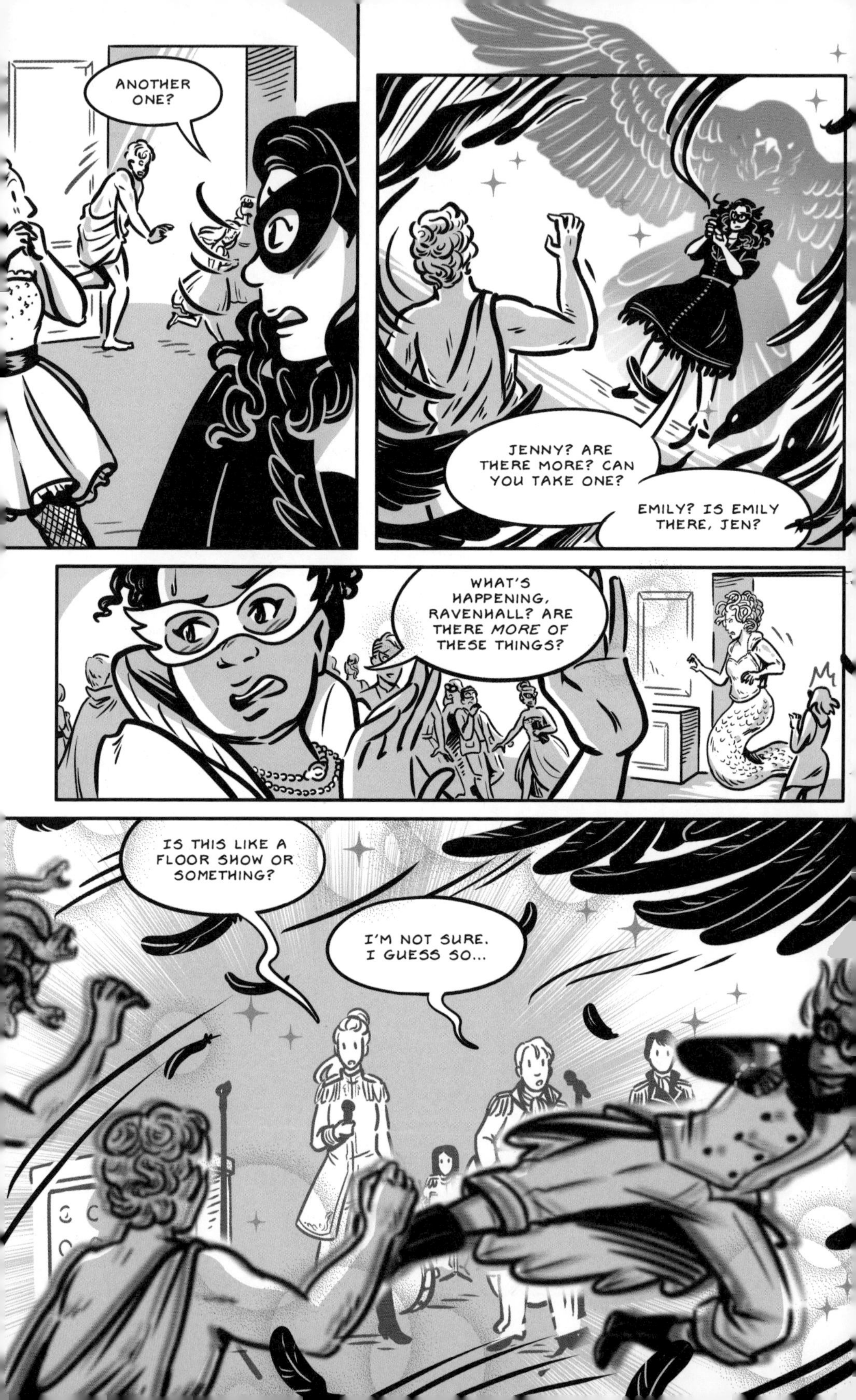
ANOTHER ONE?
JENNY? ARE THERE MORE? CAN YOU TAKE ONE?
EMILY? IS EMILY THERE, JEN?
WHAT'S HAPPENING, RAVENHALL? ARE THERE *MORE* OF THESE THINGS?
IS THIS LIKE A FLOOR SHOW OR SOMETHING?
I'M NOT SURE. I GUESS SO...

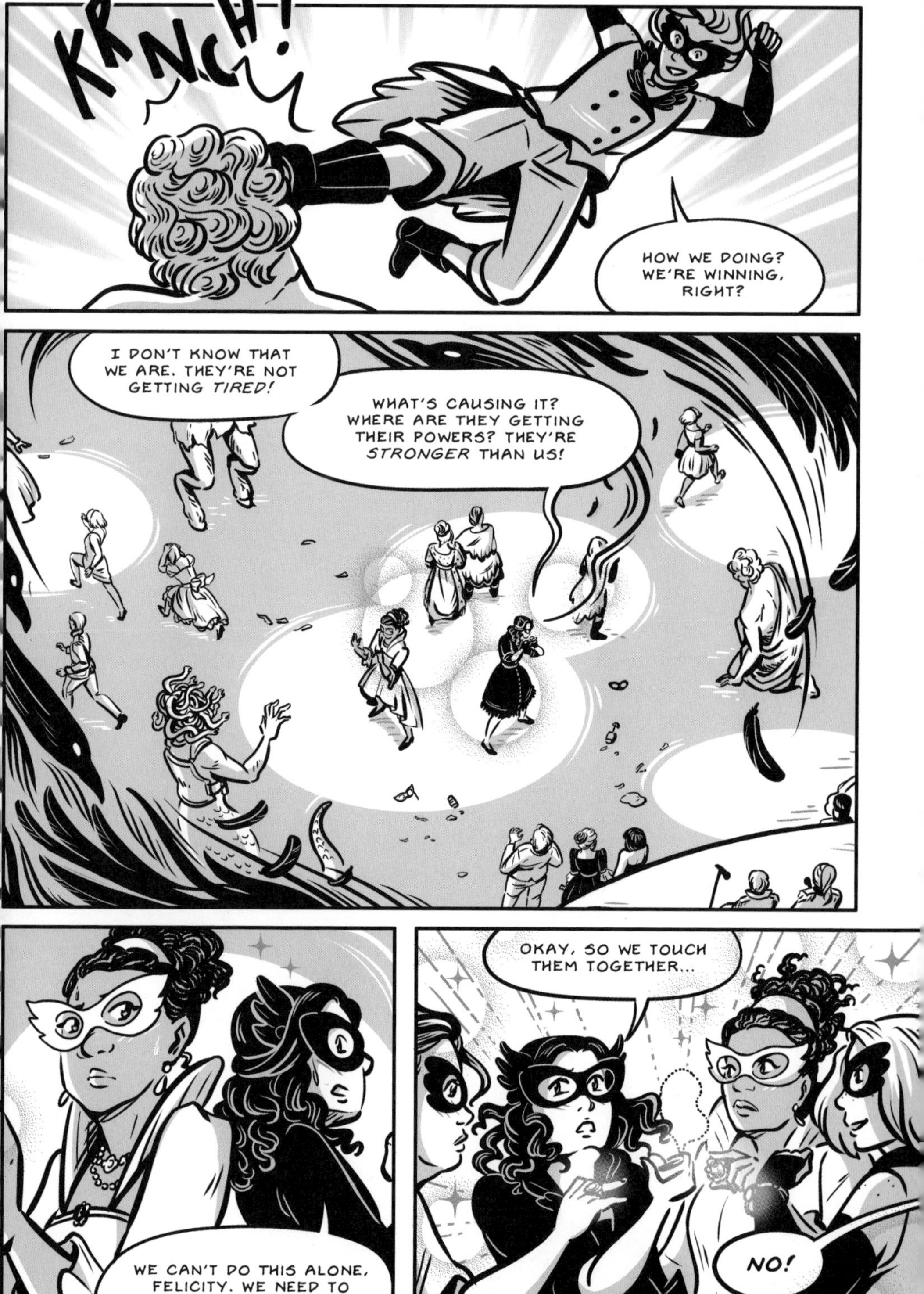
KRNCH!
HOW WE DOING? WE'RE WINNING, RIGHT?
I DON'T KNOW THAT WE ARE. THEY'RE NOT GETTING *TIRED!*
WHAT'S CAUSING IT? WHERE ARE THEY GETTING THEIR POWERS? THEY'RE *STRONGER* THAN US!
WE CAN'T DO THIS ALONE, FELICITY. WE NEED TO COMBINE OUR POWERS!
OKAY, SO WE TOUCH THEM TOGETHER...
NO!

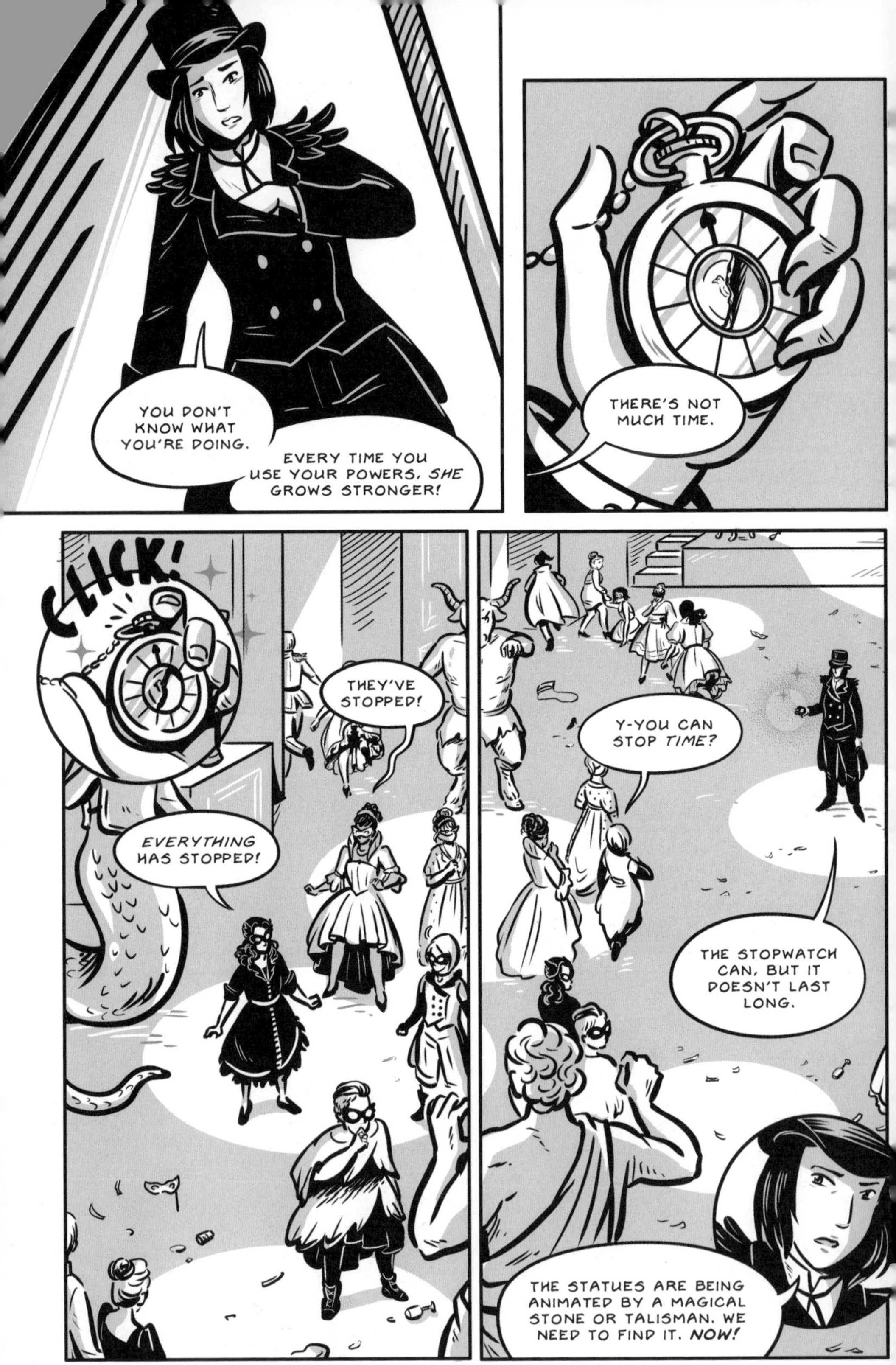
YOU DON'T KNOW WHAT YOU'RE DOING.
EVERY TIME YOU USE YOUR POWERS, *SHE* GROWS STRONGER!
THERE'S NOT MUCH TIME.
CLICK!
THEY'VE STOPPED!
EVERYTHING HAS STOPPED!
Y-YOU CAN STOP *TIME?*
THE STOPWATCH CAN, BUT IT DOESN'T LAST LONG.
THE STATUES ARE BEING ANIMATED BY A MAGICAL STONE OR TALISMAN. WE NEED TO FIND IT. ***NOW!***

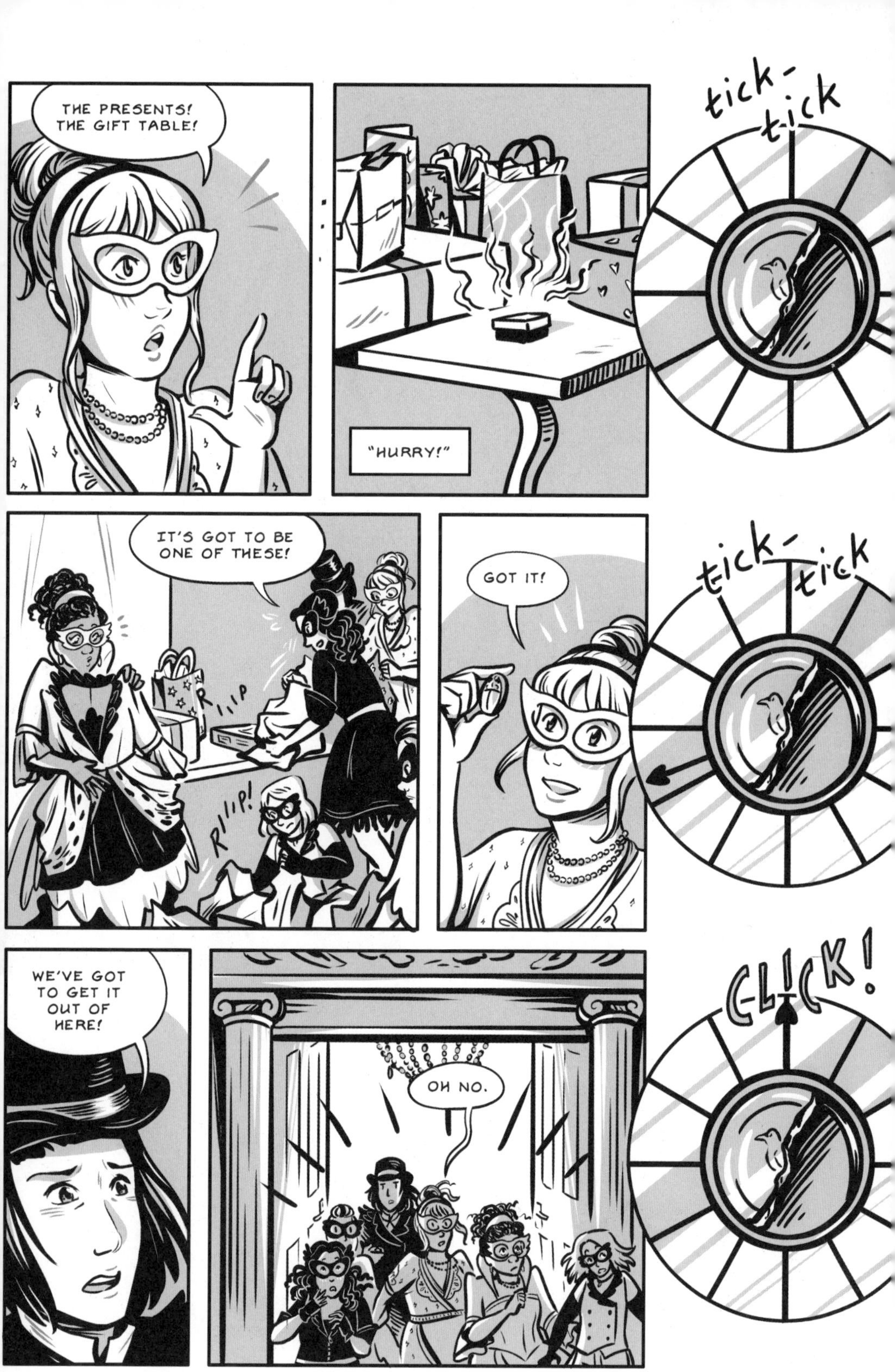
THE PRESENTS! THE GIFT TABLE!
"HURRY!"
tick-tick
IT'S GOT TO BE ONE OF THESE!
RIIP
RIIP!
GOT IT!
tick-tick
WE'VE GOT TO GET IT OUT OF HERE!
OH NO.
CLICK!

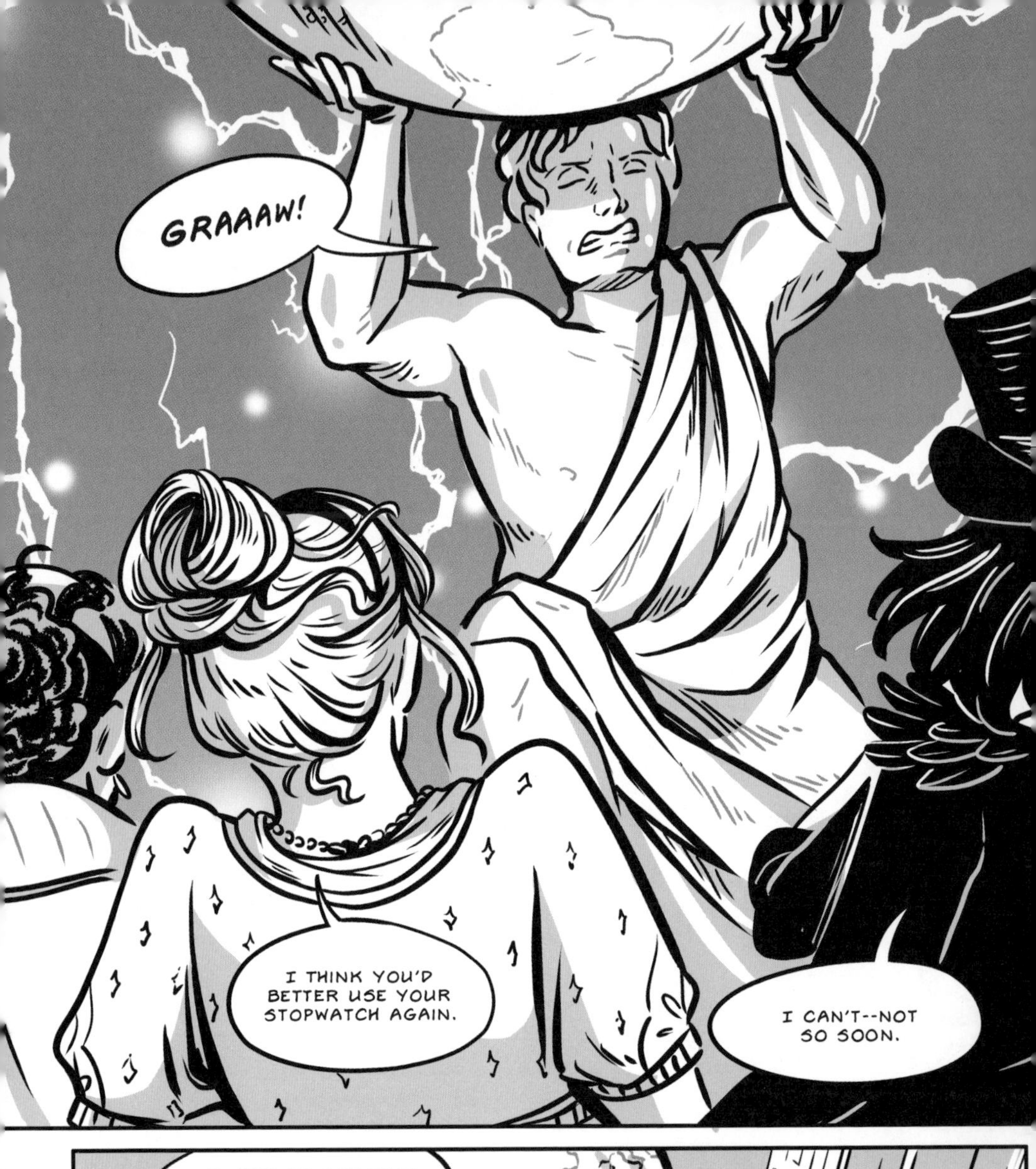
GRAAAW!
I THINK YOU'D BETTER USE YOUR STOPWATCH AGAIN.
I CAN'T--NOT SO SOON.

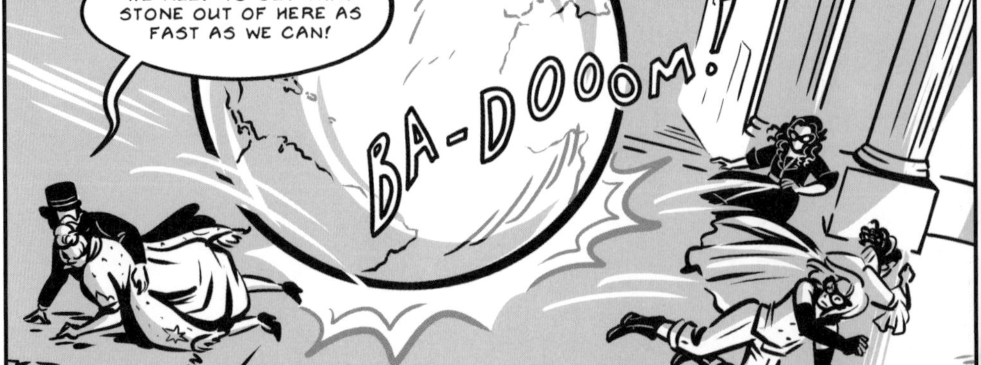
WE NEED TO GET THAT STONE OUT OF HERE AS FAST AS WE CAN!
BA-DOOOM!

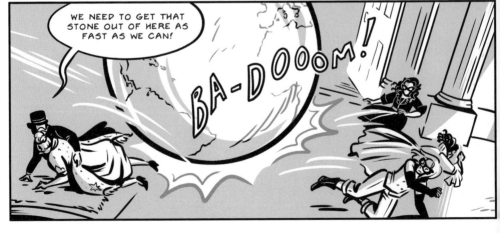

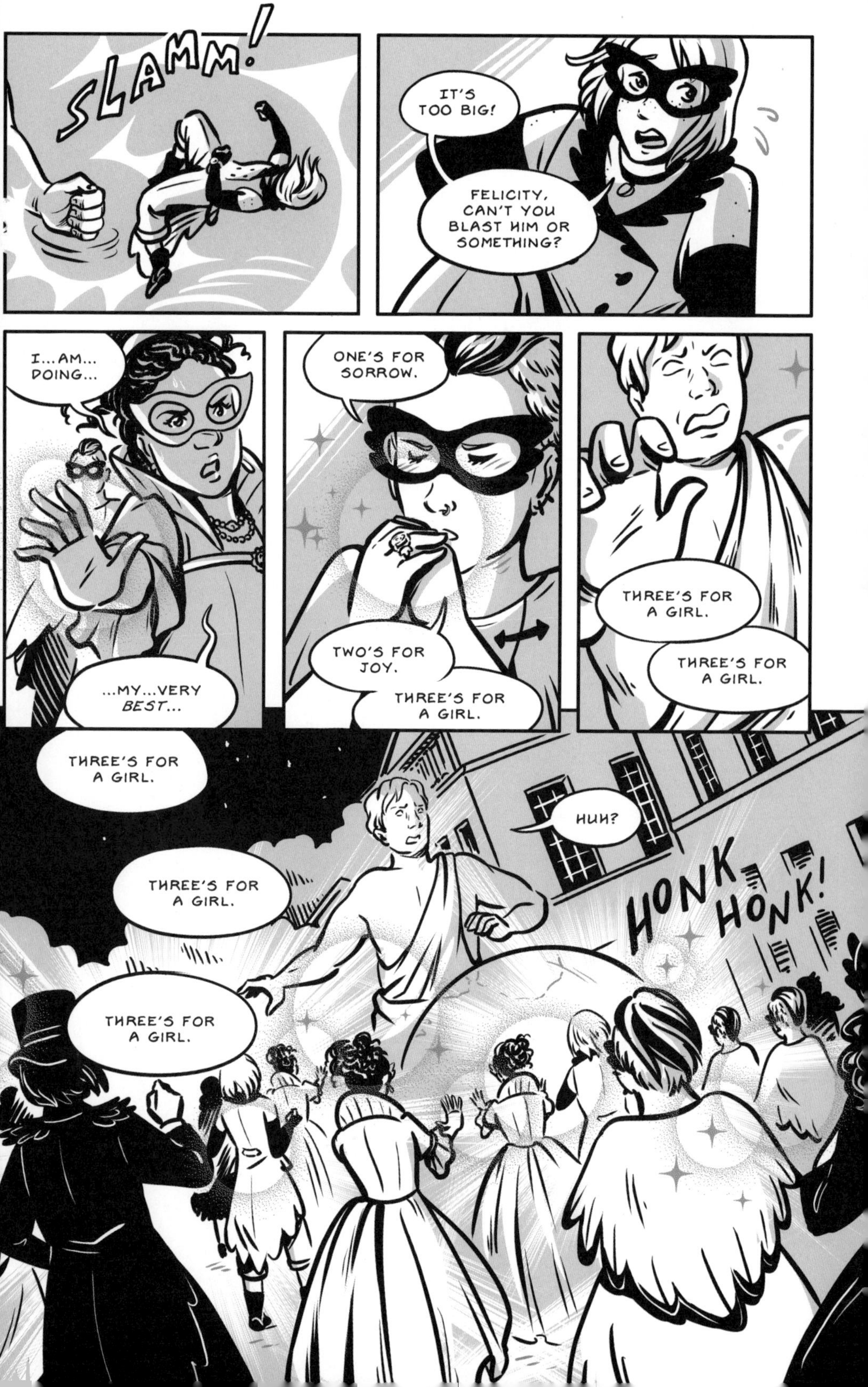
SLAMM!
IT'S TOO BIG!
FELICITY, CAN'T YOU BLAST HIM OR SOMETHING?
I...AM... DOING...
...MY...VERY *BEST*...
ONE'S FOR SORROW.
TWO'S FOR JOY.
THREE'S FOR A GIRL.
THREE'S FOR A GIRL.
THREE'S FOR A GIRL.
THREE'S FOR A GIRL.
THREE'S FOR A GIRL.
HUH?
THREE'S FOR A GIRL.
HONK HONK!

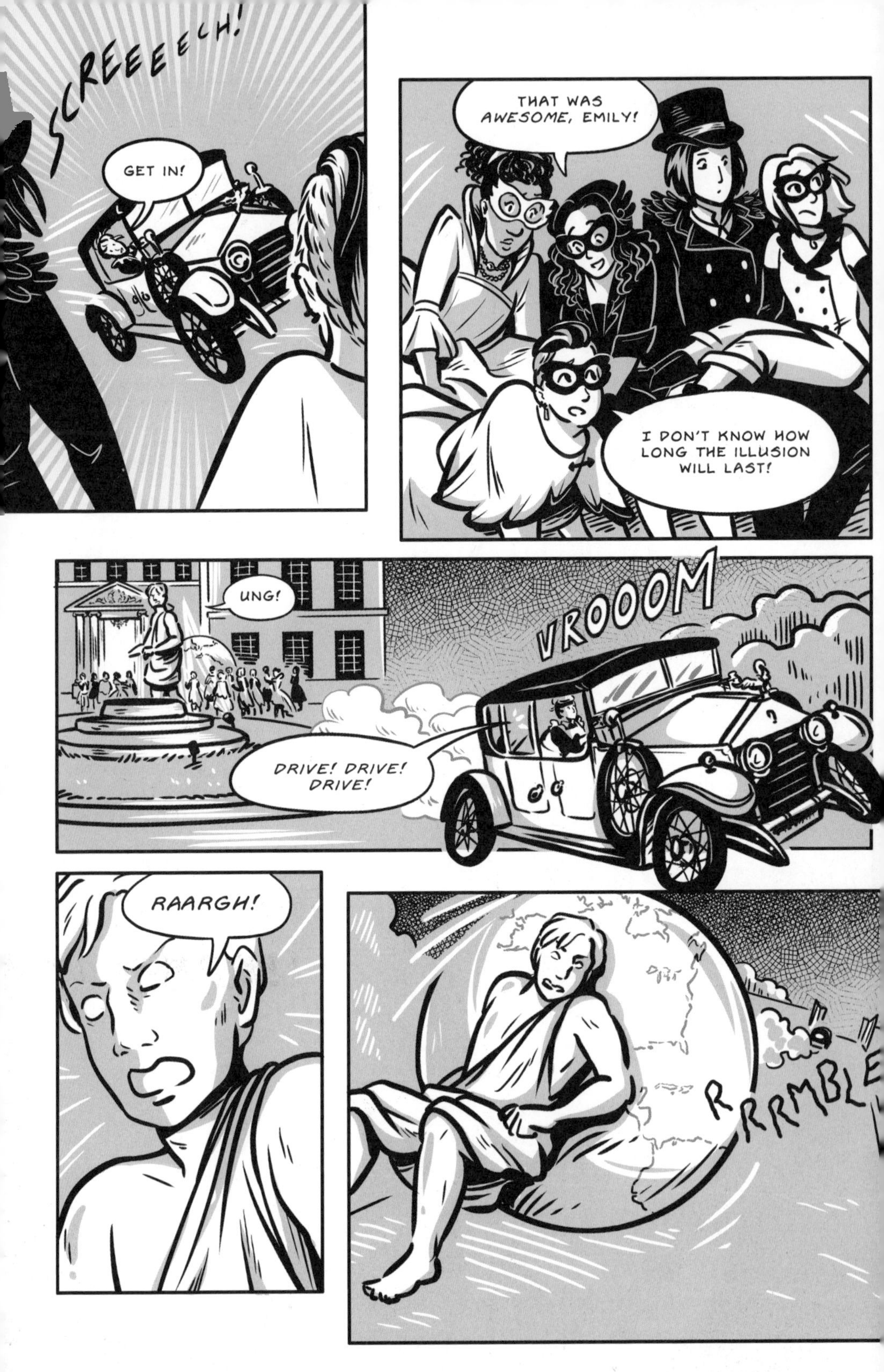
SCREEEECH!
GET IN!
THAT WAS AWESOME, EMILY!
I DON'T KNOW HOW LONG THE ILLUSION WILL LAST!
UNG!
VROOOM
DRIVE! DRIVE! DRIVE!
RAARGH!
RRRMBLE

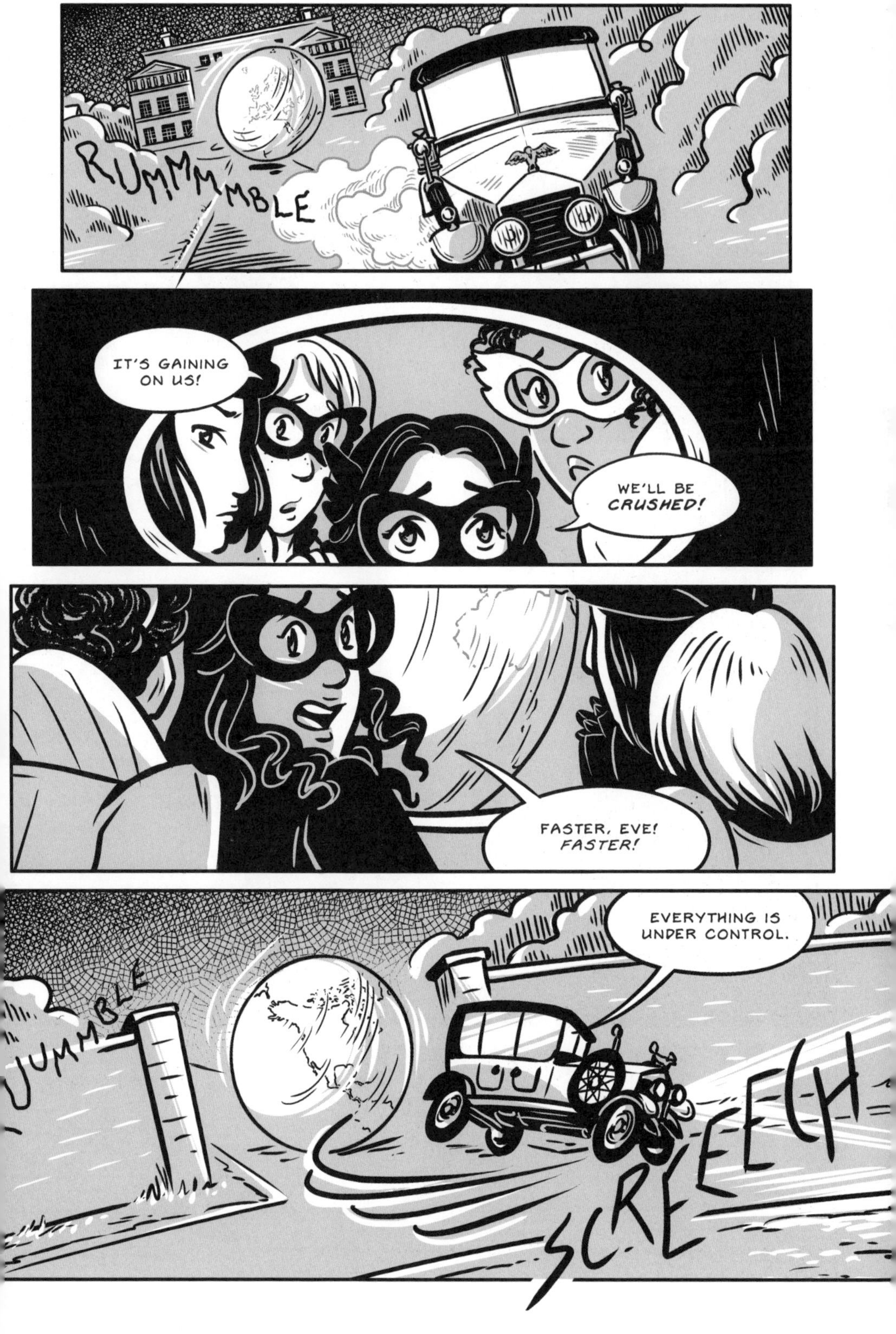
RUMMMMBLE
IT'S GAINING ON US!
WE'LL BE *CRUSHED!*
FASTER, EVE! *FASTER!*
UMMBLE
EVERYTHING IS UNDER CONTROL.
SCREEECH

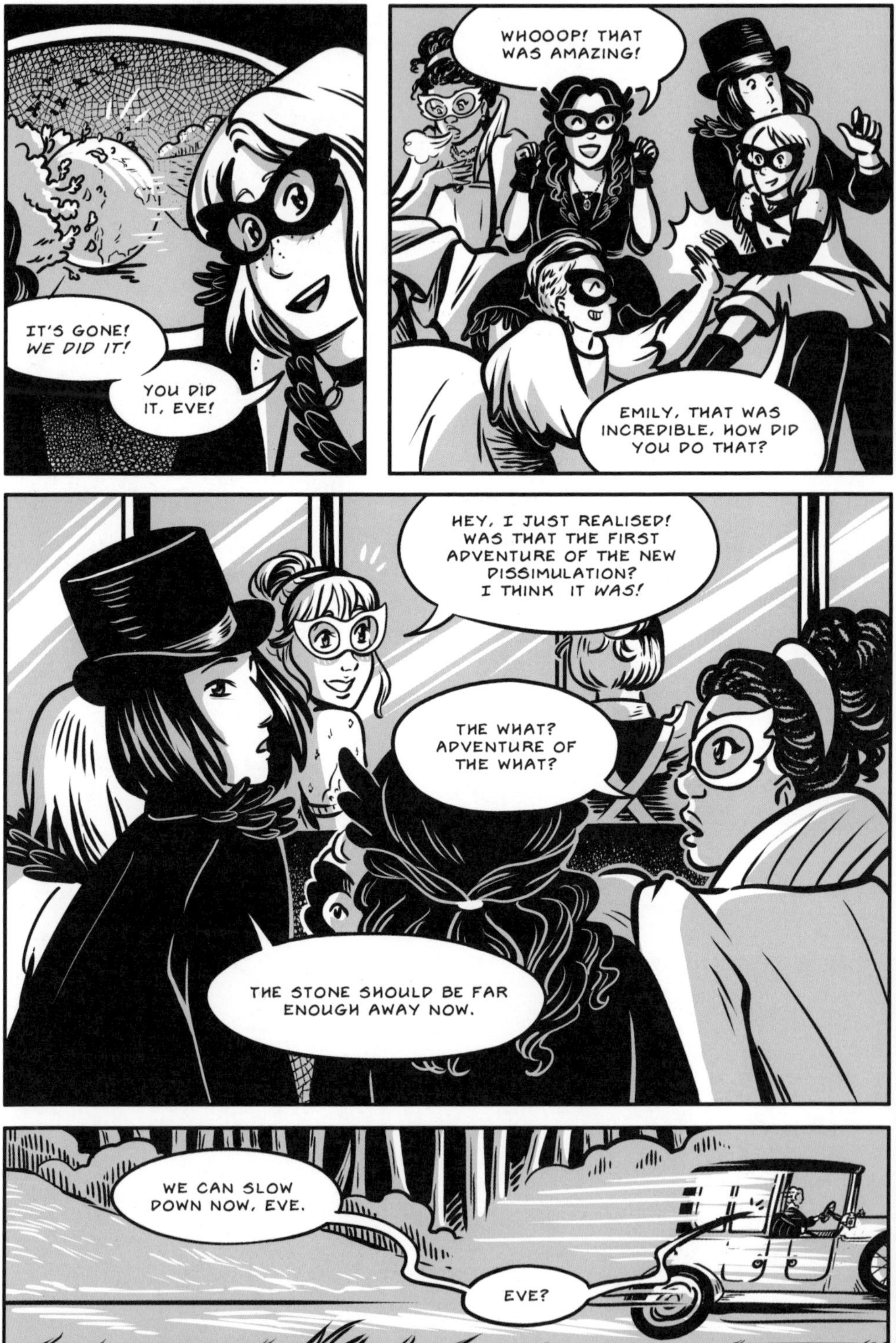
IT'S GONE! WE DID IT!
YOU DID IT, EVE!
WHOOOP! THAT WAS AMAZING!
EMILY, THAT WAS INCREDIBLE, HOW DID YOU DO THAT?
HEY, I JUST REALISED! WAS THAT THE FIRST ADVENTURE OF THE NEW DISSIMULATION? I THINK IT WAS!
THE WHAT? ADVENTURE OF THE WHAT?
THE STONE SHOULD BE FAR ENOUGH AWAY NOW.
WE CAN SLOW DOWN NOW, EVE.
EVE?

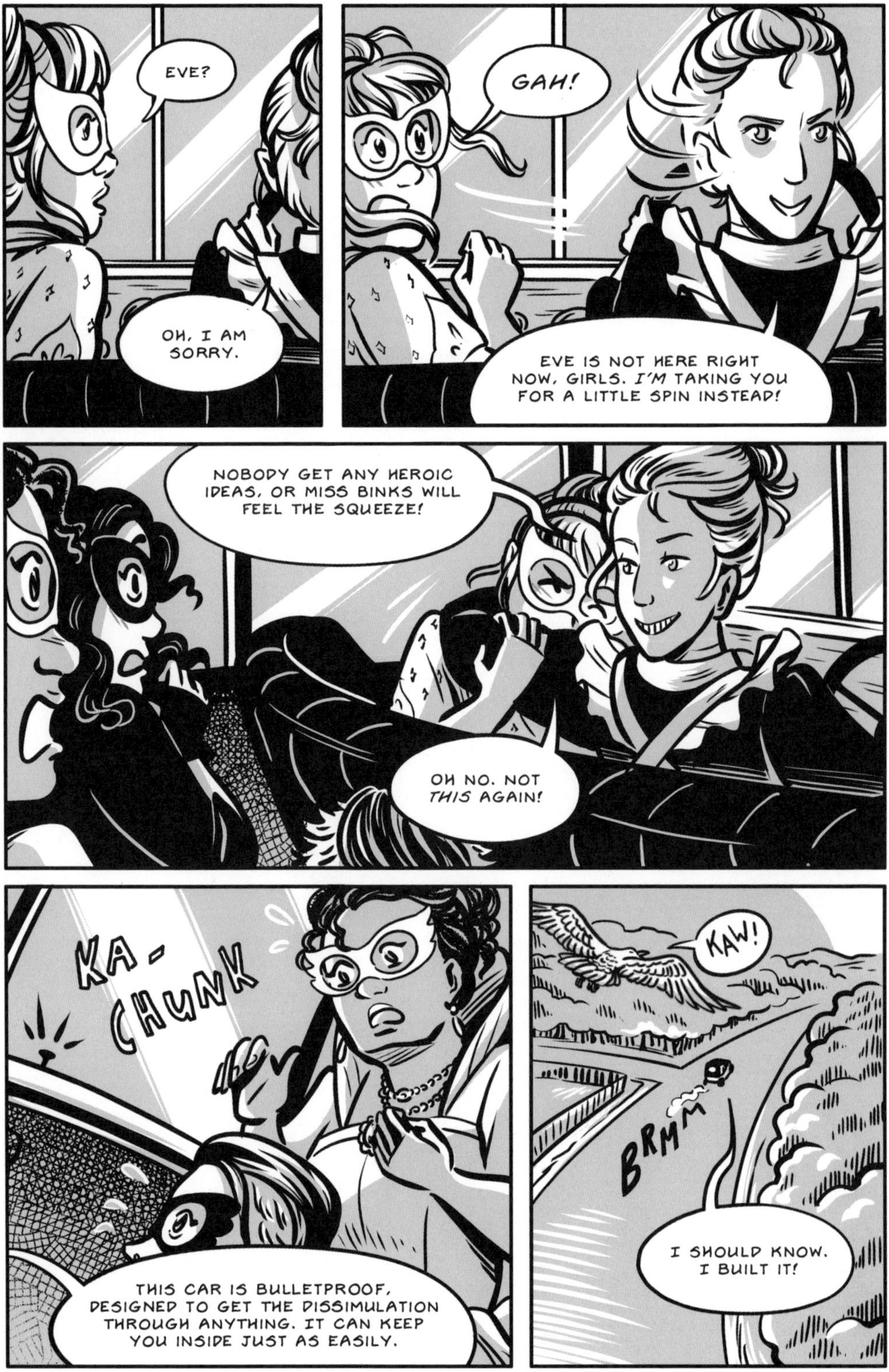
EVE?
OH, I AM SORRY.
GAH!
EVE IS NOT HERE RIGHT NOW, GIRLS. *I'M* TAKING YOU FOR A LITTLE SPIN INSTEAD!
NOBODY GET ANY HEROIC IDEAS, OR MISS BINKS WILL FEEL THE SQUEEZE!
OH NO. NOT *THIS* AGAIN!
KA-CHUNK
THIS CAR IS BULLETPROOF, DESIGNED TO GET THE DISSIMULATION THROUGH ANYTHING. IT CAN KEEP YOU INSIDE JUST AS EASILY.
KAW!
BRMM
I SHOULD KNOW. I BUILT IT!

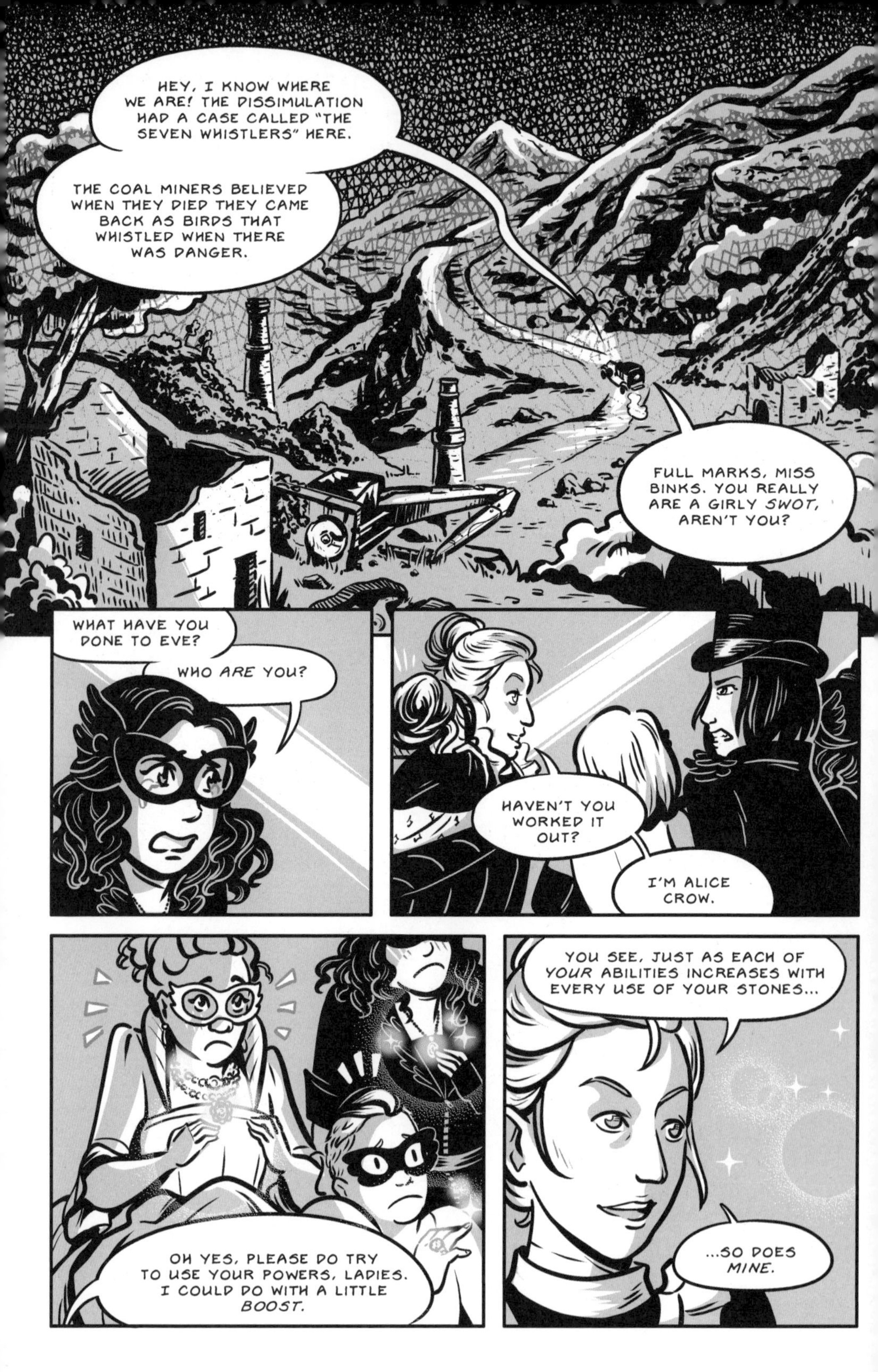
HEY, I KNOW WHERE WE ARE! THE DISSIMULATION HAD A CASE CALLED "THE SEVEN WHISTLERS" HERE.
THE COAL MINERS BELIEVED WHEN THEY DIED THEY CAME BACK AS BIRDS THAT WHISTLED WHEN THERE WAS DANGER.
FULL MARKS, MISS BINKS. YOU REALLY ARE A GIRLY *SWOT*, AREN'T YOU?
WHAT HAVE YOU DONE TO EVE?
WHO *ARE* YOU?
HAVEN'T YOU WORKED IT OUT?
I'M ALICE CROW.
OH YES, PLEASE DO TRY TO USE YOUR POWERS, LADIES. I COULD DO WITH A LITTLE *BOOST*.
YOU SEE, JUST AS EACH OF *YOUR* ABILITIES INCREASES WITH EVERY USE OF YOUR STONES...
...SO DOES *MINE*.

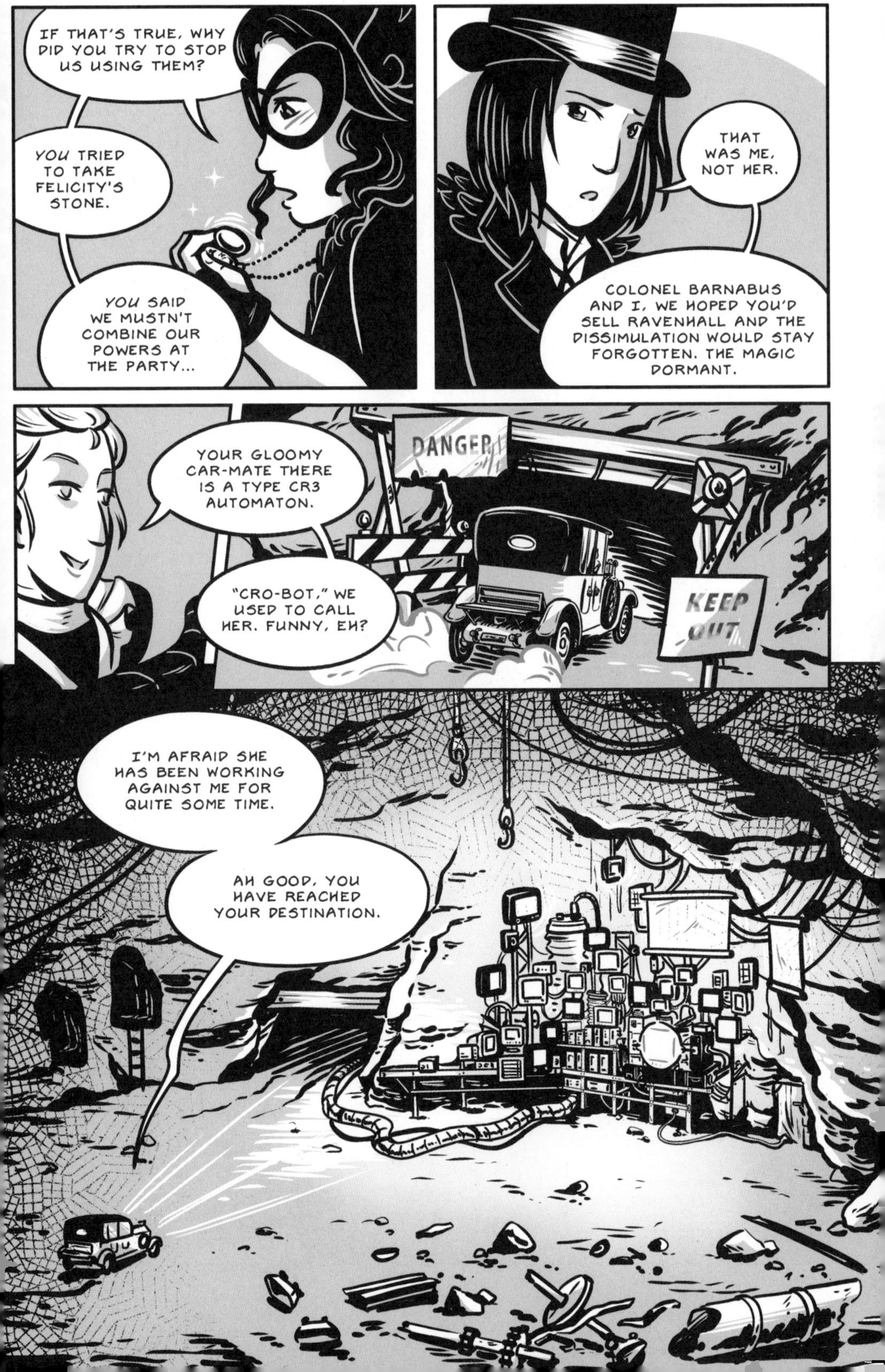

IF THAT'S TRUE, WHY DID YOU TRY TO STOP US USING THEM?
YOU TRIED TO TAKE FELICITY'S STONE.
YOU SAID WE MUSTN'T COMBINE OUR POWERS AT THE PARTY...
THAT WAS ME, NOT HER.
COLONEL BARNABUS AND I, WE HOPED YOU'D SELL RAVENHALL AND THE DISSIMULATION WOULD STAY FORGOTTEN. THE MAGIC DORMANT.
DANGER
YOUR GLOOMY CAR-MATE THERE IS A TYPE CR3 AUTOMATON.
"CRO-BOT," WE USED TO CALL HER. FUNNY, EH?
KEEP OUT
I'M AFRAID SHE HAS BEEN WORKING AGAINST ME FOR QUITE SOME TIME.
AH GOOD. YOU HAVE REACHED YOUR DESTINATION.

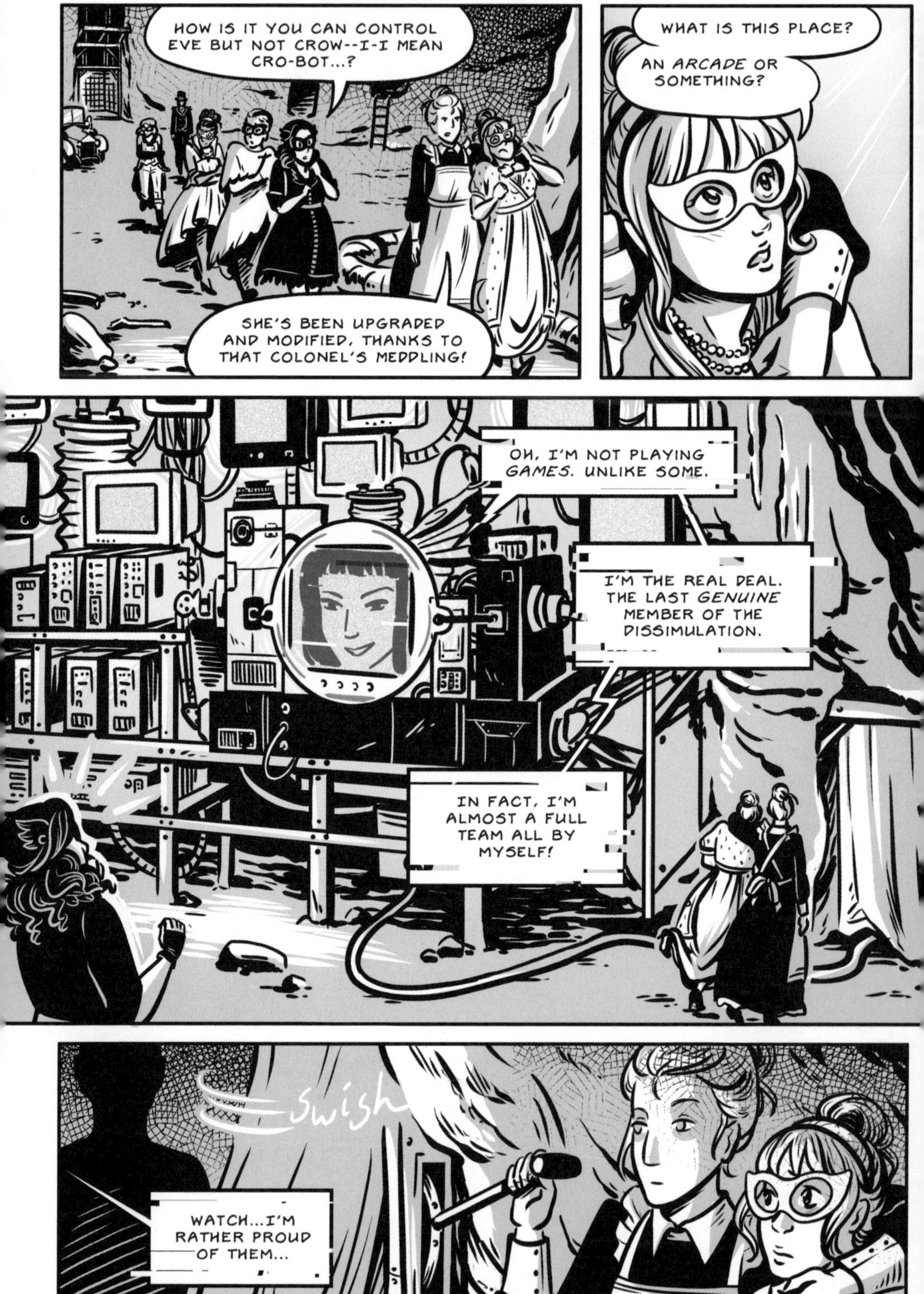

HOW IS IT YOU CAN CONTROL EVE BUT NOT CROW--I-I MEAN CRO-BOT...?
SHE'S BEEN UPGRADED AND MODIFIED, THANKS TO THAT COLONEL'S MEDDLING!
WHAT IS THIS PLACE?
AN *ARCADE* OR SOMETHING?
OH, I'M NOT PLAYING *GAMES*. UNLIKE SOME.
I'M THE REAL DEAL. THE LAST *GENUINE* MEMBER OF THE DISSIMULATION.
IN FACT, I'M ALMOST A FULL TEAM ALL BY MYSELF!
SWISH
WATCH...I'M RATHER PROUD OF THEM...

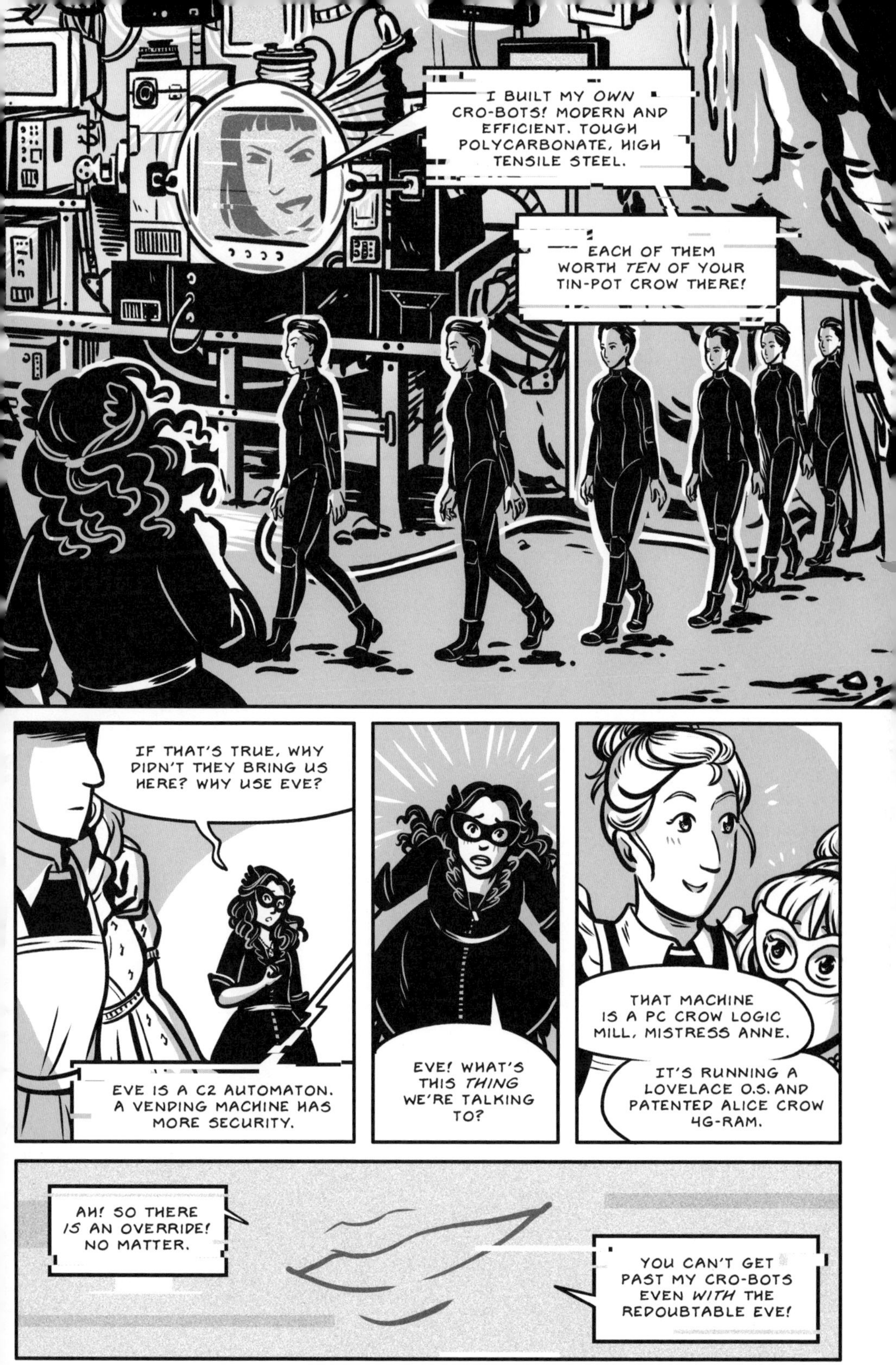

I BUILT MY *OWN* CRO-BOTS! MODERN AND EFFICIENT. TOUGH POLYCARBONATE, HIGH TENSILE STEEL.
EACH OF THEM WORTH *TEN* OF YOUR TIN-POT CROW THERE!
IF THAT'S TRUE, WHY DIDN'T THEY BRING US HERE? WHY USE EVE?
EVE IS A C2 AUTOMATON. A VENDING MACHINE HAS MORE SECURITY.
EVE! WHAT'S THIS *THING* WE'RE TALKING TO?
THAT MACHINE IS A PC CROW LOGIC MILL, MISTRESS ANNE.
IT'S RUNNING A LOVELACE O.S. AND PATENTED ALICE CROW 4G-RAM.
AH! SO THERE *IS* AN OVERRIDE! NO MATTER.
YOU CAN'T GET PAST MY CRO-BOTS EVEN *WITH* THE REDOUBTABLE EVE!

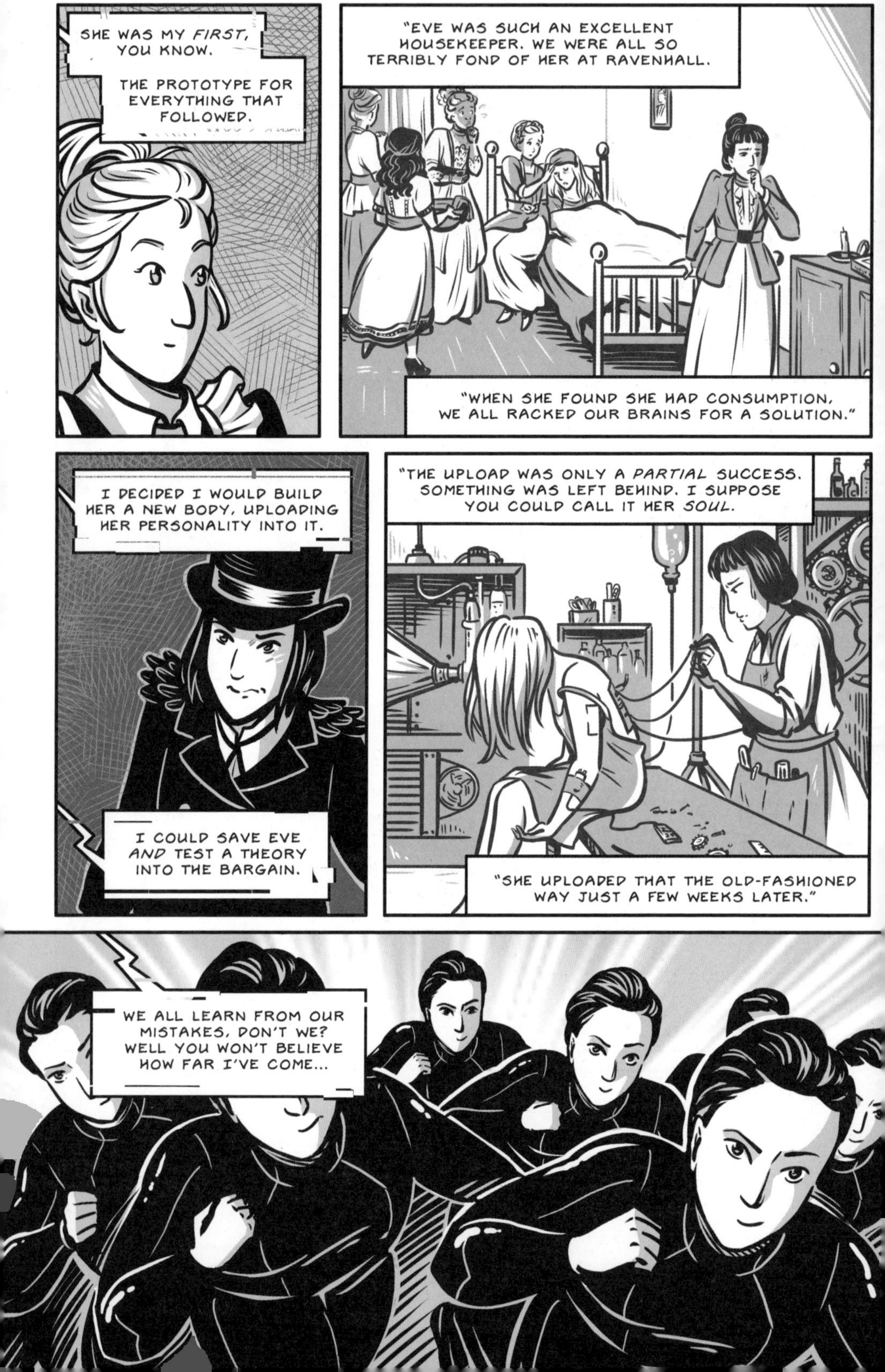
SHE WAS MY *FIRST*, YOU KNOW.
THE PROTOTYPE FOR EVERYTHING THAT FOLLOWED.
"EVE WAS SUCH AN EXCELLENT HOUSEKEEPER. WE WERE ALL SO TERRIBLY FOND OF HER AT RAVENHALL.
"WHEN SHE FOUND SHE HAD CONSUMPTION, WE ALL RACKED OUR BRAINS FOR A SOLUTION."
I DECIDED I WOULD BUILD HER A NEW BODY, UPLOADING HER PERSONALITY INTO IT.
I COULD SAVE EVE *AND* TEST A THEORY INTO THE BARGAIN.
"THE UPLOAD WAS ONLY A *PARTIAL* SUCCESS. SOMETHING WAS LEFT BEHIND. I SUPPOSE YOU COULD CALL IT HER *SOUL*.
"SHE UPLOADED THAT THE OLD-FASHIONED WAY JUST A FEW WEEKS LATER."
WE ALL LEARN FROM OUR MISTAKES, DON'T WE? WELL YOU WON'T BELIEVE HOW FAR I'VE COME...

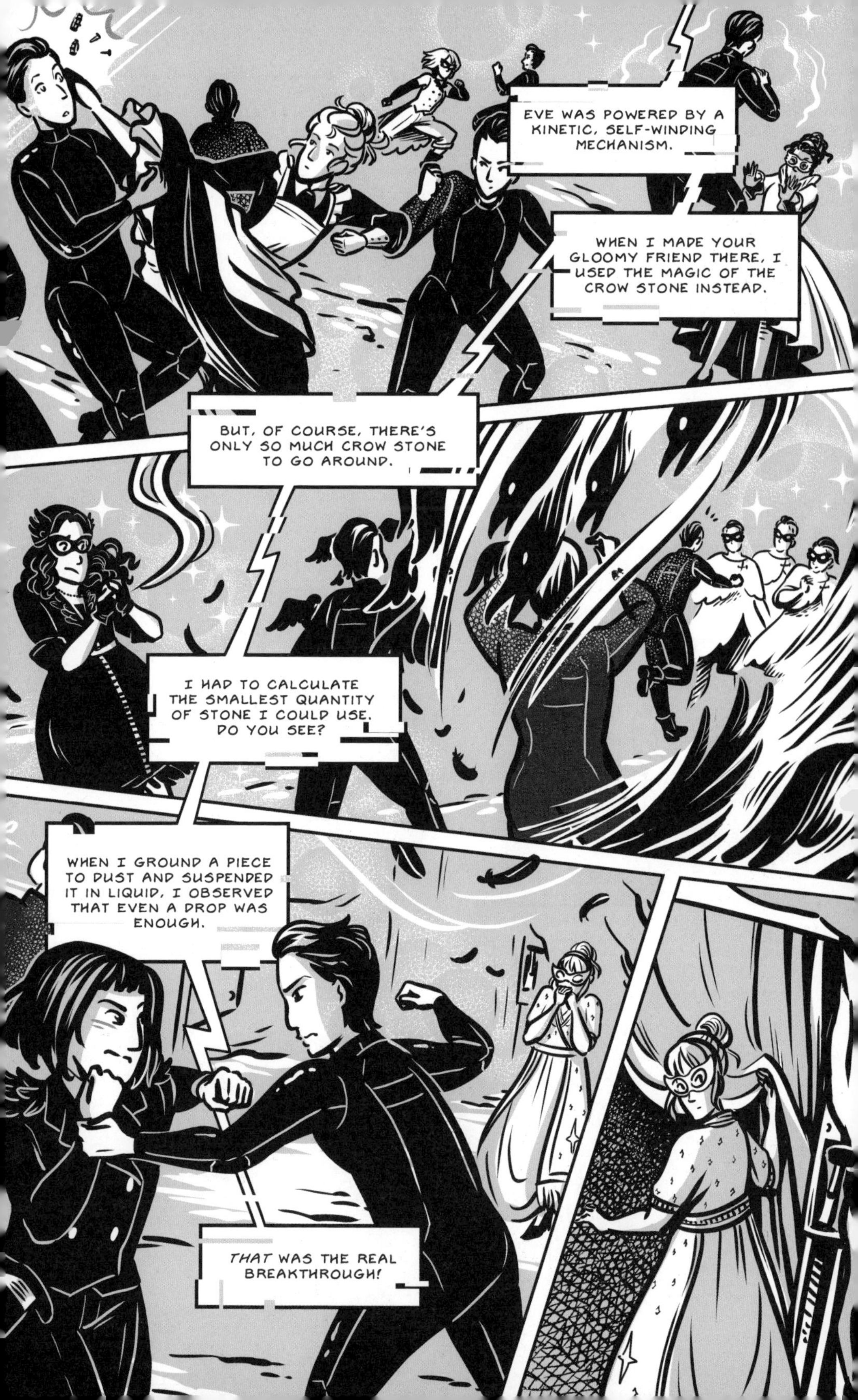
EVE WAS POWERED BY A KINETIC, SELF-WINDING MECHANISM.
WHEN I MADE YOUR GLOOMY FRIEND THERE, I USED THE MAGIC OF THE CROW STONE INSTEAD.
BUT, OF COURSE, THERE'S ONLY SO MUCH CROW STONE TO GO AROUND.
I HAD TO CALCULATE THE SMALLEST QUANTITY OF STONE I COULD USE. DO YOU SEE?
WHEN I GROUND A PIECE TO DUST AND SUSPENDED IT IN LIQUID, I OBSERVED THAT EVEN A DROP WAS ENOUGH.
THAT WAS THE REAL BREAKTHROUGH!

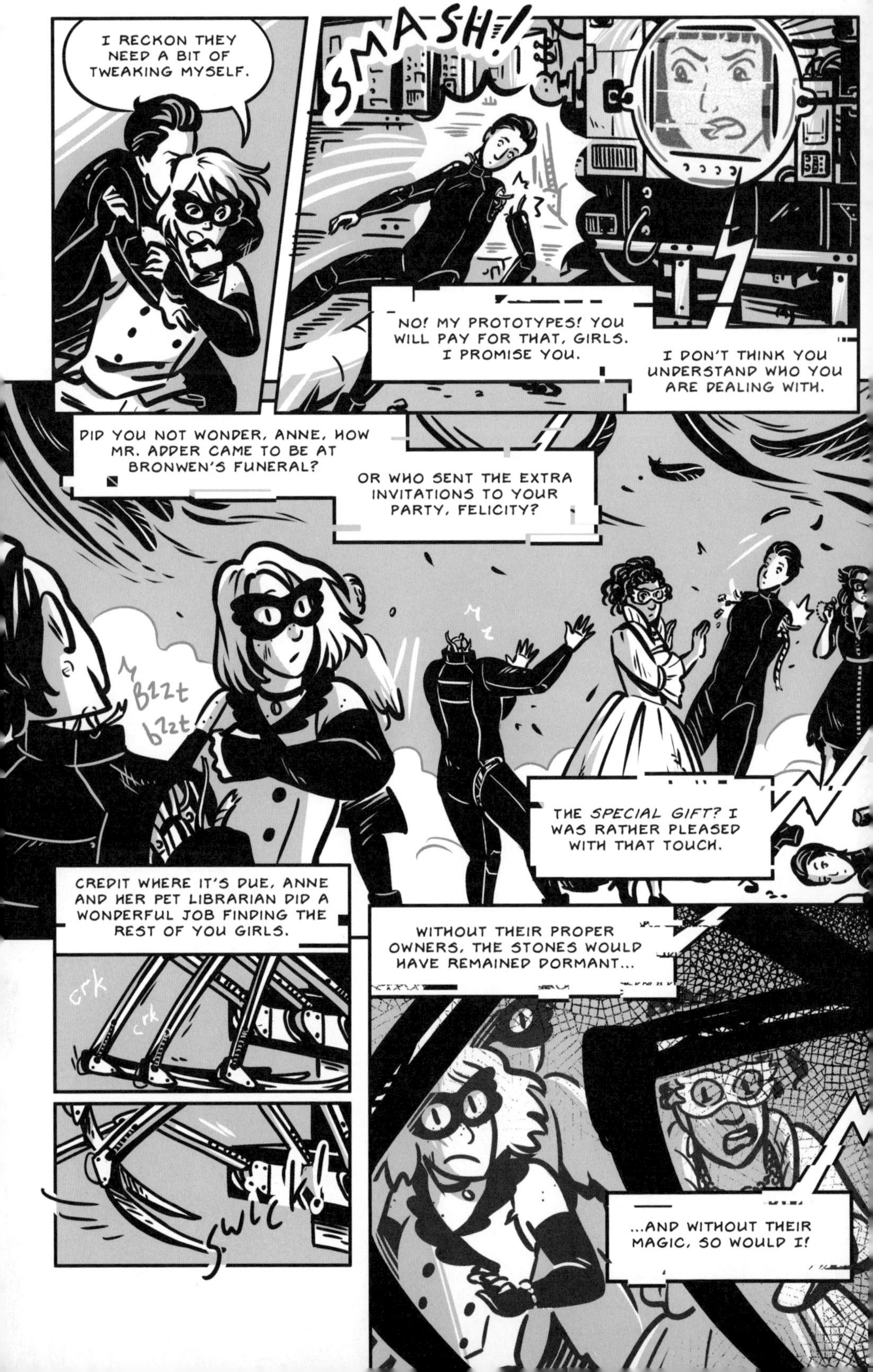
I RECKON THEY NEED A BIT OF TWEAKING MYSELF.
SMASH!
NO! MY PROTOTYPES! YOU WILL PAY FOR THAT, GIRLS. I PROMISE YOU.
I DON'T THINK YOU UNDERSTAND WHO YOU ARE DEALING WITH.
DID YOU NOT WONDER, ANNE, HOW MR. ADDER CAME TO BE AT BRONWEN'S FUNERAL?
OR WHO SENT THE EXTRA INVITATIONS TO YOUR PARTY, FELICITY?
BZZT BZZT
THE *SPECIAL GIFT*? I WAS RATHER PLEASED WITH THAT TOUCH.
CREDIT WHERE IT'S DUE, ANNE AND HER PET LIBRARIAN DID A WONDERFUL JOB FINDING THE REST OF YOU GIRLS.
CRK CRK
SHICK!
WITHOUT THEIR PROPER OWNERS, THE STONES WOULD HAVE REMAINED DORMANT...
...AND WITHOUT THEIR MAGIC, SO WOULD I!

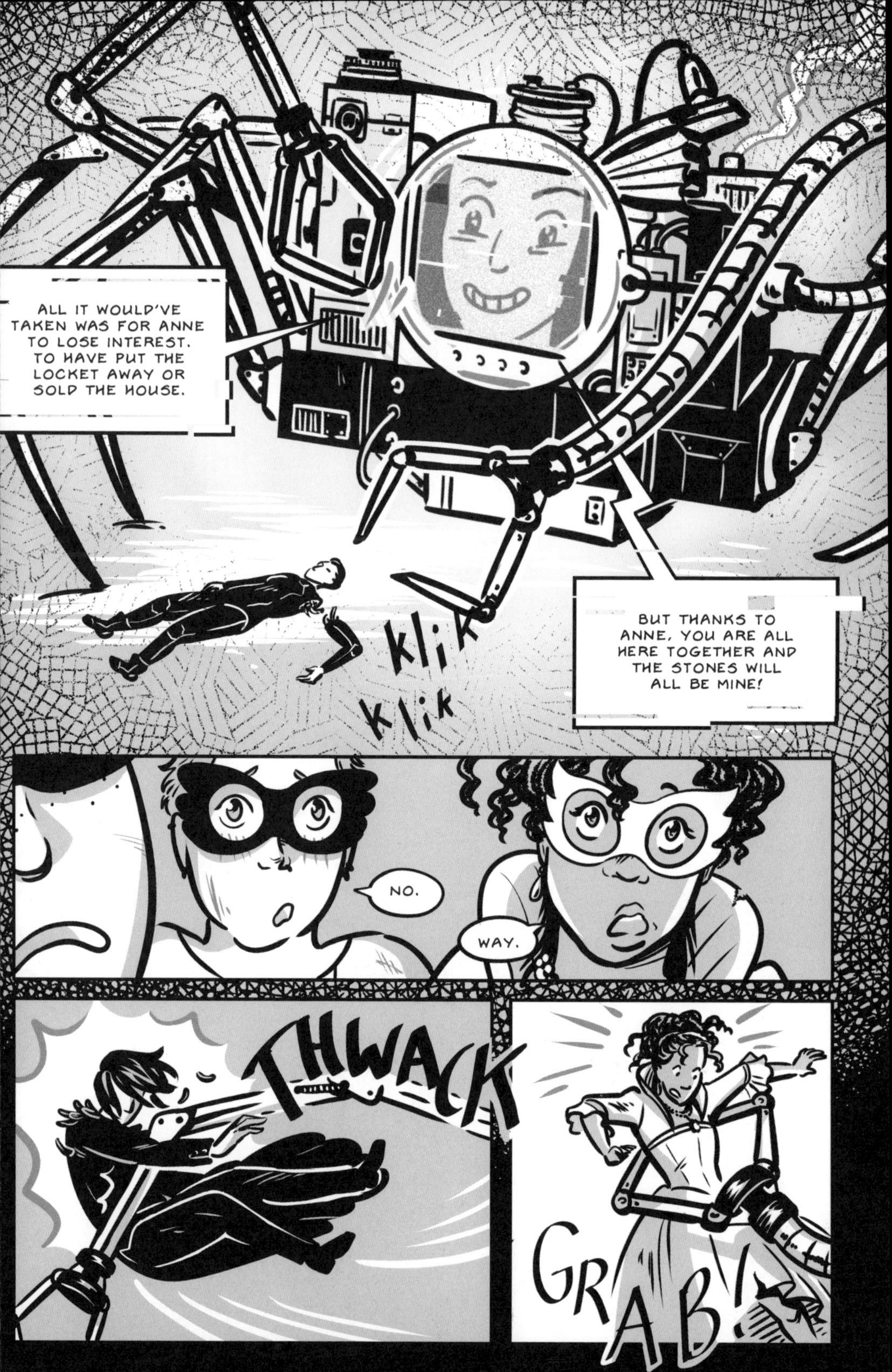
ALL IT WOULD'VE TAKEN WAS FOR ANNE TO LOSE INTEREST. TO HAVE PUT THE LOCKET AWAY OR SOLD THE HOUSE.
BUT THANKS TO ANNE, YOU ARE ALL HERE TOGETHER AND THE STONES WILL ALL BE MINE!
klik
klik
NO.
WAY.
THWACK
GRAB!

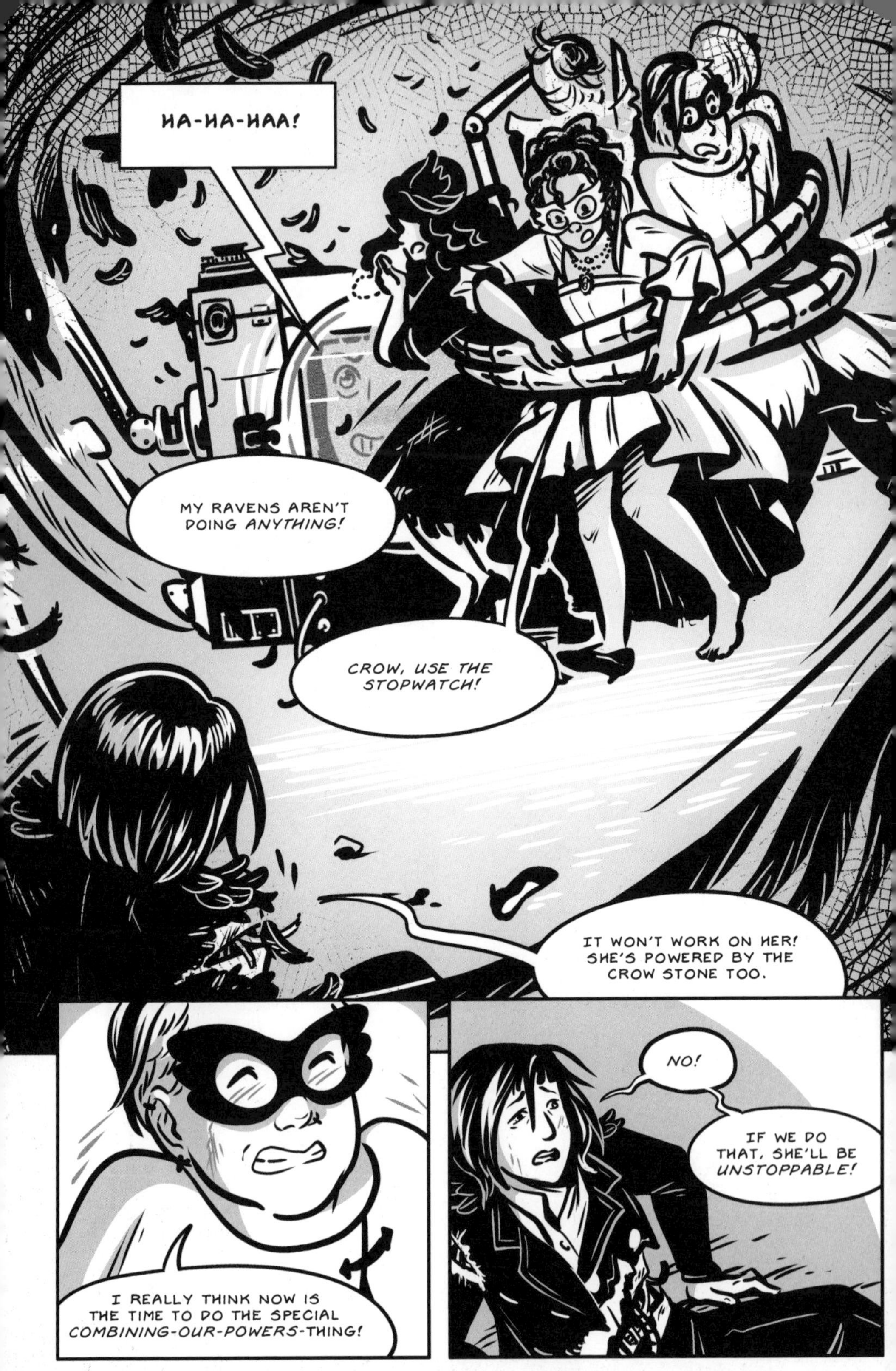
HA-HA-HAA!
MY RAVENS AREN'T DOING ANYTHING!
CROW, USE THE STOPWATCH!
IT WON'T WORK ON HER! SHE'S POWERED BY THE CROW STONE TOO.
I REALLY THINK NOW IS THE TIME TO DO THE SPECIAL COMBINING-OUR-POWERS-THING!
NO!
IF WE DO THAT, SHE'LL BE UNSTOPPABLE!

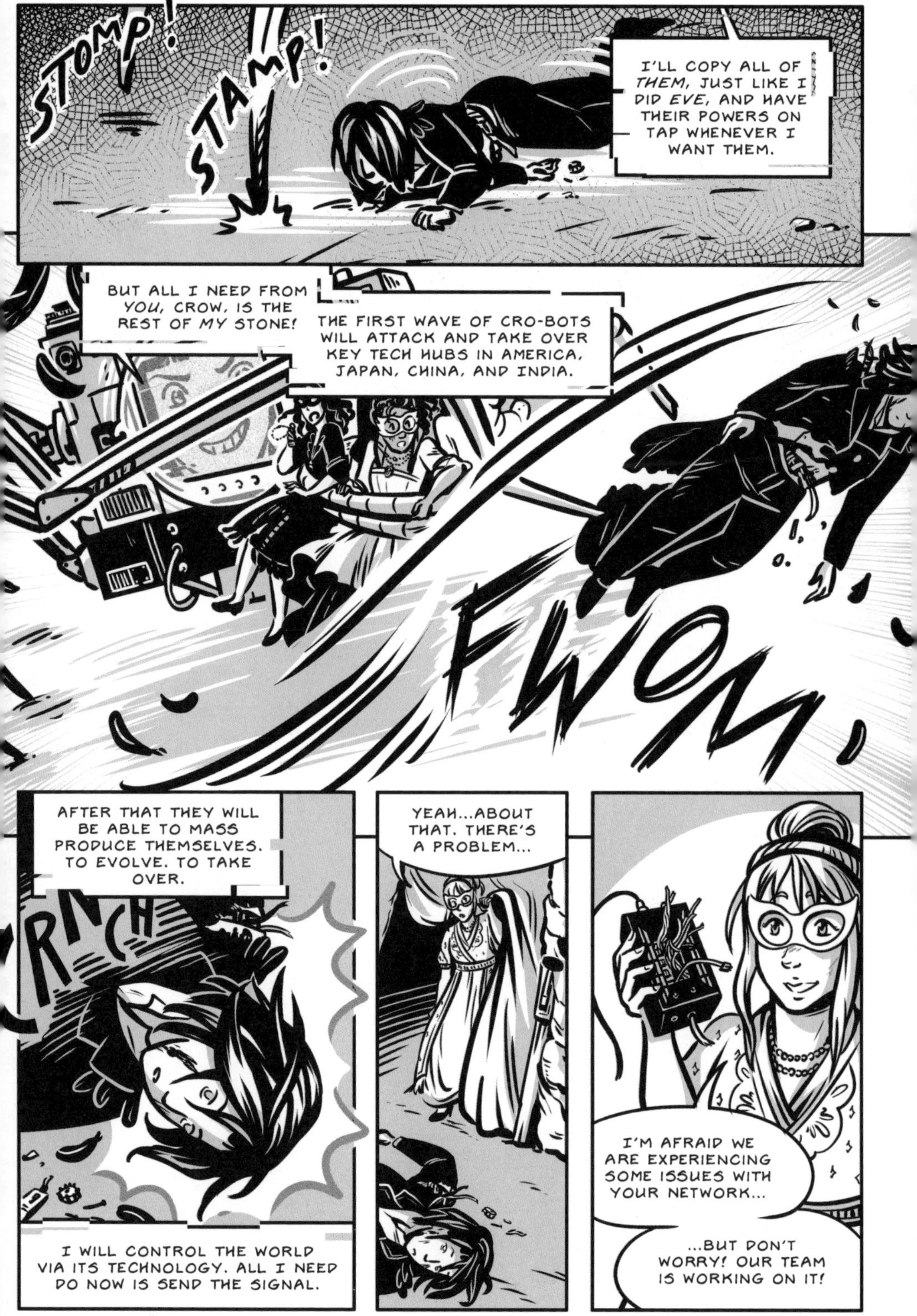
STOMP!
STAMP!
I'LL COPY ALL OF *THEM*, JUST LIKE I DID *EVE*, AND HAVE THEIR POWERS ON TAP WHENEVER I WANT THEM.
BUT ALL I NEED FROM *YOU*, CROW, IS THE REST OF *MY* STONE!
THE FIRST WAVE OF CRO-BOTS WILL ATTACK AND TAKE OVER KEY TECH HUBS IN AMERICA, JAPAN, CHINA, AND INDIA.
FWOM
AFTER THAT THEY WILL BE ABLE TO MASS PRODUCE THEMSELVES. TO EVOLVE. TO TAKE OVER.
CRNCH
I WILL CONTROL THE WORLD VIA ITS TECHNOLOGY. ALL I NEED DO NOW IS SEND THE SIGNAL.
YEAH...ABOUT THAT. THERE'S A PROBLEM...
I'M AFRAID WE ARE EXPERIENCING SOME ISSUES WITH YOUR NETWORK...
...BUT DON'T WORRY! OUR TEAM IS WORKING ON IT!

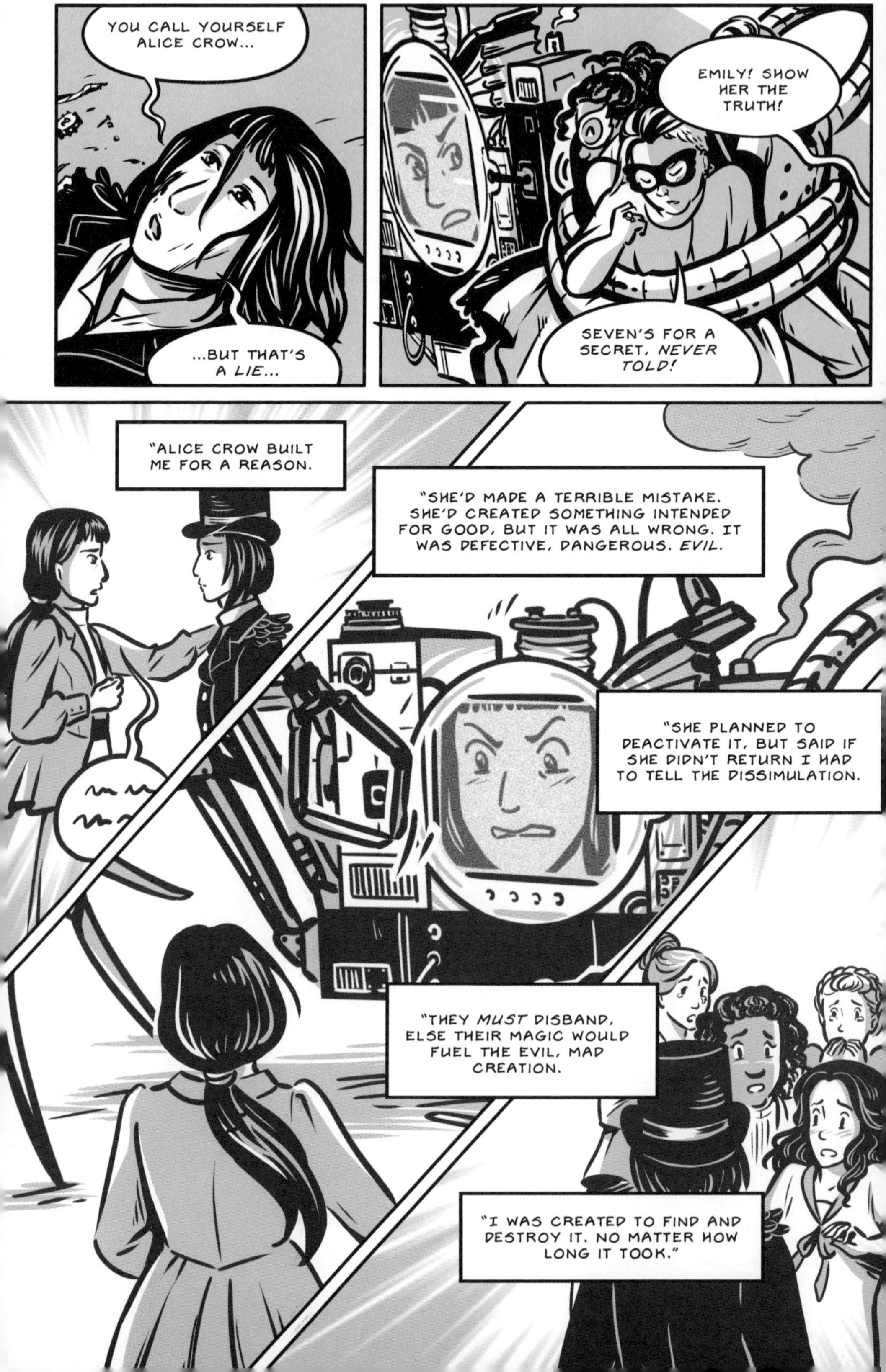
YOU CALL YOURSELF ALICE CROW...
...BUT THAT'S A *LIE*...
EMILY! SHOW HER THE TRUTH!
SEVEN'S FOR A SECRET, *NEVER TOLD!*
"ALICE CROW BUILT ME FOR A REASON.
"SHE'D MADE A TERRIBLE MISTAKE. SHE'D CREATED SOMETHING INTENDED FOR GOOD, BUT IT WAS ALL WRONG. IT WAS DEFECTIVE, DANGEROUS. *EVIL*.
"SHE PLANNED TO DEACTIVATE IT, BUT SAID IF SHE DIDN'T RETURN I HAD TO TELL THE DISSIMULATION.
"THEY *MUST* DISBAND, ELSE THEIR MAGIC WOULD FUEL THE EVIL, MAD CREATION.
"I WAS CREATED TO FIND AND DESTROY IT. NO MATTER HOW LONG IT TOOK."

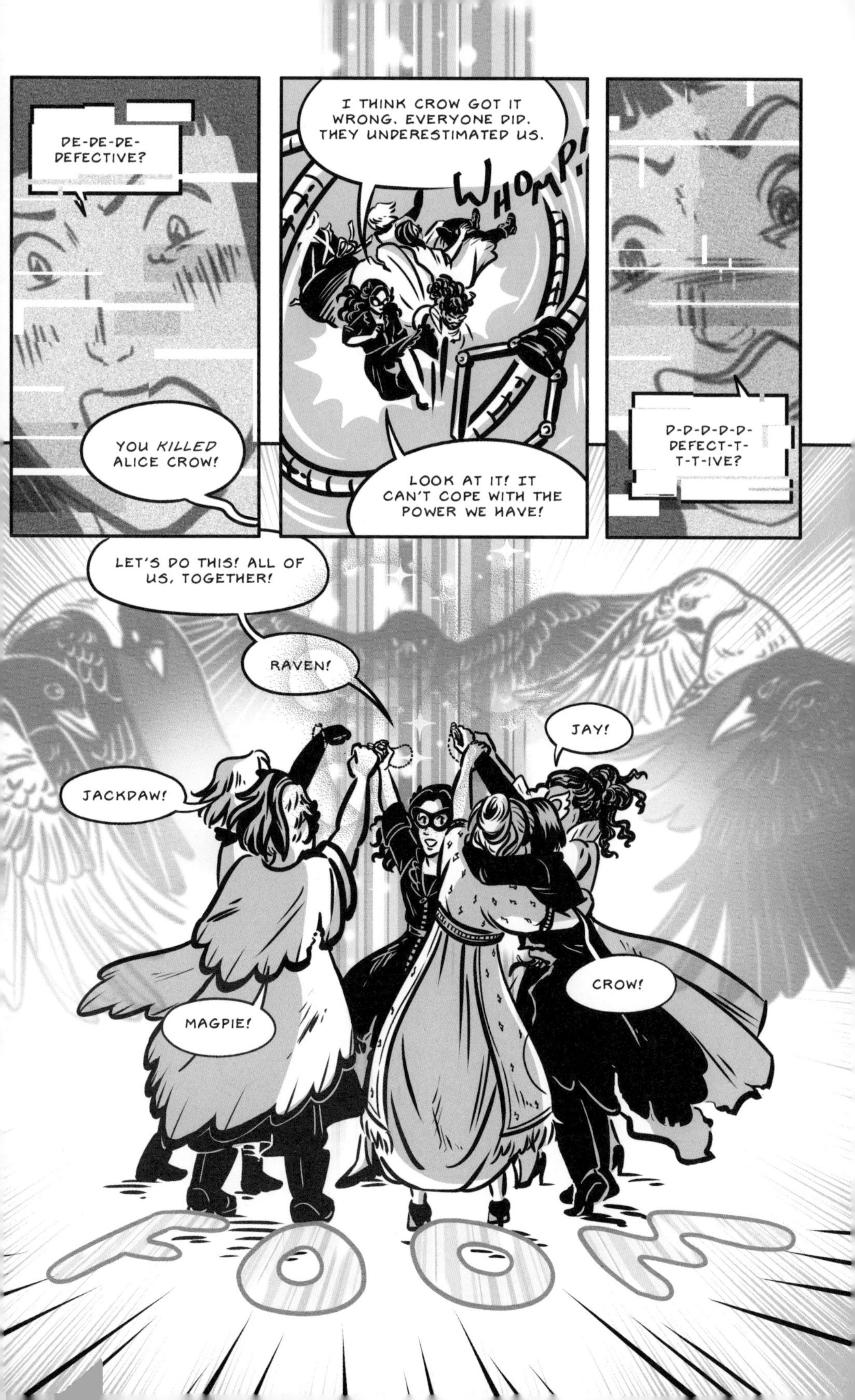
DE-DE-DE-
DEFECTIVE?
YOU *KILLED* ALICE CROW!
I THINK CROW GOT IT WRONG. EVERYONE DID. THEY UNDERESTIMATED US.
WHOMP!
LOOK AT IT! IT CAN'T COPE WITH THE POWER WE HAVE!
D-D-D-D-D-DEFECT-T-T-T-IVE?
LET'S DO THIS! ALL OF US, TOGETHER!
RAVEN!
JAY!
JACKDAW!
CROW!
MAGPIE!
FOOM

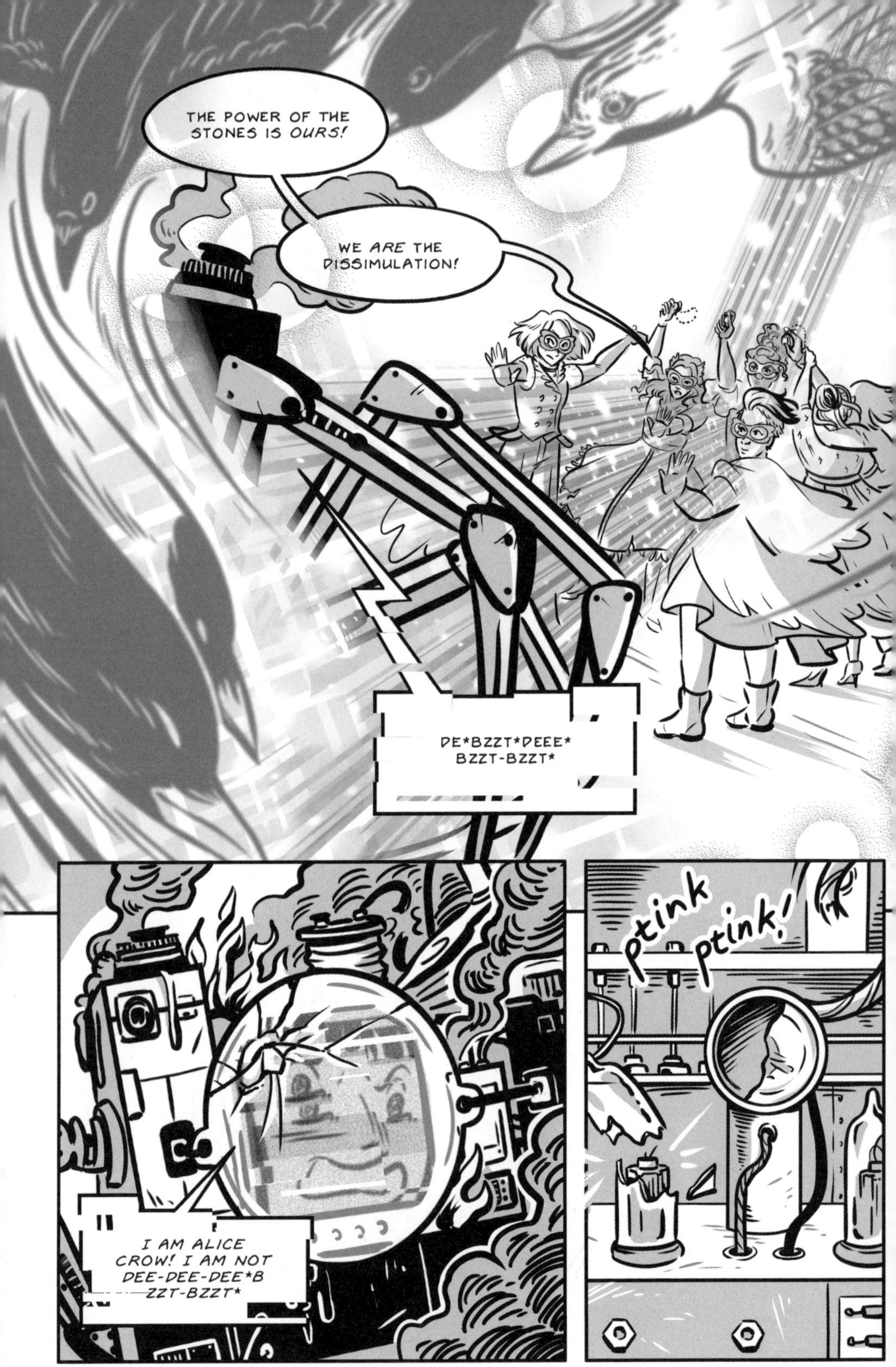
THE POWER OF THE STONES IS OURS!
WE ARE THE DISSIMULATION!
DE*BZZT*DEEE* BZZT-BZZT*
I AM ALICE CROW! I AM NOT DEE-DEE-DEE*B ZZT-BZZT*
ptink ptink!

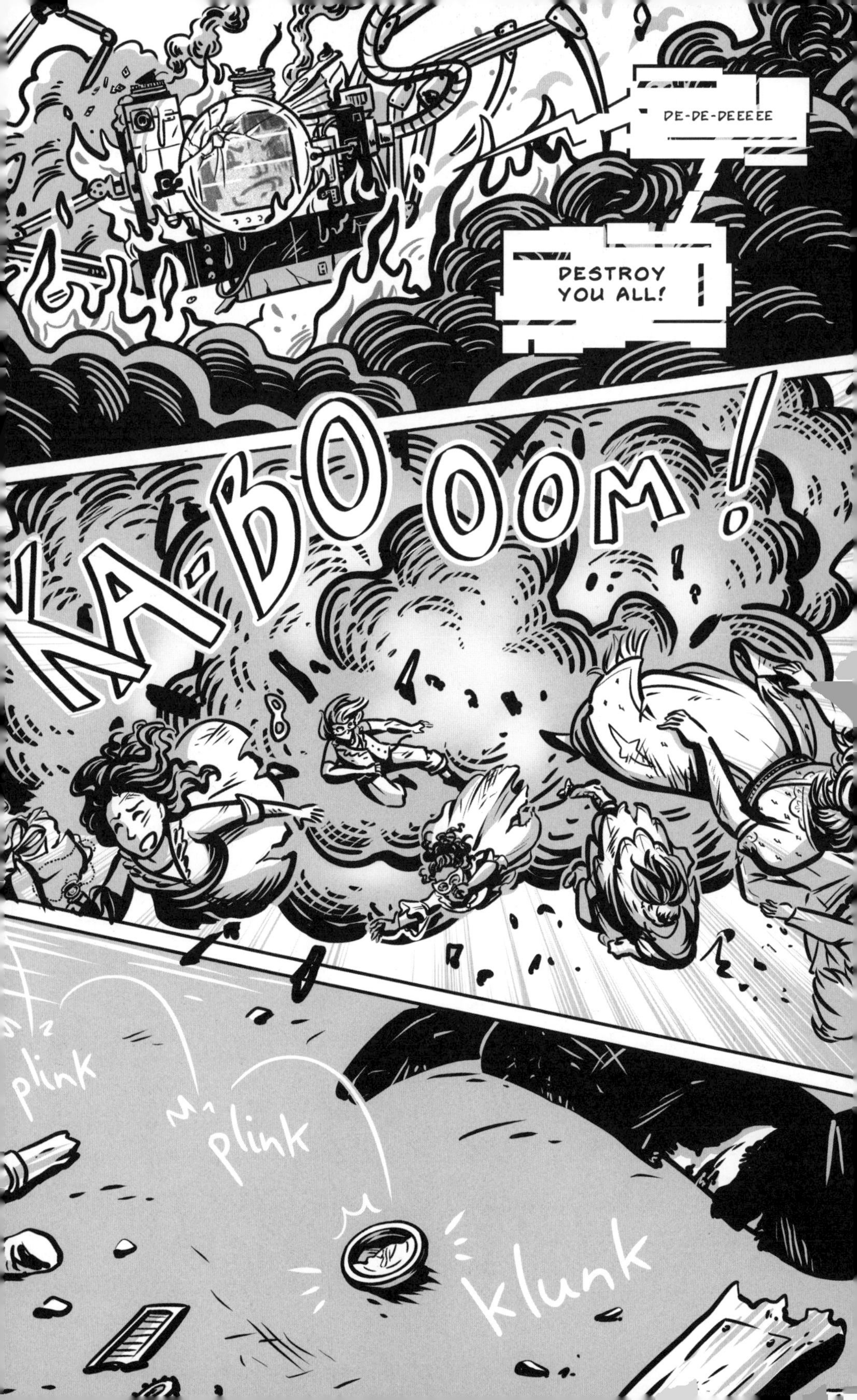
DE-DE-DEEEEE
DESTROY YOU ALL!
KA-BOOOOM!
plink
plink
klunk

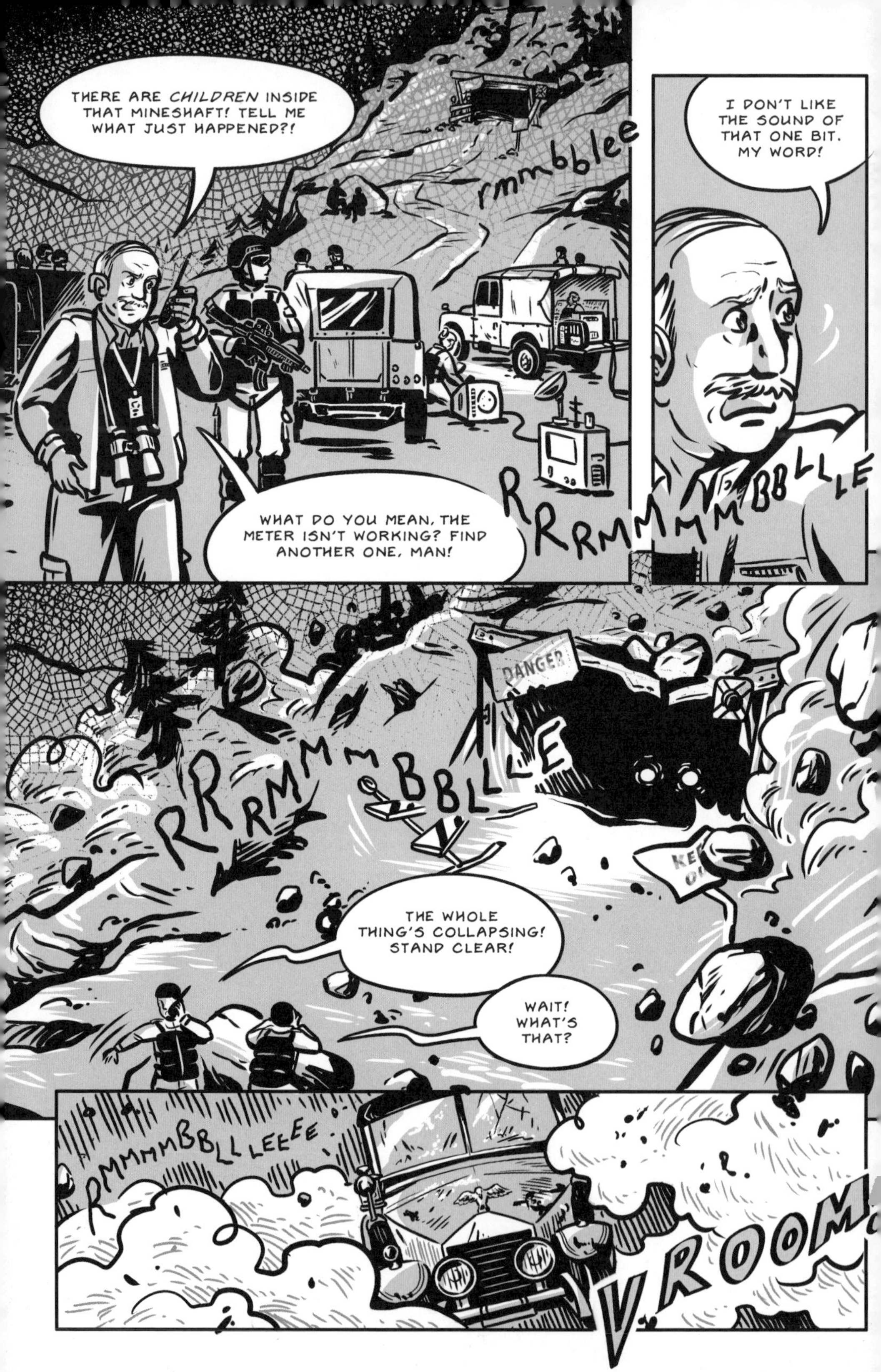
THERE ARE *CHILDREN* INSIDE THAT MINESHAFT! TELL ME WHAT JUST HAPPENED?!
rmmbblee
WHAT DO YOU MEAN, THE METER ISN'T WORKING? FIND ANOTHER ONE, MAN!
RRMMMMMBBLLLE
I DON'T LIKE THE SOUND OF THAT ONE BIT. MY WORD!
DANGER
RRRMMMMBBLLLE
THE WHOLE THING'S COLLAPSING! STAND CLEAR!
WAIT! WHAT'S THAT?
RMMMMBBLLLEEE
VROOM!

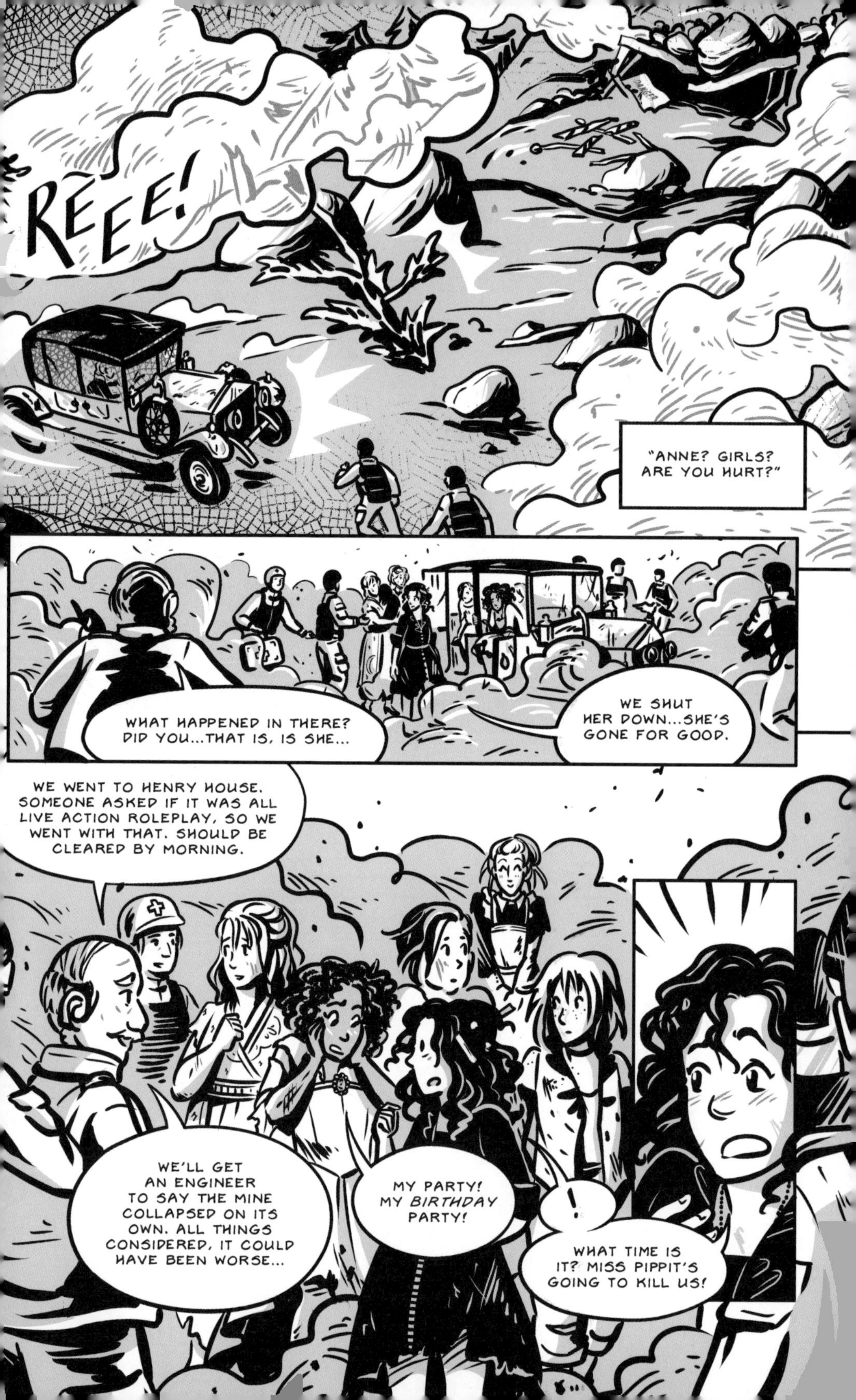
REEEE!
"ANNE? GIRLS? ARE YOU HURT?"
WHAT HAPPENED IN THERE? DID YOU...THAT IS, IS SHE...
WE SHUT HER DOWN...SHE'S GONE FOR GOOD.
WE WENT TO HENRY HOUSE. SOMEONE ASKED IF IT WAS ALL LIVE ACTION ROLEPLAY, SO WE WENT WITH THAT. SHOULD BE CLEARED BY MORNING.
WE'LL GET AN ENGINEER TO SAY THE MINE COLLAPSED ON ITS OWN. ALL THINGS CONSIDERED, IT COULD HAVE BEEN WORSE...
MY PARTY! MY *BIRTHDAY* PARTY!
!
WHAT TIME IS IT? MISS PIPPIT'S GOING TO KILL US!

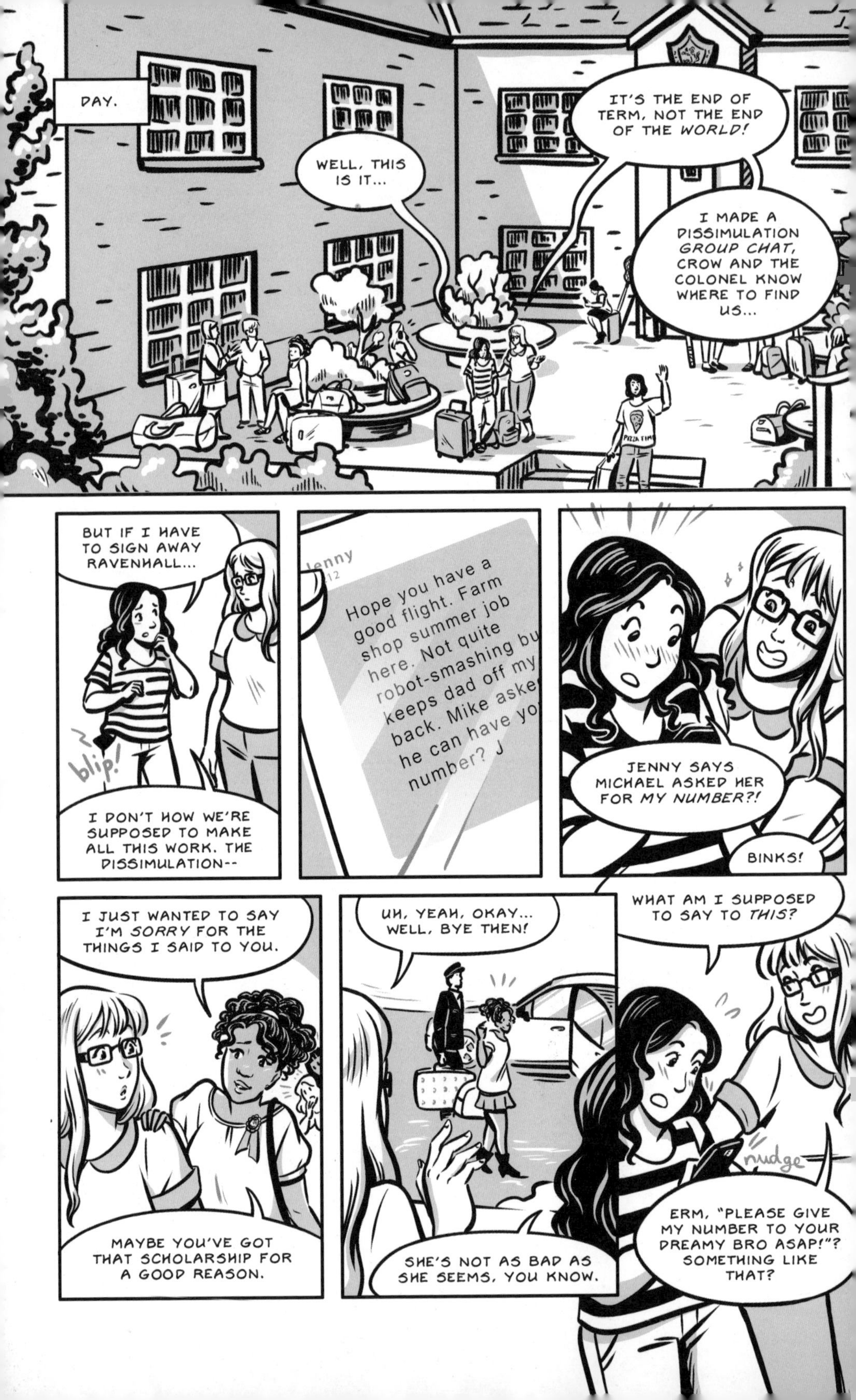
DAY.
WELL, THIS IS IT...
IT'S THE END OF TERM, NOT THE END OF THE *WORLD!*
I MADE A DISSIMULATION *GROUP CHAT,* CROW AND THE COLONEL KNOW WHERE TO FIND US...
PIZZA TIME
BUT IF I HAVE TO SIGN AWAY RAVENHALL...
blip!
I DON'T HOW WE'RE SUPPOSED TO MAKE ALL THIS WORK. THE DISSIMULATION--
Jenny
Hope you have a good flight. Farm shop summer job here. Not quite robot-smashing bu keeps dad off my back. Mike aske he can have yo number? J
JENNY SAYS MICHAEL ASKED HER FOR *MY NUMBER?!*
BINKS!
WHAT AM I SUPPOSED TO SAY TO *THIS?*
I JUST WANTED TO SAY I'M *SORRY* FOR THE THINGS I SAID TO YOU.
MAYBE YOU'VE GOT THAT SCHOLARSHIP FOR A GOOD REASON.
UH, YEAH, OKAY... WELL, BYE THEN!
SHE'S NOT AS BAD AS SHE SEEMS, YOU KNOW.
nudge
ERM, "PLEASE GIVE MY NUMBER TO YOUR DREAMY BRO ASAP!"? SOMETHING LIKE THAT?

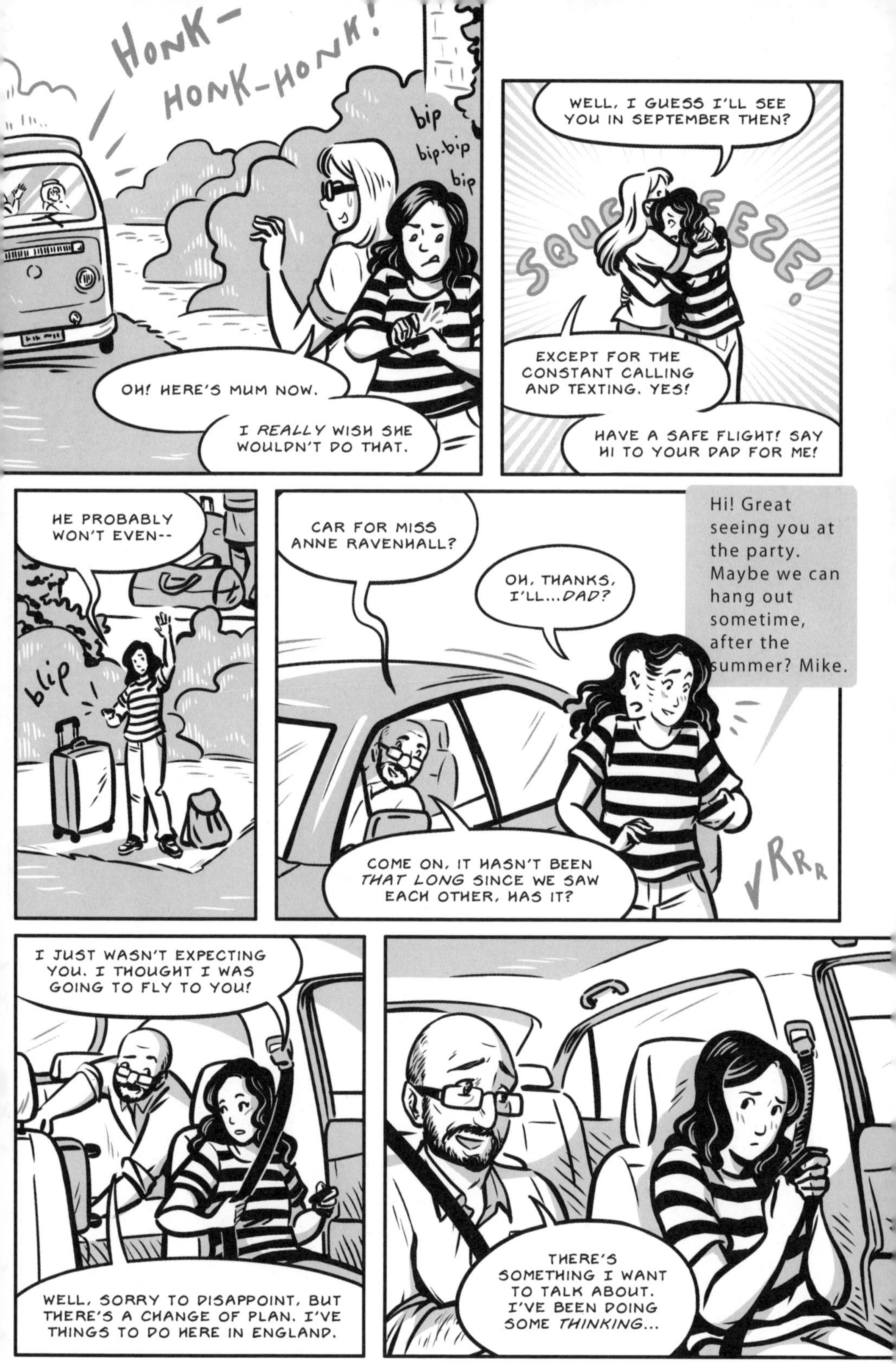
HONK-HONK-HONK!
bip
bip-bip
bip
OH! HERE'S MUM NOW.
I *REALLY* WISH SHE WOULDN'T DO THAT.
WELL, I GUESS I'LL SEE YOU IN SEPTEMBER THEN?
SQUEEEZE!
EXCEPT FOR THE CONSTANT CALLING AND TEXTING, YES!
HAVE A SAFE FLIGHT! SAY HI TO YOUR DAD FOR ME!
HE PROBABLY WON'T EVEN--
blip
CAR FOR MISS ANNE RAVENHALL?
OH, THANKS, I'LL...*DAD?*
Hi! Great seeing you at the party. Maybe we can hang out sometime, after the summer? Mike.
COME ON, IT HASN'T BEEN *THAT LONG* SINCE WE SAW EACH OTHER, HAS IT?
VRRR
I JUST WASN'T EXPECTING YOU. I THOUGHT I WAS GOING TO FLY TO YOU!
WELL, SORRY TO DISAPPOINT, BUT THERE'S A CHANGE OF PLAN. I'VE THINGS TO DO HERE IN ENGLAND.
THERE'S SOMETHING I WANT TO TALK ABOUT. I'VE BEEN DOING SOME *THINKING*...

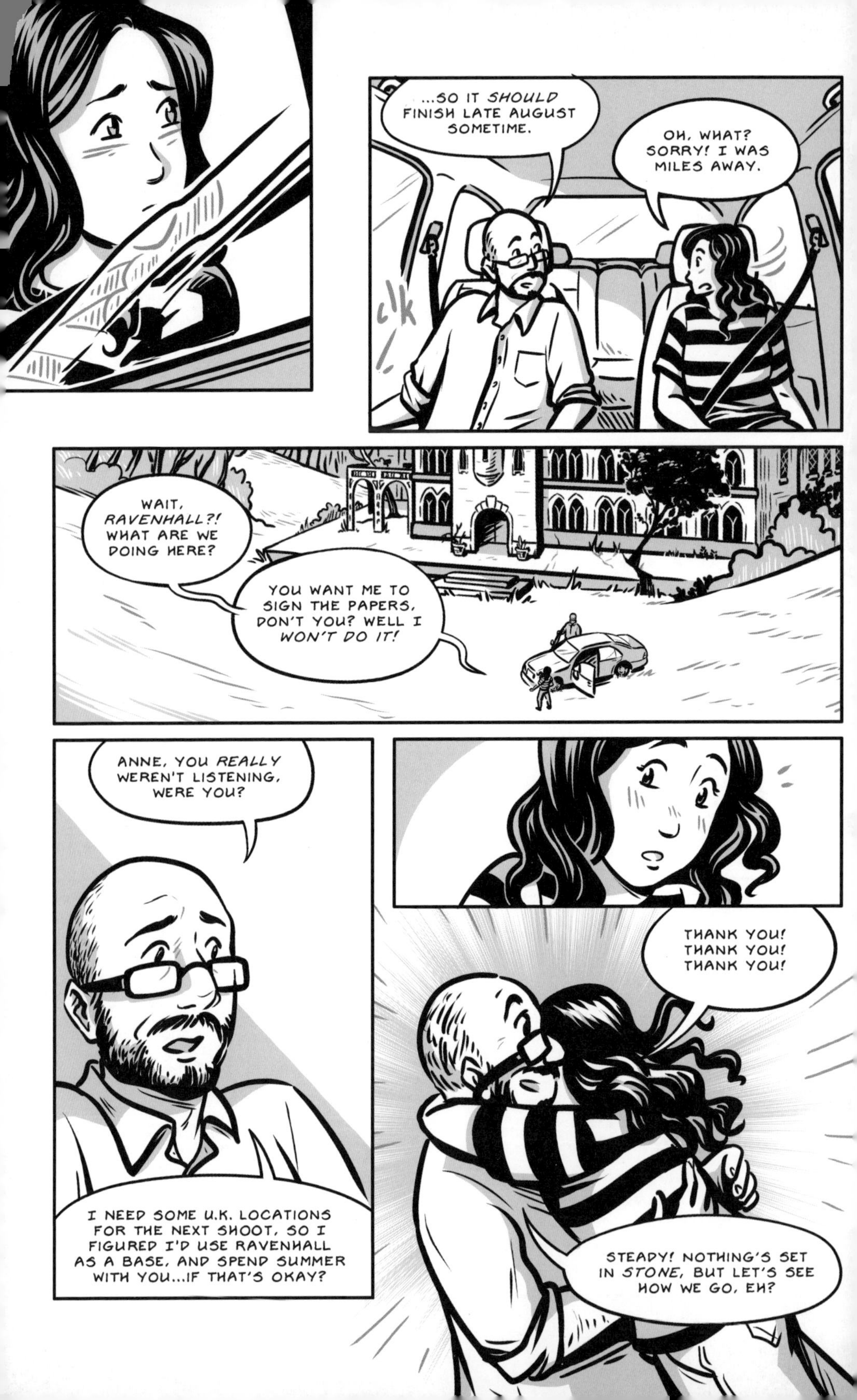
...SO IT SHOULD FINISH LATE AUGUST SOMETIME.
OH, WHAT? SORRY! I WAS MILES AWAY.
CLK
WAIT, RAVENHALL?! WHAT ARE WE DOING HERE?
YOU WANT ME TO SIGN THE PAPERS, DON'T YOU? WELL I WON'T DO IT!
ANNE, YOU REALLY WEREN'T LISTENING, WERE YOU?
I NEED SOME U.K. LOCATIONS FOR THE NEXT SHOOT, SO I FIGURED I'D USE RAVENHALL AS A BASE, AND SPEND SUMMER WITH YOU...IF THAT'S OKAY?
THANK YOU! THANK YOU! THANK YOU!
STEADY! NOTHING'S SET IN STONE, BUT LET'S SEE HOW WE GO, EH?

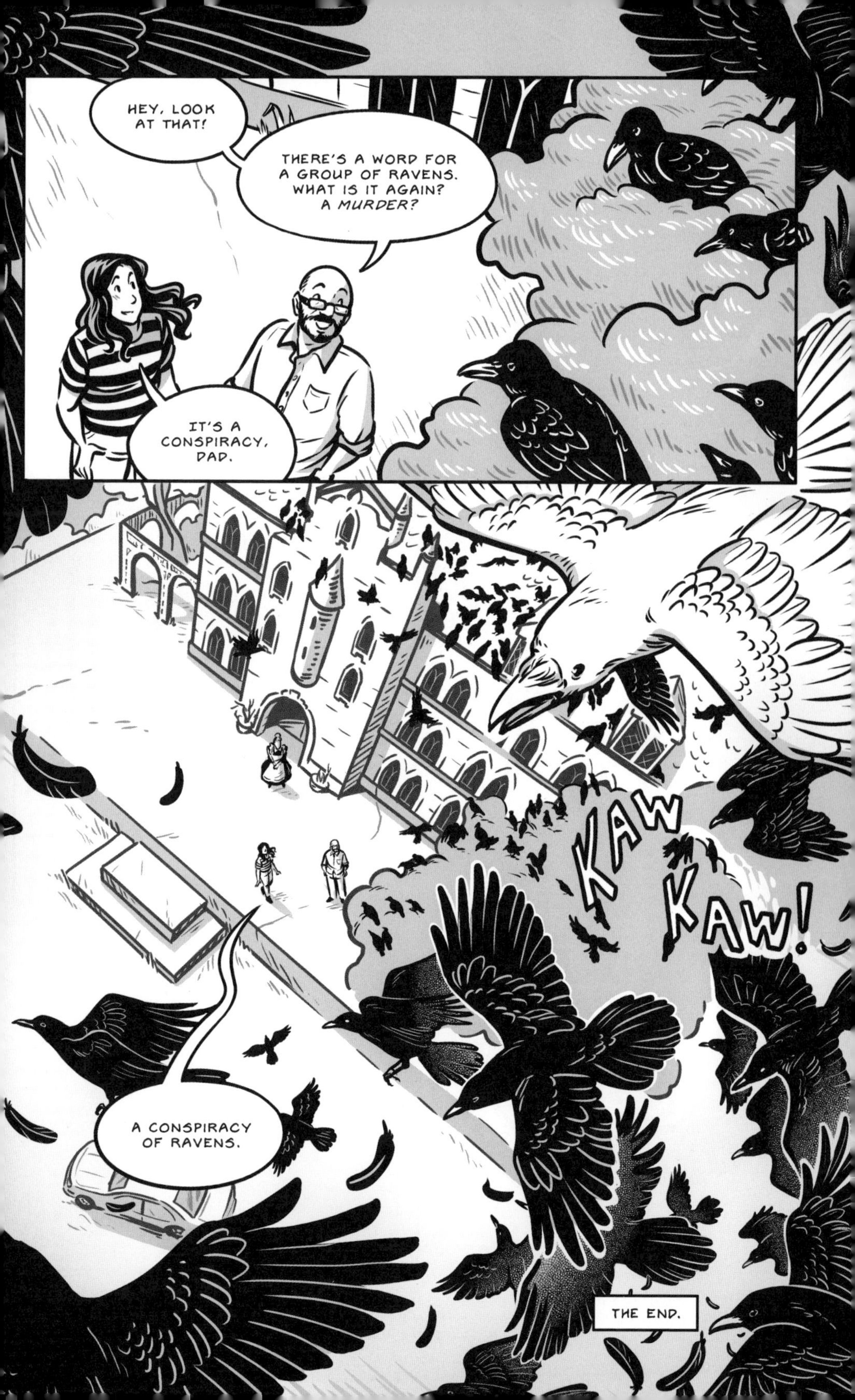
HEY, LOOK AT THAT!
THERE'S A WORD FOR A GROUP OF RAVENS. WHAT IS IT AGAIN? A *MURDER*?
IT'S A CONSPIRACY, DAD.
KAW KAW!
A CONSPIRACY OF RAVENS.
THE END.

CONSPIRACY OF Ravens

Sketchbook

NOTES BY **Sally Jane Thompson**

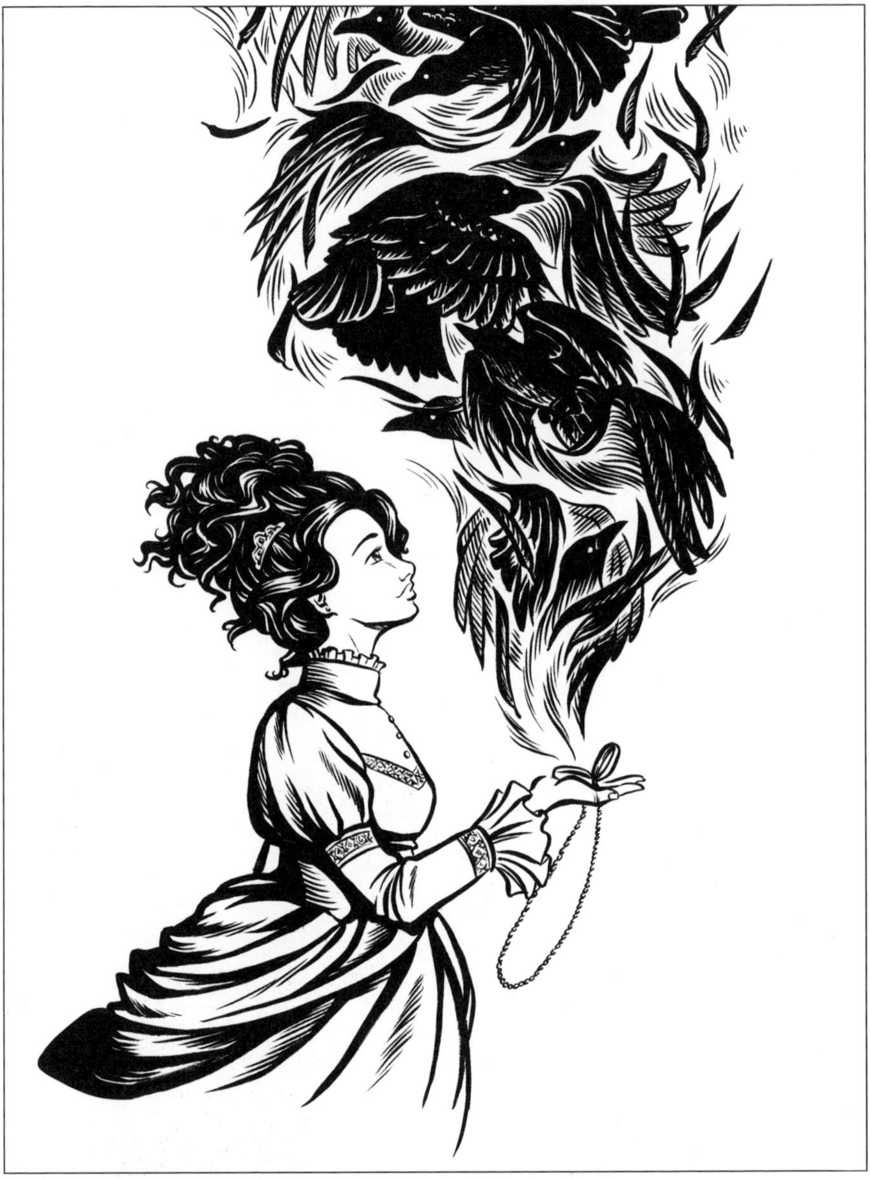

In 2012, I ran a sketch giveaway online. It was won by John, who responded with a request for themes with "Victorian stuff and corvids." This picture was the result (I love these themes too, so got a bit carried away!), and before we knew it we were trading story ideas about how good a raven/locket magical girl setup would be—"Sailor Moon via Poe." This has made it a deeply meaningful collaboration, threaded with all of our DNA from the very start.

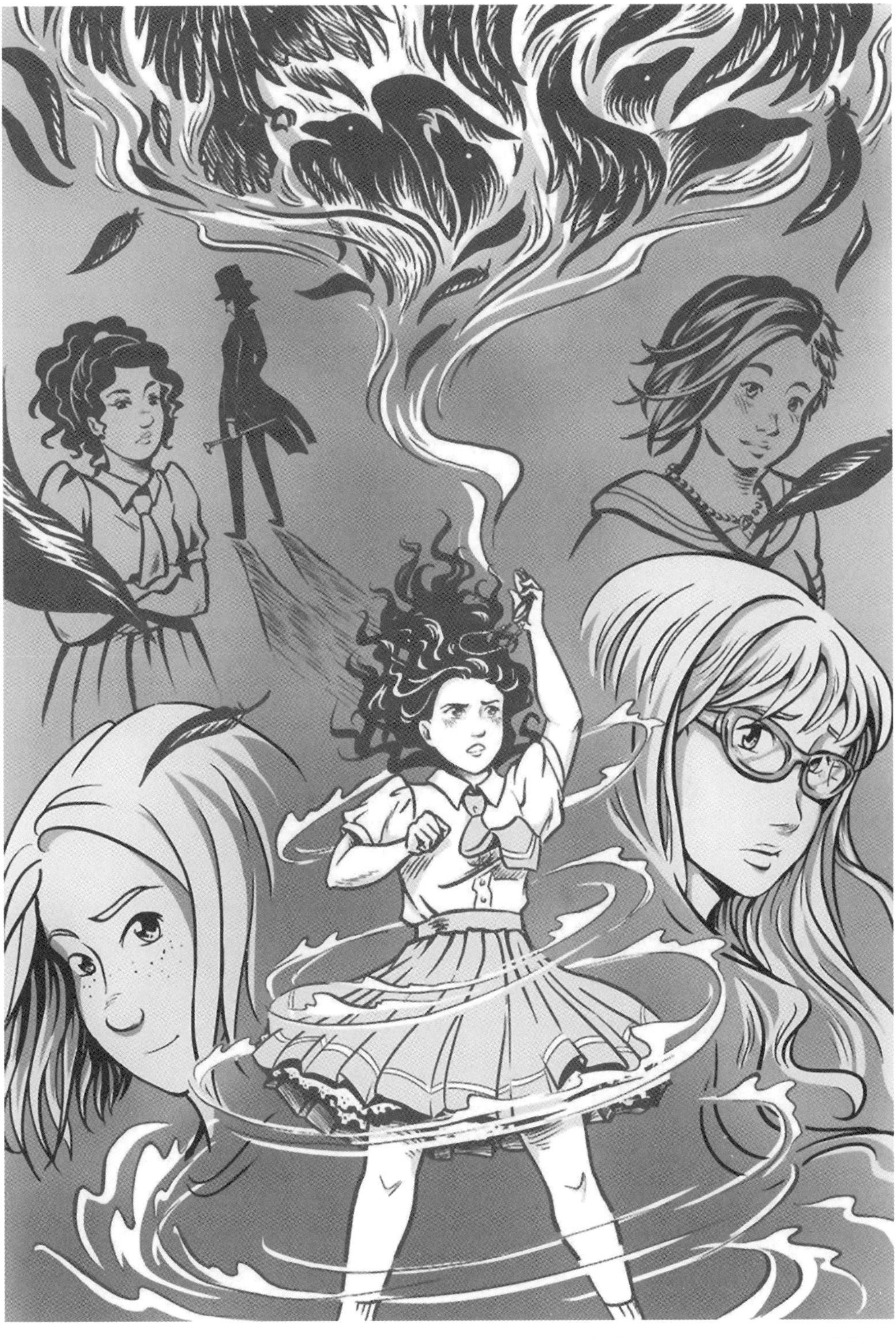

A promo illustration from the pitch package. The story went through a couple of iterations, but once we settled on a modern-day boarding school, things clicked into place, and these designs have carried through with little to no alteration for the final book.

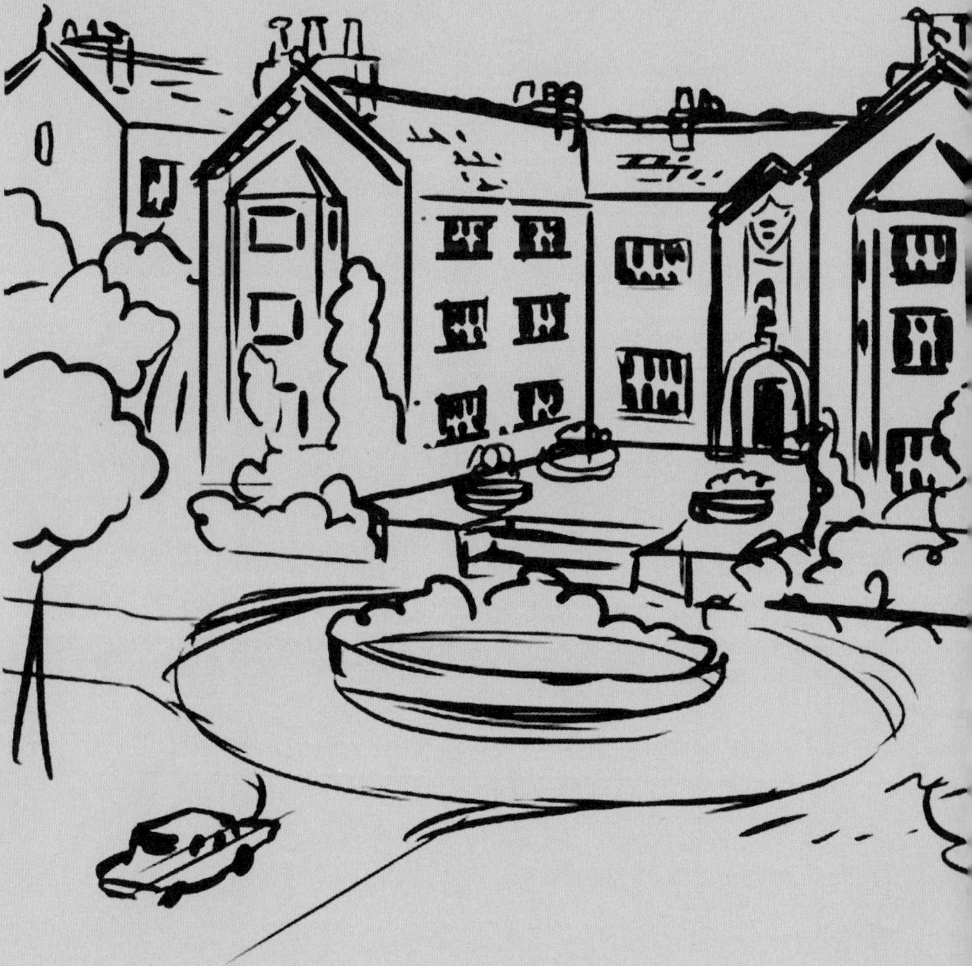

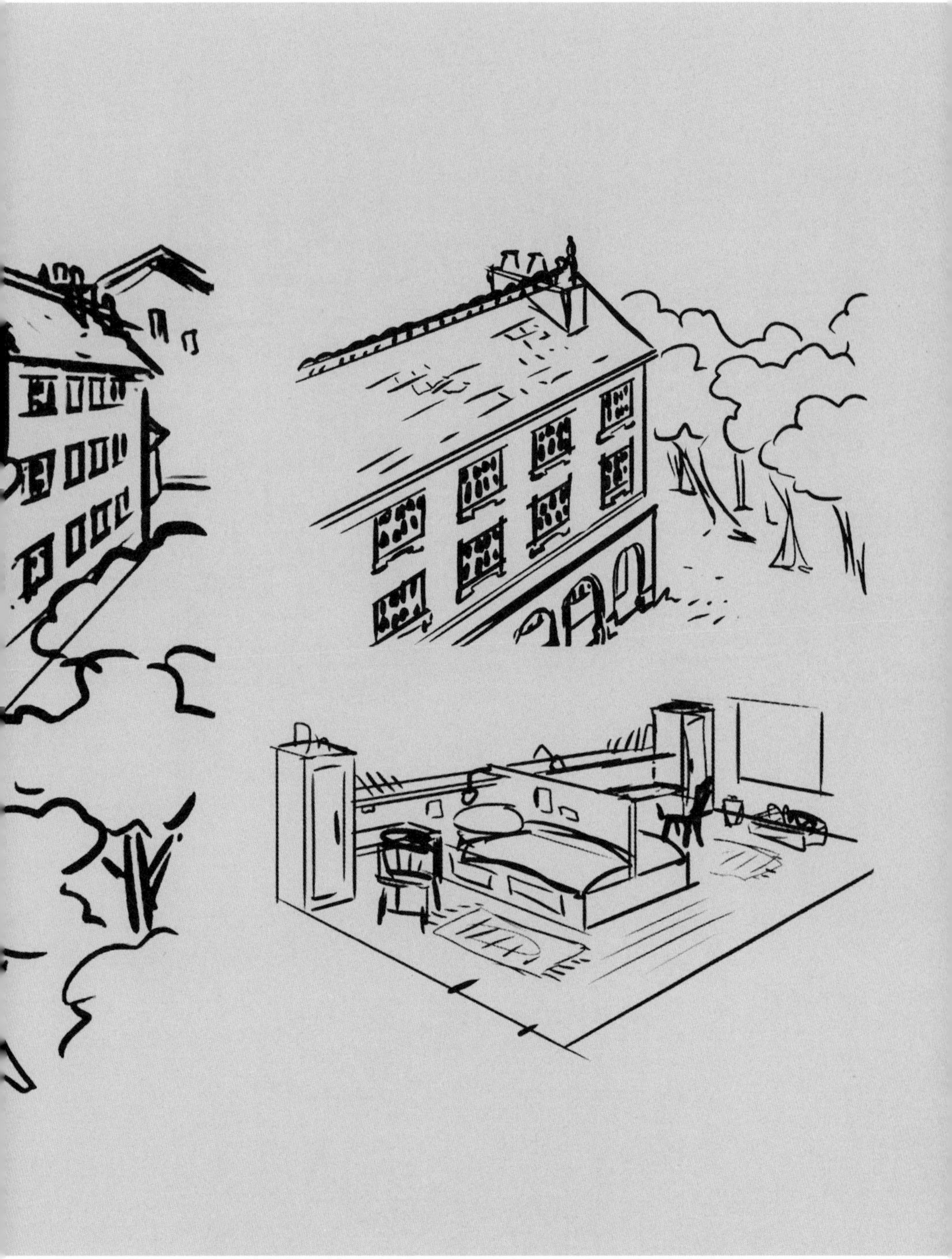

We spend quite a lot of time at Gables, so I wanted to make sure it felt like a believable school, with space beyond the classrooms and dorm rooms that we see. We tried to get across a building with lovely old bones and lots of history, but with the institutional fittings of a contemporary school. And of course, I wanted to make sure its shapes were easily distinguishable from our other important location, Ravenhall!

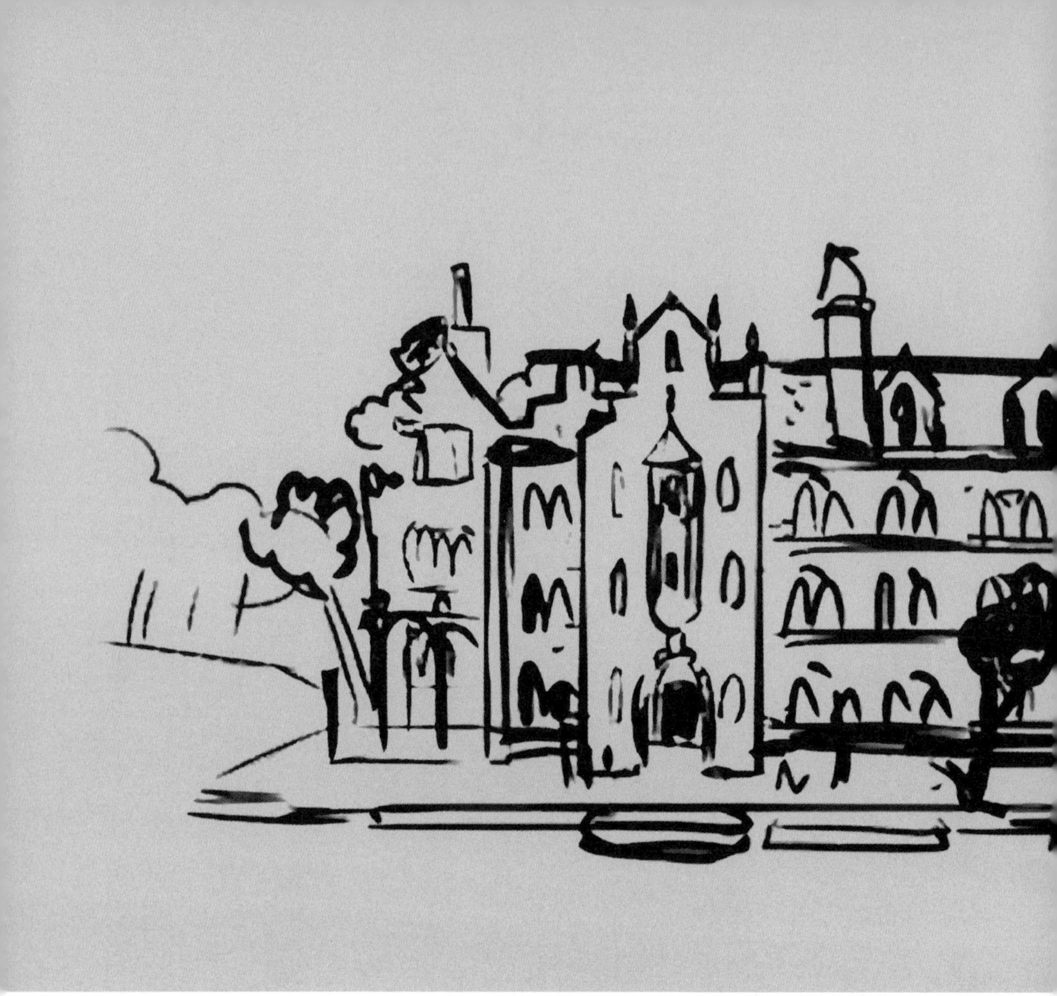

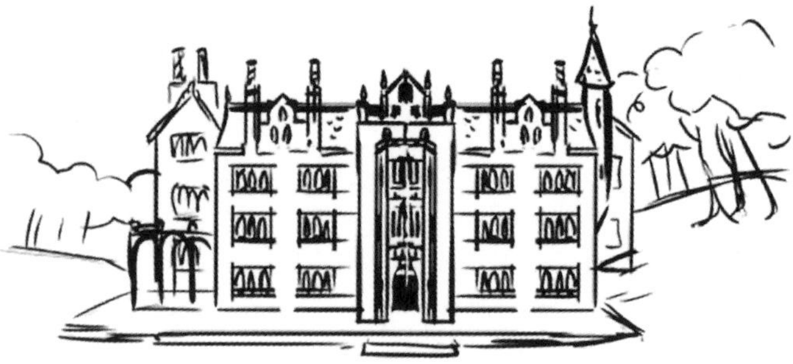

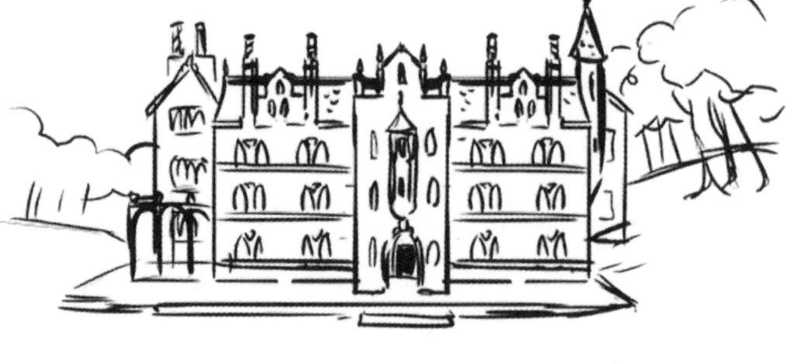

Ravenhall is such an important location to the book, I really wanted to get the right feel to it! I initially tested out both Gothic Revival and more Châteauesque influences, and decided to push the magical feel a bit with the latter, shifting the entrance off-centre a bit in the final design to make it feel a tiny bit less austere. It's a very grand home, but it is a home!

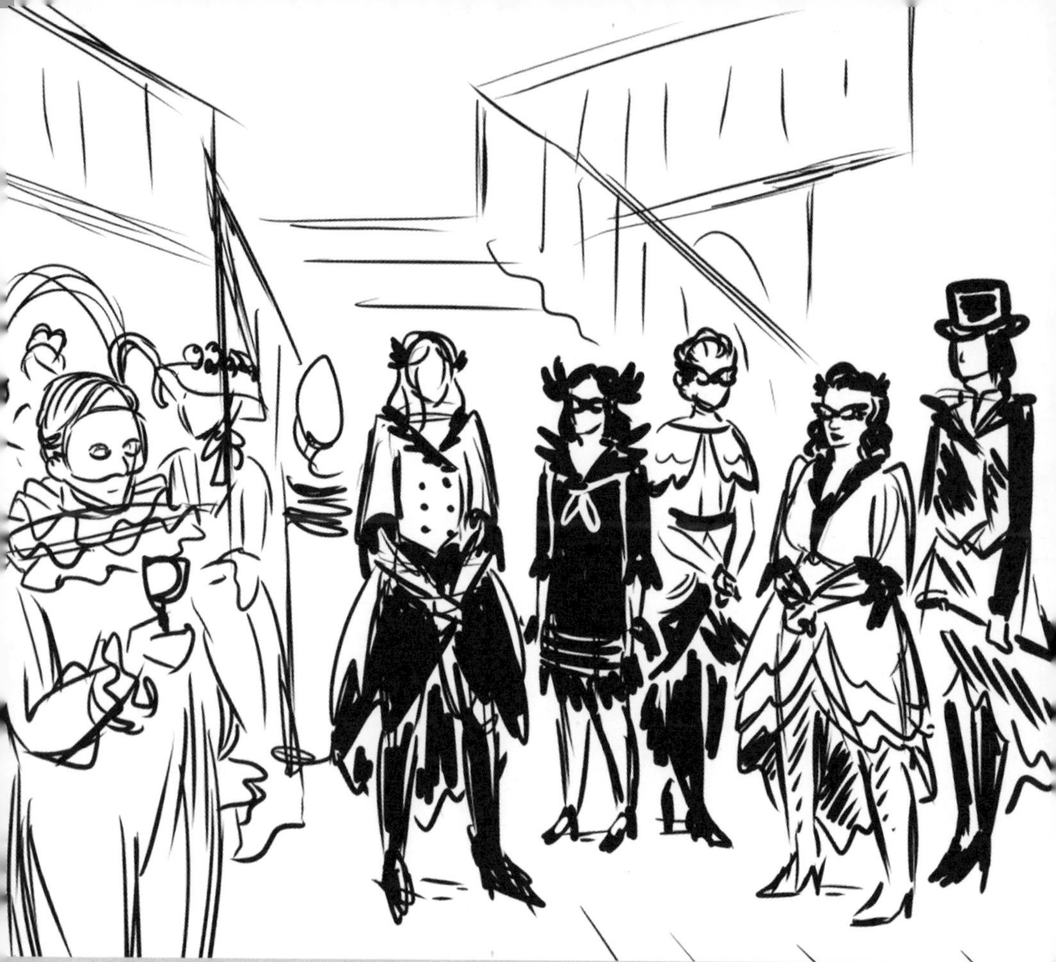

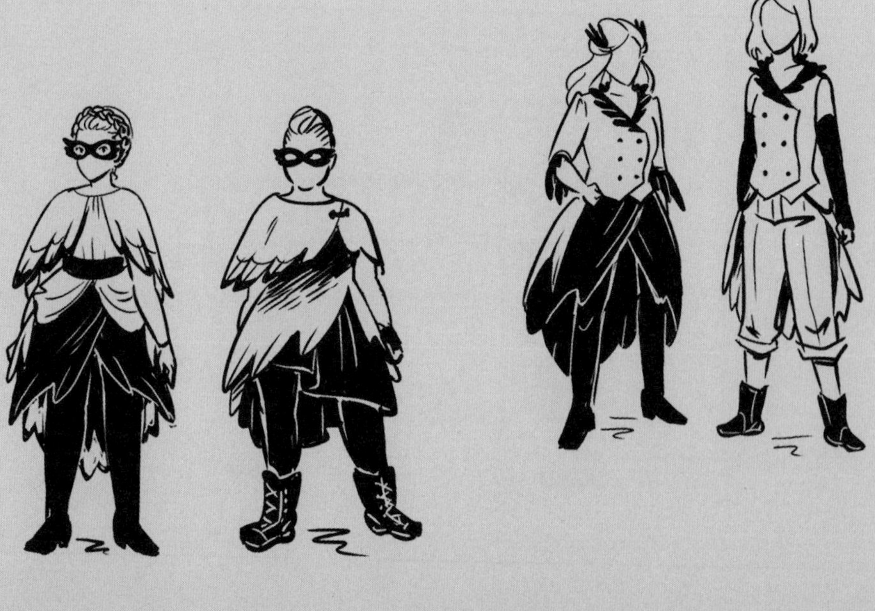

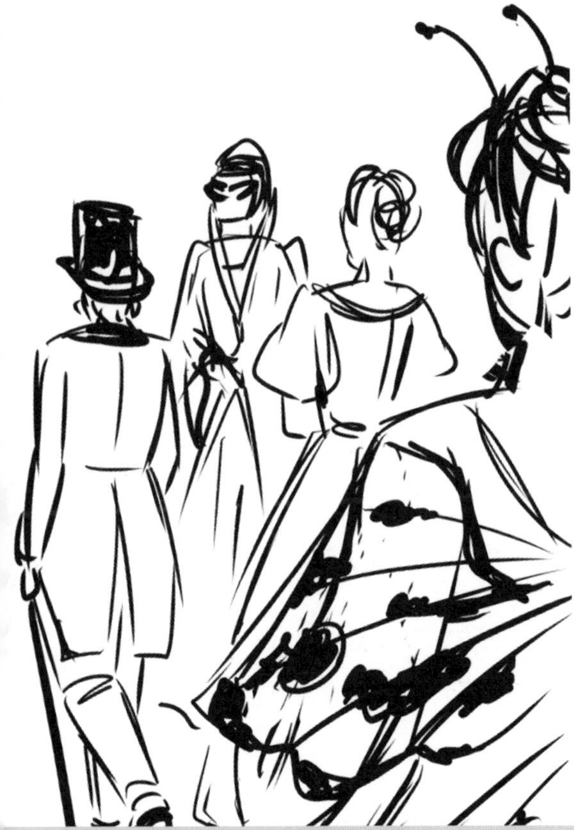

The girls' costumes were a challenge, being designed in tandem with their prior versions—something that fit both the characters and time period of the former Dissimulation but could still be modified for each of the current girls—and also referenced their bird in the design! I looked at early 1900s masquerade fashion illustrations, which were often wildly creative and didn't always match contemporary fashion silhouettes, allowing for a little more variation, daring, and active hero practicality!

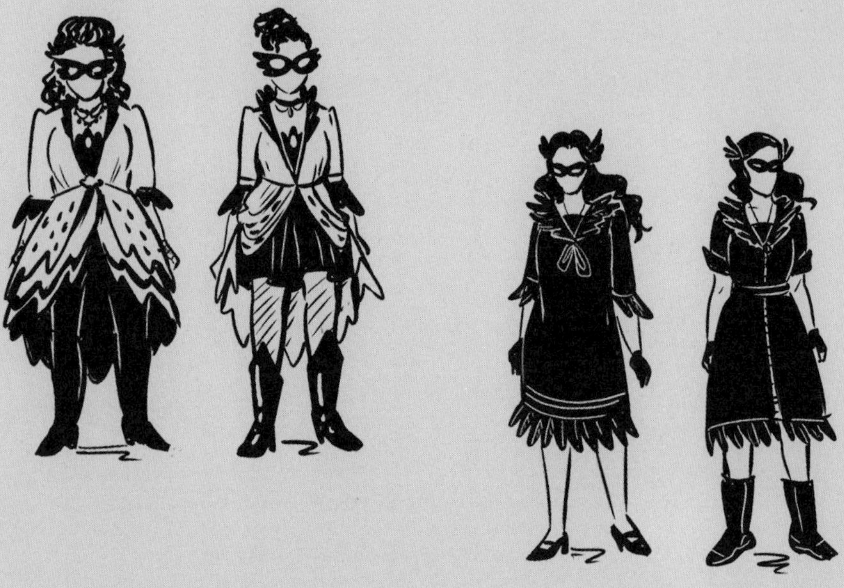

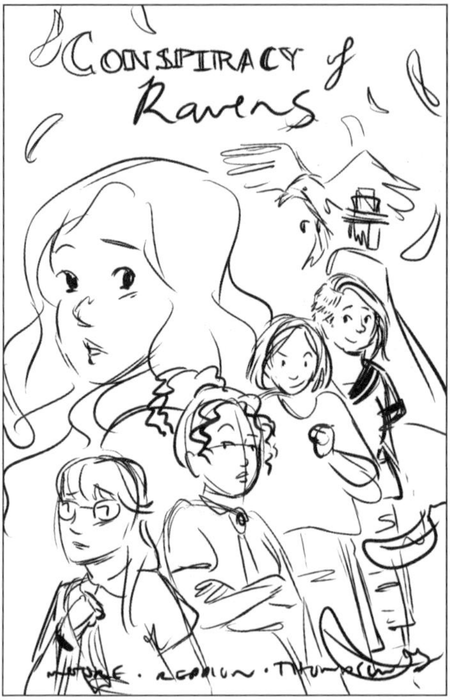
CONSPIRACY of Ravens
MOORE · REPPION · THOMPSON

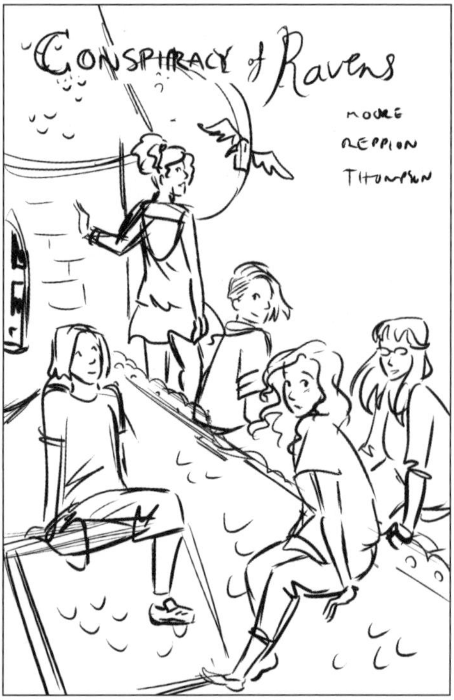
CONSPIRACY of Ravens
MOORE
REPPION
THOMPSON

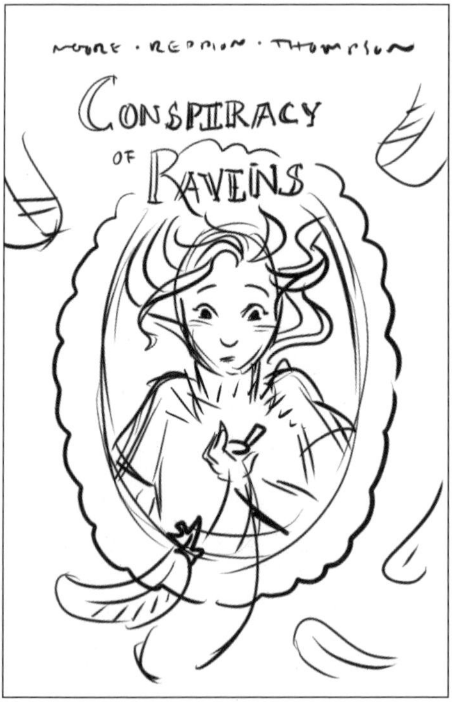
MOORE · REPPION · THOMPSON
CONSPIRACY
OF RAVENS

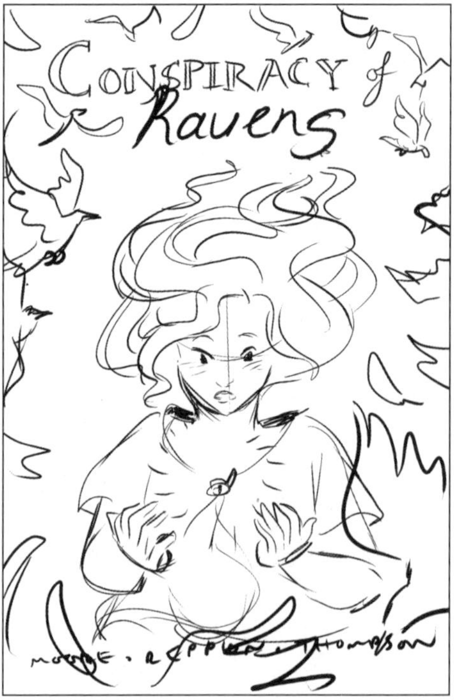
CONSPIRACY of Ravens

We had a lot of back and forth about whether to try and get the whole team on the cover (it's a team book!) or focus on trying to get a beautiful character shot that carries a sense of mystery and magic (and reads clearly on a shelf). Additionally, we needed to avoid giving the costumes away too early!

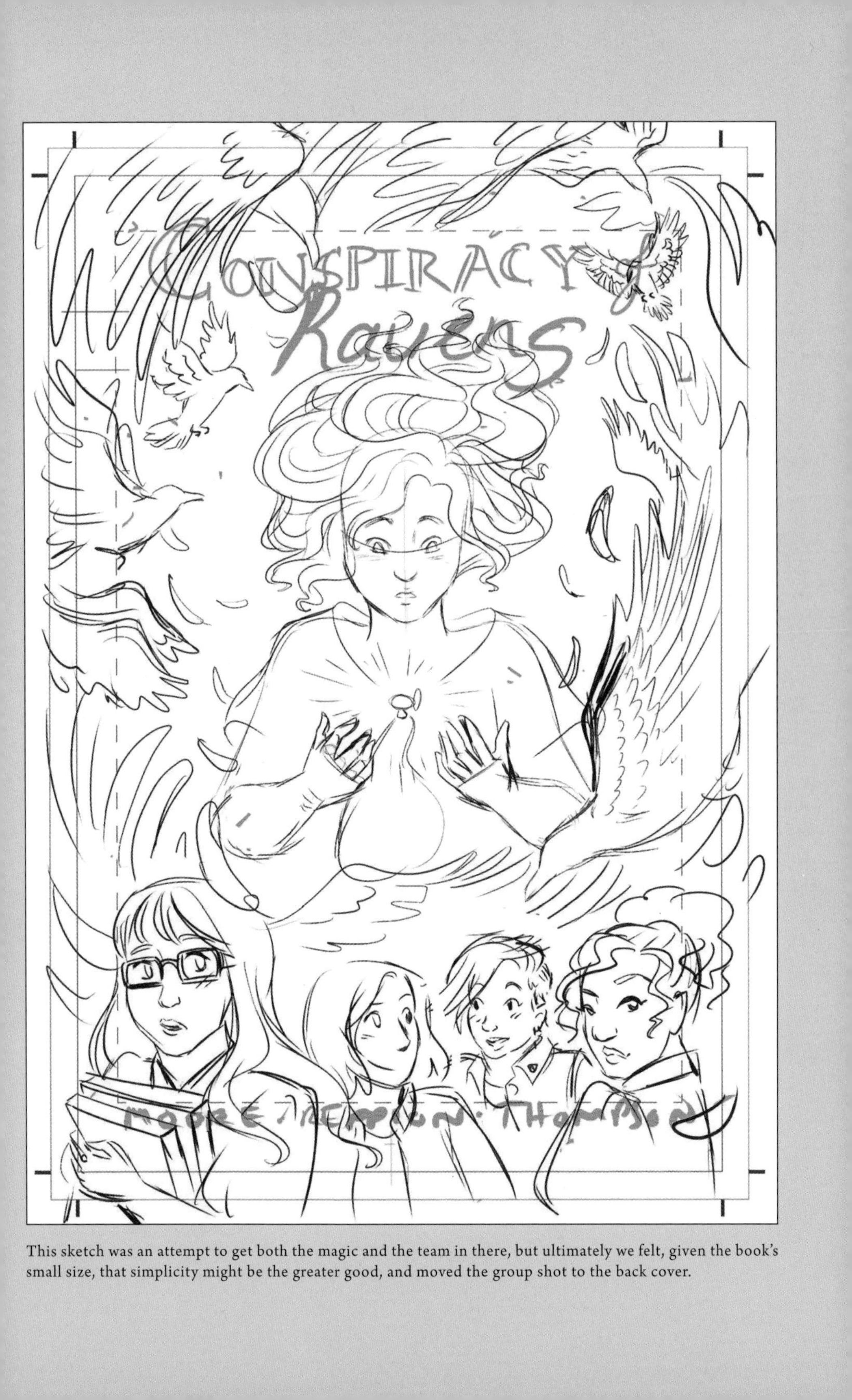
CONSPIRACY of
Ravens

This sketch was an attempt to get both the magic and the team in there, but ultimately we felt, given the book's small size, that simplicity might be the greater good, and moved the group shot to the back cover.

RECOMMENDED READING